COLE and LAILA are JUST FRIENDS

A Love Story

BETHANY TURNER

THOMAS NELSON
Since 1798

Published in Nashville, Tennessee, by Thomas Nelson. Thomas Nelson is a registered trademark of HarperCollins Christian Publishing, Inc.

Thomas Nelson titles may be purchased in bulk for educational, business, fundraising, or sales promotional use. For information, please email SpecialMarkets@ThomasNelson.com.

Publisher's Note: This novel is a work of fiction. Names, characters, places, and incidents are either products of the author's imagination or used fictitiously. All characters are fictional, and any similarity to people living or dead is purely coincidental.

Library of Congress Cataloging-in-Publication Data

Names: Turner, Bethany, 1979- author.

Title: Cole and Laila are just friends : a love story / Bethany Turner.

Description: Nashville, Tennessee: Thomas Nelson, 2024. | Summary: "Cole and Laila have been inseparable since they could crawl. And they've never thought about each other that way. Except for when they have. Rarely. Once in a while, sure. But seriously . . . hardly ever"-- Provided by publisher.

Identifiers: LCCN 2023055165 (print) | LCCN 2023055166 (ebook) | ISBN

9780840706904 (paperback) | ISBN 9780840706911 (e-pub) | ISBN

9780840706928

Subjects: LCGFT: Romance fiction. | Novels.

Classification: LCC PS3620.U76 C65 2024 (print) | LCC PS3620.U76 (ebook) | DDC 813/.6--dc23/eng/20231204

LC record available at https://lccn.loc.gov/2023055165

LC ebook record available at https://lccn.loc.gov/2023055166

Printed in the United States of America

24 25 26 27 28 LBC 5 4 3 2 1

Praise for Bethany Turner

Cole and Laila Are Just Friends

"I always thought, Once you're in love, the only place you ever fall in love again is the movies. But you can fall in love again reading this book."

—Delia Ephron, bestselling author, screenwriter, and playwright

"Deliciously romantic and laugh out loud funny, this one had me in its grip until the very end. Cole and Laila are meant-to-be perfection. I loved it!"

—Annabel Monaghan, bestselling author of *Same Time Next Summer*

"*Cole and Laila Are Just Friends* is a glorious ode to '90s romcoms, life-long friendships, and all the many twists of life that drop us right where we need to be. Full of warmth and witticisms galore, this will-they-or-won't-they love story will capture readers from the first page and spin them capably through the landmarks of New York alongside the most rootable duo I've ever encountered. Sweet and swoony, yet always rooted in human struggles (and stubbornness!), *Cole and Laila Are Just Friends* is the tight, affirming hug we all need right now."

—Nora Nguyen, author of *Adam & Evie's Matchmaking Tour*

"Hands down THE BEST pairing of first-love flutters and soul-deep friendship a romance reader could ask for—a new fan favorite! Funny, moving, and achingly adorable, Cole + Laila = relationship goals."

—Nicole Deese, Christy award-winning author

"Small town romance? Check. Friends-to-lovers? Double check. Enough romantic tension to keep you turning pages well into the night? That's a big check! I couldn't put down Cole and Laila's love story."

—Erin La Rosa, author of *Plot Twist*

"Bethany Turner has taken my favorite trope, friends-to-more, and created the most heartwarming, joy-filled, tender story. It's absolutely wonderful! Their love for each other brews from the first page all the way through to the beautiful finale. Why it takes them so long to realize how made for each other they are, well . . . sometimes falling in love with your best friends is complicated. With all sorts of pop culture references and a first 'fake' date to beat all first 'fake' dates, this book is Turner at the very top of her game. Do yourself a favor and pick up this gem of a story."

—Pepper Basham, bestselling author of *Authentically, Izzy* and *The Mistletoe Countess*

BRYNN AND SEBASTIAN HATE EACH OTHER

"Set in a charming small town and populated by well-developed, believable characters, *Brynn and Sebastian Hate Each Other* is a thoughtful and often tender exploration of two wounded souls seeking redemption and learning to trust again. I couldn't get enough of Bethany Turner's witty banter or the loyal found-family and sweet nostalgia threaded throughout this delightful story. A must-read for lovers of romantic comedy with healthy doses of pop-culture, humor, and depth . . ."

—Julie Christianson, author of *The Mostly Real McCoy* and *That Time I Kissed The Groomsman Grump*

"From the moment I heard the title and saw the cover, I knew I NEEDED to read this book. And if you are someone who loves quirky small town settings, enemies to lovers, and crisp, delightful prose, you do too! You'll be rooting for Brynn and Sebastian, not just as a couple, but as two people in need of a little redemption and maybe a life reset. This is a rom-com that brings some real depth and development but will also leave you smiling. Longtime fans of Bethany Turner and new readers alike will love this one!"

—Emma St. Clair, *USA TODAY* bestselling author

"Bethany Turner has a magical, effortless way with words, and *Brynn and Sebastian Hate Each Other* showcases this perfectly! You also get an adorable small town, enemies-to-lovers vibes, and all the feels you expect when two protagonists figure out themselves as they figure out each other. Add in a cast of unique and delightful secondary characters, and you get a feel-good story sure to delight and entertain."

—Jenny Proctor, author of *How to Kiss Your Best Friend*

THE DO-OVER

"Turner's (*The Do-Over*) latest is fun, fast, and heartwarming. This book will appeal to anyone who loves enemies-to-lovers romance and to readers who appreciate when a community plays a central role in the story."

—*Library Journal*

"Turner (*The Do-Over*) charms in a squeaky clean contemporary driven by a battle of wits between journalists . . . In addition to the appealing and endearingly flawed protagonists, Turner delivers a strong supporting cast, especially cameraman Orly Hill and generous town mayor Doc Atwater. Readers will long for a quick return to Adelaide Springs and its salt-of-the-earth citizens."

—*Publishers Weekly*

"Readers who haven't yet discovered the savvy, comedic rom-coms of award-winning author Bethany Turner are in for a treat with her latest second chance romance, *The Do-Over* . . . While romantic comedy may not be the genre for every reader, many will enjoy this light-hearted escape, especially anyone looking to drift away with a well-paced, feel-good story."

—*New York Journal of Books*

"Pitch-perfect comedic timing, a relatable heroine, and a refreshing sweetness elevate this novel above the sea of modern rom-coms. The rare author who can make me laugh out loud, *The Do-Over* is Bethany Turner at her best."

—Lauren Layne, *New York Times* bestselling author

PLOT TWIST

"Turner crafts an entertaining rom-com that spans ten years and keeps the reader guessing who will claim the heroine's heart . . . As the slow-burn romantic mystery of who Olivia will end up with builds to an amusing and satisfying conclusion, Olivia's witty narration will hold readers' attention. This is a treat."

—*Publishers Weekly*

"Turner's humorous latest has an enjoyable New Adult vibe . . . There is a happily ever after, but not the one most readers will be expecting."

—*Library Journal*

"*Plot Twist* gave my rom-com loving heart everything it could hope for: pop-culture references, frequent laugh-out-loud lines, an enduring friendship, a determined heroine to root for, and (of course) a love story with plenty of twists and turns. Bethany Turner's voice is fresh and fun, and it's a joy to read about Olivia as she grows and changes over the course of ten years. A sweet, funny read about the many kinds of love in our lives, perfect for anyone who loves love or dreams about meeting George Clooney."

—Kerry Winfrey, author of *Waiting for Tom Hanks*

"With a decade-long span of pop-culture fun, playful romantic possibilities, and the soul-deep friendships that push us to be real, *Plot Twist* is everything a reader has come to adore from Bethany Turner . . . plus so much more!"

—Nicole Deese, award-winning author of *Before I Called You Mine*

"Funny, clever, and sweet, *Plot Twist* reminds us that sometimes love doesn't look just like the movies—and that it can be so, so much better than we ever dreamed. Bethany Turner has gifted us all with another winning story with her trademark wit, wisdom, and charm!"

—Melissa Ferguson, bestselling author of *The Cul-de-Sac War*

"Bethany Turner just keeps getting better! *Plot Twist* is like experiencing the best parts of all my favorite rom-coms, tied together with Turner's pitch-perfect comedic timing, an achingly sweet 'will they or won't they?' romance, and the BFF relationship most girls dream of. Add in some Gen-X nostalgia, and you have a book you'll want to wrap yourself up in and never leave."

—Carla Laureano, RITA Award–winning author of *The Saturday Night Supper Club* and *Provenance*

"With a sassy Hallmark-on-speed hook and a winning leading lady, Turner loans her fresh, inimitable voice to her strongest offering yet: a treatise on how love (and the hope for love) paints across a canvas of fate and happenstance, and how life undercuts our expectations only to give us the biggest romantic adventures. Winsome and wise, Turner draws on beloved romantic tropes and zesty pop-culture references to provide a surprising comedy that is the sweet equivalent of Beth O' Leary and Emily Henry."

—Rachel McMillan, author of the Three-Quarter Time series and *The London Restoration*

COLE and LAILA are JUST FRIENDS

For Milo Ventimiglia's wife. For the record, you guys weren't married yet when I set your husband up on a blind date with Laila. Still . . . sorry about that. We cool?

Cole and Laila were their own thing. Longtime occupants of The Friend Zone who seemed to have taken the express train through Like Family to Me Village before setting up permanent residence in a kingdom that heretofore Sebastian had thought was only the stuff of legend: Soulmate City. (Where they diligently maintained the dual citizenship granted them by the Platonic Principality.)

—*Brynn and Sebastian Hate Each Other: A Love Story*

LAILA

My grandma Hazel always told me that big, life-changing events come in threes. Like most things she said, I took that with a grain of salt. After all, this was the same woman who spent years insisting World War II was the only thing standing between her and Paul Newman, little nuisance that it was. For years we heard about the forbidden romance between Grandma Hazel and the young Newman, who Grandma told us was working as a waiter at the lodge where her family stayed on a trip to Yellowstone when she was seventeen. There were instant sparks when he took her order for a turkey club sandwich with potato salad, and sweet nothings whispered during midnight strolls near Crystal Falls. She would sneak out after her little sister, my great-aunt Clara, went to sleep, and she and Paul would hold hands and steal innocent kisses, and she would stare into those dazzling blue eyes under a clear, full moon.

When she and her family returned to their home in Adelaide Springs, Colorado, Paul promised to write. And write he did . . . until he enlisted. She never heard from him again, and soon she met my grandfather, who ended up being the great love of her life for more than sixty years.

But that didn't stop us from jokingly referring to Newman as Grandpa Paul every time *Butch Cassidy and the Sundance Kid* came on TV. My grandfather would even pretend to be jealous and say things like, "Stay away from my woman, Blue Eyes."

It wasn't until Grandma Hazel was in her final weeks of life, and

Grandpa Clarence had been gone for a few years, that she looked up from her crossword puzzle one day and said, "*Pete* Newman. That was his name. Not Paul."

So, yeah . . . What came out of my grandmother's mouth always needed to be verified. But the "life-changing events come in threes" thing had always checked out. Jobs were lost on the same day friends passed away and homes burned down. Babies were born hours before engagements were announced and college scholarships were received. Those things wouldn't necessarily all happen to the same person, of course, but in a person's "circle of influence," as Grandma Hazel liked to call it. Within a community of friends and family.

So maybe it was superstitious hooey, but . . . yeah. I was just a little bit nervous that someone else's life was going to change on September 6. That morning, my stepmother, Melinda, had received the call she and my dad had been waiting for, finally putting a name to the symptoms she had been dealing with for months. Parkinson's. The diagnosis wasn't a surprise. In fact, having some answers had generated a fair amount of relief, even if we'd been hoping against hope for a more hope-filled answer.

And then two of my closest friends got married that afternoon. Although Brynn and Sebastian's wedding had been on the books for months.

Still. That was two biggies in the life-change column.

But by the time Brynn and Sebastian said, "I do," everyone was happy and having a great time, and I was so focused on the love and light on my friends' faces that I'd forgotten to be on the lookout for number three.

CHAPTER ONE

LAILA

"I'm pretty sure that's the last of it!" I stepped into Cassidy's Bar & Grill and kicked my foot up behind me to shut the solid-oak door just as the creaky, swinging screen door slammed closed.

Cole's head appeared in the kitchen service window. "What do you mean that's the last—" His eyes flew open at the sight of me standing just inside the door, peering at him over the mountain of precariously stacked catering equipment in my arms. His top half disappeared for a quick second, until all of him came barreling through the kitchen door. "What are you doing? I told you I'd be back to grab more." A handful of sizable strides got him close enough to grab the heavy stainless steel chafing dish sets from my hands, but rather than relieve me of them, he took a step back and sighed.

"What?" I muttered with pouted lips against the slipping fuel canisters I'd just been forced to catch.

He simultaneously groaned and laughed as he grabbed a fuel canister in each hand, set them on the table behind him, and then came back for more. "Oh, nothing. I just didn't know Laila Jenga was on the activity schedule for the evening."

"I would have planned better," I insisted once the remaining catering-grade containers of oil and wicks and such—along with three or so long-stem lighters I had slipped into the gaps between all the highly flammable things—were no longer being precariously balanced by my chin. "But by the time I realized how little was left to carry in—"

"You mean by the time good sense and a little bit of patience gave way to some good old-fashioned Laila Olivet stubbornness . . ."

"I didn't really have the wiggle room to stack things better."

"Clearly." Cole maneuvered a coffee urn out from under my arm while balancing some serving platters with his other hand.

"Be careful with that," I instructed as he prepared to lower the urn to the floor, in the second before we both heard gentle clinks reverberate from inside it.

He set the serving platters on the table and then unscrewed the vacuum-sealed lid of the coffee urn and looked inside. I watched the progression of emotions dance across his face—dismay, annoyance, frustration . . . Every last emotion accompanied onto the dance floor by humor and, more than anything, not even the tiniest tinge of surprise.

"Thank you for protecting the champagne glasses," he finally said, smiling at me as he looked up.

I waited for the follow-up, but there was none. He just kept smiling at me.

"Oh. You're welcome." I placed a couple of scalloped deli crocks into his waiting hands and then dug into the pockets of my coat, pulling out the serving utensils I had crammed in there and setting them in the crocks. "I thought you were going to make some crack about how if I had time to open up the urn, take out the coffee filters you had in there— Ooh!" I reached into the front of my dress and pulled out the package of plastic-wrapped coffee filters resting at the dress's waistband. I'd almost forgotten. Cole shook his head slowly as I handed them to him but remained otherwise unfazed. "And, you know, had time to wrap the glasses in dish towels—"

"What? You thought I'd make some crack about how if you had time to do all of that, you probably had time to just wait thirty more seconds until I came back out there to help you bring it all in?"

"Yeah." I looked up at him sheepishly.

"I would never." He spotted the basting spoon I had slipped through my increasingly deflated updo. "Can I take that, or is it the latest in maid-of-honor fashion?"

I laughed and attempted to pull it out as easily as I had slipped it in. No such luck, however. The weighty steel spoon end slipped down to my shoulder, further entangling my hair and the ridged, coated handle as it went.

"You're a mess," Cole whispered as he stepped in to rescue me. Or to rescue his catering utensil, which he may have felt ever so slightly more protective of in that instant.

"It was a beautiful wedding, wasn't it?"

"It was," he replied, but his focus was definitely still on trying to sort out the chaos on my head.

"And a super-fun reception."

He shrugged. "That I'm a little less sure of." He placed the palm of his hand flat on my head and applied some pressure as he handed me the almost-free spoon with his other hand. "Hold this," he instructed. Once I had it within my grasp, his hand returned to my head and promptly pulled out a couple hairs.

"Ouch!" I exclaimed, though truthfully the grounding pressure he had preemptively applied to my scalp kept me from feeling much of anything. "You pulled my hair out!"

"I did." He took the utensil from my hand and began unraveling the connected hair as he made his way back to the kitchen. "And I would never even consider making a crack about just how very, incredibly, overwhelmingly much you only have yourself to blame for that. Wouldn't dream of it."

The corner of my lips smirked at him, and I scratched my head at the site of impact. "That's good of you."

"What can I say? I'm a nice guy."

I rolled my eyes as he smiled widely at me through the service window. Once he turned away, I indulged in a soft chuckle. Not a moment sooner.

"So why didn't you have fun?" I called to him as I raised the coffee urn to a tabletop and began carefully removing the bridal party champagne flutes.

"Hmm?"

"At the reception. Why didn't you have fun?"

I heard the familiar roar of the commercial dishwasher coming to life. The first of several times it would have to run before Cassidy's was ready to open tomorrow for the dinner crowd.

He stepped out of the kitchen with a sigh, dish towel in hand. "Oh, I don't know. It wasn't that I didn't have fun, really. I was just more focused on making sure everything went perfectly for them. It wasn't supposed to be fun. I was working."

I turned and leaned my hip against the table as I faced him. "And since when is that not fun for you?"

Cole finished drying his hands and threw the dish towel over his shoulder. "The fun was had in the kitchen, ahead of time. At the reception I was just trying to fulfill my best-man duties while simultaneously doing all I could to keep the hot food hot and the cold food cold on the top of a mountain. Not to mention never taking my eyes off the open bar to make sure the PTA ladies stayed out of trouble. That was work."

I'd been serving the PTA group at their Tuesday night meetings at Cassidy's for years. He wasn't wrong.

"You should have let me help you more." I began shrugging my arms out of my coat, and he stepped behind me and held it as it slipped off.

"You helped plenty." He folded my coat over his arm as he stood in front of me again. "You helped so much, in fact, that I don't even know why I bothered hiring those fancy-schmancy waiters from Denver. I *thought* the point was that you were going to focus on being maid of honor."

"Um, hello. First of all, if you have any doubt as to whether or not I more than adequately fulfilled my maid-of-honor duties, you need only ask me how many times I reapplied Brynn's makeup due to tears and/or wind. Spoiler: The answer is approximately seventy-two thousand. And second, don't give me that. You hired fancy-schmancy waiters because this was your first celebrity wedding, and you didn't trust me not to spill food on Hoda and Jenna."

"Allow me to say once again: Brynn and Sebastian invited neither Hoda Kotb nor Jenna Bush Hager to their wedding, Laila."

"But *why*, Cole? This makes no sense to me."

"You know as well as I do they just wanted it to be family and close friends—"

"Yes, but they both know Hoda and Jenna. I guess I just don't see how you can know Hoda and Jenna and *not* consider them close friends. I mean, I've never met either one of them, but I would be willing to make them the godmothers of my future children right here and now. No questions asked."

"Some things do indeed defy understanding. Regardless, you're the best waitress I've ever seen, and you never spill food." He turned to carry my coat to the door to hang it on the coatrack. While he was straightening it, he looked out the window toward our vehicles. "I mean, look at that. You managed to close the doors and still carry all that stuff in, and all you lost were a couple unrelenting strands of hair. That really is impressive."

"Thank you. Now don't you feel bad about all those things you thought but didn't say?"

I crossed into the kitchen and opened the refrigerator door. Truth be told, as fun as the day had been, watching two of my favorite people so happy and so in love and being celebrated by all the people who mattered to them, it had been a lot of work. I'd been too busy to eat—a fact I hadn't really thought about until I found myself practically inside the fridge, rummaging around, the sound of my growling stomach reverberating as I lustfully eyed an unopened pack of raw bacon in the back on the top shelf.

"When was the last time you ate?" Cole asked, his voice distant and tinny, like he was calling to me from the outside of the cave I was lost in.

Hmm . . . When . . . Good question . . .

"On the drive up the mountain, I guess." It had been too warm during the day to put my coat on, so I'd thrown a poncho on over my dress, like I was in the front row of a Gallagher show, bracing myself for all the watermelon smashing. Hadn't spilled a drop of that peanut butter sandwich, thank you very much.

Ooh! Whipped cream!

I grabbed it and stood from my crouching position, beginning to remove the safety seal from the can's plastic lid as I shut the refrigerator door behind me.

Cole laughed and snatched the can out of my hands just as I lifted it upside down and prepared to shoot it straight into my mouth. "I think we can do better than that. Here." He reached behind him and set the whipped cream down, then handed me a storage container of food. *Real* food. I pulled back the plastic lid and was hit by the delicious scent of rosemary. And thyme, maybe? Didn't know, didn't really care. All that mattered was it smelled amazing and Cole Kimball had made it, so I was sure it *was* amazing.

"You're the best!" I hurried out of the kitchen and set the food down on the bar before hiking my dress up above my knees and hopping onto a barstool. Then I dug my fingers straight into the tender, aromatic chicken breast, which tasted even better than it smelled. I moaned in satisfaction. "I didn't realize you had any left," I mumbled with my mouth full, stuffing a steamed baby carrot in to make it even fuller.

"There wasn't much." He grabbed a glass from above the bar, filled it with Sprite from the soda gun, and set it in front of me. "I sent a veggie tray with Maxine for Prince Charlemagne."

"Seriously, Cole, there are vegetarians in Aspen who don't eat as well as that bearded dragon."

"And Jo gathered up a smorgasbord of cake, cookies, and eclairs to drop off with my grandfather."

"Oh, good." I took the napkin and fork he handed me and quickly wiped off my hands before diving into the mashed potatoes. With the fork. I'm not a barbarian. "He'll have something besides pie for breakfast for a change."

"Variety is the spice of life." Cole chuckled, but the humor faded quickly as he studied me. "And I made a couple plates for Larry and Melinda. Dropped them off on my way back into town."

It wasn't as if my dad and stepmother had ever really been out of my thoughts throughout the day, of course. Or even over the course of the past months as Melinda's voice had grown gravelly and the nervous energy we'd teased her about for years morphed into an unmistakable tremor, however slight. But the mention of their names brought them to the forefront once again.

"Thanks for doing that."

"Of course."

"Did they seem okay?"

"Yeah. Your dad was asleep, so Melinda and I talked for a couple minutes. You know how she is. She's just ready to get to work. She's already ordered a bunch of books and supplements, and she's looking forward to going to Denver to meet with the neurologist at the end of the month. I think she's a lot more worried about Larry than she is herself."

I nodded as guilt washed over me. I shouldn't have gone all day without checking on them. No, I didn't have cell signal at Adelaide Gulch, and no, I didn't so much as find time to get onto the wooden parquet dance floor. Right about the time Lucinda and Jake Morissey were trying to pull me out there for the Cupid Shuffle was when I'd had to go shoo away a fawn that nearly hit the scavenging jackpot with Cole's cheese and fruit charcuterie board.

Still. I should have gone straight over to check on them when I got back into town.

Cole leaned onto the bar across from me and lowered his head to try to catch my downcast eyes. "She's worried about you too. So am I, for that matter. You doing okay?"

"Yeah," I responded as I looked up at him. And I meant it. "I'm really glad Dad has something to work with now. You know how he is. He hates feeling helpless." I swallowed down the argument in my mind that we were still going to be helpless bystanders far more than seemed fair to Melinda.

"Must be hereditary." He studied me. "Want to talk about it?"

I shook my head. "Not right now." I set down my fork, my appetite suddenly satisfied—or forgotten. I'm not sure which. "Thanks, though."

"Do you mind if I change the subject for a minute, then?"

"Please!"

He stood up straight, and his face took on a completely different countenance. His bottom lip was caught between his teeth, and his eyes darted around the room. "Okay, I want your opinion on something."

I took a sip of my soda and nodded.

"And I want you to be completely honest."

I snorted in response to that unnecessary request, causing a few carbonation bubbles to burn their way through my sinuses, resulting in Cole throwing another napkin at my face while laughing at my pain.

"I know, I know," he continued. "But really, Lai. I know you'll be honest, but I don't want you to sugarcoat anything or try to be considerate of my feelings or anything like that. If this is a stupid idea, I'm counting on you to tell me."

I raised three fingers to communicate my commitment to tell the truth via "Scout's Honor," though I got hung up for a moment thinking I might have just volunteered as a Hunger Games tribute instead. When in doubt, use words.

"What sort of friend would I be if I didn't stand at the ready to point out your stupidity as needed?"

The nervousness on his face was replaced by a warm smile as he sidled up next to me at the bar. I turned on my stool so I could face him and prepared to listen and honestly respond, but the assuredness that had overtaken his eyes made me fairly confident whatever was about to come out of his mouth wouldn't be stupid at all.

"Okay, so I've been thinking. Adelaide Springs is growing. Between the attention Brynn and Seb have brought to it and the success of Township Days, more and more people are visiting, and it looks like people are even starting to stay. To actually move here."

They were indeed. The combination of an It power couple calling Adelaide Springs home and the revival of a kitschy annual festival that was just weird and wonderful enough to attract attention from social media influencers and YouTubers (who obviously hadn't played a role in Township Days' first incarnation, starting in 1975) had already resulted in the town's biggest population boom since they found silver in Adelaide Canyon in 1889.

Early indications were that the population would surpass five hundred before the end of the year.

"And obviously no one can blame Andi for closing up the Bean Franklin. I mean, her sister died. Of course she's going through a lot and dealing with things. But Wray's been dead for weeks now, and we've barely heard from Andi at all. We don't know when she's coming back. Or even, at this point, *if* she's coming back. And, of course, if she does, there's more than enough business for everyone. But with the Bean closed, there aren't any other restaurant options for breakfast and lunch, and I'm afraid we're going to start losing tourists to Alamosa or something. So I was thinking—"

"You should open Cassidy's for breakfast and lunch!"

His shoulders fell. "Wow. Nothing like letting a guy build up to a joke and then stealing the punch line."

I gasped and covered my mouth with both my hands and then reached down and rested my hands on his knees. "I'm so sorry. I just got excited. Forget I said anything. Go ahead. You were thinking . . ." I chewed on my bottom lip to keep myself from interrupting again, and I felt the contained energy begin to bubble at my feet, which were suddenly rocking up and down on my barstool's footrest.

He laughed and leaned in and kissed me on the cheek before standing and going back behind the bar. "Just tell me it's not stupid, and I'll forgive you." He tossed me the can of whipped cream, which he had very wisely brought out with him.

I caught it and jumped down from the stool. "It's *so* not stupid, Cole! Cassidy's is ready for this. *You're* ready for this. *I* feel stupid for not thinking of it and telling you to do it." I shot some whipped cream into my mouth as the possibilities swam around in my head. "You need Wi-Fi," I insisted, enunciating as well as I could through the cream. "For the breakfast crowd, especially."

He motioned for me to give him a hit, and I filled his mouth to overflowing as I rambled on about needing more staff and maybe having a trivia night and creating punch cards for frequent customers. He leaned against the wall and crossed his arms, listening to every word I said, until I finally paused long enough to shoot the nozzle into my mouth for a refill.

"So you're with me on this?"

I tilted my head and actually went to the trouble of swallowing before speaking. "Of course I'm with you on this. I'm with you on everything. Always. And this is also just a fabulous idea, so I'm pretty sure I'd be with Prince Charlemagne on this, if *he'd* thought of it first."

The smile returned to Cole's face, and I knew I'd told him exactly what he needed to hear. "Who says he didn't? I don't give away veggie trays for nothing, you know."

I nudged my shoulder into his chest, then slipped my arms around his torso. "I'm so proud of you. This is going to be great. Seriously."

He sighed and wrapped his arms around my back before leaning his cheek down onto my head. "It's going to be a lot of work."

I scoffed and pulled away to look up at him. "Nah. Not really. Not compared to all the work you've put in already." I separated myself from him and turned to face the door into the kitchen. "Remember when that led to nothing more than rows of shelves and stacks of boxes? And remember when there was just that one lamp hanging from the ceiling, with the bulb we had to turn on with the chain, like we were in an old-timey interrogation room or something?" I shuddered at the memory. I'd spent the first half of my life creeped out by that dark, dingy storeroom.

I turned back to face him. "Your dream and your vision and your hard work turned Cassidy's into *this*. And it's about to get even better."

He nodded once. "Thanks, Lai."

I shrugged. "What sort of friend would I be if I didn't point out your brilliance?"

The smile returned to his face. "Well, then . . . here is the real test of friendship. You'll point out my stupidity, and you'll point out my brilliance, but are you willing to help me deglaze stained pans while wearing . . ." He reached down and grabbed the fabric of my skirt between his fingers. "What is this? Taffeta?"

"Beats me. But I do happen to have a poncho for just such an occasion."

I headed toward the door to grab the poncho from my car but stopped short at the sight through the window of Mrs. Stoddard walking up the steps and onto the porch. Cole noticed her at the same time I did and hurried over to open the door.

"Hey, Jo," he greeted her as she stepped inside. "What's up?"

"Hi, kids."

Kids. She'd been our teacher all through school, right up until high school graduation. Never mind that we'd been out of high school for more than twenty years. Half the people in Adelaide Springs called us kids, and I figured they always would.

"Sorry to barge in so late."

"No problem," Cole assured her with a smile that quickly fell away. Just as familiar to us as Mrs. Stoddard the strict educator was Mrs. Stoddard the caring adult who was completely invested in our success and committed to our well-being. The warmth and concern in her eyes informed us it was *that* Mrs. Stoddard standing before us. "Is everything okay?"

Grandma Hazel always said big, life-changing events came in threes. I really wish she'd been right about Paul Newman instead.

CHAPTER TWO

COLE

For a couple hours, people had been trying to come up with nice things to say about his grandfather. They'd walk by the casket, spend the appropriate amount of time staring at the top half of the body of an old man who was wearing a suit for the first time since his wedding day, and then walk up to Cole and say, "Bill was one of a kind," or "This place won't be the same without him." Both statements were true, but Cole wasn't sure what he was supposed to do with either one of them.

It wasn't that Bill Kimball had been a bad guy. He was just a grump. A textbook curmudgeon. The emotional love child of Oscar the Grouch and pretty much every role ever played by Ed Asner. But just like Oscar and Lou Grant and Carl Fredricksen in *Up*, you always knew there was a heart under there somewhere. At least Cole always knew. There were probably a lot of people in Adelaide Springs who weren't so sure about that. Plenty of kids who had feared him, far too many young adults who had been offended by his lack of verbal filter, and even a handful of peers from Bill's generation who had long ago given up on befriending him.

And those had been the people passing by the casket. They'd made an appearance during the visitation time—out of respect for Cole, maybe, or at least so word wouldn't get around their small town that they hadn't bothered to show up—and then made an excuse why they couldn't stay for the memorial service itself.

That didn't bother him a bit. And it certainly wouldn't have bothered his grandfather. The people who mattered hadn't even made their way to the casket yet, but they'd been there. All day. Sitting in the pews of the little church, checking on Cole every so often to see if he needed some coffee or some help getting away from a particularly clingy half-hearted mourner. And while people stood in his space, attempting to come up with nice things to say, he kept his eye on the people who mattered and noticed that no matter how engaged in conversation they were or how focused elsewhere they seemed, they always had an eye on him.

And then there was Laila. His lifelong best friend was an eternal optimist and the sunniest person he'd ever met, but she was struggling today. Truthfully, she'd been struggling ever since Mrs. Stoddard broke the news that when she'd gone to Spruce House—the assisted living center where Bill had lived for about six months—to drop off his desserts, she'd discovered he'd never awakened from his evening nap. It was as if Laila was absorbing and carrying all of the grief she assumed Cole was feeling or resisting. Or maybe she was just expressing her own grief in a very Laila sort of way.

That's what Cole was pretty sure *he* was doing. Expressing his grief in a very *Cole* sort of way. Which, admittedly, hadn't yet proven to be very expressive.

Today, the "very Laila sort of way" meant she had shifted into hostess mode, and he was grateful. Not only did it take some of the pressure off him to meet and greet and be hospitable, but it also kept her busy. It wasn't that he minded her asking him how he was holding up. He appreciated it and knew she genuinely cared. But how many more times would he have to tell her he was fine before she believed him?

He *was* fine. Whether Laila believed him or not.

"How are you holding up?"

Cole groaned and faced her as she stepped up beside him and checked in on him. Again. "Lai, the man was ninety years old and had had two strokes in the past six months. He ate pie and ice cream with every meal—quite often *for* every meal—for the last ten years.

Yes, he was my grandfather, and yes, I loved him. Miserable old man that he was, I'm going to miss him. But this is not a traumatic loss. I knew it was coming."

She studied him intently, and he knew she was surveying the damage. Looking for chinks in the armor, imperceptible to anyone but her. He smiled in response to her concerned, compassionate eyes, his momentary irritation with her forgotten.

"I really am fine. But thank you for caring so much. Thanks for all you're doing."

She wrapped her arms around him and leaned her head on his chest. "Of course I care. And I'm not doing anything you wouldn't do for me."

He smirked against the top of her head. "I *have* done it for you. Or are you forgetting the top-notch buffet I prepared for Happy Gilmore's celebration of life?"

She pulled back and looked at him, humor and lightness radiating from her shimmering eyes for the first time in days. "That kitty litter quinoa *was* delicious . . . no matter how disgusting the name."

The fact was Laila had had to say goodbye more often than he had. And not just to cats—though there really had been *so* many cats. There had also been beloved grandparents, aunts and cousins who had died far too young, and a mom who hadn't died but whose departure after divorce had required its own grief and period of mourning. And each time, Cole had been her shoulder. Her rock. When they'd felt deserted by friends, it had been *their* loss, each time. And each time, Laila had mourned in her Laila sort of way, and Cole had mourned in his Cole sort of way. In those situations, the Cole sort of way had always been easy to define: take care of Laila and find healing as he helped *her* find healing. Until now, he'd never been alone at the center of the loss. He supposed it wasn't surprising, really. Laila had always had more to lose.

"How are you doing, kid?" Doc Atwater came up beside them with a refreshed cup of coffee in his hands. After years of pumping his bloodstream full of the stuff—black and "strong enough to press a man's shirt from the inside"—he had given in to the mounting pressure from his daughter Addie and Jo Stoddard (the only person in town who never hesitated to give medical advice to the town's doctor) and made the switch to decaf a while back. Cole could tell from the bold aroma emanating from the cup in his hands that Doc had determined today was not a day for trifling around with the stuff from the pot with the orange lid.

"I'm fine." He turned toward Doc as Laila focused her attention on straightening the late-season wildflowers arranged on the casket. "I'm good, actually. I mean, if one more person who didn't really know him tells me my grandfather was a teddy bear, I may no longer be able to resist a *very* inappropriate outbreak of laughter, but otherwise . . ."

Doc chuckled. "Bill certainly wasn't the unfeeling man he wanted everyone to believe he was, but a teddy bear he was not." He took a sip of his coffee and paused long enough to savor it. "He sure loved you, though."

Cole looked down at the shoelaces of the fancy boots he'd had to buy as part of his wardrobe as Sebastian's best man. The boots he'd thought he would hate but had ended up loving. He hadn't given Sebastian enough credit—and he'd temporarily forgotten that the man had somehow found a way to fit into Brynn's high-class, star-studded, designer life without ever letting himself (or Brynn) lose touch with the slower, methodical simplicity of Adelaide Springs. The boots could have been the mascot for their combined life.

Cole hadn't been looking forward to his grandfather's funeral, of course, but he did have to admit he was glad to have another opportunity to strap on the boots. And right now, they were proving especially useful as something to focus his attention on.

"I know he did, Doc. Thanks."

"And he was proud of you. I hope you know that."

He was pretty sure he did know that. Not that his grandfather ever would have come right out with those words. That wasn't his way. But things would slip out every now and then. A smile that seemed to be reserved just for his grandson when no one else could see. A "Yep, that's what I would do," in response to the way Cole had handled a situation with a food vendor or a drunk customer at Cassidy's. Sometimes Cole would show Bill the profit-and-loss statements for the restaurant and be met with nothing more than a nod and a firm slap on the shoulder. It may not have been much, but Cole knew what was being communicated.

Bill had owned Cassidy's since the 1970s, and for more than thirty years, it was just a bar. A hole-in-the-wall, backwoods bar for locals. But from the time Cole was a teenager, he'd always dreamed that it could be more. The building itself was a beautifully built corner-post log building, fortuitously surrounded by some of the most beautiful pine trees and aspens on earth on a secluded but easy-to-access piece of land, just off the main road. For years, Cassidy's—much like Adelaide Springs, and maybe like Bill Kimball himself—just existed for itself. After Cole's grandmother passed away when he was sixteen, his grandfather started spending all his time there. Not drinking. No, Cole couldn't remember ever seeing his grandfather drink more than a sip for a New Year's toast. Work was how he numbed the pain.

It was around the time of high school graduation that Cole finally mustered up the courage to share his dreams for Cassidy's with his grandfather. What if it was more than just a bar? The huge storeroom could become a kitchen. They could refinish the floor, which had been scuffed up beyond recognition during country line dancing's heyday, and add a few four-tops. Maybe a six-top. There weren't a lot of food options in town, after all. Andi had just opened the Bean Franklin, but that was only for breakfast and lunch. Maxine Brogan made the best tamales you'd ever tasted, but you couldn't exactly count the way she sold them (wrapped in aluminum foil, out of an original Igloo KoolTunes cooler under an umbrella on her porch) as a legitimate business. Cassidy's had a real opportunity to make a mark.

Cole's ideas had been shot down, of course. Time after time after time. So, in his early twenties, he left home for the first time in his life and went to Boulder to get his culinary arts degree. His thought had been that he would pick up more knowledge and improve upon his natural ability in the kitchen, and then he'd go somewhere else to live out the dreams he'd had for Cassidy's. His stubborn old grandfather was never going to come around, after all. But his two years in Boulder—just 173 miles away as the crow flies, though the drive took nearly six hours—had clarified for him that his window had closed. Not his window for being able to leave Adelaide Springs, but his window for wanting to.

Not that he ever told his grandfather that. Not when the man who had helped raise him suddenly seemed willing to consider implementing some new ideas if it meant his only grandchild—the last family he had in Adelaide Springs—wouldn't go away again.

He'd been silently staring at his nothing-that-costs-this-much-is-supposed-to-be-this-comfortable boots long enough that Doc read the cues and changed the subject.

"Is your mom going to be able to make it back in time?"

Cole caught himself and turned a disappointed sneer into an indulgent grin before he looked up. "You know how she is, Doc. 'Funerals are just a stopgap toward closure, and the souls of our loved ones deserve to be released from the burden of our sadness.' Or something." He shrugged. "She's been checking in with me a lot, but as far as actually showing up . . ." That sneer sure was determined. "I don't think that's exactly her style."

The oak double doors at the end of the aisle groaned open for the first time in a while, and Cole looked up with his well-rehearsed smile—the one that said, "I'm just barely holding it together, of course, but seeing *you* has made everything a little bit better"—to see who had shown up for their tour past Old Man Kimball's casket. He couldn't imagine there were many people left in town.

He hadn't expected to see two of his favorite people, who were supposed to be somewhere off the Amalfi Coast right about then. Laila gasped behind him. Cole didn't gasp, but he felt the same sort of surprise at seeing Brynn and Sebastian walking toward him, all in black. Surprise, yes. And gratitude. Love, certainly. But also the tiniest bit of frustration.

"What are they doing here?" Cole muttered.

He met them halfway down the aisle. He hadn't quite formulated words in his head yet. He wanted to say something about how he couldn't believe they were letting his grandfather's death ruin their honeymoon. But before he could say anything, Brynn was on her tiptoes, and her arms were wrapped around his neck.

"He was a miserable old man who seemed to look for every opportunity to torment me," she whispered before she pulled away and looked into his eyes. "From the time I was six years old, I can't remember him ever saying a kind word to me, and I'm sure he was awful before that too. I just can't remember. He was quick to point out my mistakes, and he *never* commended me on a job well done. And yet . . . somehow . . . I knew he was looking out for me. You know? I knew he was cheering me on. Somewhere. Deep down." She cleared her throat. "I'm really going to miss him."

Cole chuckled and wrapped his arms around her waist to pull her against him again. "I know. Me too."

CHAPTER THREE

LAILA

"I'm so glad that's over," Cole exhaled as he collapsed into a wooden chair at a table in the center of Cassidy's, laid his head back, and closed his eyes. He'd finally been chased into the dining room to join Brynn and me. Sebastian could cook pretty well and would do just fine preparing some burgers for the four of us, but Cole was never a fan of giving up his kitchen. Nevertheless, relief seemed to permeate through him as he allowed himself to relax for the first time in days.

"Do you need a drink or something? Can I get you anything?" I asked.

His eyes remained closed as he shook his head. "Thanks, I'm good. It's just nice to have a moment to myself."

Brynn and I looked at each other and smiled, completely understanding he wasn't passive-aggressively hinting for us to go home. To spend a little time with just the Sudworths and me was to be able to completely unwind. There were no pretenses or polite-smiles-for-the-sake-of-appearance necessary among the four of us.

"Hey," Brynn started, sitting up straighter in her seat. "Was that Lottie Carlson I saw pulling out of the church parking lot right about the time Seb and I got there? How's she handling things? I bet she's heartbroken."

Cole chuckled, head still back and eyes still closed. "She told me to call her if I need a grandma hug."

Laughter burst from Brynn. I thought I'd gotten my own giggles out after overhearing her say it—and overhearing Cole respond by asking, "How is a grandma hug different from a normal hug?"—but I found myself losing it all over again.

Charlotte Carlson had been a few years ahead of us in school, so she had to be all of forty-five now, at the oldest. She'd had three short-lived marriages to increasingly exotic men who always whisked her away from Adelaide Springs. Each time, the people of the town had been cajoled into big au revoir send-offs and bridal showers before she got married in some far and distant land. And each time she got divorced, she'd suddenly just reappeared in the flow of everyday life again, like none of it had ever happened. After the third divorce, she'd changed tactics and begun pursuing local men. Cole had been in her crosshairs for a while and had kindly but efficiently communicated his fears of ending up the subject of an unsolved mysteries podcast if he so much as had dinner with her.

Let's just say that from there, Lottie had started chasing an older demographic. And since Cole's grandfather was the oldest, most financially solvent single man in town, it hadn't taken her long to zero in.

"She wore a veil, Brynn." I was still giggling as I pictured it. "Like, an actual black veil like you'd see in the movies."

"No!"

Cole nodded and opened his eyes. "Yep. She was straight-up dressed like Diane Keaton at Vito Corleone's funeral in *The Godfather*. It was quite remarkable."

"Who?" Sebastian asked as he came from the kitchen carrying a platter of burgers on buns. "Lottie?"

"Got it in one," Cole answered. He adjusted his posture to get ready to eat, loosening his tie as he did.

Seb set the platter in the center of the table and took his seat between Brynn and Cole. "I suppose poor Doc will be next in her widower crosshairs."

"Well . . ." We had the restaurant to ourselves, but that didn't stop me from looking around to make sure no one would overhear. "I suspect Doc may not be on the market much longer."

Brynn's eyes flew open, and she leaned in to get the scoop, but Cole shook his head. "Don't encourage her, Brynn. She's about to fill your head with theories based on *zero* evidence and no semblance of fact whatsoever—"

"Jo?" Seb asked as he reached in, grabbed a burger, and placed it on Brynn's plate and then got himself one.

"Yes!" I squealed and pointed at Cole. "Yeah, no semblance of fact . . . Whatever! You see it, too, don't you, Seb?"

"Of course." He jumped up as he realized he'd left the bag of potato chips on the bar. "I've always seen it."

Cole rolled his eyes. "They're just friends. They've been friends for—what—sixty-some years?"

"At least," Seb confirmed.

"So what makes you think that all of a sudden—"

"Except it wouldn't really be all of a sudden, would it?" Brynn interjected. "Seb's always seen it. I see it. Laila sees it. Something's been developing for a while."

Cole seemed to consider the possibilities for a moment. "Still," he finally said between bites. "When you know someone that well, what would it take to flip that switch?"

Sebastian raised his hand. "Am I the only one who would rather not think of Doc and Jo flipping any switches?"

"If you know what I mean . . . ," I said in the most innuendo-laced tone I could, causing Seb to shudder and Cole to cover his ears and call out, "La-la-la-la-la-la! I can't hear you. I can't hear you!"

"As fun as it is to picture the senior citizens in our lives in flagrante delicto—"

"Gross," Cole muttered just as Sebastian asked his wife, "Is that really necessary?"

Through her giggles, Brynn stood and raised her glass. "To Old Man Kimball, who may not have always been a barrel of monkeys but who made a huge impact in my life and the lives of so many. He came through for me more than once, and I'll always be grateful. Most important, he helped shape one of my favorite people in the world. Any man who can raise you to be the man you are, Cole, can't be all bad."

Cole chuckled and cleared his throat before standing and raising his glass. Seb and I joined them.

"To Old Man Kimball!" we all said in unison before taking a drink.

We began sitting back down, but Brynn shot up again. "Ooh! I almost forgot!" She dug into the pocket of her black pencil skirt and pulled out some crumpled bills and some coins and set them all on the table.

"What's that for?" I asked as Seb began laughing.

"*That*," she responded, "is six dollars and forty-two cents I owed Bill for some whiskey glasses I broke in 2001."

Cole laughed as he reached across the table and scooped the money into his hand. "I know it's a symbolic gesture, but you're rich, and I have absolutely no qualms whatsoever about taking your money."

We sat around laughing and eating and sharing memories of Bill for a few more minutes until the bell over the front door began ringing.

"Sorry," Cole called out as he turned to face whoever was entering. "We're not open today. Family situat—" A familiar face appeared around the doorframe. "Oh, hey, Doc."

"I'm sorry to interrupt."

"Not at all." Cole stood. "Why don't you join us?"

Sebastian was already heading to the kitchen. "It will just take a minute to throw another burger on the grill."

"Nah, thanks, Seb. I appreciate it, but Jo already fed me."

Brynn and I looked at each other knowingly—mischievously—causing Sebastian to roll his eyes at us before he said, "How about a cup of coffee, then?"

"That I won't say no to."

Cole had already pulled a fifth chair up to the table, between him and me, by the time Doc finished his walk across the room to us. I leaned in and hugged Doc as he sat, and Brynn stood from her chair to come around and do the same. We had all just seen each other not even an hour ago, but Doc had been like another parent to all of us. There was just something about losing one of the parental figures in your life that made you want to hold the ones you had left a little closer.

"Thanks, Seb," he said with a nod as Sebastian set the cup of coffee in front of him and went back to his seat on the other side of Cole. "I really am sorry to break up your time together. I know it's a little more difficult to come by these days."

That was true, though Cole and I had all the time in the world together, of course. We'd worked together at Cassidy's at least four days a week, every week, since he'd convinced his grandfather to invest in his dream of turning it into a restaurant. And what had that been? Ten years now? Fifteen, maybe? There had been lots of times over the course of those however many years that he'd apologized there weren't other opportunities for me there. That there weren't ways for me to "move up." Well, no . . . there wouldn't be, would there? Moving up in Adelaide Springs wasn't really a thing.

Someday, maybe I'd be able to convince him I was okay with that. I loved waiting tables at Cassidy's. I loved having the opportunity to chat with pretty much every tourist passing through town—because, seriously, where else were they going to eat? I loved our constant carousel of regulars, be it Fenton Norris, who always watched whatever ball game was on television and talked about the weather with whoever else wandered in, or Neil Pinkton, twenty years old and inching toward his own definition of adulthood by sitting at the bar with the old men, drinking a soda. Mostly I loved playing my small part in Cole's success.

For a few years, the team had gotten even better. I really wouldn't have thought that was possible, but having Sebastian behind the bar had made the whole thing click into place at a new level. I mean, he'd resurrected the karaoke machine, for goodness' sake.

Once in a while we still got him behind the bar and on the stage, but of course he and Brynn lived in New York a good part of the time these days. And now that Sebastian was a journalist again, even when they were in town, we didn't see them nearly as often. He was writing or working on his podcast. Now that they were newlyweds, it seemed unlikely their time would magically free up for their friends. And how long would it be before they had kids?

Would they have kids? Did they even want kids? It was sort of difficult to imagine, honestly. They'd both be great parents—I was absolutely sure of that—but with their busy lives, I didn't expect they'd make time to add a kid to the mix anytime soon. They already had Sebastian's dog, Murrow, who traveled the globe with them—or at least with *him* when they traveled the globe in separate directions. A little human Sudworth child might not travel so well. And if they didn't expand their family *soon* . . . Well, they weren't exactly spring chickens.

None of us were, of course, though I was a few months younger than Brynn and Cole, and we were all a few years younger than Sebastian. What did that make me? A summer chicken? *Early* summer at best. Though, really, who was I kidding? The countdown to forty had begun. I'd be thirty-nine in a week, and then we'd start turning forty. *Forty*. Cole, then Brynn, then me. Nope, not a single spring chicken in the bunch.

Though . . . should I think of myself as a late-winter chicken rather than an early-summer chicken? We'd had a lot of animals growing up, but never chickens. I couldn't say with absolutely certainty that I understood the metaphor.

"Earth to Laila, " Cole teased melodically from across the table. "You still with us?"

I looked up in surprise at the sound of my name. "I was just . . ." I shook away the stupor. "Sorry. What did I miss?"

"Doc was telling us his reason for stopping by."

"As I was saying, after the funeral, I went to the bank to get Bill's will out of my box." He reached into the inside pocket of his jacket. "Not sure if you knew he asked me to be his executor?"

Cole chuckled. "I didn't even know he had a will."

"Yeah, always has had. This one is new. He updated it just a few months ago."

Cole eyed the yellow envelope with curiosity. "A few months ago? Why? Nothing's changed."

Doc shrugged. "The only thing that changed, I figure, is he finally started believing he was a mere mortal after all. After the strokes and everything. The other one was pretty old, I think. He probably just wanted to make sure everything was current and in order."

"Do you know what's in there?" Cole asked.

"No. We can find out now, if you want . . ."

I raised my hand. I'm not sure why. I just wasn't sure I was part of the moment enough to speak freely during it, I guess. Still, I didn't take it so far as to wait to be called on.

"Sorry, but does there not have to be some sort of will reading or something? I always picture these things taking place in an attorney's office."

"That's just a device invented for the movies." Sebastian smiled. "Certainly more dramatic than an envelope being pulled out of Doc's pocket, but unless there are beneficiaries contesting bequeathments or things being held up in probate, it's typically a pretty nondramatic thing."

"I did call your mom," Doc said to Cole. "As next of kin I figured she had the right to know everything first. She said to just go ahead and get with you—"

"And I can let her know how much money she gets?" Cole filled in the rest of the thought. When Doc raised his hands in a way that clearly communicated, "Nothing so crass as that, but for all intents and purposes, you nailed it," Cole laughed. "Well, alright, then. Let's do this thing. Let's find out how many more orphans can have their lives changed by a generous endowment from the Cassidy Dolan-Kimball Foundation to Save the World."

CHAPTER FOUR

COLE

Doc looked around the table and then back at Cole. "I'm pretty sure I know the answer to this, but just to be sure . . . Are you okay with everyone being here?"

His friends all jumped up, maybe a little bit horrified that they hadn't even thought to ask whether they were welcome to stay for the awkward business-and-legality part of the day, but also, it seemed, a little bit horrified at the thought of leaving. Brynn and Sebastian started rattling off lists of things they needed to go do while Laila refused to meet Cole's eyes. Her mouth was moving, but he had no idea what she was saying. She was probably just copying Brynn and Seb's excuses.

Actually . . . yeah. That was it. He was able to make out the faint echoes of ". . . laundry . . . pack . . . Murrow . . . *Sunup* . . ." coming through her mumbles, though none of that had anything to do with the reality of her life.

They all hated the thought of not being there for him, and Cole loved them for it.

He laughed and pointed a finger down toward the chairs. "Sit down, you numbskulls." No other explanation was necessary, and the three of them sat back in their seats without another word.

"Okay, then," Doc began with a fond twinkle in his eyes. He slipped his fingers into the seal of the envelope and opened it up, then pulled out the trifold of white pages. Four pieces of paper. Maybe five.

Cole didn't expect to feel any sadness right then, but all of a sudden, his throat constricted and he bit down on the right side of his bottom lip, just to keep things in check. Ninety years of life and family and investments and prudence and being a cheapskate but also surprisingly generous (not that Bill Kimball ever would have allowed most people to know that) and loving a town an irrational amount despite being its most unyielding critic . . . This was what was left to show for it. Whatever was in those four pieces of paper. Maybe five.

"Scoot." He looked at Laila to his right, instructing Sebastian to make room for her. Without another word being spoken, Brynn scooted into Laila's seat, Sebastian scooted into his wife's former chair, and Laila sat down next to Cole, grabbing his right hand in both of her small, delicate ones.

"I'm fine, Lai," he whispered to her.

"I know."

How had she always been able to do that? To detect his mood, correctly assess it, and provide the perfect amount of support in less time than it took most people to slip off their shoes when they walked in the front door of their homes at night?

In their group, Cole was known as the protective one, but at least when it came to him, Laila was a one-woman triage unit.

He squeezed her hand and looked to Doc. "Ready when you are."

Doc folded the papers back on their creases to straighten them out and then pulled his reading glasses from the outside chest pocket of his heavy-duty denim jacket. He slipped them over his ears and cleared his throat. "Let's see here." His eyes skimmed the first few lines before he muttered, "Legal jargon. Ah, okay . . . here we are."

Lowering his foot to the floor, he sat up straighter in his chair, running his finger along the words at the bottom of the first page and then flipping to the second. "The house located at 23394 County Road 14, Adelaide Springs, Colorado . . ." He looked up and smiled at Cole. "It's yours, of course. Along with everything in it."

Cole released a breath he hadn't realized he'd been holding. He certainly wasn't sure *why* he had been holding it. It had never even occurred to him that there was a chance the house wouldn't be his, but he'd also never thought of it in those terms. To think of it in those terms would have been to acknowledge, in some small way, that it wasn't his already. No, his name might not have been on the deed, but apart from his two years in Boulder, he'd never lived anywhere else. His earliest memories were in that house with his grandparents and his mother. Then his grandmother had died, and his mother went off to chase her restless desire to save the world. And eventually his grandfather needed more care than he could give, so Grandpa went to Spruce House, and Cole lived in that big house alone. He'd probably known they'd never live together again. They'd probably both known that. But they never discussed it. And Cole hadn't so much as repositioned his grandfather's chair from right in front of the fireplace where he liked it.

Cole nodded. "That's very generous."

Doc's eyes continued skimming the pages, and about the time he flipped over to page three, they started growing wide. Wide and full of bewilderment.

"What is it?" Sebastian asked.

Doc looked up from the pages. "You're all in here."

"What?" Brynn and Sebastian asked in shocked unison, while Cole just shook his head and smiled. That had been the story of his life. For nearly forty years, every single time he'd thought he had his grandfather figured out, the old man did something that surprised him. Genuinely surprised him. Maybe it was finding a bunch of wrapped Christmas gifts in the closet and realizing they weren't for him but for the kids of some of the miners who were clinging to desperate hope they wouldn't have to relocate their families when the last of the silver mining dried up in the late eighties. More than once it had been the way his miserly stubbornness had been overruled by compassionate humanity and he'd used his vote as a member of city council to actually make people's lives better. And how many times had Cole been ordered into the car after school, grumbling and full of resentment that his video game time was being taken away from him, only to end up having one of the best afternoons of his adolescence sneaking around with his grandfather, pretending to be invisible superheroes on a mission to pick up trash and pull weeds without being spotted?

Of course he'd wait until he was gone to display his heart and reveal his true feelings for some of the people he liked to pretend vexed him more than any others. Cole didn't know why he was surprised.

Doc chuckled and looked at them over the rims of his readers. "I think I'll just read this part aloud. It's unmistakably Bill's voice." He looked back at the papers and cleared his throat. "'To Sebastian Sudworth, I leave my Benjamin Homer Brass Barreled American Flintlock Pistol, crafted in Boston, Massachusetts, circa 1775, along with certificate of authenticity. Credit where it's due.'" Doc looked at Sebastian. "That's all it says. No actual credit given, it seems, but—"

"Yeah, I get it." Sebastian nodded and studied his hands resting on the table while the outbreak of a smile threatened to overtake the twitching corners of his mouth. "That means a lot."

In the three years or so that Bill Kimball and Sebastian Sudworth had served together on the Adelaide Springs city council, they'd only voted the same way a handful of times. The most notable had been in support of the new plan Brynn and Sebastian had hatched to bring back Township Days in a way that was sustainable, affordable, and forward thinking. Oh, Bill still complained every chance he got, of course, but by bringing back Township Days, Sebastian had finally earned the old man's respect. Credit where it was due.

"'To Brynn Cornell,'" Doc continued, and Brynn froze in her seat at the sound of her name. "'I forgive a debt in the amount of $6.42, valued at approximately $41.30 when adjusted for inflation and accrued interest.'"

The entire table erupted into laughter, and Brynn stood from her seat and reached across the table. "Hand it over, Kimball. I'm free and clear, baby. Free and clear." Cole pulled the money from his pocket and handed it back to her as Brynn continued laughing.

"'To Laila Olivet,'" Doc resumed, being the adult in the room, as always. But this time the chuckling continued and the uneasiness that had originally accompanied the seriousness of the occasion seemed to be gone. At least it was until Doc said, "Oh. Well . . . Hmm."

Everyone snapped back to attention, but Laila still attempted to keep things light. "I'm pretty sure I paid him back for everything *I* ever broke, Doc. Everything he knew about, anyway."

Doc smiled at her and held the document to his right so Cole, who was craning his neck, could see what had caused Doc's reaction. Cole's eyes flew open as he looked quickly to Doc and then back to the paper.

"Okay, now you're freaking me out." Laila exhaled a shaky breath. "What does it say?"

Cole faced her, his eyes no longer wide but his grin getting wider by the second. "My grandfather left you ten thousand dollars."

The color drained from her face in an instant. "What? What are you talking about? Why would he . . . *What?!* What does it say? Did he say *why*? That doesn't make any sense!"

"It says, 'To Laila Olivet I leave ten thousand dollars.'" Doc raised his gaze over his glasses again and smirked. "You know Bill. He always had a way with words."

"That's too much. I can't accept—"

"Of course you can," Cole argued. "It's what he wanted. And as to *why* . . ." He hadn't seen it coming, but it actually made all the sense in the world to him. "You know you were his favorite." He was filled with affection for her—and his grandfather—as he watched her grapple with her emotions. Bill Kimball had been a man who didn't like many people and had no trouble finding fault with all of them. All of them except for the wife he had loved and lost.

Cole's grandmother aside, Bill had thought Laila Olivet had fewer faults than all the rest.

Doc resumed reading. "And then there's a little bit of money to your mom, Cole. And some of your grandmother's belongings, it looks like. Engagement ring, some other jewelry, a fur coat . . . those sorts of things. Then it looks like everything else . . ." His voice faded. "That can't be right," he said under his breath as he flipped from page three to page four and back again. His eyes met Cole's. "Everything else goes to the town, with a good portion earmarked for Township Days."

Cole snorted. "Sounds right to me. I'm surprised there wasn't some sort of stipulation in there that Brynn's $6.42 debt forgiveness must be accompanied by an unbreakable vow to always support the festival and give it top-of-the-hour coverage on *Sunup*." He began looking over Doc's shoulder. "So how much is 'everything,' anyway? I know he had a few stock investments and some money in the bank, but—"

"One point eight million."

Silence echoed around the table. Everyone stared first at Doc, as if trying to make sense of the words he had just said, and then at Cole, as if he'd been holding out on them. Big time. For their entire lives, in some cases.

Of course it didn't take long at all to observe the slack-jawed confusion Cole knew his face expressed and realize that if anyone had been held out on, it was him.

"I'm guessing you didn't have any idea Bill had that sort of money?" Sebastian asked him.

Cole raised his eyebrows and shook his head. "If you'd have asked me what sort of liquidity he had left, after the house and investments and all that, I would have guessed a hundred grand. Maybe two if he was savvier than he let on."

And the thing was he *had* suspected his grandfather was savvier than he let on. No surprise there. For all the ways he struggled with technology and railed against advancements and a changing world and such, he also dropped names like Steve Jobs and Bill Gates into conversations often enough that Cole would sometimes tease him by asking if he had Rupert Murdoch on speed dial.

Bill would respond by acting like he didn't understand the concept of speed dial.

But one point eight million? How was that even possible?

"An amount like that is going to change everything for Adelaide Springs," Brynn whispered—in excitement and fear, Cole guessed. Cole understood the tone because he understood the sentiment.

"Is there any sort of instruction, Doc?" Cole asked. "Apart from supporting Township Days, I mean. Did he say anything about a trust being set up or how to spread out payments to the town, or anything like that?"

Doc shook his head. "Doesn't look like it. Not in here, anyway. But obviously there's got to be more paperwork somewhere. I guess I'll have to get with his lawyer—"

"I have his number." Cole pulled out his phone. "I'm assuming it's the same firm we used in Grand Junction when we set up medical power of attorney."

Doc reached into his inside jacket pocket again and pulled out a pen and handed it to Cole. Cole wrote the information on the envelope the will had been in and handed it to Doc. "Here you go. Let me know how I can help with any of that."

"Same here," Sebastian chimed in, and Brynn nodded her agreement. "Something like this has the potential to make it all too big too quickly if we're not careful."

Laila's quiet, shaky voice broke through the ongoing speculation. "What about Cassidy's?"

Huh. Cole hadn't given any thought to Cassidy's. Yes, they were sitting right in the center of it, but it hadn't been on his radar even so much as his grandmother's fur coat (which his mother had already sworn she would sell, the proceeds going to an animal rights charity). His grandfather's house had been just that—his grandfather's house. Never mind that Cole had never received his mail anywhere else or that nearly every paycheck he'd ever earned had contributed to the utilities and upkeep. Never mind that on the odd occasion he had a day off from Cassidy's, he would find himself on a ladder or in the attic or mowing the yard. It was his grandfather's house.

But he couldn't remember the last time he had thought of Cassidy's Bar & Grill as his grandfather's business. Cassidy's was his, and he suspected his grandfather had seen it that way for even longer than he had.

And now he just had to hope that a long-standing shared view wasn't going to cause any unnecessary problems.

"Did he forget to include Cassidy's in his will?" Cole asked. "What happens then? Will it have to go to probate or something?"

"You may get your movie drama after all," Brynn teased Laila from across the table.

Cole chuckled and envisioned just how nondramatic that might be. *People's exhibit A: Cole's Bacon Cheeseburger with Cassidy's Sauce. On the menu since 2016. Can anyone else in the entire world recreate the recipe for Cassidy's Sauce? No? The defense rests. Case dismissed and bon appétit!*

Doc wasn't laughing. He had flipped to the fifth and final page, and it was holding all his attention. And just like that, the seriousness of Doc's expression captivated the attention of everyone else at the table.

"What is it, Doc?" Sebastian finally asked, after everyone's eyes had shifted around to each other several times and his had landed on Cole. "What's wrong?"

It wasn't until Cole heard the question from Sebastian's mouth that it clicked that something was, in fact, wrong. Sebastian was the keenest observer he'd ever known, and Cole was suddenly afraid he was missing something.

"He did leave Cassidy's to me, didn't he?" The thought of any other alternative was unfathomable, but that didn't stop his brain from spiraling down a list. Not of worries, but of possibilities. If he had to, he'd buy it. From whom, he had no idea—the town, maybe?—and with what money he had even less of a clue. But the house was his and had been free of debt for twenty-five years or more. His credit was good and his reputation was spotless.

The more he thought about it, he wasn't all that concerned. He had a little bit of lingering guilt that he hadn't helped his grandfather keep a better eye on things, but he would just have to live with that. He would have insisted on more than just medical power of attorney if he'd known wills were going to be rewritten in the last months of his grandfather's life, but he'd seemed more together than anyone in his condition had any right to be.

It was what it was. If "everything else" was going to Adelaide

Springs, that must include Cassidy's. He'd figure out a way to pay what the restaurant was worth—and to him, it was worth whatever it took.

Besides, he thought as he looked across the table and a smile returned to his face, two of his best friends were loaded. They would make a sizable donation to his GoFundMe account.

"Cole, I don't know how to explain what I'm looking at here." Doc's voice was grave as he looked up from the papers in his hands and met Cole's eyes. "It looks like he sold it."

The complete difference in terminology from what had just been flooding his brain—the difference between leaving something as an inheritance and selling it—didn't register. "Okay, so who do I need to talk to? Do I make an offer with city council, or—"

"No, listen to me, son." Doc turned and placed his hand on Cole's shoulder and transmitted the complete weight of his caring, compassionate nature as his eyes bored into Cole's. "Bill sold Cassidy's Bar & Grill. Months ago, it looks like. To an investment group of some kind."

Gasps escaped from Laila and Brynn, while Sebastian scooted his chair from the table, the legs scraping against the wood floor and teetering to maintain their balance as Seb faced away from his friends and muttered his frustrations toward the log wall.

As for Cole, he didn't know what to say. What was he *supposed* to say? Ultimately, as Laila squeezed his hand and Doc held his gaze as stoically as he could and Sebastian wandered in a way mildly reminiscent of a caged animal and Brynn held her tongue and her breath, he said the only thing that made any sense at all to him.

"No." He shook his head, and a confused chuckle escaped. "No. There's been some sort of mistake. For all the things he . . . I mean, I know he wasn't exactly . . ." Cole let out a deep breath. "No. He never would have done something so cruel. Without even telling me? No way. Not a chance. I'm sorry, Doc, but you're wrong."

Doc set the papers down on the table in front of him. "I can't tell you how much I wish I was."

CHAPTER FIVE

LAILA

"I can't believe Bill would do this," Sebastian was saying about twenty-five minutes later. Doc and Cole had left to track down the rest of the paperwork to try to make sense of whatever was happening, and after twenty-five minutes, those were the first coherent words to come out of Sebastian's mouth. I'd never seen him so angry.

I hadn't gotten to anger just yet. Or sadness. Or understanding. Certainly not understanding. I was just worried about Cole and anxious for him to get back with answers.

"It'll be okay." Brynn had shifted into fixer mode. The part of her personality that had won her the reputation as America's Ray of Sunshine had been activated. One of her best friends had just had his life yanked out from under him, another was feeling powerless and confused, and her husband was exhibiting a temper that she jokingly said was usually reserved for her alone when she accidentally blurted out the Wordle for the day before he got there on his own. Everything in her nature forced her to try to step in and make things better for the people she loved. "I'm sure there has been some sort of misunderstanding."

"But what if there hasn't?" I asked.

"Then he'll buy it back." Brynn shrugged as if it were the most obvious suggestion in the world.

Sebastian sighed and rolled his eyes. "I'm sorry. I love you, but that's absurd. I'm pretty sure every dime Cole has ever made has gone right back into Cassidy's." He looked across the table at me for verification. "Right?"

"Probably," I whispered. "And I know it wasn't cheap to get his grandfather into Spruce House. I could be wrong, but I got the impression Cole was paying for most of that."

"Yeah." Sebastian nodded. "He had talked about not wanting to have to liquidate Bill's investments . . ." His voice trailed off, and he began fuming as the heat returned to his face. "And that's the thanks he gets. He busted his tail to take care of Bill so that Cassidy's wouldn't have to be sold. And it just got pulled out from under him anyway."

Sebastian began to stand from his chair, probably to begin another furious round of pacing around the building, but Brynn got up first. She stood behind him and placed her hands on his shoulders and held him down.

"I'm sure he can get a loan." Sebastian opened his mouth to offer some argument, but she didn't let him voice it. "Or we'll give him the money."

"Yeah, right," I replied, laughing for the first time in a half hour or so. "You know he won't take your money."

Brynn considered that, but the Ray of Sunshine could not be deterred. "He may not take ours, but he'll take yours."

I laughed again. "Are you kidding me? Do you remember those huge dill pickles at the movie theater in Alamosa? He loved those things, and I tried to buy him one every single time we ever went—from junior high on—and I never got to. Not once. He'd either pay me back or insist on paying—for the pickle *and* my popcorn, it should be noted." My laughter faded as I considered the reality before us. Before *him*. "But I don't know. Maybe you're right. Maybe this would be different."

Of course, even if my stubborn best friend would accept my help this time, we still had one major issue before us. "I'm no real estate magnate, but I'm guessing Cassidy's would cost more than those dill pickles?"

Brynn gave Sebastian's shoulders one final squeeze and returned to her seat at the table. "We'll give you the money, obviously."

"And pretend I've been a secret millionaire all these years? How'd that happen?" Yes, I had faithfully waited tables at both Cassidy's and the Bean Franklin for pretty much my entire adult life, but most people in Adelaide Springs tended to show their appreciation in ways that were much more personal than money. Magda Sorenson tipped me with a dozen farm-fresh eggs every single Tuesday when she came for Cole's chicken-fried steak dinner special, and though I didn't cook, I could boil water. Hard-boiled eggs were my snack of choice most days. And I hadn't bought hand soap in nearly a decade, because every time I ran out, all I had to do was mention it to Susan Singer when she was in there picking up her garden salad with a side of sunflower oil. One of her homemade goat-milk soap bars would inevitably be waiting for me on my front step when I got home.

I'd always been pretty good about saving my money, if only because there wasn't much to spend it on in Adelaide Springs. I had a nice car and my own little house on a couple of acres at the north end of Elm Street. Yes, I'd bought the house from my dad and Melinda—who lived less than a mile away on the south end of Elm—but it was mine. Or it would be in about four more years. That wasn't too shabby, right? I'd have the mortgage on a house I loved completely paid off before I turned forty-five. How many single, small-town waitresses could say that?

And since the internet in Adelaide Springs had become more reliable, thanks to the Sudworths working their connections to get a fiber network installed, I'd been treating myself to Netflix and getting caught up on all the shows of the past decade or so that I'd never cared enough to sit still for while they buffered. (If all you know about *House of Cards* is that Robin Wright is in it and you *love* Robin Wright, I recommend you skip it. I'm permanently scarred by seeing the darker side of Princess Buttercup.)

What's more, I had splurged last year on the Singer Quantum Stylist 9985 sewing machine. Do you hear me? The 9985! The one with a color touch screen and thirteen different buttonhole styles.

Thirteen! That baby came with 960 built-in stitches and a twenty-five-year warranty, so clearly I was doing okay for myself.

But if Cole's grandfather really had done the unthinkable and sold Cassidy's out from under him, my 850-a-minute high-speed stitching capabilities weren't going to make much of a difference.

"We'll have to loan him the money," Sebastian said as he scratched his jawline where his five-o'clock shadow was beginning to show. "With interest."

"Oh, come on," Brynn objected. "We're not going to charge him interest."

I didn't know exactly how wealthy the Sudworths were, but it was reasonable to assume they could buy Cassidy's Bar & Grill many times over. In addition to their lucrative day jobs, they'd both had memoirs on the *New York Times* bestseller list for the better part of a year, and I knew Brynn had just landed another huge book deal and was the new face of orange juice. Not *all* orange juice, obviously, but one of the big brands. I couldn't remember which. If the state of Florida or wherever could have nailed down her endorsement for oranges in general, the entire world would have said goodbye to vitamin C deficiencies. Everything she touched turned to gold.

So there's nothing to worry about, I reminded myself. *Brynn and Seb will fix this.*

"No, he's right," I told her. "He's not going to want anyone's charity. Even to hold on to Cassidy's. It's going to have to be beneficial for you guys, too, or I'm pretty sure he won't even consider it."

We all sat quietly, considering the possibilities, until Brynn's eyes flew open and she pounded her fist on the table. She turned to face Sebastian, who was already giving her his full attention in anticipation of whatever brilliant thing she was about to come up with. Brynn may have had the reputation of being bubbly and cheery and all of that, but Sebastian knew, as I did, that she was a semimaniacal freak-of-nature genius underneath all the pop-culture references and TikTok video obsessions.

"Let's go corporate." She threw her hands up in the air as she said the words, then crossed her arms over her chest and sat back in her chair as if there was nothing more to say on the matter.

And I guess that's why the Sudworths made such a good team. Because Sebastian was tracking.

"Yes." He grabbed her face in his hands and planted a quick kiss square on her lips. "Yes. Of course. That's it."

Brynn and I had always been pretty good at speaking the same language too. In high school, we would make plans to sneak out of our houses at night right under our parents' noses. (I mean, sure, we'd do the sneaking right under their noses, of course, but most teenagers could do that. It was the *planning* right under their noses that was really impressive.) And when it came to John Mayer songs, it was like we had our own private language that would have made zero sense to the rest of the world.

"What's the one that always makes me hungry?"

"'Why Georgia'?"

"Yes! Thank you. Although, come to think of it, I think I'm in more of a 'Heartbreak Warfare' mood."

"So . . . tater tots?"

"Perfect."

But this? I didn't have a clue what she was talking about. "What does that mean? 'Corporate'?" I looked to Sebastian, since he had been the last to speak, but he gestured for Brynn to take the floor and share her idea.

She leaned forward onto her elbows. "If we take our feelings for Cole out of this, it's still easy to see that buying Cassidy's right now would be a super-smart investment. I haven't looked at the books or anything, but it's obvious that business has picked up over the past couple of years."

Sebastian nodded. "Right. Adelaide Springs is growing. There are going to be more restaurants soon. There will have to be. But Cassidy's is the standard bearer."

"He won't be able to argue with us wanting to invest and make things as good as they can possibly be before the population boom really hits." She smiled at me and then rested her hand on Sebastian's forearm. "Actually, we should probably think about buying up some of the empty houses out on the county roads."

"And the downtown storefronts." Sebastian pulled his phone out and began tapping away. "Whoever bought Cassidy's from Bill—this is probably just the beginning. We need to do all we can to keep the properties local. I can't believe we didn't think of this before."

Okay. I got it. I was all caught up and couldn't deny they'd probably stumbled upon the most Cole-friendly approach to fixing this mess. It was easy enough to fill in the gaps. They, along with Cole and whoever else, would own shares of Cassidy's. Or percentages. I mean, it wasn't going to be traded on the stock market or anything, right? Okay . . . so multiple people would own it, and then when Cole's percentage made enough money, as Brynn and Sebastian were confident it would, it seemed, he could buy everyone else out. Yeah, if he was going to go for anything, that was probably it.

But as I watched them buzzing with excitement—looking up addresses on their phones and throwing out numbers to each other that made as much sense to me as an unquantifiable John Mayer hunger scale would mean to most people—I just felt sad. Like something had been lost that would never be reclaimed. Sure, maybe Cole would ultimately be the sole owner of Cassidy's. All the hard work that he had poured into the place—the literal blood, sweat, and tears he'd devoted to what I was pretty sure would go down as the love of his life—would still, somehow, all be worthwhile. With Brynn and Seb working in Cole's corner, Cassidy's was going to reach new levels of success he hadn't even dreamed of. I didn't have any difficulty believing that. Cassidy's could still be his legacy, as he'd always wanted it to be.

But no one and no amount of money or success or legacy would ever be able to rid him of the moment when, in his mind, all his deepest fears were confirmed. The ones he had only ever shared with me, I was fairly certain. Maybe Brynn and Sebastian could fix the situation, but what was it going to take to fix Cole? Would he ever again believe anything other than what now probably appeared to him to be the cold, hard, indisputable truth? I couldn't believe it was true, but from Cole's perspective, *of course* he was going to believe that as the adopted son of Bill Kimball's stepdaughter, he was an outsider. Never fully connected. Easily disregarded. The grandfather whose needs Cole had always put before his own had never counted him as his real family after all. Who was ever going to be able to convince him of anything else after this?

"I want to invest." I made the declaration with as much certainty as I'd ever said anything in my life, I was pretty sure. At least since 2010, when I'd stood up in the theater at the end of *Extraordinary Measures* and confidently declared Brendan Fraser was going to win an Oscar. (My timing may have been off a bit, but who's laughing now, suckers?)

I'm not sure what they had been saying to each other—or to me, maybe?—right then, but they were suddenly silent as I jumped up and ran over to grab my purse from behind the bar. I pulled my phone out and clicked on my banking app, did a little figuring in my head, and hurried back over.

"How big a share will twenty-five thousand dollars get me?"

They stared at me for a moment, and then Sebastian pulled his eyes away, and I was suddenly a little embarrassed. These were two people with whom I always felt comfortable being who I was, for better or worse, but at that moment I wanted to be who I was but with a more impressive investment portfolio.

"I know it's not much."

I looked down at my favorite heels—the ones I had picked out in Denver three years ago when Cole took me shopping for my birthday and told me to pick out the pair I loved most, no matter the price. I knew he meant it, but I also knew I'd rather he spend his money splurging on appetizers *and* dessert at Cheesecake Factory, so I only looked in the clearance section. And there I'd found my favorite pair of shoes of all time, which I'd worn while waiting tables and at Brynn and Seb's rehearsal dinner, right there in Cassidy's a little over a week ago, and on more than one occasion while sitting on my deck reading a book. They were a translucent sort of pale pink with a glittery effect. They reminded me of the jelly shoes I'd been obsessed with as a kid, except they had a kitten heel that made me feel like a cross between Cinderella running away at midnight and Peggy Olson on *Mad Men*, after she came into her own and started writing ads for Heinz Baked Beans and such. (Again, better internet has opened a whole new world to me.)

Right now, my favorite heels were making me feel like I didn't belong at this table of power investors. I loved them, but what had they cost? Thirty-two bucks, I think. Don't get me wrong—it had been completely worth it, being able to sit across the table from Cole an hour later, feeling sorry for Cinderella that she'd not taken advantage of a little bibbidi-bobbidi magic to conjure up some Tex-Mex Eggrolls and Very Cherry Ghirardelli Chocolate Cheesecake. But Brynn probably wore Louboutin pumps to walk to the end of the driveway and check her mail. I'd never been jealous of her until that very moment, when I wished I had a closet full of shoes like that to sell.

"I don't know when I'll actually get the ten thousand Bill left me, come to think of it." I really wished I could quit my feet from shuffling. I was going to scratch up the wood floor with my stupid, cheap kitten heel if I wasn't careful. "So, right now, I can do fifteen grand."

I sighed. *Quit talking, Laila. And stop* thinking. *This isn't getting any better.* "And most of that's in a CD, so I'll need a few days to close that out."

How much would the early-closure penalty take away?

Here, guys . . . I have about a buck fifty-two to contribute to the cause.

"I love you so much," Brynn whispered.

"I really wish I could do more."

"Are you kidding? This is amazing. *You're* amazing!" she exclaimed.

Sebastian met my eyes, which I'd finally raised from my feet. "You know Cole won't want you to do that." I began to protest, but he didn't give me the chance. "But don't you take no for an answer. You hear me?"

I grinned and nodded. "I hear you."

Just then we heard the rumble of Cole's Jeep Wrangler as it pulled into Cassidy's gravel parking lot. I ran to the door to try to catch sight of him before he knew I was looking. Before he had a chance to put on a carefully constructed face to alleviate his friends' concerns. Brynn and Sebastian cleared their throats and shuffled behind me, preparing the stage for their presentation, if necessary, and probably hoping to sell it as a perfectly constructed, carefully considered earnest calculation while still somehow making it look like it just came to them off the top of their heads and was really no big thing.

He was going to see straight through it, of course. He'd see straight through all of it. But I was confident he'd eventually accept the help.

Or I *was* confident until the glare on his windshield from the setting sun stopped bouncing back into my eyes and I was able to see him clearly for the first time. He looked unconcerned. Carefree. Happy, even. His lips seemed to be pursed in a whistle, and though his eyes were showing the exhaustion that had accumulated over the course of the week, the creases at the corners of them seemed to be tilting upward again. He parked the Wrangler between my Subaru Outback and Brynn and Seb's brand-new Bronco Sport—a wedding present from Brynn because she refused to keep riding around in the 1974 orange-and-white Bronco Seb had been borrowing from Andi Franklin pretty much since he'd moved to Adelaide Springs—and stepped down with an undeniable spring in his step.

My entire body released the tension I hadn't been aware I was holding as I let out a trembling breath. "It's okay," I called over my shoulder. "It must have been a mistake."

"Are you sure?" Sebastian asked, standing to try to peek out the window. "I don't think we should get our hopes up—"

"Seb." I turned and faced him, a beaming smile on my face. "Trust me. It's fine."

If there was one thing I was more of an expert on than the long-ignored talents of underappreciated movie stars of the nineties and early aughts, it was Cole Kimball. Everything was going to be fine now. I'd bet two *Encino Men* and a *George of the Jungle* on it.

CHAPTER SIX

COLE

"Hey, Lai," Cole greeted as the bell over the door jingled. She ran to him so quickly he didn't even have time to open his arms for her. His right arm was behind him, shutting the door, and his left arm was crushed between their bodies. He laughed as he carefully pulled his left arm out and wrapped it around her shoulders. "What's this about?" he whispered into her hair. She pulled away from him, but his arm stayed around her shoulders as he looked down at her face, full of so much emotion he didn't know how to interpret it all. The laughter was gone in an instant. "Are you okay?"

She nodded and smiled. "I'm okay if you're okay."

Cole's head tilted away from her as his elevated eyebrows caused his forehead to wrinkle a bit. "Yeah. I'm great."

He'd spent the entire drive back from his house—*his* house . . . how weird—making sure he would present as *great* for Laila. He knew she'd be there waiting, chomping at the bit to learn whatever bits of information he and Doc had been able to unearth.

He looked toward where they all had been sitting when he left. Yep. Sure enough, Brynn and Seb had stayed too. He'd figured that would be the case, but he'd sort of been hoping he'd be proven wrong about that one. Fat chance. The type of friends who ended their honeymoon early to show up for a grandparent's funeral weren't the type of friends to wander off and wait for you to text them as soon as your life careened out of control.

"Hey, guys. You didn't have to stick around. You must be wiped.

Isn't it the middle of the night Italy time? When was the last time you slept?"

He felt a perfect opportunity for borderline risqué honeymoon humor slipping away from him, but he'd spent the few minutes on the road back to Cassidy's preparing himself for *great. Normal. Peppy*, even. Sophomoric humor or any discernible level of innuendo was currently out of reach.

Sebastian shrugged. "You know us. We are well acquainted with the life of crossing time zones and catching z's standing up."

"How'd that go?" Brynn asked. She'd nodded along with what Seb was saying, but Cole could tell she wasn't really listening to a word of it. Her eyes were darting between him and Laila, trying to interpret the moods, he figured.

Cole squeezed Laila's shoulders one more time and then released her. She sat back down at the table, probably expecting him to join her and begin regaling them with a tale of senior citizen folly and small-business ownership intrigue. He wasn't sure how much folly was involved. His grandfather hadn't made choices Cole agreed with or even understood, but there didn't seem to be any indication he had done anything other than exactly what he'd intended to do. Maybe what he'd *always* intended to do. And as for intrigue . . . Well, he and Doc hadn't had any trouble at all tracking down the documents they needed. It had all been stacked right there on a desk in an office his grandfather hadn't stepped foot in in months. In a house he'd surely known he would never return to.

Maybe if Cole had allowed himself to be as clear minded, if he'd brushed away sentimentality and operated in the cold, callous manner his grandfather had clearly prized, he wouldn't have left the office untouched when Bill moved into Spruce House. He could have discovered the neatly folded tablecloth that had been yanked out from underneath him without even causing the candlesticks to wobble or the pieces of silverware to clink against each other. He might have seen the light before he was left with nothing but resentment toward a dead man.

"It was fine," he called over his shoulder as he turned and headed to the bar. He took his jacket off and threw it over a barstool as he approached. "Anyone need a refill? I don't care how tough *you* are, Seb . . . your wife survives on espresso and Red Bull."

Cole poured himself a cup of coffee but then thought better of it. This night was probably going to be restless enough as it was. He grabbed a can of ginger ale and carried it over to the table along with the mug of coffee, which he placed in front of Brynn.

"He's not wrong," she muttered to Sebastian before greedily gulping down the hot liquid.

"So?" Laila turned to Cole as he sat next to her and rested her fingers on his forearm as he popped the lid to his can. "It was all a mistake . . . right?"

He felt them all lean in, and the room grew silent apart from the second hand ticking on the clock above the door and the wind outside creating a faint howl. "Um . . . no, actually. Cassidy's Bar & Grill is now owned by something called Weck Management Group, LLC, and there's this other company called Alpine Ventures that serves as the manager of the LLC."

Laila's hands fell away like deadweight, and he raised the cold can to his lips and drank for as long as his breath would hold out.

"When?" Sebastian asked. "When did he sell it?"

"About seven months ago. Not long before the first stroke." Doc had been very meticulous in verifying the timing, and it had definitely been before the strokes. Before medical power of attorney. Before Spruce House. They couldn't even claim his grandfather hadn't been in his right mind.

Of course Cole knew that up until the morning of his death, the man had been as mentally sharp as he'd ever been. It was bad enough that he might never know *why* his grandfather did it, but he'd even been robbed of the gift of questioning whether he'd meant to.

"I . . . I . . ." Laila stammered next to him, and he looked at her. All the color had drained from her face apart from her lips, which were beginning to grow very pink as she bit down on them. "I don't understand. How could he . . . Why would he . . . He can't . . ." She shook her head. "No. That can't be right."

Cole sighed. "Well, it is. Looks like control transfers on October 1."

Brynn's eyes flashed to her watch on her wrist and then back to Cole. "Two weeks? So . . . what? Are you saying you have to be out of here in *two weeks*?"

He guzzled the little bit of ginger ale left in the can and set it down on the table in front of him. "Yep."

He was having a difficult time believing anything apart from the worst about his grandfather right now—basically everything most people who ever met Bill Kimball had believed all along—but he did have to believe he would have told him. If he hadn't died. He would have at least communicated his two weeks' notice personally, right? Wouldn't he at least have given Cole an opportunity to get his personal effects out of the building that had been like a second home to him—sometimes more like a first home—for most of his adult life?

Had Alpine Ventures agreed to keep the employees on staff? Maybe there was some such agreement. Surely his grandfather hadn't been as careless with Laila's well-being and the futures of everyone else who worked there part time as he had been with his grandson's, had he?

Had he thought Cole would keep working there? Had he actually thought he would stay quiet and share his recipes and become a glorified—or maybe not glorified at all—line cook for the new owners?

Had he assumed that Cole would, because what other options did he have?

"Let's buy it back." Brynn catapulted from her chair. "This isn't fair, Cole. Let's buy it back. And I don't want to hear any of your stubborn reasons why you can't accept our money. Just in the time you were gone we came up with about ten different ways we could make this happen, and if you don't like any of them, we'll come up with ten more."

Sebastian reached over and placed his hand on the calf of her leg, no doubt attempting to offer some calming, grounding presence. "She's right. Let us help you. And before you say anything, you should know we think this needs to go farther than just Cassidy's. Who is this Weck Management Group? And what'd you say the other one is? Alpine Ventures? What are they wanting to do with the place? This was one of the debates we had over and over in the beginning, when we were first considering bringing back Township Days. We want Adelaide Springs to grow, but not at the expense of what makes the area special."

"Exactly!" Brynn exclaimed, the coffee apparently kicking in, if the restlessness of her twisting hands was any indication. "They don't get to move in here and turn Cassidy's into an Applebee's. I won't stand for it, Cole! I won't!"

Cole laughed then. He couldn't help it. There was nothing funny about any of it, apart from how absurdly activated his friends had become while he found himself checking out more and more by the second. But there was still something laugh-worthy about Brynn—a girl who had once publicly proclaimed that she hated everything about her hometown—plopping her clenched fists on her hips and standing up against beloved chain restaurants everywhere.

And then there was the friend who didn't seem to be activated at all. He tilted his head to look at Laila. "What? You're not going to go stand in the picket line with Norma Rae over there?"

Her bottom lip was still between her teeth, but she unclamped it long enough to whisper, "I don't know what to say."

There was no one in the world he was more himself with than Laila. There was no one else who had seen him at his best and his worst and everything in between and never judged him for any of it. And of course the same could be said in reverse. But this time he'd made the decision to be *great* for her for exactly this reason. She needed to believe he was fine so that she would be fine. Apparently she wasn't buying it, and if Laila wasn't going to pretend along with him, he wasn't sure how long he could muster up the energy.

Cole ran the palms of his hands roughly across his eyes and attempted to eradicate the way Laila's heartbroken vulnerability made him feel. "Well, I suggest we start figuring it all out tomorrow." He managed to plaster a congenial smile on his face by the time his hands left his eyes and he began rising from his seat. "Sudworths, go home. Get some rest."

He began walking toward the door, and Sebastian was the first to willingly oblige the hint. "We're supposed to fly out tomorrow, but if you need help getting packed up or figuring out a plan or—"

"Oh, definitely!" Brynn's heels clopped along the wood floor as she hurried behind Sebastian. "We can stay."

Nope. We're still going for great. Just a few more minutes and then you can feel all the things these horrible, wonderful, evil people you love are making you feel.

"Seriously, I'm fine. If you have time for brunch or something before you go, that would be nice. Maybe I can use up all the good ingredients before the new owners take over." *Too soon.* "Say ten o'clock?"

"We'll be here." Sebastian stuck his hand out and Cole shook it, and then Seb ushered Brynn out the door.

Cole didn't close the door right away because he expected Laila to be right behind them. But there she was, still sitting at the table, not making any move to go.

"Now will you please talk to me?" she asked as soon as they were alone.

"What do you mean? I've been talking to you."

"This is me, Cole."

"Yes, Laila, I know. But I don't know what you think I'm supposed to be saying that I'm not already—"

"If you need time to process, that's fine. Anyone would understand that. If you're not ready to talk, I get that." She twisted in her chair and crossed her arms across the back. "But you've been pretending ever since you got back here, and that's not something you ever do. That's not something *we* ever do. Not with each other. Brynn and Seb are gone now. You can quit pretending."

He took in a deep breath and exhaled, all through his nose. His jaw was a little too clenched right then for his mouth to participate in the breathing.

"You're right." He resisted the urge to slam the door and gently closed it instead. Because she *was* right. They had an entire lifetime of complete authenticity between them, and she deserved better than he was giving her right then. It was time to stop pretending. "But see, the thing is, I'm just trying to survive until you go. I need to be alone, and alone doesn't mean you and me. I do need to be my own person sometimes. Separate from you. You get that, right? Can't you just read the room like everyone else and go home now?"

Any other time, in any other circumstance, he would hate himself for being the reason her eyes turned instantly red and her bottom lip began trembling, but right then he knew he really was showing her as much kindness and love as he was capable of. He would owe her an apology, and he would willingly deliver it later. He'd make her all the chocolate-chip pancakes she could eat tomorrow morning, and soon he would turn to her for all the comfort he knew she would so willingly give. But right now, he needed to be alone. Because, at the end of the day, he was. Alone. Abandoned. Forgotten. And he wanted to wallow in the pain of that for just a little while before Laila attempted to convince him it wasn't true.

"Sorry." She mouthed the word, but the sound didn't make it across the room. She cleared her throat and stood from her chair—her straight, confident posture reminding him what a jerk he was being, though he was certain that wasn't her intent—and then walked toward him, lip still trembling but head held high. She grabbed her coat from the rack and avoided his eyes as she walked to the door.

He opened the door again, and unlike his best friend, he couldn't keep his eyes from drifting to the floor. "I'm sorry, Lai." He'd needed some time to feel the pain, and he'd inadvertently made it so much more accessible. But no matter how jerky he was allowing himself to be, he couldn't let her unnecessary apology to him be their final spoken words to each other for the day. "I promise it's not you."

He knew he still owed her an actual heartfelt apology. And at least one entire can of whipped cream on those pancakes.

CHAPTER SEVEN

LAILA

"Hang on! I'm coming, I'm coming . . ."

I wasn't sure what time it was, but the sun wasn't all the way up, so it was definitely too early for anyone to be pounding on my door like I was the suspect hiding in a crack house on an episode of *Law & Order*.

I thought I had grabbed my bathrobe from the end of my bed, but as I stumbled out of my room and attempted to pull it on, I realized I'd grabbed my pajama pants instead. *Hang on.* I looked down at my legs—my *bare* legs, unfortunately—and things started to rush back. Well, okay, there was no rushing. My brain does not rush first thing in the morning. But the details of the night before did begin meandering into place with the slow, steady swagger of an old cowboy of a bygone era, traipsing across the Old West in too-tight chaps and boots with jingling spurs.

I'd gotten too hot in the night. September was one of those weird months in Colorado during which you had to turn on your furnace and your swamp cooler all in the span of one day. Whatever you began the day or the night wearing would rarely be sufficient for the span of time that inhabitants of other climates took for granted. Okay, I'd gotten too hot and taken off my pants and that meant . . . Yep. I had been about five seconds away from opening my door in just a tank top and my underwear. Awesome.

"Be right there!" I yelled, but of course I was just on the other side of the door, so the delay (and the yelling) was starting to seem a bit silly.

I slipped one leg into my pajamas and then hopped on that foot as I attempted to get the other leg in while simultaneously leaning forward to look through the peephole.

Glasses!

I couldn't see a thing, of course, except for a fuzzy shadow in the predawn orange haze that was beginning to bounce off the mountains and the clouds.

Shoot. I turned and began hurrying back to my bedroom to grab my glasses off my nightstand and called over my shoulder, "Who is it?"

"Lai, it's me. Open up."

Cole had seen me every which way. With split pants after jumping on a trampoline, in bathing suits through every stage my body had ever gone through, and in the hospital, high on morphine after a tonsillectomy, attempting to sneak out of my room because I thought Noah Wyle in an episode of *ER* on my TV was diagnosing me when he said, "I'm afraid we have to amputate." Typically hearing his voice on the other side of the door would have put a speedy kibosh on all the pretenses surrounding opening the door in a presentable manner. But among the details that had sidled up next to me with a leisurely "Howdy, ma'am" were memories of crying myself to sleep in full makeup. Contacts came out, pajamas went on . . . and that was it for my day-end beauty regimen.

Not that that mattered either. After a cute, single, nice guy roughly my age named Michael Perry moved to Adelaide Springs in 2014 and then dumped me after five months because he needed to "get back to civilization," Cole took to calling me McStreaky because of the mascara-stained state of my face for a solid week. But that was fine. Being called McStreaky made me laugh. *Cole* made me laugh.

There hadn't been many times in my life when Cole had been the one to make me cry. I just couldn't stand the thought of piling that guilt on him on top of everything else he was dealing with.

"Just a second!" I needed to grab my glasses, make sure I was at least mostly dressed, and now I needed to wash my face too.

Of course none of that was as important, in the mind of my cat Gilbert Grape, as feeding him forthwith. He curled between my ankles, and to avoid stepping on him, I lifted my left foot. But that meant I was left to balance on my right foot, and my right foot was still covered by the hem of my pajamas, since I hadn't gotten them pulled all the way on yet. My foot gave way against the white-oak laminate wood flooring in my foyer, and my legs went flying. I landed on my back and I heard Cole's panicked voice respond to the thud by asking if I was okay, but at that moment I was only concerned by two things:

1.   *Had I landed on Gilbert Grape?*
2.   *What was that noise I heard that sounded suspiciously like a key turning in my lock?*

I instinctively reacted to both concerns at once, turning over onto my stomach to look for my cat and attempting to bar the door shut with my admittedly-feeble-in-the-best-of-circumstances upper-body strength.

"What in the . . ." Cole peeked around the door after opening it as far as it would go—ultimately not blocked at all by my brute strength and determination but by my head, which got bonked before he realized what was awaiting him inside—and then slid through the opening. "Lai . . . talk to me. Are you okay? Laila?"

"I'm fine," I muttered into my hair, which was all piled up between my face and the floor. "Is Gilbert Grape okay?"

"What?" he asked as he lowered himself to the narrow space in the hallway foyer beside me.

"Gilbert Grape!" I shouted through another mouthful of hair. "Gilbert Grape!"

Forgive me for not being able to better articulate my thoughts right now, Cole, but you're the one who made enough sense of my drug-induced paranoia to explain to doctors that I didn't need a psychiatric evaluation, we just needed to turn on something less threatening than an ER marathon. Connect the dots!

"Yeah, he's fine. He's on the cat tower with Cocaine Bear." He gently brushed the hair away from my face. Or he attempted to, anyway. It was still all over the place. "What happened? I'm afraid to move you. Did you hit your head? Should I call Doc?"

There was no hope for further postponing the inevitable. I rolled over onto my right side and faced him and his adamant "Careful! Careful!" instructions.

"How many times do I have to tell you? I am *not* naming him Cocaine Bear. I refuse. His name is Shang-Chi."

A smile—and a whole lot of relief—overtook his face. At least I was pretty sure that was what I was seeing. He was basically still a blur. "What have you gotten yourself into here, kiddo?" He sat down in the extra space I had made by rolling over and crossed his legs. His fingers made further attempts to clear the hair away from my face and check for damages. "Seriously, are you hurt?"

I exhaled. "I have no doubt I'll be needing some aspirin and a hot bath later, but otherwise I'm fine. I just slipped trying to pull up my—" I groaned and rested my forehead on his knee. "Okay, be honest but kind. How naked am I?"

He chuckled and reached down just below my hip and pulled the elastic from my pajama pants up to my waist. "Not at all, now. Although if you were a man, that flap would be pretty worthless for you back there."

My hand flew to my bottom to discover my super-comfy junior men's pajamas from Old Navy were, in fact, on backward. Ah, well. In the grand scheme of things, it really could have been so much worse.

I snorted as the thought went through my head, and then I gave in to an all-out giggling fit. Cole laughed with me, just because it was contagious and all so ridiculous, I guess, and asked what was so funny.

"I actually just thought, 'Ah, well. Could have been worse.'" The giggles completely overtook me again. "How could this *possibly* have been worse?"

He kept laughing as he said, "Easy. I mean, in addition to the possibility of blunt-force trauma to your head and a squished cat and all that, you might not have had your contacts in yet. If the Sophia

Lorens had gotten broken in this whole kerfuffle, *that* would have been a tragedy. I know I never would have gotten over it."

I had horrible eyesight, but I was fortunate enough to have had roughly the same horrible eyesight since middle school. I'd gotten contacts freshman year, and for nearly twenty-five years, I'd had the same oversize, pink plastic Sophia Loren glasses that no one apart from Cole and people related to me by blood had seen me in since. I'd insisted for years that they were bound to be back in style again some-day, as all fashion trends were, but once again our improved internet capabilities and a lot of Netflix bingeing had completely changed my life. When Barb from season one of *Stranger Things* sported the exact same glasses, the legend of the Sophia Lorens grew in both stature and adoration. At least as far as Cole was concerned.

"Fear not. The Sophia Lorens are safely stored on my bedside table, which was part of the problem to begin with."

"Oh, I see. So you can't see me at all right now, can you?"

I squinted and leaned forward, and he mirrored me until our noses were two inches from each other and his good-natured ribbing finally came into focus. I began pushing myself up with one hand and pushed his face away with the other. He laughed softly and stood to help me to my feet.

Ouch. My hand went to my behind. Nope, that wasn't going to feel better as the day went on, that was for sure.

Cole put his hand on my lower back, and I winced slightly, caus-ing him to move his hand to my elbow.

"I should call Doc so he can check you out. Just to be safe."

I shook my head and stretched my arms over my head, leaning to one side and then the other. "I'm fine. Really."

"But you might have cracked a rib or something."

"I didn't."

With his shoes on, he was easily nine or ten inches taller than I was barefoot, and he used his height advantage to examine my head again. "And you're sure you didn't hit your head? Concussions can be sneaky buggers."

I chose to ignore "sneaky buggers," though it really cried out for some teasing, and instead decided to change the subject entirely. "What are you doing here, anyway? I was sort of sleeping, you know."

His eyes grew wide. "This was my fault. Oh, gosh, Lai . . . I knew it was early, but I didn't even think about you still being asleep. I'm sorry."

"No, it's fine."

"It's not." He guided me into the living room and helped me onto the couch. "As much as I hate to ask: Is it safe to assume the return of McStreaky is my fault too?"

Oh. That. In all the kerfuffle, as he'd called it, I'd rather pleasantly stopped thinking about all of that. Well, for better or worse, I had a moment to think about it now. A quick one. The words, "Hold that thought," spilled out, and then he vanished from my very nondescript view.

What to say when he got back . . . I shook my head for my own benefit as the thoughts and emotions crystallized in my head. There was no choice, really. I didn't want to inflict guilt on him—and I would do what I could to avoid that being the outcome, though I knew him well enough to know he was already inflicting it upon himself—but I couldn't very well be upset with him for cutting me out and not communicating and then turn around and do the same to him.

"Here you go, Sophia." The huge glasses appeared in front of my face.

"Thank you." *For adding the benefit of sight to this disastrous morning and still calling me Sophia rather than Barb. I'm eternally grateful.*

"No problem. Anything else I can get you? Want me to make some coffee? Or I can bring you a bag of frozen peas or something for your back."

I patted the couch next to me. "Just sit."

He did as I instructed, most of a seat cushion away, but turned so that he was facing me and his propped-up knee was nearly touching mine. "I really am sorry, Lai."

"And I really am fine. Admittedly, my thirty-eight-year-old body is already telling me this isn't like when we were kids and we'd take turns rolling down the ski slopes and not have so much as stiff muscles getting out of bed the next morning, but I'm not hurt. Really."

"Well, just give it another week or so until you're thirty-nine like the rest of us. Trust me—it *sucks*."

I laughed. "And just think about poor Seb. In his *forties*. I mean, I know we didn't grow up with him, but doesn't it make you feel ancient just knowing that someone we *did* grow up with is married to someone in their *forties*? It drives home the sad truth that it's just around the corner for all of us."

Cole's laughter dissipated into the air, but the smile remained as he watched me giggle, and then that became more subdued as well. "I don't know what I'd do without you."

I shrugged. "And you'll never have to figure it out. But—"

"But I really hurt your feelings last night. Didn't I?"

I smiled gently to soften the blow. "Yeah."

"You know that would never be my intent. But I . . . I'm sorry, and I know it's not our typical way, but I really did just need to be alone."

"I get that." I nodded and slipped a couple of fingers from each hand up under my lenses to rub my eyes. *Note to self: Don't even look in a mirror until you get out of the shower. What you see will not help anyone.* "And I'm sorry that maybe I wasn't the most sensitive to that. But it wasn't you wanting to be alone that bothered me so much as the 'read the room like everyone else.'" I reached over and gently punched his knee. "I'm *not* everyone else, Cole. And that was the first time in a very long time that you made me feel like I was."

He grabbed my hand just as I began pulling it away from his knee and raised his eyes to look at me sheepishly. "Forgive me?"

"Well, that depends. What are you making for breakfast?"

He'd never questioned whether or not he'd attain my forgiveness, of course. And I would never want him to. All the same, relief flooded his features as he leaned in and kissed my cheek, then hopped up and walked across the room toward my kitchen—stopping to give Gilbert Grape and Shang-Chi a little chin-rub love.

"Whatever you want, as long as you've got the ingredients in your fridge."

I heard the water running in my kitchen sink as he washed his hands, so I followed in after him before speaking so he could hear me. "I thought we were meeting Brynn and Seb at Cassidy's."

He shook the water off his hands and grabbed my self-made hippopotamus hand towel from the knob on the cabinet door. "Change of plans. That's what I wanted to talk to you about, actually." He rested his hip against the counter and faced me.

"Oh, really?" I crossed my arms in mock frustration. "Yeah, makes total sense that you'd wake a girl up to tell her she's not getting the brunch food she was promised. Rob her of her sleep *and* her little sausages-wrapped-in-croissant pigs-in-a-blanket things. You always have had a way with the ladies."

He groaned and opened up the refrigerator, looked around inside it, and then groaned again. "I'm pretty sure I can still pull something together, but yeah . . . sorry. You're not getting anything quite as ostentatious as pigs-in-a-blanket, unless the pigs come in deli-ham form and the blankets are . . . ." He stood up and looked around my kitchen. "I don't know . . . ground-up Cheez-Its? Oh, hang on! You have eggs?"

"Yeah, Magda's. I already hard-boiled them."

He closed the carton and stuck it back on the shelf. "When was the last time you bought any groceries?"

I shrugged. "Not sure if you've heard, but my best friend's a chef. I live on leftovers."

He closed the fridge and opened the cabinet above the stove, going straight to the unopened box of pancake mix he'd bought me months ago in an attempt to convince me I, too, could mix floury stuff and water, drop it in a pan, and have my favorite breakfast food in front of me, ready to eat, just moments later.

As for the success of his lesson, I repeat: the box was unopened.

"Do you have chocolate chips?"

My eyes widened. "Always!" I pulled a chair from my two-seat kitchen table and placed it beside him. Then, using his shoulder for a boost, I climbed up and grabbed the airtight glass cylinder from the cabinet above the fridge. That was where I kept my favorite guilty pleasure foods. The brilliant thought behind that, of course, was that if I had to go to a little extra effort to access them, I wouldn't go through them as quickly.

"Okay," Cole said as I handed him the half-empty container. "And how old are these?"

"New bag. Just opened yesterday."

He grimaced, and at first I thought he was being judgy about how many semisweet morsels I had eaten in a day, but then I realized he was grimacing in response to whatever expression was on *my* face. Probably a grimace, come to think of it.

Oh. Yeah. That hurt. Getting up on the chair hadn't been too bad, but as soon as I began stepping down, my lower back began throbbing.

"Here, let me help you." He put his hands at my waist to lift me down, but I put my hand on his head to stop him.

"Not yet. Hang on." I took a couple slow, deep breaths until the throbbing lost its intensity. "Just let me stand here a sec. I'll be fine."

From the time we were all kids, Cole had been our protector. He was the one who insisted on walking the girls to our doors, even though the only real possible threat was the occasional bear or mountain lion—which, let's face it, wasn't going to honor Cole's chivalry and recognize that the girls should be eaten last. Still, he insisted. Every single time. He'd made more pots of chicken noodle soup in his lifetime than half the grandmas in America combined, and he'd gotten into more than a couple fights in his time standing up for someone he loved. So I knew that what he perceived as my stubbornness in refusing to let him take care of me was killing him. And if I hadn't known that just because I knew Cole, his wrinkled brow and eyes that hadn't blinked since the grimace overtook his face may have given it away.

"Maybe some ice or something would be good," I relented.

He snapped into action and carefully slid the chair, with me still standing on it, a couple inches to the side so he could open the freezer. His exasperated sigh quickly reminded me what he would find in there.

Just ice cream.

"How do you not have even one single bag of frozen vegetables? And even if you live off the spoils of someone else's hard work, don't you ever want ice in your water? This is not an acceptable way for a grown adult to live, Laila."

I dissolved into giggles. He was genuinely so disappointed in this side of me, and though it wasn't necessarily a conscious decision, the never-ending amusement I found in his disappointment filled me with enough joy that on some level I probably did do it on purpose.

"Yeah . . . this is hilarious," he muttered. Then, before I knew what was happening, he had wrapped his arms around my knees and carried me back over to the refrigerator, lifting me a few inches higher until my bottom was even with the open freezer. "Sit."

"What? What do you mean?"

"*Sit*," he repeated, and I did as I was instructed, though I didn't at all understand why I was doing it. But then, in an instant, the frigid air washed over me, and the thick blocks of way-past-due-for-defrosting ice caused my sore muscles to relax. Or maybe I just went numb. Either way, it was magical.

Cole helped me slide a little farther back into the freezer, until my folded arms were hunched over my knees, and then he stepped back a bit. His chest pressed against my dangling legs to stabilize me, and his eyes were even with mine. "How's that feel?"

I relaxed my neck and lowered my forehead onto his shoulder. "'You're a wizard, Harry.'"

"And you're a dork, Laila." His shoulders fell as tension released from them, a direct result of finally being permitted to help me, I knew.

"I bet you feel silly now." I stopped worrying about holding myself in position and rested my weight against him.

"I'm not the one with my rear end stuck in a freezer, but I'll bite. Why should I feel silly?"

"For making fun of me for having my pants on backward. I tell ya, if the pharmaceutical companies ever get wind of how genius this is and the sort of money they could be making, men's pajama pants will no longer be available over the counter."

CHAPTER EIGHT

COLE

"See . . . I don't care what you say . . ." Laila barely slowed down as she stuffed chocolate-chip pancakes into her mouth. "I could never make something this good. It's not as simple as you like to pretend it is."

How had they been having this same argument since they were teenagers? While she was in the bathroom washing her face and putting in her contacts, he had made an earnest attempt to covertly track down ingredients to make literally anything else. Maybe not instead of, since the least he owed her was her favorite breakfast food, but in addition to. He was a trained chef with more than a decade of experience creating recipes and stretching inventory as far as it could go. If he'd found so much as a potato, he would have been off to the races. But he had found absolutely nothing else to work with. Cole found that to be equal parts frustrating and endearing.

"Pancake mix. Water. Chocolate chips. Heat. Spatula. I'm not downplaying my talents here, Lai. That's legitimately all there is to it."

"Sure. Those are the components. But, I mean, using your own logic, water should be even easier to make. Two simple ingredients, right? But you wouldn't be all shocked and dismayed if I wasn't able to pull hydrogen and oxygen out of my cabinet and make water, would you?"

The corner of Cole's lips tightened as he watched her and attempted to keep the smile from appearing too soon. The familiar back-and-forth banter was something he counted on, and the moment he appeared to relent and give up the fight, they would dissolve into laughter and move on to something else. And today, especially, he knew the something else was going to be a bit less carefree than their recurring flapjack feud.

He nodded and took a sip of his coffee. Thank goodness she at least kept coffee in stock. "Truthfully, yes. I think I would."

"Oh, come on, Cole. How in the world could you expect me to know how to make H_2O? Now you're just being ridiculous."

He contorted his face in offense as a dramatic gasp escaped. "I beg your pardon? I am *not* being ridiculous. For one thing, you're smart enough to figure out whatever you want to figure out, and I really wish you would stop selling yourself short. But perhaps just as important, while we're being scientific and all, are you forgetting that you are the one who just threw out a hypothesis"—Or theory? No . . . some other science-y word. How was he supposed to know? He'd mostly cheated off of Laila in science class—"and in this hypothesis, you store hydrogen and oxygen in your kitchen cabinets. I believe it's reasonable to believe, by this same logic, that you would have some sort of idea what to do with them."

She pointed her fork at him, three layers of pancake on the end. "Aha! See? You just inadvertently argued against yourself. I have pancake mix and chocolate chips in my cabinets, and yet I have no idea what to do with those ingredients."

"Exactly, Laila. I made exactly the point I meant to make. You have pancake mix and chocolate chips in your cabinets, and I stand by my assertion that it's completely reasonable to believe you would know what to do with them."

She paused for a moment and then slumped back in her chair. "Oh." She stuffed the three layers into her mouth and chewed. "Well, be that as it may, *this*, my friend, is not science. It's art. You are an artist. And . . ." Her eyes suddenly took on a sparkling quality as she sat up straight again. She knew she had him beat. Actually, Cole saw, in the moment before she voiced her new argument, where she was going with it, and the smile finally overtook his face. Yep, she was right. She had him beat. "If I had some finger paints and a canvas board in my cabinet, you wouldn't expect me to be able to paint the *Mona Lisa*."

Boy, she sure was smug when she knew she was right.

"Touché." He raised his hands in surrender. Although, considering what an artistic freak of nature Laila could be, he wouldn't put it past her to do more with those simple components than what da Vinci had pulled together. Nevertheless, point well made.

How was it possible that they'd been having this argument since they were teenagers, and he never seemed to get tired of it?

He also never seemed to win.

He stood as she slid her final bite around in the syrup on her plate, stuffed it into her mouth, and set the fork down on the plate with a satisfied sigh. Cole took her plate along with his own and walked them over to the sink. She had a dishwasher—an extremely underutilized dishwasher—but he chose to run some hot water in the sink and wash the sticky plates by hand. He needed a moment with his back turned to her to prepare himself for the conversation they were about to have. He knew Laila well enough to know that right now, in the next few moments, was his best possible time to broach a difficult topic. She was riding a chocolate-chip pancake high. A chocolate-chip pancake high of his making. He could do no wrong in her eyes right now.

"So, um, I did come over to apologize, of course, but there's something else I was hoping to talk to you about. Do you have a few minutes?" He knew she did. He'd canceled their ten o'clock.

"Sure. What's up?"

As if he had just received a cue that his human was going to be hurt if this other human who gave off definite "dog person" vibes wasn't careful, Cocaine Bear chose that moment to swirl his massive Ragdoll body between Cole's ankles in a way that always reminded Cole of "Figure Eight," clearly the creepiest of all *Schoolhouse Rock* songs.

He gently nudged the cat away—as gently as a cat that weighed the same as a seven-month-old human *could* be nudged if you hoped to get your point across—and cleared his throat. "I decided to close Cassidy's."

Laila was silent, and he almost turned to face her to try to interpret her thoughts, but he was pretty sure he already knew them. Or at least the "Goonies never say die" spirit behind whatever her thoughts might be at that moment. He wasn't really any more interested in talking through all of that than he had been the night before.

"What do you mean you decided to close Cassidy's?" Her voice was soft and shaky. "You mean you're not even going to *try* to hang on to it?"

Alright. Here we go.

He set the two clean plates in the rack and rinsed off his hands—meticulously, stalling as much as he could—before drying them off and turning to face her. He didn't want to fight with her, and if it was up to him, he wouldn't. He hated disappointing her. He'd *always* hated disappointing her. The worst part about it was always the way she would insist he could never disappoint her. But he could. He had. And he was about to again.

"No. I'm not. But what I mean is I'm closed. Now. It's over, so there's no point trying to talk me out of it. I got in touch with the new owners—"

"Hang on." Laila stood up and took a step toward him and then stopped and turned back. Ultimately she spoke from exactly where she had been standing to begin with. "You went from finding out this huge, life-altering news to 'I'm done. Who do I need to talk to?' in . . . what?" She glanced at her wrist and then realized she wasn't wearing her watch yet. "Twelve hours? Without thinking it through? You just . . . made that decision?"

"In case you've forgotten, the decision was made for me. And if there *were* further decisions up for grabs, they were mine to make. And *of course* I thought it through. Have you ever known me not to think things through, Laila? But it didn't take me twelve hours. I was on the phone with Alpine Ventures about an hour after you guys left last night."

And then he was on the phone with Sebastian, canceling brunch and taking the first step toward what came next about twenty minutes after that.

She gasped. "Cole, what did you do?"

He threw his hands up in the air. It's not as if he had expected anything other than this exact reaction, but for some reason he'd still rushed over there this morning excited. Excited that something in his life was about to change. Excited that a new path had popped up in front of him like one of those secret pipes to Bowser's castle he used to lose his mind over when he was playing *Super Mario Bros*. Excited to bring her in on the decisions he had made, because the truth was it *had* felt wrong not to talk it through with her. Or if not wrong, weird. Super weird.

"I made sure I ended up in the best possible place I could with the hand I was dealt. That's what I did. I convinced him to buy the appliances—"

"Oh, Cole . . ."

There it was. There was her disappointed voice. But it was the only thing that had made sense. He knew that.

The appliances were his. Four years ago, he'd completely modernized the kitchen, and foolishly thinking that Cassidy's would someday be his, he hadn't wanted to rely on his grandfather for anything else. He'd gotten the loan in his name, using his Jeep Wrangler as collateral. It hadn't been *enough* collateral, of course, but a flawless relationship with the bank, a loan officer who had gone to prom with Cole's mother back in the day, a down payment that he scraped together in part by selling all those now-valuable Nintendo gaming systems that had taught him to look for secret pipes, and a nearly suffocating interest rate had come together to get it done. And then he'd paid the loan off in forty-two months instead of sixty when Cassidy's began turning into exactly what he always knew it could be.

"What else was I going to do? At least now I have something to live on while I figure out where I'm going to go."

She clutched her stomach and sank back into her chair. "You mean while you figure out what you're going to *do*."

He'd known last night. When he'd flipped through the stack of bereavement cards in the back seat of his vehicle to find the business card he'd received and rather carelessly dismissed after Brynn and Seb's wedding, he'd known. When he'd hurt her feelings by giving her the brush-off, he'd known. When he'd called Sebastian and asked if he could be a tagalong, he'd known. Maybe it hadn't really cemented in his mind until this morning—this morning when he woke up and everything felt different, and it dawned on him that the thought of *different* was causing everything in him to speed up rather than slow down—but he'd known.

"No, Lai." He shook his head, and he wanted nothing more than to tear his eyes away from hers so he wouldn't have to witness the pain and confusion he was inflicting on her, but as she'd reminded him, that wasn't who they were. "There's nothing for me here anymore."

It would have been so much easier to avoid eye contact. To not say the real things. To let the pain lie there until it didn't matter so much that it was worth talking about. That's what other people did, right?

Not Laila. And not Cole when Laila had anything to say about it.

"You're not really going to make me say it, are you?" She was refusing to so much as blink and break the eye contact between them. "You're not actually going to make me say what should only ever be said in a Reese Witherspoon movie. Are you?"

"Look, I know what you're—"

"*I'm* here, Cole. *I* am. And, okay . . . maybe I'm not enough—"

"Lai, I didn't mean—"

"But how dare you?" She stood from her chair again, and there was such passion and pain in her words. She was gearing up for the fight. She was there for it. But the way she stood so gingerly, clearly proceeding with caution to keep her sore back in check, made Cole want nothing more than to somehow make the fight go away. "How dare you say there's nothing here for you?"

The fight had left his own voice, but none of the circumstances he was facing had changed. "What am I supposed to do? Cooking is all I know—"

"So cook." She crossed her arms and said it as if it was the most obvious solution in the world. Easy. What's the problem?

"Oh. Okay. Thanks. Hadn't thought of that. Why didn't you say so sooner?"

She rolled her eyes. "Sarcasm is such a good look on you, Cole."

"About as good as blind, cheerful, oblivious optimism is on you, I'd imagine."

Nope. When it was just the two of them, they certainly weren't those people who avoided saying the hard things in order to avoid conflict.

Cole took a step toward her. "There is one other restaurant in town, and it's currently closed. And even if it weren't, after Andi gets back, you know that wouldn't work either. She does the cooking at the Bean, and she's not going to give up her kitchen. Nor would I want her to."

"Why not? Apparently giving up kitchens isn't any big thing. Takes less than an hour to decide to do it, right?" Laila took a step away from him. Not to put distance between them, it was immediately revealed, but to lean back against the kitchen wall for support. "I think she'd be happy to have you."

Cole sighed. "Laila, would you please go sit down on the couch and relax? I'll bring you some aspirin—"

"Once Andi gets back to town," she continued as if he hadn't spoken at all, "you know she's going to need some help getting things going again. And with Sebastian not working at Valet Forge anymore, she's probably going to be spread pretty thin anyway. I'm sure she would be thrilled if—"

"You're not listening to me!"

Cole had raised his voice for the first time, and Laila took note. That much was obvious. She may have remained unmoving against the wall, but her eyebrows darted up and stayed up. And her cheeks appeared to be on fire.

The cats had taken note, too, it seemed. Well, Cocaine Bear had. Gilbert Grape remained unaffected on his perch directly across from the open door of the kitchen, next to the east window in the living room where he was soaking in the morning sun, in the middle of the most thorough bath that any cat's toes had ever received. But Cocaine Bear was definitely staring at him as if deciding whether to go straight for the eyes or if it would be better to slip something in his drink when he wasn't looking.

That was why he'd suggested naming him Cocaine Bear last year when Laila adopted him from the shelter in Grand Junction. Laila thought he was just trying to be funny, but no. It was this. The way the animal always seemed to have drug-fueled rage and murder in his eyes whenever he looked at Cole. Of course the cat *loved* Laila, so the version of him that she saw made even Shang-Chi—the former valet parking attendant / reluctant superhero—seem a bit too edgy.

Anyway, duplicitous felines aside, Cole had raised his voice, and Laila looked none too pleased about the fact.

"How many times do I have to tell you I'm fine? Stop babying me, Cole. This is about you, and you don't get to yell at me because I'm not taking your expert advice when you are clearly not listening to anyone about anything. There isn't a single person who knows you and loves you who would think this is a good idea. Not even one. Not that you *asked* anyone, I'm sure." And then she added in a grumble under her breath, "Stubby McStubbornson."

He would almost be amused if he wasn't currently so frustrated with her. "I actually meant you weren't listening to what I was trying to tell you about *me*."

His voice was soft now, but her cheeks hadn't gotten any less red. It would have been nice to think the anger had been replaced by embarrassment—not that he relished the thought of embarrassing her, even if right now maybe she sort of deserved it—but he figured nothing had been replaced. Nothing was gone. All of the emotions were just piling up and compounding on top of each other.

"Okay," she responded, sitting back down in her chair—and

working harder to cover up the grimace that resulted. "Go ahead. I'm listening."

She was the most important person in the world to him. He couldn't remember far enough back to know if there had ever been a time when that wasn't the case, but he felt fairly confident that a deep search through the archives would have come up empty anyway. There wasn't a particular moment that he remembered. There wasn't a singular moment when something had shifted and somewhere deep in his subconscious his soul had whispered, "She matters more than the rest." It had just always been. He'd always known.

There were five of them who'd been born within ten months of each other in this tiny, insignificant town with—until the past couple years—an ever-shrinking population and shockingly few opportunities to meet anyone new. But he loved those other four, and apart from a few rebellious moments that he assumed weren't all that different from what every other teenager experienced, he'd always been okay with his small but perfect circle, with Laila at the center of it. At least from his perspective. That hadn't changed when Wes and Addie fell in love, and it hadn't changed when Cole and Brynn tried dating each other for a few disastrous—and in retrospect, hilarious—weeks in high school. When Brynn left after graduation and Wes took off a few months later, and then ultimately Addie joined the air force, it was just the two of them after a lifetime of five. And they were devastated.

But it was somehow still okay.

"That was a crappy thing I said. Sorry."

"Which thing? You've said a lot of crappy things today." She huffed and crossed her arms, which just made him smile. Apparently he was done fighting.

"The Reese Witherspoon movie thing. Of course you're here. And of course that's important. But . . ." He pushed himself off from the counter behind him and ran his fingers through his hair before sitting down next to her at the table. "I don't know what to do with this, Lai. I don't know how I'm supposed to drive by Cassidy's—heaven forbid anyone I know ever wants to meet there for dinner—and just be okay with it."

She leaned in and placed her hands on his on the table. "Then why not fight to hold on to it? I know you don't want to accept any charity or anything. I get that. But it's Brynn and Sebastian. They could pay whatever the new owners wanted, and what's more, you *know* how happy it would make them to do it."

He knew she was right. Seb had tried to sell him on the idea last night when they spoke on the phone. But Seb's thinking, even being the good guy and supportive friend that he was, wasn't clouded by the glass-half-full outlook on life the way Laila's was. It had been easy to make him understand why he couldn't accept his generosity, no matter how much a part of him wanted to. Laila was going to be a tougher sell.

Cole studied her hands on his until he intuitively sensed that he was about to lose the silence. If he didn't speak soon, she was going to mistake his silence for contemplation. But he was done thinking it through. The decision was made. "Cassidy's isn't really the problem though, is it?"

"What do you mean?"

He squeezed his eyes shut as tightly as he could, but he couldn't block out the moment he'd never be able to escape. He tilted his head upward and peeked at her with one eye. "It doesn't matter what happens now. Even if the new owner called me today and offered to cancel the whole deal, how would I ever get over the fact that this happened at all? How am I ever supposed to forgive him for this?"

"I know." Her voice was soft. As much as his dismissal last night had hurt her, he figured her compassion for the pain she knew he was feeling and refusing to talk about was actually the primary culprit of the long night written across every inch of her face. "But isn't that going to be the case whether you stay in Adelaide Springs or not? Isn't it *always* going to suck?"

He chuckled painfully. "Now *there's* that legendary Laila Olivet optimism I was counting on."

"I'm just saying—"

"No, I know." Cole nodded. "And you're probably right. But I feel like right now I have to get away from here. I feel like if at least I'm not living in a house where his things are still everywhere, unable to avoid Cassidy's, unable to avoid memories and dreams I've had for the future assaulting me on literally every corner . . ."

"Yeah."

"I think it's better to at least start trying to find an existence a little less saturated in torture and misery, you know?"

They sat unmoving and silent until Cole turned his hand under hers palm up so their fingers could intertwine. "But seriously, ignore that crappy straight-out-of-a-badly-written-movie stuff I said earlier." He tapped the side of her hand with his thumb. "Being away from you is going to be its own brand of torture and misery."

"*Thank you!* That's all I wanted to hear you say. Was that so hard?"

He smiled at her and savored the comfort of just *being* with her. Just for an extra second. If he'd had any idea just how quickly everything would change, he would have grabbed a lot of extra seconds along the way. Every chance he had.

But with a sigh he acknowledged the end of the painfully short extra second. *Just rip off the Band-Aid, Cole.* "I met this chef at the wedding. A friend of Seb's. Or the wife of a friend . . . something. Anyway, she really liked my food."

Laila beamed at him. "Of course she did."

"She offered me a job."

Cole watched her take in a sharp breath and put in the necessary effort to lock her supportive smile and wide, interested eyes back in place in the same instant as that breath. "Oh." Her eyes were growing wider and wider. Not in wonder or excitement, he knew, but because she was putting every effort into stabilization rather than allowing her features and her emotions to crash to the floor. "Um, well, of course anyone would be lucky to have you. Um . . . where is her . . . Where does she—"

"Williamsburg." In his haste to rip off the Band-Aid, he'd been a little careless. He quickly realized his mistake as her shoulders relaxed and unmistakable relief softened every shadow across her face. "In Brooklyn. New York."

Laila's hand rolled out of his, landing with a thud as her knuckles hit the table. Along with her smile. His heart. So many different thuds all tied up in one woman's sadness. "Oh, sure. Of course. That makes more sense. Are there even any restaurants in Williamsburg, Colorado? Is *anything* there apart from the prison museum?"

Cole hadn't thought about that prison museum in a long time, but it had been a highlight of one of his favorite Colorado exploration trips with Laila. They'd been in their late twenties and endlessly amused by the department store mannequins, with their lipstick smiles and their "Trust me . . . you'll look as good in these prison stripes as I do" poses playing the parts of incarcerated prisoners.

"I think Williamsburg is technically a little bigger than Adelaide Springs."

"Then go there. Start over. Do for Williamsburg, Colorado, what Cassidy's has done for Adelaide Springs. Or go work in some trendy place in Pueblo. Denver. Whatever." She began running her finger across her bottom lip, maybe in an attempt to keep from chewing it to pieces. "If you really have to leave home, there are tons of options closer to—"

"I haven't committed to anything yet, but I think it would be foolish not to at least—"

"Hang on." She raised her hands in the space between them as her feet pushed back and the legs of her old wooden chair groaned in squeaky compliance with her desire to add to the space. "You're actually considering this."

"I texted her this morning. Set up a meeting for next Monday."

"As in a week from tomorrow?"

"Yeah." Cole tilted his head and spoke softly, still confident in his decision but feeling every last ounce of excitement he'd awakened with that morning dripping out of him. "I'm going to New York with Seb and Brynn. Just to familiarize myself with the place for a few days. And then in a week I'll meet with her—"

"You've lost your mind!" Laila bolted from her chair but instantly seemed to realize she shouldn't have. Her hand flew to her lower back as a jolt of pain resulted in a groan and tightly squeezed eyes, and Cole stood in response to her obvious discomfort. He tried to usher her back to her seat, but of course she wasn't going to let anything get in the way of her telling him off. "You just went from zero to sixty on the road to a midlife crisis, and—"

"Lai, sit down." His arms were outstretched to her, but she ignored them.

"Don't you think this is just a little bit hasty, Cole? Are you seriously going to up and leave home the moment things get a little tricky?"

He wasn't sure if it was her words or the fact she was no longer ignoring his attempts to aid her and had begun swatting at his arms instead, but he felt his adrenaline begin to pump.

"Seriously, Laila? A little tricky? You think this is the moment that things got 'a little tricky'? From my perspective, I'm up and leaving home because it's the only option I have right now, having been betrayed by the man who raised me. I have no choice but to leave home because everything I had planned for my future—*everything*—has been ripped out from under me. You understand that, right? 'A little tricky.'" He collapsed onto the edge of the chair and muttered under his breath, "Potato, potahto."

They stared at each other, and as her furrowed brow smoothed, Cole felt his pulse regulate again.

"I know," she muttered. "Sorry. I'm being selfish."

He shook his head. "No. It's not that."

"Well . . ." She sat back down in her chair and scooted it up to the table again. "It's a little bit that. So I'll try not to be. Selfish, I mean. But I need you to understand that from my perspective this is—"

"Coming from nowhere. I know."

"Heartbreaking. I was going to say heartbreaking." She looked down at her hands, resting in her lap, and then raised them to the table and lifted her eyes back to his, which were studying her with concern. "So tell me about this chef. She was at the wedding?"

"Yeah. I guess her husband and Seb were in the field together, in Syria or somewhere, years ago." Cole settled back into his seat. "She said my baby quiches are better than the ones Wolfgang Puck makes for the *Vanity Fair* Oscar party. She used to work for Wolfgang Puck, I guess. And she called my Monte Cristos 'le dernier cri,' and I'm not entirely sure what that means, but she definitely said it like it was a good thing."

Laila chuckled. "Oh, come on. Don't act like you didn't look it up first chance you had."

"It's French for 'fashionable,' basically. Which I found a little ironic since that obnoxious wedding planner Brynn consulted with in the beginning called the idea of mini Monte Cristos 'gauche.'" He shrugged. "I think this chef—Sylvia Garos is her name—tried every single thing I made for the wedding, and she loved it all. She's opening her own restaurant, and she offered me a job on the spot. I mean, not to be the head chef or anything. Obviously. She's the head chef. But just to go and be a cook, I think."

Laila squinted her eyes and studied him until Cole asked, "What?"

"Why didn't you tell me any of this?"

Finally. An easy question.

"Because, first of all, by the end of the night, Grandpa was gone. Lots of things went by the wayside. But even more than that . . ." How had all that hope and all that potential been so real just a few days ago? "It didn't seem urgent to tell you about it because there was zero chance I was even going to consider taking the job. The truth is, as she praised my quiches and Monte Cristos and some of these other foods that I had so little experience with, compared to steak and burgers and everything . . . That's when I really started thinking seriously about opening Cassidy's for breakfast and lunch. I thought maybe I could do it. Maybe I was good enough. And the first chance we had to talk, that was what I needed to talk to you about. I needed to know if you thought I could handle it." He cleared his throat. "If *you* thought I was good enough."

Cole didn't have crises of confidence very often. Not when it came to his cooking, anyway. He knew what he was doing in the kitchen, and he got better all the time. Prior to culinary school, everything he'd learned had been taught by his grandmother. She'd taught him how to crack eggs with one hand and how to properly whisk, and by the age of ten he'd known every possible way to prepare a chili pepper. He could take those babies from the garden to any southwestern dish you were craving, by way of roasting, blistering, pickling . . . you name it.

But the most important thing she'd taught him was to trust his instincts. She'd told him that some people had the intuition needed to cook that way—to not be reliant on recipes and precise measurements—and some people simply didn't. His mother and grandfather didn't, Grandma had informed him. But she had also instructed him that anytime they went to the effort of cooking for him, he was to rave about whatever they prepared and finish off every last bite. For Cole and his grandmother, cooking was fun. For his mother and grandfather, it was work. But they put just as much love into that work as he and his grandmother put into their fun.

The results of that sort of love sometimes just didn't taste as good, but he was never to tell them that.

"You know I think you're good enough," Laila whispered and then cleared her throat, and her voice grew stronger. "You know I think you're the best. And that's part of the reason I think it's such a mistake to go to New York. You could do anything. Cook anywhere. And I think you're selling yourself short. I think it's a mistake to accept the first thing that came along—"

"I haven't accepted it. Not yet. But I think it would be a mistake not to meet with her." He really wished he could stay with Laila forever in the land of Yet to Fully Grasp the Situation. "But regardless, I *am* leaving, Lai. I'm not staying in Adelaide Springs. I'm going to New York with Brynn and Seb just to figure out if I could stand to live there, and to meet with Sylvia, but . . ." He leaned in and looped her index finger, which was nervously tapping on the table, in his. "It's difficult to imagine I won't take this job."

"But what if a better offer comes along?"

"Better than an up-and-coming, James Beard Award–winning chef whose mentor is Wolfgang Puck and who already loves my food offering me a job in the kitchen of a restaurant in one of the trendiest neighborhoods in America, where there's already an eight-month waiting list?"

A frown overtook her lips. Well, Laila's version of a frown, anyway. She'd never really mastered the expression. Whenever she attempted it, it always ended up looking like she'd had a bad Botox experience. And somehow it was still adorable.

"Okay . . . I didn't know any of that. But still. You know you're going to miss being in charge of your own place. Don't take this sitting down, Cole. Open up a restaurant in Williamsburg, Colorado, instead," she pleaded. "Whoever's in charge of dressing and posing the mannequins at the prison museum has to eat *somewhere*."

He laughed and released her finger. "You know, you could always come with me." Laila smiled in the exact same instant that the laughter fell from Cole's face. "You should come with me. I can't believe I didn't think of it sooner."

She quirked up her face and studied him and then rolled her eyes. "Be serious."

"Don't I *look* serious?"

This was the answer. He was sure of it.

"You need sleep." She gathered the silverware from the table and stood to take it all to the sink. "I'm supposed to be the one who wears my heart on my sleeve and acts out of emotion and all of that. You're the one who keeps us all from making really stupid decisions like this one."

"This isn't stupid."

She dropped the utensils in the soapy water he had left in the sink and then turned to face him as they plopped. "My life is here, Cole."

"I know I haven't had the heart to officially lay you off yet, but you've been able to connect the dots and realize you're currently as unemployed and destitute as I am. Right?"

"I'm not destitute. I just inherited some money, it seems. That will get me through for a while." She shrugged. "And I'm only unemployed until the Bean reopens. If I have to, I'll pick up odd jobs. I'm not picky."

"If that's the case, you can pick up odd jobs anywhere."

"But that doesn't change the fact that this is home. And I have a house I love. And cats. And I couldn't possibly leave my dad and Melinda right now. Not with . . ." She swallowed hard as her entire face tightened. Cole understood every single thing she was feeling and opened his arms to her, and she accepted his offer.

"Of course. You're right. I'm sorry."

He laid his cheek on the top of her head as she rested hers against his chest. "I *could* go with you, you know. I mean, just for this little trip with Brynn and Seb. If you want me to."

Well, *that* was just the most unnecessary sentence anyone had ever spoken.

"Of course I want you to!" He pulled back from her, beaming from ear to ear—an expression of joy that was not mirrored in front of him. "I'm sorry I didn't think of that. I was just so busy—"

"Having a midlife crisis and resisting the urge to buy a sports car? Yeah, I know."

Cole laughed and released her from his arms. "Seriously, Lai, this will be fun."

"I have to be back before Melinda's appointment next week."

He nodded. "Definitely. And if you want, we can even pretend the plane is a boat and the clouds are water." That had almost worked the first time they flew on a plane, when they unearthed Laila's crippling fear of flying approximately five seconds after takeoff. But they'd been in second grade then. Cole wasn't too convinced the tactic would work this time.

"Or we could take a train to New York. That could be fun."

Cole chuckled. "Yeah, and we might even get there before it's time to come back."

She swallowed hard. "No, it will be fine. We'll do the pretending-it's-a-boat thing. But I do have one more favor to ask of you."

He smiled and reached down to grab her hand. "Name it."

"Can we also pretend that at some point throughout the course of this nightmare of a morning I went to the trouble to turn my pants the right way?"

He chuckled, tilted his head around to survey the flap on the back of her pajama bottoms, and shook his head. "Oh no. I'd sooner walk to New York than play along on that one."

CHAPTER NINE

LAILA

I stepped out of the shower an hour or so later to, I kid you not, the sound of someone pounding on my door. Seriously, what happened to the courtesy text my generation was supposed to be so fond of? On top of that, didn't I have a doorbell? I mean, I was pretty sure I did, but I was really starting to wonder if I was remembering incorrectly. Well, this time whoever it was would just have to wait. I'd learned my lesson.

"Laila, are you here?"

Oh, good grief. In true horror-film fashion, the call was now coming from inside the house. Brynn's voice being the call, as it were. I might have learned my lesson about not rushing to the door in a precarious state of undress, but there was still a lesson to be learned regarding not handing out my house key to everyone I knew.

I cracked the bathroom door open a sliver. "Are you alone?"

"Hey! Yeah. I have something for you."

"And Sebastian's definitely not with you?"

She laughed. "Um . . . I'm pretty sure."

I pulled my bathrobe from the hook on the back of the door and pulled it on before opening the door wider. "What's up?"

"We just talked to Cole. He told us you're coming to New York!"

I sighed and toweled off my hair enough that it wouldn't drip on the floor before stepping into the hallway and walking toward my bedroom. "Yeah." I didn't even have it in me to fake enthusiasm.

"Here." She reached into her jacket pocket and pulled out a bottle of pills, opened it, and gave me one. "Take it about thirty minutes before the flight. It will help take the edge off the nerves and keep you from puking before we get to the end of the runway."

"One pill can do all that? Does it also fight crime?" I chuckled and set it on my dresser. "Thanks, Brynn, but I'm not sure there are enough pills in the world to make me feel better about this trip."

"This is perfect, Laila. You realize that, right?"

"Why? Why is it perfect? Nothing about any of this seems perfect to me. If anything, I'm just helping him dive deeper and deeper into his little escape plan. I don't even know why I said I would go."

Because he's acting completely irrationally.

Because sometime over the course of the next few days, regardless of where he is, he's going to start thinking clearly, and I need to be there for him when he does.

Because I can't stand the thought of today being the beginning of goodbye.

Brynn grabbed my hand and pulled me to sit on the edge of the bed. "Think about it. This is a good plan. Right now, he's just needing some distance. And, you know, his emotions are heightened and everything. So it's extreme. But if he spends a few days in Manhattan, then it will almost be the end of the month. The new owners will be in Cassidy's, and Bill's stuff has to be out of Spruce House—"

"And who's going to take care of that if Cole and I leave town?"

Brynn raised her hand and swatted that little detail away like a fly. "They're talking to people now."

"Who's they?"

"Seb and Cole, of course. Come on, don't act like that will be any big deal for this town. You know they'll all step in and do whatever they can to help. Mrs. Stoddard and Doc will have it all taken care of in no time, and Cole won't have to be there for it at all. So he can get the distance he needs without making any sort of big, irrational, impulsive decision."

I groaned and fell back onto the bed, which actually hurt more than I would have thought. But the pain I was feeling in my back just helped accentuate the misery coursing through the rest of me. "Cole's entire state of being is one big, irrational, impulsive blob of decision-making right now."

And that, of course, was why I had to go with him. But New York? I'd never been east of Kansas, and until that morning I'd had no intention of breaking that nearly thirty-nine-year streak.

Oh yeah. Nearly thirty-nine.

I scrunched up my nose. "I hate that I'm going to be away from home for my birthday."

She gasped and lay down beside me on her side, propping her chin up on her hand. "Are you kidding? I think that's one of the best parts! It's going to be amazing. We can go to a Broadway show and some unbelievable dinner somewhere. I'd suggest we eat at Daniel— it's my favorite, although Sebastian insists it's pretentious. Or maybe Bar Pitti, which is definitely pretentious, but I've never once gone there without seeing Beyonce and Jay-Z, and that's not nothin'."

I had no idea what she was talking about. Well, mostly. Like any other reasonable human on planet Earth, I spoke the language of Beyonce, but everything else she was rambling on about—prix fixe and Fotografiska and *Kimberly Akimbo*—sounded as strange and horrifying as that one time Cole explained foie gras to me.

"Brynn!" I cut her off in the middle of a soliloquy centered around Skinny Dennis, which I *think* she was maybe saying was a honky-tonk dive bar in Brooklyn, though I was really too afraid to ask. I would just trust that I hadn't accidentally zoned out while she was referring me to a person by that name. "I'm sorry. I love you, but this sounds sort of awful to me. And you know that as awful as it sounds to me, if Cole was in his right mind right now, he wouldn't even be entertaining the idea of moving to New York. He's Colorado through and through, and he will absolutely hate all of this. He's literally going to kiss the ground when he gets back to Adelaide Springs."

"Yep." A pleased-as-punch grin spread across her face, and I suddenly understood why she thought the trip was such a good idea. "I'm counting on it."

⁓

"As I live and breathe," Cole greeted me with a laugh as I rolled my suitcase out of the airport and toward the plane. He, Brynn, and Sebastian were standing just beside the steps talking to Steve, the pilot who regularly flew the Sudworths on their connecting flights to and from Telluride. "Is that Laila Olivet I see, all packed and ready for her adventure in the big city?"

"I can't believe we're doing this."

Seb rushed over to me and whispered, "I'm really glad you're coming," then took my backpack off my shoulder and my suitcase from my hand. "I'm counting on you to make Cole stop and breathe for at least two seconds."

"And I'm counting on you to keep your wife sane for, hopefully, the entire trip," I whispered back. "I don't know who Skinny Dennis is, but I'm okay never making his acquaintance."

Seb chuckled and walked my bags over to Steve as Cole and Brynn surrounded me.

"I'm so happy!" Brynn squealed and hugged me tightly enough that Cole winced.

"Be careful," he told her. "Did she tell you about her fall this morning?"

Brynn released me and backed away as if Cole had just said, "Did she tell you she came down with a bad case of the bubonic plague?" "No. What happened?"

I rolled my eyes. "It was nothing. Really. Besides, you know . . . Doc gave me something."

Cole's eyes darted to Brynn and then back to me. "Like, a pain pill?"

I nodded. "Yeah, I think it's starting to help."

I felt Cole grab my elbow then. At least I was pretty sure it was

Cole who did it. And I was pretty sure it was my elbow. *Elbow . . . elbow . . . elbow . . .*

"Hey, Lai?" Brynn asked, stepping back toward me. "You didn't take that other pill I gave you, too, did you?"

"Oh no," Cole muttered as his arm slipped around my waist. "What did you give her?"

"Just something for her nerves. For the flight. I didn't know she was going to take anything else."

Brynn said something else that I didn't quite catch, and then I looked behind me to see what Sebastian had done with my bags. But when I turned around, he was gone. And so was Steve. And the airplane!

"Why is she saying 'elbow' over and over?" Sebastian's voice asked from . . . *somewhere.*

"It was my dad," I responded, as if that answered all of life's questions. "Did you take the plane?" I asked Dad as he walked toward me. "We're going to need that in order to fly, I think."

I heard Cole exhale. Like a big, heavy exhale. Like, "Hhhhggggg-hhh." That's my best guess at how to spell it.

"Larry, you drove her here?"

My dad laughed, and then the plane was back. I'm not sure how he did it. "Oh yeah. Doc gave her some pills for her back, but he said they might just make her a little drowsy. I forgot this one doesn't have much tolerance for anything."

"Larry, I'm afraid this one's on me," Brynn confessed.

She was already laughing a lot, but she started laughing even more when Cole said, "Great. We have to make two connecting flights today, and Laila's high as a kite."

Elbow . . . elbow . . . elbow . . . elbow . . .

⌒

My first memory of New York City will always be sitting on Brynn's enormous rolling suitcase, being anchored on each side by Brynn and

Sebastian and pushed from behind by Cole, as a huge I Heart NY sign came into view. It was right about then that the world came into focus again, and not a moment too soon, I figured. Brynn and Seb were used to making less conspicuous journeys through public spaces, I was guessing, and people were beginning to take note.

Have Brynn Cornell and Sebastian Sudworth drugged and kidnapped a woman? Should we call the police? Should we ask if we can take a selfie with them? So many choices!

"Hey there, Sleeping Beauty," Cole greeted me over my shoulder. "Have a nice flight?"

"Can you walk now, Lai?" Brynn asked with a slight huffing quality behind her voice. "There's an escalator coming up, and as much as I want to believe you won't end up at the bottom a little sooner than we intend for you to, I really can't make any promises."

The world may have come into focus a few moments earlier, but that was the moment when my brain caught up.

"Oh my gosh!" I jumped off the suitcase and looked back at the three of them—Cole and Sebastian grinning mischievously, clearly amused by the entire situation, and Brynn drenched in sweat, her hair having lost all its body, and her cute green dress displaying unmistakable pit stains. "I'm so sorry. How long have I . . ." Okay, maybe my brain hadn't *completely* caught up yet. "We're in New York."

"What gave it away?" Brynn asked, the huffing having been replaced by thinly veiled snark.

I guess I deserved the snark, considering that in addition to the giant I Heart NY sign we were stopped beside and the images of the Statue of Liberty, the Empire State Building, and yellow taxi cabs all over the walls, Frank Sinatra's "Theme from *New York, New York*" was blaring across the PA system so loudly we were having to shout at each other to be heard.

"How did we even get here?" I was so confused. The last thing I remembered clearly was settling into a seat next to Cole on the tiny plane out of Adelaide Springs, and then . . .

No. That was it. That was the last clear memory. After that I could *sort of* remember Cole trying to force-feed me a smoothie, and I may have asked a TSA officer who was frisking me if she had any Jolly Ranchers, but otherwise I had blinked, and I was on the complete other side of the country.

"It wasn't without its challenges," Cole responded, that amused, indulgent grin still on his lips. "But as Brynn and I told Seb, as two people who have experienced the all-out paranoia and vomiting fest that is flying with you when you're sober, this wasn't so bad. I'll check with Doc and see if there are any long-term risks, like odds of permanent brain damage or needing a liver transplant. Otherwise, you're repeating this cocktail for the flights home."

"Throw in a glass of Chardonnay," Sebastian added, "and you might just be able to check her with your luggage."

About twenty-five minutes later we had collected our bags and were following Brynn to the curb where a car waited for us. I'd been alert for less than half an hour, and I was already in sensory overload. I had bumped into more people waiting with Brynn in the line for the bathroom than I had gone to school with, and everything was so loud and bright. It was one o'clock in the morning there, and I was already homesick for 11:00 p.m.

But I had to admit the car was nice.

"I've never taken an Uber before." I'm sure that statement came as a surprise to absolutely no one. "I didn't expect them to be so classy."

"Hey, Malik." Sebastian patted the shoulder of the driver who was opening the doors for us all. "Sorry to get you out so late."

"Not a problem. As if I was going to pass up the chance to be the first to hear about the wedding and honeymoon." Malik smiled at me and gave a little nod. "Here, may I take your bags, ma'am?"

"Oh." I looked at Sebastian, who was now making his way back to the trunk to stow his own bag, and decided to follow his lead. "That's okay, but thank you. My name's Laila, by the way." I put my hand out and he shook it.

"Very nice to meet you, Ms. Laila. I've heard a lot about you." Cole stepped up beside me, and Malik initiated a handshake between the two of them. "And Mr. Cole—"

"Just Cole's fine. Thanks."

"Here." Malik took my suitcase from beside me and put his hand out for Cole's as well. "I insist." Cole handed it to him, and Malik joined Sebastian in the back.

I leaned in and whispered to Cole. "My mom's always talking about taking Ubers when she travels, and she made it sound pretty sketch. But this is nice."

"Hey, Malik!" Brynn greeted him with a brief hug and then handed him the massive suitcase that had recently been, for all intents and purposes, my stroller. Malik lifted it with one hand as if it weighed nothing and slipped it into the cargo area in the back.

"Welcome back, Ms. Brynn. Was Italy completely perfect?"

She sighed. "It really was. We brought you a postcard. I know it would have been better if we had actually mailed it from there, but we forgot."

"I'm honored you thought of me at all."

"Of course!" Brynn turned to Cole and me. "Malik is our favorite driver. He thinks of everything."

"You're too kind, Ms. Brynn." He tilted his head down and added, more softly, "I have some Red Bulls for you in the cooler."

"Bless you!" Brynn opened the passenger side door in the front, stepped up, and leaned in with her bare-below-the-knees legs dangling out. Sebastian quickly stepped in front of her less than ladylike position to protect her from prying eyes and a camera shutter or two.

"I swear, woman," he muttered. "You're the worst at being famous of anyone I know."

"Please, please." Malik ushered Cole and me toward the third row of the vehicle. "Make yourselves comfortable. There are waters for you there, and of course the energy drinks if Ms. Brynn is willing to share."

"Nope!" Brynn hopped back down onto the ground and gave Sebastian a quick kiss on the lips—and the camera flashes lit up the darkness.

Malik smiled at me and offered me his hand to help me climb in. "Is anyone hungry? Do we need to make any stops?"

"What's even open this time of night?"

I regretted it as soon as I said it. Even before Sebastian and Cole started snickering. I was going to have to be very careful not to come across as a country bumpkin every time I opened my mouth.

"I mean, I know stuff is open. I just don't know how that works. Is *everything* open? Or just like . . . pizza and hot dogs . . . and . . ." What were other New York foods? "Pretzels and stuff?"

I climbed in after Cole and couldn't contain a moan of pleasure as my body seemed to become one with the supple dark brown leather.

"That's it," he said as he leaned his head back and let his arms flop to the sides. "I'm moving here." Panicked tightness grabbed at my throat, but it didn't last long. "We live in this Cadillac Escalade now, Laila. Please have someone forward all our mail." He sighed and closed his eyes.

I copied his relaxed posture and settled in. "This isn't an Uber, is it?" I asked the question softly enough that only Cole could hear me. Country bumpkin protocol had been activated.

"I'm guessing not."

Sebastian helped Brynn into the second row and then climbed in behind her and shut the door. They buckled their seatbelts, and I muttered to Cole, "I suppose we should buckle up too."

"Nah. The Escalade would never betray us by leading us to our death. It's fine."

I laughed and sat up, reached across him and pulled the seatbelt down and clicked it into place, then did the same for myself. "But what a way to go if you're wrong."

CHAPTER TEN

COLE

His eyes didn't stay closed much longer. As Sebastian and Brynn regaled Malik with tales of Vietri Sul Mare and the Amalfi Cathedral and boat excursions and grottos galore, he and Laila sat in awed silence as Manhattan spilled out before them. He'd spent a fair amount of time in Denver, and of course he'd lived in Boulder for a couple years. He'd traveled throughout the Four Corners states pretty extensively and had even gone to LA with his mom when he was younger. Once, when he was twenty-three, he'd driven all the way to Houston so his grandfather could reunite with his brother, Burt, one more time. And he and Laila had spent one of her birthdays in Vegas. But none of that could ever prepare anyone for what his brain was trying to make sense of in New York.

It wasn't just that it was bigger than he'd pictured it or that he couldn't see the tops of skyscrapers that rose up past the clouds. It was that every direction he looked was familiar . . . and yet unlike anything he'd ever experienced. They gawked at the recognizable highlights of the skyline—the Empire State Building, the Chrysler Building, other buildings that they knew but had no idea what they were called. Cole had never so much as imagined what it would be like to visit New York. He hadn't spent time studying coffee table books of NYC architecture, and he certainly hadn't watched as many movies as Laila and Brynn had—though he was suddenly anxious to track down some locales from *Home Alone 2*—but he still somehow felt like he'd been plucked up from his everyday existence and dropped into the middle of something he'd experienced in a dream and forgotten about by the time he awoke.

"Cole." Laila's voice jolted him from his wonder, though her voice was barely strong enough to form his name. Nevertheless she got his attention, and he turned to follow her gaze out his side of the vehicle.

It was a strange thing to have lived in a place like Adelaide Springs during a scary, uncertain time like 9/11 and everything that came after that day. They'd sat in Mrs. Stoddard's classroom and watched the coverage all day like everyone else the world over, and it had been shocking and heartbreaking, of course. But it had also felt so distant. Like it impacted them, but it also had so very little to do with them. The closest anyone in town got to knowing someone directly affected by the attacks was Lucinda Morissey's dad having spent some time working at the Pentagon, though he had long ago retired from the Defense Department and had moved on to installing xeriscaping in the Tucson area. Doc Atwater and his late wife had taken a trip to New York for a medical conference once, and Doc said they had bought tickets for *Phantom of the Opera* at the half-price TKTS booth in one of the twin towers. That was it, as far as anyone knew.

Before anyone knew any facts, the citizens of Adelaide Springs had sat around speculating and theorizing just like everyone else had—Where had Flight 93 been heading? What would be the terrorists' next target?—but there wasn't a single theory, realistic or otherwise, that put them in direct danger. Security was supposedly heightened around the Hoover Dam, and Fenton Norris had speculated the ultimate target was Area 51, but that was as close as the fears ever got to them. As relatively conscientious teenagers coming of age in a suddenly very confusing world, Cole and his friends had been less relieved by that and more stricken with guilt: when they probably should have been counting their blessings that they were able to go to sleep in peace, breathing in clear, ash-free air and not having lost a single person they knew, much less loved, they dreamed of getting out instead. They didn't feel protected. They felt sheltered. Agitation sparked rather than grateful peace.

And now the World Trade Center was just out their window, reflecting the moonlight that pierced the clouds the shimmering building rose into. Cole couldn't tell how far away it was—he didn't know how to compute the size of the city, only that skyscraper ratios and proportions skewed differently than the mountains he was used to— but he figured he could walk there without breaking a sweat. And since he'd be taking that walk at sea level for a change, he was almost sure of it.

"Brynn, how did you ever get used to this?" Laila asked.

Brynn turned in her second-row seat to face them, just as Malik slowed down and then shifted the vehicle into Park. "Who said I have?" The driver's door opened, causing the interior light to come on, and the smile was evident on Brynn's face.

She jumped out when Malik opened her door, and then it was Sebastian's turn to look back at Cole and Laila in the third row, still staring out the window, though their view of the tallest of the buildings had been blocked by much shorter buildings that were still taller than any they'd ever stepped foot in. "For the record, your mountains have a similar effect on those of us who grew up with the man-made wonders. I'll never get used to having fourteen-thousand-foot peaks outside my window. Peaks that are . . . what? Seven or eight One World Trades stacked on top of each other? I'd imagine there are days when you don't even notice them anymore."

Sebastian climbed out on his side, and then Brynn poked her head back in to add, "I'm so excited that you guys are here. Seriously. I can't wait to show you the city." And then she grabbed another Red Bull from the cooler and trilled, "Let's go!"

Cole sighed as he unbuckled his seatbelt. "She doesn't mean tonight, does she? She *can't* mean she wants to show us the city *tonight*."

Laila laughed and climbed out the door. "Hmm. Who's wishing they'd been passed out all day now, huh? See? I knew exactly what I was doing."

⁓

Thankfully Brynn's middle-of-the-night tour of the city was brief.

"So this is Tribeca. JFK Jr. and Carolyn Bessette lived . . . oh, I think about eight doors down that way." She pointed to the right of the redbrick building she was standing in front of. Sebastian and Malik had already gone inside with all the luggage.

"You 'think'?" Laila asked. "Who do you think you're talking to here, Brynn?"

Cole hadn't necessarily been able—or even tried—to keep up with all of the girls' celebrity crushes through the years, but he vaguely remembered *one* of them dramatically refusing to eat or shower or something until JFK Jr.'s plane was found. They would have been fourteen or so, right? It certainly made the most sense that the boy-crazy, pubescent, and yet somehow still mature-beyond-her-years Brynn Cornell of his recollections would have been the one conducting the round-the-clock vigil.

Her sheepish grin shone under the streetlamp. "Okay, yeah. They lived exactly eight doors down that way. I can make it there in eleven seconds. Nine if there aren't any lookie-loos around, and I don't have to be extra careful not to trip. Wanna see?"

Cole laughed. "How many energy drinks did you consume, woman?"

Brynn looped her arm in his. "Come on. Let's go. Run with me."

"I have *zero* interest in that. Maybe less than zero. I mean no disrespect to the deceased celebrities that none of us ever met, but I'm exhausted. Right now, all I want is to—"

"Did you tell him that the *Ghostbusters* firehouse is just across the street?"

Cole's head snapped toward Sebastian, standing on the black

metal landing in front of the building that, presumably, was where they lived, though there was a sign for a pediatrician on the door. So far, New York didn't make a whole lot of sense to him. But *Ghostbusters*? In a world of chaos and confusion, *Ghostbusters* would always make sense.

"What are you talking about?"

Malik laughed and stepped down from the landing after telling Sebastian good night, and then cordially said goodbye to everyone. He pulled the Escalade away, and the street was quiet and mostly dark again.

Brynn kept holding on to Cole's arm and pulled him out slightly into the empty street. She pointed in front of them. "See number twenty? That's John-John's apartment. Then there's that bar on the corner. And then see right there? Across Varick Street? That brick building with the red—"

Holy crap. "Race you there."

Brynn guffawed. But even as she laughed, she hiked her skirt a little farther above her knees, looked down at the sensible-by-Brynn's-standard-but-definitely-not-meant-to-be-run-in heels she was wearing, and lowered her body into the stature of a sprinter, waiting for the pistol to fire.

"Ready, set, go!" Cole shouted, too quickly, taking Brynn by surprise and bringing an abrupt end to her laughter.

Cole's exhausted, time zone–confused, thirty-nine-year-old body that had been lugging his comatose best friend from sea to shining sea all day took in a couple lungsful of sea level–dense oxygen and ran like the wind toward a relic from what had been *his* obsession when he was fourteen.

Yesterday afternoon he'd been in mourning.

Last night he'd been abandoned.

This morning he'd been lost and wandering.

But now? Now he was running toward his boyhood fantasy of taking on the Gatekeeper. Not a bad way to turn around a crushing hand being dealt, all in all.

CHAPTER ELEVEN

LAILA

"I have to say, it's just weird to think of you two as condo people."

We were in the elevator heading up to their seventh-floor penthouse. *Penthouse.* As in Seb pushed the button that said "7PH," and that was them. Top floor. The *entire* floor. Upstairs from a pediatrician's office, down the street from the *Ghostbusters*, and, most important, around the corner from Taylor Swift. Literally around the corner. "You can see her roof from our roof," Brynn had said, as if that was a normal thing to say.

"Honestly, I think it's weirder to think of you as Cadillac Escalade people," Cole chimed in.

Brynn laughed. "We're *not* Cadillac Escalade people. We just needed more space because you guys are here."

"But you have a driver!" I argued. How were they so chill about all of this? "You had your driver bring your bigger car because you needed more space."

"Don't be silly," Brynn said. "Malik is not 'our driver.'" She used her air quotes liberally, but the "silliness" she was insisting we were exhibiting wasn't clear to me yet. "And the Escalade is not 'our bigger car.' He drives for the network, and yes, he does drive us around fairly often, but only to and from the airport and to the studio and stuff like that."

"And what sort of vehicle does he usually drive you in?" Cole asked, an amused grin on his face.

Brynn blushed and looked down at her feet. "Oh, I don't even know, really. It's just some little—"

"It's a Mercedes S-Class," Sebastian interjected. "Give it up, Brynn. In New York, we are Cadillac Escalade people, and they know it. We're also condo people. There's just no denying it."

"And that's awesome," I insisted, though I really had no idea if it was or not. That remained to be seen, I supposed.

The elevator doors opened, and we were all met by the *clickety-clackety* of little dog paws running against hardwood floors. "Murrow!" We all greeted the tiny Havanese in unison, and Sebastian bent over to pick him up. Sebastian had already been up, of course, to bring in our luggage, so I guessed Murrow's enthusiasm was really directed at Brynn. She reached over and scratched behind his ear and cuddled him in Sebastian's arms, and Murrow's excited yelps confirmed my suspicions.

Yeah . . . that was another thing. Murrow usually traveled with them, but after the wedding Murrow had come back to New York with Brynn's assistant. East of the Mississippi, the Sudworths were also personal-assistant people. *Weird.*

I'd begun making my way over to say hello to Murrow, but Cole stopped me with a hand on my elbow. "Look at this place," he whispered.

There was a lot to see, but I followed his eyes and tried to take it all in from his perspective right then. He was looking up at a staircase that led to a mezzanine in the center of the condo. That mezzanine not only featured a den or office or something, by the look of it, but was surrounded by massive windows with unobstructed views of the city outside. We'd been craning our necks outside before we came in, wanting to catch one more glimpse of One World Trade in case we weren't going to have such an easy opportunity to stare at it later. Who'd have thought that all we'd have to do was look up and around a winding staircase inside our friends' home?

"Is that a door up there?" Cole asked me. "Where does it go? Out to their helipad?"

I chuckled softly as Brynn came up behind us. "Do you like it?"

I turned to her. "Do we like what? New York? It's sort of hard to say—"

"No, the apartment. I was . . . well . . . I know it's stupid, but I was a little nervous, actually. I was afraid you might think we're sort of pretentious or something."

"Weren't you there for the 'Cadillac people' conversation?" Sebastian was kneeling on the giant curved tan-leather couch with Murrow by his side. "They do think we're pretentious."

There was enough humor in his voice, and we knew and loved each other enough, that I understood it was all very good natured. Nevertheless, I felt guilty. The way Cole's mouth tightened and puckered as he pulled his eyes away from Brynn's made it pretty clear he did too.

"No, of course not," I insisted. "You're not pretentious. It's just . . . I mean . . . *wow*. This place is crazy, you guys. I just can't really wrap my head around it."

Cole chimed in. "I was making a lame joke to Laila a minute ago, but as long as you and the neighbors don't actually have a helipad on the roof, I think we'll adjust."

Brynn shook her head. "No. Definitely not. No helipad."

"Besides," Sebastian added, "the neighbors aren't allowed on the roof." He laughed and stood up as Murrow jumped down. "Want to get settled in your rooms?"

Brynn clapped in excitement. "Ooh! Yes! Okay, now they aren't quite finished yet. And we only really have one guest room. Lai, you can stay in there. Cole, we'll put you in the—" Her mouth clamped shut and she seemed to just manage to stop the words she was going to say before they escaped. "The, um . . . Well, it's just a den, really. Or, you know, an office. Yeah, it's an office. With a bed. Just a little separate from the other rooms—"

"What is it, really?" Cole asked, bending his neck to look around Brynn at Sebastian.

"Yeah, it's a maid's quarters. But don't worry. We don't actually have a maid. We're not *that* pretentious."

⌒

A couple minutes later we had moved my luggage into a modestly sized guest room that could have passed for a guest room in a middle-class noncelebrity home in Colorado Springs or something if not for the skylight that didn't reveal much of the city but displayed a perfect view of the roof. Brynn and Sebastian's roof that—he wasn't kidding—the neighbors weren't allowed on. Yes, it was the top of the entire building that quite a few people lived in and that rich little Manhattanite kids presumably visited when they had a cold or got marbles stuck up their noses, but Brynn and Seb owned the roof. Including north, south, and west terraces, one of which gave them direct line of sight to Taylor Swift's roof.

The walls of the guest room were painted with a leftover design Brynn called "if Monet had painted the jungle room at Graceland," which I actually sort of loved, and the bed was also left over from the previous owners. It had a canopy tent over it, but not like something we had actually camped in. Oh no. It was tan and tasteful and reminiscent of photos I had seen of Ernest Hemingway on safari in Africa. (Brynn wouldn't tell me whom they had bought the condo from, but she did go so far as to say, "I'm not saying it *wasn't* a former Sexiest Man Alive, his *Gossip Girl* wife, and their ever-expanding brood.")

I could hardly wait to see what awaited Cole in his maid's quarters, so I ran after them, circled around the mezzanine stairs, passed the dining alcove, made a right at the full-height wine refrigerator, shimmied past a built-in shelf full of Emmys and who knew what other glittery hardware accolades, did a quick double take at what I'm pretty sure was an actual Picasso on the wall, and then I arrived. Just as Brynn said, "Oh no! Why would she put everything in here?!"

Cole's maid's quarters—smaller, tasteful, and sadly devoid of nineteenth-century-impressionism-meets-Elvis interior design—were crammed to the hilt with wedding presents.

Brynn pulled her phone out and began texting. "I'm so sorry, you guys. I told my assistant we had two people coming to visit . . ." She nodded her head in resignation as she read the text that popped up in front of her. "She thought you were a couple. I guess I didn't specify. She just wanted to get the wedding gifts out of the way." She stuffed her phone back into the pocket of her dress and looked at Sebastian with a pained expression. "Does the couch pull out?"

Sebastian chuckled. "Do you mean the circular one that you insisted on because it would form an intimate conversation nook? No. No, it doesn't. But if Cole wants to curl up like a horseshoe all night, I'm sure it will be very comfortable."

She shot him a look that we'd seen *a lot* when they were planning the wedding. "Thanks, Seb. That's helpful." Sighing in frustration, she pulled her phone out again. "The Roxy Hotel is only a block or two past *Ghostbusters*. I'll call and get you a room for tonight, and then tomorrow we'll—"

"Don't you dare." Cole stepped into the doorway and wrapped his arm around her. "I bet I can just bunk with Laila." He glanced at me and shrugged.

"Ooh!" I clapped my hands and then raised them in the air excitedly. I knew he was hoping I would go along with the suggestion so we could keep Brynn from going to any trouble or feeling bad, but I didn't even have to feign enthusiasm for the idea. "Yes! Let's do that!"

"It's really not a problem to get a hotel room. I don't want you guys to be cramped."

Cole scoffed. "Are you kidding? The five of us used to cram into Doc's fifth wheel, remember? We'd spend weeks at a time in that thing over summer break, and I'm pretty sure it was smaller than that tent bed Ryan Reynolds bought for his kids."

"I never said it was Ryan Reynolds!" Brynn protested.

He laughed. "My bad. Just making wild guesses."

"It's really not a problem, Brynn. We're mountain kids, you know. I'm pretty sure we can rough it in your luxurious penthouse for a little while. I'm actually a little excited."

I was more than a little excited, truth be told. I hadn't had a sleepover in years, unless you counted Cole falling asleep on the couch when I made him watch *The Crown* with me.

Sebastian flipped the light switch and ushered us all out before closing the door to the maid's quarters. "Great. That's settled. Let's go to bed." He grabbed Brynn's hand and began pulling her toward their bedroom, which we hadn't even seen yet.

"I'm sorry it's been such a long day." I hugged each of them. "Thanks so much for everything, and for letting us crash for a little bit. Don't let us get in your way. Anything we need to know about? Which towels to use or anything like that?"

Cole grabbed my arm and pulled me back toward the room, calling over his shoulder, "We'll figure it out. Good night!"

"Good night!" Sebastian echoed.

Brynn groaned. "Seb, hang on," she whispered and then hurried over to me and pulled me aside, into the marble kitchen. "You're really sure you're okay with this?" She spoke so quietly I had to lean in to hear her.

"Of course. Why wouldn't I be?" I didn't see any need to whisper, so I didn't. "I probably just need to call my dad and check in, and then I might take another of those pills Doc gave me for my back—"

"Give them to me." Cole appeared around the corner just a split second before Sebastian did.

"You can't be trusted with those things," Sebastian added.

I rolled my eyes. "I told you I didn't know I couldn't take them together. Now I know. Brynn only gave me the one happy pill, anyway, and the ones for my back will be fine."

Sebastian raised his eyebrows, and Cole nodded. "Don't worry. I'm on it." And then Sebastian held Brynn's fingers again and began pulling her away from me.

"Boys, go away," Brynn instructed, and they did as they were told—Cole quickly and efficiently, Sebastian with an agitated groan.

I smiled and leaned in. "What's up?"

She rubbed her hands up and down my arms and lowered her voice again. "I just . . . well, I mean . . . I guess I just know emotions are running sort of high for you right now. For both of you. Bill dying . . . everything that happened with Cassidy's . . . Cole thinking he needs to move away . . ."

"Yeah?"

She studied me intently, her head tilted and her eyes narrowed. And then she seemed to shake it all off, and the seriousness was replaced by a smile as she wrapped her arms around me. "Forget it. I think I'm just exhausted. But I'm so glad you're here."

I hugged her back. "Love you."

"Love *you*," she replied. She began walking away and then turned back one more time. "Just leave the lights on, or do whatever. We can control them from—"

"Enough already." Sebastian swooped in and scooped her up into his arms, causing Brynn to giggle all the way until they were out of eyeshot and earshot.

CHAPTER TWELVE

COLE

"Sebastian is about to collapse, I think," Laila said as she entered the room after taking out her contacts, washing her face, brushing her teeth, and doing all the other bare-minimum nighttime requirements. "He just gave up and carried Brynn to bed . . ." The last four words dissipated into the air as realization dawned. "Ah. He's not wanting to sleep."

Cole chuckled as he searched through his suitcase for his toothbrush and toothpaste. "No. I don't believe he is."

Laila picked up her backpack and sat down with it beside her on the bed at the opening of the tent. "Well, I feel dumb."

"Don't. You were passed out and gloriously unaware of them being unable to keep their hands to themselves on Air Newlywed today. Speaking of . . ." He reached his hand out, palm up.

She rolled her eyes. "Oh, good grief, Cole. I'm a grown woman who is perfectly capable of—"

"Do you remember when you got your wisdom teeth out and called the Sarah McLachlan number on TV and paid for the immunizations of about three hundred cats?"

She scoffed. "It wasn't three hundred . . ."

"And do you remember going on Ticketmaster after your tonsillectomy and hatching your mercifully short-lived plan for us to spend our summer following Edwin McCain on tour?"

"I really liked that 'I'll Be' song back in the day," she muttered and then dug into her backpack, grabbed the bottle of pills, and handed it over.

"Don't take it personally. It's not your fault that so much as three ibuprofen instead of two turns you into Courtney Love at Chateau Marmont." Cole bit his lip to avoid laughing at her. "How is your back now? Do you need one before bed?"

"I'm starting to feel pretty sore, I guess."

He pressed down on the lid and tipped one out into his hand before setting the bottle on the Art-Deco-meets-Ikea desk where Blake Lively's kids probably used to do their homework. He handed the pill to her. "What do you think we're supposed to do about water? Do you think they keep the Perrier on tap, or is that just for the domestic and local craft brews?"

She snorted and pulled her nearly empty CamelBak bottle out of the side pocket of her backpack. She managed to swig out enough water to swallow the pill. "Isn't it crazy? I mean, I'm so happy for them, but I just can't get over it. They're *not* pretentious is the thing."

"Eh . . . Brynn's a little pretentious. But in a lovable way."

"Yes. That's very true." She twirled the bottle around and watched the few drops of water at the bottom swirl around. "I'm just really happy they have each other. And I think the part that's craziest to me is that they make as much sense together here as they do back home. Even though their lives are so different here."

When her eyes stayed focused on the bottle and didn't rise to meet his, and didn't move on to other things, he took a deep breath. Then he picked up her backpack and set it on the floor before squeezing in next to her in the opening of the tent.

"Hey, Lai?"

"Hmm?"

"Why did you agree to come? I mean, *really*."

She shrugged but still didn't look at him. "It's okay that I did, right? I mean, you wanted me to?"

"Of course I did." That was true. Now he couldn't even remember why he'd ever been thinking of coming without her. "But I want you to do lots of things that you don't do."

She finally raised her eyes to look at him. "Like what?"

"Oh, I don't know." Cole looked behind him to make sure the space was clear and then pushed himself back with his hands until his feet dangled off the side of the bed. He kicked his shoes off onto the floor and scooted himself the rest of the way in and rested his back against the wall. "Learn how to cook, for one."

The right corner of her lips rose, and her eyes began to twinkle. "That's different."

"How?"

She leaned over and untied her pink Converse high-tops and slipped them off and then scooted back to join him in the tent. "If I thought it really mattered to you, I would." She tilted her chin to look him straight in the eyes as she said it, brimming with sincerity.

But Cole wasn't buying it.

"No, you wouldn't."

The left corner of her lips matched the right. "Okay, probably not. Though maybe I'd subscribe to one of those food-delivery things where they give you all the ingredients and you just have to throw them together. That I could handle, I think."

"Lai, that's still cooking. They just do the shopping for you."

"Yeah, but don't they give you the step-by-step instructions? I think that would help."

"You mean a recipe? Again . . . that's cooking."

Her eyebrows fell. "Oh. Then, no . . . probably not that either." She leaned her head over and rested her temple against his shoulder as it bounced up a little from his chuckle. "But I can't think of much else I wouldn't do for you, Cole Kimball."

Her hair, up in her signature strategically messy bun, which had become increasingly flighty after a long day of travel and the addition of humidity to the mix, tickled his jawline. He laid his head down on hers, and they rested there in a posture so practiced and familiar. "Same, Laila Olivet. Same."

They sat there another minute, maybe two, listening to the sounds of the city outside. Those certainly weren't the ambient night sounds they were used to. Aspen leaves quaking and coyotes howling had been replaced by car horns honking and occasional sirens in the distance. Even in the middle of the night in Tribeca. Not that he knew where Tribeca was, really. Close to One World Trade but a lot farther from the Empire State Building, it seemed. Home of the *Ghostbusters*. Beyond that, he looked forward to exploring and learning more. He really couldn't remember the last time he'd been somewhere completely new. Vegas was a lot, but Vegas still offered him touchpoints of southwestern cognizance. New York already felt so unfamiliar and daunting.

He couldn't remember the last time life had felt uncertain. But for the moment, he wasn't worried about it. He knew he'd have to worry soon enough, but for the moment he was with his favorite person in a tent where Deadpool had probably told his kids bedtime stories. That was enough for now.

"I have to be honest with you about something." His voice was soft and scratchy, but he didn't bother trying to do better. "I'm still hoping to convince you to move with me. Here or wherever I end up going. I think, in a way, I'm sort of hoping you realize it doesn't matter where we are, as long as we're together. Even though I know your reasons for not coming with me do actually matter." He reached his hand up and brushed some of her flyaway strands out of his face and then kept his arm around her shoulders. "Is that manipulative?"

"Yes. Just like it's manipulative that I'm pretty sure I really only came on this trip to make sure you have such a horrible time that you never want to leave Adelaide Springs ever again."

He laughed. "At least my manipulation was going to lead to a great vacation for us both. You're over there making plans to throw me in front of a subway car or something."

She gasped. "I would never!"

"Well, you know . . . not enough to kill me."

Cole felt her head begin to lift under his cheek, so he rose up and met her eyes.

"I was really just thinking more along the lines of homesickness and maybe a little food poisoning from a bad slice of pizza or something. You didn't have to go all dark with it."

Her eyes were beginning to droop and Cole knew he only had a few good minutes with her before the pill kicked in completely. He'd go take a shower, and she'd be asleep before he got back. The next time they talked there would be light streaming in, and they'd encounter new views and everything might feel a little different after sleeping to different sounds. Brynn and Seb would be there, and then by tomorrow night his room would probably be cleared out of wedding gifts, and they might not have these final sleepy moments together that had always been some of his favorites. On camping trips and movie nights and evenings when they just lost track of time. It was possible they'd never have these final, sleepy, perfect moments together ever again.

"Hey, Lai?"

She laid her head back on his shoulder. "Hmm?"

"What if while we're here, I don't try to convince you to go, and you don't try to convince me to stay? What if we don't even think about all that stuff?"

Was that even possible, for either one of them? Was it even possible, when he was only here to try to cement a decision for which he'd already begun leveling the land and installing the footings? He was sure willing to give it his all if she was. "What if we just spend time together and try to make it the most special week and a half we've ever had together? And then, well . . . *whatever* happens, we'll always have this trip. You know?" Cole knew that "whatever happens" would involve him leaving Adelaide Springs. He just couldn't see any way around it. But he was willing to not think about that for a little while if it also meant he didn't have to think about how it was equally certain she wouldn't be going with him. "Do we have a deal?"

"Do you know what I just realized?" she asked, her words beginning to slur.

Cole chuckled. He'd lost her. "What's that?"

"This is Brynn and Seb's first night here together. The wedding and then the honeymoon and then back to Adelaide Springs . . . We totally crashed their first night as husband and wife in their new home. That's monkey punky monkey punky."

He was pretty sure those last few words hadn't been accurately transcribed by his brain, but they were his best guess.

"I bet they'll forgive us." He kissed the top of her hair. "Get some sleep."

He carefully lowered her head to a pillow and straightened out her legs and helped her slip under the covers. Then he climbed out and shimmied her over to the edge of the bed and removed her Sophia glasses. He'd have to climb back over her to get into the tent after his shower, but he didn't want her to wake up panicked and confused from her drug-induced sleep and not understand what she was doing in the darkness of a tent, with the sound of more massive jet engines flying overhead every hour than either one of them had ever seen in their entire lives. All the Edwin McCains and Sarah McLachlans in the world might not bring peace amid that freak-out.

He turned off the light and then felt around for everything he needed for his shower, though it only took his eyes a few seconds to adjust. The light shining in from outside was as bright as the moon on a clear night in their mountains, camping under the stars. And suddenly the tent made sense, though he couldn't imagine why you would want to shield your eyes from the New York nightscape any more than you would in Colorado.

"Hey, Cole?" Laila whispered as he made his way to the door.

"Yeah?"

"We have a deal."

CHAPTER THIRTEEN

LAILA

I woke up on Sunday morning to the smell of bacon, the sound of traffic, and the weight of Cole's forearm resting on my hip. And I was immediately able to make sense of all of that and put it into context, so the pill must have worn off.

If there'd been any doubt about that, the ache in my back confirmed it.

It had been a long time since I'd watched him sleep. I used to do it all the time when we were kids. Okay, that sounds creepy. It's not like I was Edward Cullen sneaking into his room and disappearing before he awoke, of course. It's just that when we all had sleepovers or went camping when we were little, Cole was always the last to fall asleep. It was like it wasn't physically possible for him to pull back on the rpms until whoever was in his care was safe and settled. Not that we were ever in his care. Not really. Not officially. There was usually an adult around somewhere—Doc or Cassidy or my mom and dad or Wes's mom—but that meant nothing to Cole. Truthfully, when the five of us got together, it meant very little to any of us. It didn't matter how many times we were shushed or told to go to sleep, we couldn't help but laugh and talk and play silly games into the night. After a while the adults stopped trying. And then eventually the adults stopped tagging along.

The thing is they were right to trust us. Even as we became teenagers together, they were right to trust us. When the five of us were together, it was about *the five of us*. Together. And we weren't ever going to do anything to jeopardize the privileges we had earned.

In some ways I think it was hardest on Cole when the lives of the other three fell apart. He never said so—not in so many words, anyway—but I was pretty sure he felt like he had failed them. In his mind I think it was somewhat his fault that Brynn was gone, Wes was gone, and Addie was heartbroken by the time I turned eighteen—the last one, bringing up the rear. It was ridiculous, of course, but it was also part of what made Cole *Cole*.

So, Cole being Cole, when we all got together for camping trips or sleepovers, he was the last to fall asleep. As a result, he was the last to wake up. I couldn't keep track of all the times in my life that a sleeping Cole was the sight that awaited me when I opened my eyes, but it had been a long time.

The arm across my hip had never happened before. At least not that I remembered. He was on his right side, and I was on my left, and I was closest to the edge. It didn't take long for even *that* context to all click into place and make sense. I could remember absolutely nothing from the moment I'd lain down, but I had little doubt that Cole feared I would slip off in the night and adopt some dogs with sad eyes. Thus the restrictive arm.

Honestly, giving away all my money to the care of neglected pets was probably always a risk for me—with Schedule IV controlled substances in my system or not.

My left arm was bent up under me and my hand was resting on his forearm in front of his face on his pillow, but I slid my hand to rest on his chest, as gently as I possibly could. His breathing was deep, and it lulled me into its rhythm pretty much instantly once I could not only hear it but feel it under my fingertips. Even breathing came easier when I was with him, and I wasn't ready to accept that soon enough I'd have to adjust to doing it without him. He had to snap out of his single-minded determination to leave Adelaide Springs. He just had to.

But for the next ten days, I wasn't allowed to do any coaxing. *That* I remembered from the night before. We'd made a deal, and I would honor it.

A tear formed in the inside corner of my right eye, tickling my lashes until I had no choice but to blink. And once I blinked, the tear ran down my nose. And then there were more, streaming down onto my pillow, and I was biting the inside of my cheek to try to avoid making any sound that would wake him up. But then, while I was doing all of that blinking and crying and stifling, I noticed something about his face. At least I thought I did. It took me just a second to be sure. I leaned in as close as I could so I could see him clearly—where were my glasses, by the way?—and held my breath so that I didn't breathe directly on him.

He'd shaved. I couldn't remember the last time he'd completely shaved away his facial hair. For the past several years—or longer, I guess, since he'd really started growing it when Sebastian came to town rocking a pretty great-looking beard of his own—he'd been sporting what I had taken to calling the Chris Hemsworth in Lockdown. He always kept it neatly tailored, but he wasn't one of those guys with balms and special boar's-hair brushes and derma rollers and such. Nah. Cole just had style. Always had. And whoever his birth parents were, they had blessed him with thick, dark hair. And eyelashes that somehow fanned out and curled perfectly without any effort whatsoever. I, somehow, always managed to have one eyelash on each eye poking straight into my pupil and a couple that were just a little bit longer than the rest and continually practicing their downward-facing dog yoga moves. My lashes weren't horrible, I knew, but there was just enough chaos happening to occasionally make me feel like I was a newbie bank robber who had accidentally slipped fishnets over my head. Cole had no such chaos on his face.

But, admittedly, over the past week since his grandfather died, his facial hair had been somewhat neglected. I had still liked it. Some gray had started slipping in amongst the black. (And wasn't it interesting how gray hair among my peers could be distinguished and sexy, and yet every gray strand I found on my head was carefully followed down to the root and yanked out with a maniacal, "Die, sucker!"?)

(Also, while we're at it, why are gray hairs thick enough to use as fishing wire? Asking for a friend.)

Now his beard was gone and I was a little bit sad. But mostly I was fascinated. Enthralled. He was twenty-five again. Okay, maybe thirty. A whole lot younger than me, that much was certain. The hair on his head was a completely silver-free zone, and when he wasn't looking sad and he wasn't laughing and showing those lines around his eyes that I liked to believe I had helped create, looking at him transported me back to a different time. A simpler one, I guess. Right then I was remembering visiting him in Boulder when he went to culinary school. Two years he'd been away from home. The longest two years of my life, probably. But it hadn't felt like the end of anything. I hadn't been worried about the future. I'd been excited by the possibilities. The idea of him never moving back to Adelaide Springs didn't scare me then like it did now. Why was that? I'd known it was a possibility. In fact, it had been very likely.

I guess maybe then I didn't feel quite so much like he was all I had. Like he was all I *wanted*. I'd just wanted great things for him, and I'd wanted great things for me. And wherever those great things took us, nothing would change.

How could I have thought nothing would change?

Back then, one or the other of us had driven the five hundred miles round trip at least once a month, and those weekends were everything. He'd practiced his new cooking techniques on me and made the most delicious things I'd ever tried. Things I couldn't pronounce. And he'd teased me about how I couldn't pronounce them— things like *bruschetta* and *crudités* and *au jus*—and I didn't care one bit as long as he kept stuffing my face. We'd gone out to trendy hotspots and tried to act like we fit in, and then we just laughed so much about trying to fit in that we stuck out like sore thumbs.

And that's when I'd really started sewing. Huh. I'd sort of forgotten that. It had all started because Cole had a T-shirt from every place he'd ever been that sold or gave away T-shirts. National parks and coffeehouses and his school, sure, but also ten-minute oil-change places and rallies for political candidates he'd never heard of and marching band competitions that we'd gone to in Grand Junction. Not that either of us cared about marching band competitions, but sometimes we were just desperate to get out of Adelaide Springs.

"Each one is a memory, Laila," he would say to me as he threw his newest T-shirt over his shoulder like a bartender throwing a towel. "There is no reason whatsoever why I would ever remember that we were here. It would just be a forgotten day. But now I'll never forget."

While he was in Boulder I'd go over to his house in Adelaide Springs to visit Cassidy or his grandfather, or under the guise of watering his Christmas cactus (which I had forgotten to water and accidentally killed years before when he was on vacation with his family, but it had now been twenty-three years or so and I wasn't sure he had noticed yet), and I'd sneak into his closet and steal a few of the T-shirts from the pile. When he moved back home, I gave him the quilt I had made as a graduation gift.

I hadn't thought about that in years.

"Can I help you?" he muttered, and I shrieked a little. Right then my eyes were dead-on even with his lips, about an inch away, and I'd been so focused on Cole of the past that I'd forgotten to be considerate of the sleeping Cole of the present.

I pulled back and raised my eyes, probably about as abashed as I ever was with him. So not very abashed at all, really. But I did feel a little silly. "You shaved."

His eyes fluttered open the rest of the way, from the slits he had first peered at me through. "I did."

"I was just . . . you know. Looking." I began to pull away and slip over to my side of the tent, but his hand was still on my hip, and he applied a little pressure to keep me in place.

He leaned his face in so his eyes were right in front of mine. He'd been blessed with great hair, great lashes, and perfect eyesight. I usually found each of those perfections very annoying. "And what do you think? Have I made a huge mistake?"

"A mistake? No. Though I do think it's borderline cruel for you to shave ten years off your face the week I catch up with you in age."

I lifted my hands to feel his skin's new smoothness. "Can you grow it back by Friday?"

"Absolutely." His left arm stayed strung over me as he pulled up his right arm, leaned on his elbow, and propped his head on his hand. "Should I just forgo the Chris Hemsworth in Lockdown and commit fully to the Jeff Bridges in *True Grit*? As a birthday gift, I mean."

"It would be the considerate thing to do, yes." His eyes were locked with mine, and those creases were decorating the corners again. Thank goodness. If he lost those mementos of age and laughter and *us*, I might never recover. But the smooth face I could get used to. "No, I suppose I'll allow the new look. Even through my birthday, if you want. You look handsome. Of course, I expect you to completely dress the part. Let's see . . . what other style characteristics need to accompany the return of young Cole Kimball?"

Like I said, Cole had style and always had. Admittedly, I liked the current Cole style more than some of that which had existed in yesteryear. As he'd shifted more and more into the role of running a business—while still having to handle all the cooking and occasionally wait tables or tend bar—he'd adopted a casual professionalism that made him possibly the best-dressed man in Adelaide Springs (though my dad could wear the heck out of a bolo tie), but he never looked out of place. Fitted T-shirts, long-sleeved button-ups with the sleeves rolled up, an occasional fitted jacket over one of those fitted T-shirts . . . He would have fit in just as well pretty much anywhere.

"I'm sure I could track down some baggy shorts somewhere. And I *definitely* still have my skate shoes."

I laughed. "Rein it in, Marty McFly. The time machine on your face didn't take you *that* far back." His eyes were sparkling beneath his lashes, and his lips were twitching in unison with the twitching of his fingers against my hip. "What is it?" I asked when he'd been staring at me that way just a little longer than was normal.

His eyes darted away and then back so quickly I probably wouldn't have caught it if I wasn't so close to his face. But when they came back, the smile had turned into an expression I wasn't sure I recognized.

There was a different dilation to his pupils. A different curve to his lips. Of course I probably just wasn't used to seeing his lips on such unobstructed display.

"I was dreaming about you."

"Ooh! Tell me!" I lowered my hands from his face and rested them on his chest. "Let me guess. Did you dream that I could cook? I don't know why this is such an obsession for you, but, I mean, I guess you could try to teach me how to make rice or something. Rice is easy, right? Don't they even call it 'easy rice' on the package? I like rice. It wouldn't be completely inconvenient to know how to make rice, I suppose."

Even lying down and relaxed, his shoulders slumped in visible frustration with me, causing a giggle to rise to my chest. "They call it 'easy rice' because it was basically a scientific breakthrough on par with getting a man to the moon to invent a foolproof way to cook rice. Cooking rice—really cooking it and doing it well—is not easy, Laila. It's not easy at all."

I shrugged. "The microwave stuff isn't so bad."

Cole sighed. "Anyway, no. You weren't cooking in my dream. Even my subconscious knows the difference between 'could only happen *in* a dream' and 'too fantastical for *even* a dream.'"

"So what was I doing?"

His eyes seemed to glaze over for a moment, and then he cleared his throat and backed up against the wall. As he did, he moved his hand from my hip to his own and caused my fingers to fall from his chest to the bed. "Zelda."

He wasn't quite as close now, so I had to squint in order to study him and try to make sense of the words. "'Fitzgerald' or 'Legend of'?"

"'Legend of.' You were Link from *The Legend of Zelda*, and you were traveling all across Hyrule looking for Korok Seeds."

"You know I don't know what any of those words mean."

"You had the pointy little ears and everything. It was cute."

He shook his head and chuckled as he sat up with his back against the tent wall as he had last night, except his knees were pulled up to his chest and his arms were crossed over them. Now I *really* couldn't see him, so I sat up next to him, but as soon as I slid into position, he pushed himself out of the bed and jumped to his feet.

"Did Seb make breakfast?" He bent over his duffel bag and pulled out a sweatshirt. "It smells good. Do you need in the bathroom?" He slipped his Peyton Manning hoodie on over his T-shirt and then straightened it all out over his joggers. "If you don't mind, I just want to get in there real quick. Brush my teeth and such. Although it probably would have been more considerate if I'd done that *before* I breathed my morning breath all over you, huh? Sorry about that."

"Oh, gosh, I bet mine's horrible—"

"It's not. I mean, I didn't notice anything, so it can't be too bad, right? Alright. I'll meet you out there."

What was happening? I hadn't heard him string that many words together since seventh grade when we had to recite the Preamble to the Constitution and he could only remember it if he dumped it all out at once, in one big secure-the-blessings-of-liberty-for-ourselves-and-our-posterity breath.

"Cole?" I called out to him just as he shut the door from the other side of it.

He poked his head back in. "Heya. What's up?"

I laughed at him. Not *with* him but *at* him. "You're being weird. Why are you being weird?"

"I'm not being weird. You're being weird."

I squinted at his blurry silhouette. "No dice, home slice. I'm just being my normal amount of weird. You're being, like . . . *weird* weird."

"I think I'm just excited about the trip and stuff. Can't wait. See you out there."

"Hang on!" This time I stopped him before the door shut. "Can you get me my glasses? Or at least tell me where they are?"

"Oh! Sorry." He hurried over to the built-in bookshelf by the window and picked them up, then stretched his hand into the tent with them. But before I could grab them, he opened them up with both hands, leaned into the tent, and gently placed them on my face.

As my eyes adjusted and he came into focus, he rested a hand on either side of me on the bed. He kept his face close to mine as he smiled. "I'm really glad we're doing this. This trip, I mean. I'm . . . I'm really glad you're here."

I tilted my head and raised my hand to rub his smooth cheek with the back of my fingers. And then I responded truthfully, suddenly as sure of this one thing as I was pretty much anything else in my life. "Me too."

He stretched in enough to kiss me on the cheek and then maneuvered out of the tent, and then the next sound I heard was him whistling Billy Joel's "New York State of Mind" as the door was closing behind him again.

Weird.

CHAPTER FOURTEEN

COLE

It was possible that *The Legend of Zelda* had not factored as prominently into Cole's dream as he had declared. There had been no swordplay or rupees or evil warlords, and it wasn't quite so cerebral as to feature different branches of parallel timelines. Though the skimpy little tunics weren't too far off.

Neither were the different branches of parallel timelines, come to think of it. Cole sort of felt like that's what was racing through his brain right then, jumbling up his reality and making him feel as weird as Laila seemed to think he was acting.

In that way that dreams sometimes do, it had felt like a completely accurate snapshot from life and an unquestionable work of fiction, all at the same time. It was definitely Laila, and he was pretty sure it was him. But not because he ever saw himself. He just felt it all. They were in a bedroom that he knew was theirs, together, in a house that he knew was *theirs*, though nothing was ever stated to inform him of that. It wasn't a room he'd ever actually been in, he was pretty sure, and he had no reason to think it was a room that truly existed, but while he slept, he was as familiar with that dream bedroom as he was with his real-life room in his real-life house. And in the dream, Laila's laugh was the same, and her eyes were the same, and her hair was the same, and the way she looked at him felt normal, and the way he touched her wasn't awkward at all. But he was pretty sure she'd never actually looked at him like that in real life. He was positive he'd never touched her like that. He'd have remembered. If he'd ever touched her like that, Earth would have shifted on its axis and never recovered. How could the world ever have righted itself after *that*?

Look, it wasn't like he'd never had dreams about her before. *Those* sorts of dreams, even. It wasn't like he was proud of it, but the fact remained that he was a red-blooded, healthy, breathing male who was attracted to women and who happened to have a beautiful woman as his best friend. This same beautiful woman had been his best friend when he was a pubescent teenager, so no, this wasn't a first. And though he'd always done all he could to prevent those thoughts from slipping into his head, there was only so much that could be done. He didn't have control over the forbidden territory his mind trespassed into while he slept.

He'd always strived to be a gentleman, even when he was young and obnoxious. He'd been brought up to respect women. To respect *everyone*, actually. But his grandparents—his grandmother especially— had always placed special weight on how he needed to treat women. Not because women were weaker or needed his help or because it was his responsibility as the heir apparent in a patriarchal society. Nah. Nothing stupid like that. Even his grandfather, who rarely had the time of day for anyone he met, didn't buy into any of that rhetoric. He was an equal-opportunity curmudgeon.

As far back as he could remember, Cole had felt deep affection for women. Sure . . . like *that*. Again, red-blooded, pubescent, yada, yada. But he also understood now as he probably didn't then that the reverence he felt for the women in his life wasn't necessarily shared by most other boys his age. But then again, a lot of other boys probably hadn't hit the women-worth-revering jackpot quite as often as he had.

Cole was the only child of a single mother who had adopted him on her own, persevering over a system that didn't make it easy to do so. And he was the beloved only grandchild of one of the kindest, most remarkable women ever to live, in his opinion. Cole's mom, Cassidy, was the child of his grandmother, Eleanor, and her first husband, Cormac Dolan—a despicable man, by all accounts. Eleanor had spent years making excuses for the man, but when he transferred his abuse to Cassidy for the first time, all of Eleanor's excuses imploded. She had some family money and may or may not have pocketed more than her "fair share" of *Cormac's* family money. That's how Eleanor had told the tale to young Cole, with a glimmer in her eye, and even then, he'd felt fairly certain she deserved more than whatever she made off with.

Without any real plan apart from escape, she and Cassidy had headed west. Slowly. Exploring everything that intrigued them. They made it all the way from Evansville, Indiana, to Adelaide Springs, Colorado, where they stumbled upon a four-day spectacle of Revolutionary War reenactments, more than thirteen hundred miles west of the war's westernmost battlefield. On the second evening of Township Days, they'd met Bill Kimball, dressed in his regimentals and a tricorn hat. The rest was Cole's history.

Laila was his history too. And his present. Every other person he had ever truly loved had let him down at some point. They were human, and he tried not to hold that against them, but he could go down the list of the ways their humanity had broken his heart. Brynn and Wes had left without saying goodbye. Addie had broken her promise to keep in touch. His grandmother had died too soon. His mother had sought ways to fill the holes in her own heart while disregarding the holes in his. And his grandfather . . . Well, Cole hadn't come up with a short, easy way to categorize that one yet. But Laila had never broken his heart.

"Hellooo . . . Earth to Cole." Brynn's voice interrupted his reverie. Or his mindlessness. It interrupted whatever was happening in his head, thank goodness.

"Sorry. Did you say something?"

Brynn was standing beside him at the island in the kitchen, holding a coffeepot. "Need a refill?"

"Oh. Yes, please. Thanks." He held his cup out, and she filled it.

"What's up with you?" she asked as she returned the pot to the countertop next to the stove. "You were quiet all through breakfast."

"Was I? Sorry. Just tired still, I guess."

He was glad that Sebastian didn't seem to be paying any attention to the conversation. He was sitting in the center of that horseshoe-shaped sofa, facing away from the kitchen with his nose in the *New York Times*, Murrow curled up asleep beside him. The less Sebastian was aware of how distracted Cole was, the better. Seb wasn't one to pry, but he rarely had to. That was the problem with one of your closest friends being a brilliant journalist with all sorts of Pulitzers and stuff. He tended to get to the heart of things a little too quickly sometimes, and when you were once again surprised by his insight and investigative acumen, he'd just say things like, "Yeah, Syrian president Bashar al-Assad had a similar response when I got *him* to admit he'd never read *Charlotte's Web*."

"Did something happen with you and Laila?" Brynn's eyes lit up as she leaned over the island toward him.

"What?!" Cole motioned her away with his hands and shushed her as he looked behind him. Could he still hear the shower running? Check. Was Seb still focused on his paper? Double check. "No!" he whispered emphatically as he moved closer to her. "What are you even . . . I mean, what are you talking about? Something happen . . . like what?"

Nice job, Cole. You said all the right things. If only you'd said them in the right order.

Yeah, he hadn't handled that so well, and he knew it right away. If he'd had any question about that, Brynn's eyes, which now seemed to be taking up her entire face except for the little part at the bottom reserved for her O-shaped lips, would have answered the question pretty quickly.

"Oh my gosh, Cole. *Did* something happen? I was just joking. You know . . . because I've been asking off and on for our entire lives. I didn't actually think—" She covered her mouth with her hands and then spoke quietly through her fingers. "Is this finally happening? For real?"

"No!" He looked behind him again. Shower. Newspaper. No meteors shooting through the sky or other signs of the apocalypse. He just needed to breathe and rein her in. "No, Brynn. Nothing happened."

He laughed a little bit in a way he hoped communicated, *Oh, Brynn, whatever shall I do with you?* Casual and unaffected, as he had been a million other times throughout his life when someone got it in their head that there *had* to be something romantic going on under the surface of his and Laila's relationship. "I'm just worried about her. Her back, I mean. She can't take those pills during the day, obviously, so I was just thinking maybe we should ease into the sightseeing slowly. But I know she won't want to be the reason we don't do something. You know?"

"Oh." Her eyes and lips bounced back to their normal shapes as order was restored. "I was thinking we could hit up some museums. Do you think that would be okay?"

"Sure. Yeah, I bet that will be great. I'm probably worrying for nothing."

With that bit of business taken care of, Brynn began showing Cole some of her new kitchen appliances. Apparently, the jet-lagged newlyweds had been up at 4:00 a.m. opening wedding gifts.

Sebastian's paper rustled as he began folding it up, and then he brought the topic back around. "Still thinking MoMA and then tea at BG?"

Cole wasn't sure if it was New York Seb or Married Seb or Back to Being a Journalist Seb who had started saying things like "MoMA and then tea at BG," but regardless, he was going to need more time to adjust.

"I think so," Brynn responded and looked at Cole. "I think Lai will really like BG. It's on the seventh floor of Bergdorf Goodman and just down Fifth from MoMA." Cole stared at her blankly, and she smiled. "Museum of Modern Art."

"And Birddog Newman?" He was playing up his "Thank God I'm a Country Boy" status for effect a little bit, but not too much. "What's that?"

"Bergdorf Goodman. A department store. I think Laila's mind is going to be blown. And then maybe we can—"

"Did you call for a table?" Sebastian asked.

Brynn shook her head. "I'm sure they'll be able to get us in."

He stared at her. "Seriously? You're just going to leave sitting by the window to luck? I'm not sure I even know who you are anymore."

She slapped herself on the forehead. "Oh my gosh, you're right." She turned to Cole and put her hand on his forearm. "There's a great view of Central Park. Okay, I'll go call. Be right back." She pulled her phone from her pocket as she rushed to their bedroom.

Cole chuckled as he watched her go, but the humor faded quickly. "So, tell me. What happened with you and Laila?"

Cole repeated his shushing and waving-away panic from before as he hurried over to the couch. "Nothing! Nothing happened." Crap. He'd done it again. "I seriously don't even know what you guys are talking about. Happened *how*?"

Not smooth. Not smooth at all.

Sebastian crossed his ankle up over his knee and grinned. "Brynn's name makes things happen pretty quickly in this town, so you can hem and haw if you want, but she's probably going to be back here in about—"

"I had a dream." Cole looked around one more time and listened for the shower yet again, and then sat across the horseshoe from Seb and leaned in. "A *dream*. You know?" Heat rose to the top of his head. There were not words for how much he hated this. All of it. The fact that it had happened, definitely, but mostly that he was having to talk about it. "About Laila. Nothing happened. It was just a dream. But I guess it sort of weirded me out. That's all."

"Well, yeah. I would think so. Knowing someone as long as you two have known each other, and then all of a sudden . . . *that's* in your head? That could really mess with a guy."

"Yeah. Exactly." Cole released his breath and leaned against the back cushions of the couch. Okay. This was okay. He could talk to Seb about this. *Of course* he could talk to Seb about this. Seb would contribute sanity to the situation. This was good.

Sebastian chuckled. "Honestly, it's sort of shocking that this is the first time that's happened."

"Well, I mean, it's . . . not." He sat up again and leaned his elbows onto his thighs. "It's not like it's happened a lot, of course. But . . . a few times . . . through the years."

"Oh. Gotcha." Seb picked up his folded newspaper and reinforced the crease. "That's not fun. I bet that's led to lots of uncomfortable post-dream interactions, as much as you and Laila are together."

Cole dismissed the idea with a shake of his head and a slight shrug. "No. Not really. I've never given it much of a second thought. I know I can't control what happens while I'm asleep, but I am pretty good at erasing the images once I'm awake, I guess."

"Huh. Yeah. That's good." The paper went still in Sebastian's hands as he raised his eyes and met Cole's. "So what was different about this time?"

Heaven help President Bashar al-Assad if he ever had an inappropriate dream about *his* best friend.

Sebastian had gotten right to the heart of it. Of course he had. Man, that was annoying sometimes. From the look of it, Murrow took after his human. He was staring up at Cole with the same inquisitive and confident furrowed brow. *Good job, Seb. You can put our new Pulitzer Prize next to my food bowl.*

And as much as Cole didn't want to spend any time analyzing or talking it out, he couldn't deny that he was now being forced to consider the sticking point that probably needed to be addressed. What *had* been different about this time? He couldn't pinpoint much that stood out about the dream itself. Not that he'd had the same dream before. The dreams had spanned from the absurd to the ridiculous through the years, as dreams are known to, but the only thing absurd about this one had been the intimacy between him and Laila. There weren't any pink elephants or flying Doc Atwaters or cameo appearances by Steve Harvey on the set of *Family Feud*.

"We asked one hundred people, and the top four answers are on the board: What's the fastest way to make things painfully uncomfortable between two single adults who are just friends and happen to be sleeping next to each other in an enclosed tent bed that used to belong to Blake Lively Jr.?"

"I guess . . ." He paused. Water was still running. Brynn was still out of the room. Murrow was still salivating over the scoop he and Sebastian were about to land. "I woke up and she was there. You know? And I am so comfortable with her, Seb, I can't even tell you. This isn't some sitcom episode where one person turns their head and tries not to look or pretends not to look while the other changes clothes. We've spent so much time together and know each other so well, we have a rhythm. Even in the situations that are a complete break from routine, like being in New York, we have a rhythm. She can change clothes three feet away from me and she doesn't ask me not to look, because she knows I never would. That's . . ." How could he describe something that was so set-in and sacred that he'd never given it much thought? "I would never want to do anything to jeopardize that. Not ever. Her trust, I mean. The *level* of trust. The comfort."

Cole's hand went to his chin and scratched, almost out of compulsion, as he thought of her squinting to see him and leaning in and stroking his face. "But this morning, I was sort of touching her when I woke up."

"Touching her?"

"Yeah. Nothing major. My arm was just sort of across her, making sure she didn't fall out of bed or anything. As you've now witnessed, pain pills make her loopy. Always have. But I didn't want to put her on the inside of the tent in case she woke up in the night and the darkness and unfamiliar surroundings spooked her."

Sebastian shifted his propped-up foot back to the floor. "Got it."

"So, yeah. I was touching her. And her face . . ." Cole chuckled and looked down and began scratching behind Murrow's ears. He'd evidently grown bored with the interview. "She was, like, an inch from me." He looked back up at Seb, smile still on his lips. "She's blind as a bat, you know. She was noticing that I had shaved, but in order to really see, she was, like, *right there*." He put his hand in front of his face to demonstrate.

Sebastian released air through his teeth and leaned in to talk even more quietly. "That sounds pretty intimate."

Cole shrugged nonchalantly in the exact same moment that he felt the panic rising in his chest again. Here was where it got tricky. "Yes and no. I mean, yes. But . . . the physical contact wouldn't have felt so intimate if I hadn't still been waking up, I think. Waking up *from* the dream. And there was this moment that I had to actively think about and put effort into the stuff I *never* have to think about. The stuff that's always been as built-in as breathing."

"What do you mean?"

Cole swallowed hard. "I mean . . ." He spoke through tight lips and clenched teeth. "I kind of started to . . . pull her closer. Against me. You know? There was a split second when I almost . . ."

Nope. He trusted Sebastian, and if there was anyone he could talk to about this, it was him—since his absolute *most* trusted confidant had a bit of a conflict of interest where this particular situation was concerned. But he couldn't tell him about the split second when he'd had to fight against every instinct in his body, raging and rebelling inside him, telling him to pull her beneath him and pick up where the dream had left off.

He swallowed again and shook his head. Unfortunately, when he did, the image in his mind didn't budge. "I've just never had to think about that before."

Sebastian took a deep breath and let it out slowly. He opened his mouth to speak but closed it quickly as Brynn came back into the room.

"We're all set for BG."

"Then what are you thinking for dinner?" Sebastian asked.

She leaned her hip against the kitchen island. "We have reservations at Gabriel Kreuther. Cole, you're going to flip out over this place. Some of the best food I've ever tasted. I don't know if you like caviar, but—"

"I was thinking Bar SixtyFive at the Rainbow Room." Sebastian's expression turned down in visible disappointment.

Brynn guffawed. "The Rainbow Room? Are you kidding? I mean, it's good, but it's *so* touristy." By way of explanation, she added to Cole as an aside, "It's on the sixty-fifth floor of Rockefeller Center, and I think everyone always thinks they'll see a celebrity."

"Are you seriously rolling your eyes?" Sebastian asked his wife, then looked over at Cole. "We had dinner there with Jimmy Fallon and his wife about a month ago, and Paul McCartney and Ringo Starr were eating together with *their* wives, two tables over. Besides," he added as he turned back to Brynn, "our friends here *are* tourists. And if someone with a lot of pull could get us a table by the south window, right across from the Empire State Building, that might make a pretty spectacular impression . . ."

She sighed. "Fine." She pulled her phone out of her pocket again and huffed back off to their bedroom.

Sebastian watched her go with a besotted grin on his face. "I almost feel bad about that. She's right. You would have absolutely flipped over Gabriel Kreuther. Ah, well. We'll have time." He turned back to face Cole, and then they both froze as the sound of the shower shut off. Confident that Laila wasn't coming out right away, Seb leaned in a bit and whispered, "Are you going to be able to handle all of this? Being with her round-the-clock and everything?"

Yes, Cole was weirded out. That much was true. And it was true that he had been thrown off balance. But he and Laila had made a deal. They had the entire length of the trip to make memories and pretend that the saddest separation of their lives wasn't going to be waiting for them after this vacation. He wasn't going to ruin that. And, strangely enough, it was thinking of all that in response to Seb's question that made him feel as if his equilibrium was returning.

He chuckled to himself as he felt the panic subside. Throwing his hands up in the air, he relaxed into the back cushions of the couch again as the rogue adventures of his unconscious mind began to make sense. "It's because I'm scared of losing her. That's all this is." He would have chastised himself for being so dumb about it all—for panicking and allowing it to affect him the way it had—if the relief hadn't felt so good that there wasn't even room for disparaging emotions. "I think my brain's just working overtime to figure out a way to make things work—especially since we made a deal not to try to convince each other of anything while we're on the trip. And then you throw in being around you two, who are still on your honeymoon, essentially, and the tent bed and all of that . . ."

He exhaled deeply and then reached over and punched Seb twice on the knee with his knuckles. "Thanks, man. I'm fine. I was just making a big deal out of nothing."

"If you're sure . . ."

"Totally sure. I mean, I still need to clear my head a bit, I guess. But this is Laila we're talking about. Yes, to answer your question, I can absolutely handle all of this. I've been with her nearly round-the-clock for the better part of forty years. This morning was weird." Laughter spewed from him as he thought again about how ridiculous he had been. "But it's over. Now it's back to normal, and there's no reason whatsoever why I would have any other inappropriate thoughts of her flood my brain while I'm asleep. But if they do . . . so what? Whatever my dreams try to do to me has absolutely nothing to do with reality. I've got this all under control."

"Hey, guys?" Laila called from the bathroom door that had just cracked open. "Who's out there?"

Cole smiled indulgently and rolled his eyes at Sebastian. She probably needed help reaching something or for someone to bring her something she'd forgotten. This was Laila. And they had a rhythm.

"Just Seb and me right now. Need something?"

"No, it's fine. Just . . . Seb, close your eyes. Are they closed?"

Sebastian quirked his eyebrow in confused amusement and then closed his eyes and covered them with his hands for good measure. "Yeah, they're closed."

The grin spread across Cole's face as he turned on the couch to face the direction of her voice. *What is she up to?*

"Okay, good." And then she streaked out of the bathroom wrapped only in a fuzzy gray towel knotted tightly around her at her chest and stretching down to the middle of her thighs. Her hair was wet and stringy, ringlets bouncing off her back as she ran out of the bathroom, across the room, and back to her bedroom, trilling, "Keep 'em closed! Keep 'em closed! Keep 'em closed!" all the way. It happened so fast. Cole turned away as quickly as he could, but obviously not soon enough.

And then he couldn't help but look at her again as she reached the bedroom door and said, "I have my contacts in now, so I can officially declare that the clean-shaven NYC edition of Cole Kimball is a total hottie." She winked at him and called out, "Thanks, Seb! You can open your eyes now!" as she shut the door behind her.

Sebastian uncovered his eyes, and though he hadn't seen a thing, the context clues—which now included a trail of intoxicating scents that had been transported with Laila on a stream of steam, along with a gobsmacked Cole trying to remember how to breathe—probably made it easy enough to connect the dots. He cleared his throat, adjusted his position on the couch, and opened his *New York Times* again.

"So glad you've got it all under control."

CHAPTER FIFTEEN

LAILA

Day one in New York wasn't quite like I'd imagined it would be. It was great and all, but none of the movies and television shows I'd ever seen—certainly not *Friends*, which I had assumed had taught me everything I needed to know about Manhattan life—were from the perspective of celebrities taking their layperson friends around town.

I'd been excited to go underground to ride the subway, just like Phoebe when David Arquette's nice-guy stalker mistook her for her twin sister, Ursula. But I guess the subway has grown increasingly difficult for Brynn, who has collected a few crazed fans of her own. Don't get me wrong, though. Malik was awesome, and it was nice to see him again.

And I know it was a fictional show (and thirty years ago, or whatever) but I was also really hoping to spot some sort of real-life version of Joey's VD poster, just so I could joke about it with Brynn. But you didn't really see a lot of VD posters when you were driven from VIP entrance to VIP entrance of MoMA and the Met in a Cadillac Escalade.

And obviously I didn't expect to go to Central Perk and sit on the orange couch while Phoebe performed "Smelly Cat" and Gunther manned the bar, but I'd thought I was at least guaranteed some slam poetry in Greenwich Village or something. The odds were statistically in my favor that Brynn would need to replenish the coffee in her bloodstream at some point during the day.

But instead, we had tea. *Tea.* As in high tea. Tea and crumpets. As in Devonshire cream and preserves. And it was delicious. And beautiful, of course. And looking out at Central Park was probably my favorite part of the day, although even then I just wanted to get down there and be a part of it. Sitting there having tea, I felt like I had been flown directly to Buckingham Palace to watch a live cam of New York. It just wasn't what I had in mind.

On top of all of that, Cole was still being weird.

"How were your scones?" I asked him as we wandered through Bergdorf Goodman after tea. We hadn't been wandering together, for the record. I'd had to catch up with him and eventually tracked him down in a room that, bewilderingly enough, seemed to be devoted to men's pocket squares.

"Delicious. But is it just me or are the ones Andi serves at the Bean just as good? Maybe even a little better?"

"Thank you! Yes!" I looked around to make sure Brynn and Seb weren't around. "I'm so glad you said that. I mean, yeah . . . everything was good. But for the price?"

"Insane." He shook his head. "I know they have money, but—"

"Why would anyone charge that much for a cup of tea? I swear it tasted the exact same as Celestial Seasonings, straight out of Colorado."

"But those cucumber sandwich things were actually something special."

I smirked. "Are you telling me you couldn't make some just as good for about a buck fifty?"

"Oh, I could," he acknowledged. "But I hadn't thought of it, you see. So they deserved the money once." He raised his arms and spun around slowly as he proclaimed, "Thank you, Birdjosh Groban, for the inspiration to cut off the crust of the bread. I honor you this day."

I laughed just a little too loudly and had to apologize to an uppity-looking sales clerk who looked at me like I was an unruly child, which entertained Cole greatly. But when I leaned into him to share the laugh, his smile faded a bit and he took a step away, turning his attention to the pocket squares once again.

I knew exactly what was going on, of course, though I had no idea how to address it. How do you address the tension when the issue causing the tension is the one issue you've agreed not to discuss? It had been a great idea, the whole temporary hiatus of real life, but he clearly hadn't stopped thinking about it any more than I had. It was almost like if he couldn't talk to me about what he anticipated as the next steps of his future, and he couldn't try to sell me on leaving Adelaide Springs, too, then there wasn't anything to talk about.

"So, contemplating a pocket-square purchase, are you?"

"I have been meaning to up my pocket-square game for a while. Don't act like this is news to you."

I reached down and ran my fingers across a blue plaid one. "I like this one. And it *totally* doesn't look like just a handkerchief at all."

He turned and faced me. "Okay, seriously, are they not just handkerchiefs? I've really been staring at them, trying to figure out what differentiates them from handkerchiefs. I'm assuming you don't blow your nose on these. I guess? Maybe because they're silk and wouldn't hold the snot very well. But couldn't you just buy a handkerchief and decide not to blow your nose on it, and then you'd have a pocket square?"

"Wow." I shook my head. "You really don't get it at all, do you?"

"Hey, guys! There you are!" Brynn came hurrying up behind us, and I couldn't help but notice snooty clerk didn't clear her throat at her. "Did you find anything you want to buy, or are you ready to move on?"

"Move on to where?" I asked at the exact same time Cole said, "Apparently I'm not pocket-square people."

His comment was missed by Brynn, but I bit my lip to keep from laughing as she responded to me. "I think we have just enough time to take in the Guggenheim before dinner."

Another museum. Awesome.

"Oh. Okay. Sure. Um, yeah . . . I think I'm ready."

"Hey, Brynn . . ." Cole leaned in and whispered as he moved closer to us both. "There are people over there taking your picture."

She didn't even look over her shoulder. "Yeah, sorry about that. Probably another reason to move on." She looked over at snooty clerk. "Thank you. Have a nice day."

"You too, Ms. Cornell. Thank you for visiting. If you or your friends need anything at all, please don't hesitate to let us know."

Cole and I looked at each other, wide eyed, and then walked out on either side of Brynn. As we made our way down the escalator, the two people with their phones out became about six or seven people with their phones out, and one or two guys with professional-looking cameras that I guessed were paparazzi or something. She smiled and waved at some of the people with phones and completely ignored the guys with cameras. They didn't push it too much, but that didn't stop Cole from stepping off the escalator in front of both of us and then putting his body between us and the photographers all the way to the exit, where Sebastian was waiting to lead us to Malik.

We climbed into the Escalade just outside the VIP entrance of Bergdorf Goodman and took off immediately, but came to a screeching halt when I yelled out, "Stop the car!" Well, we hadn't even gotten away from the curb yet, so maybe it wasn't quite a screech. But the intensity of it all in my mind merited a screech. We'd forgotten Cole.

I turned around in my third-row seat, where I sat alone, to look through the rear window, but he wasn't standing out there waving us down or running after us. "Where's Cole?" I asked as I turned back to face them all in a panic. "We need to go back."

An entire lifetime I'd managed to keep track of him, but all it had taken was one lousy day in New York to turn me into Kevin McCallister's parents, carefully keeping track of every detail of my life except whether or not my entire family made it onto the plane.

"I'm right here, Lai," he said from the front passenger seat.

I jumped at the sound of his voice and met his eyes as he tilted his head and waved. I felt my pulse begin to steady and my heart slide out of my throat and back into my chest where it belonged. "Oh. Good. Sorry. Sorry, Malik. Sorry, you guys." I sank back into the seat and exhaled out the last of the frantic breaths. "My bad."

"Sorry it was so chaotic getting out of there." Brynn reached behind her and squeezed my knee before facing front again with a sigh as we pulled onto Fifth Avenue. As an aside to get Sebastian caught up, she said, "Just some photographers."

She kept talking—something about how she was used to it, but she sometimes forgot what a shock it could be to others who weren't—but first things first: Why was Cole sitting in the front with Malik instead of in the back with me?

Cole smiled at me in a way I think was supposed to be reassuring before he turned back to face front again, but I didn't feel reassured. Reassured that the paparazzi hadn't kidnapped him to hold him for ransom until Brynn agreed to pose for pictures for TMZ or something? Well, sure. That was a relief, I suppose.

Don't go all crazy. It's probably nothing. It was just the easiest way to get in. The fastest, certainly.

Yeah, I could positively reinforce myself Stuart Smalley–style to my heart's content, acting confident that I was good enough and that I was smart enough and that Cole really did like me, but he was definitely avoiding me. It wasn't like we'd never sat separately from each other in a vehicle. We weren't *that* codependent. But this on top of wandering away from me at the mall. (Yeah, yeah . . . I know Brynn said it was just one store, but you can't convince me that place wasn't a mall. All that was missing was a Radio Shack and a Wet Seal. And yes, before you ask, it's possible I hadn't been to a mall since 2003.) And at tea he'd talked to Sebastian the entire time. And I don't think he'd talked to any of us at breakfast that morning. Which, yes, could have meant it didn't have anything to do with me.

But I knew it did. I could feel it.

I watched the buildings and the yellow taxicabs outside my window in a stupor until Brynn's phone rang. Actually *rang*. She checked it all the time, and there were always little vibration sounds happening, and she would look at it and then ignore it or fire off a text. But this was an actual ring, turned up on high volume, and everyone stopped talking in response.

"Hey, Colton," she said and then put her hand over the bottom of her phone and whispered, "Sorry!" before turning to face out the window.

"Executive producer of *Sunup*," Sebastian explained to us softly. "Not technically Brynn's boss anymore on *Sunup3*, but he's sort of the big boss. Usually only calls if he needs something." He rolled his eyes good-naturedly.

"Tonight?!" Brynn flipped her head around to meet Seb's eyes. "No, I can't. We have friends in town . . . Well, yeah, but not like that . . . They're staying with us, Colton. They're our guests. I can't just . . ." She sighed. "Yeah. No, of course. Alright. Okay, yeah, let me talk to Sebastian and let you know. Thanks. Talk to you in a bit." She clicked the End button on her phone and then let out a soft but aggravated groan. "Well, that sucks."

"What's up?" Seb asked as he reached over and ran a strand of her brunette locks through his fingers. "What does he need you to cover?"

Brynn closed her eyes and shook her head. "Oktoberfest. Irvine has the flu or something. Crap!" She glanced at Cole in the front seat and then turned around and faced me. "I'm so sorry. I have to go over there and step in. I won't be back until Saturday." She started talking to Sebastian in a softer, more intimate tone. "You can come, of course, but I don't know what to do about—"

"You guys would be okay, wouldn't you?" He looked from Cole to me and then back again. "You can make yourself at home at our place. And Malik, do you think you could be available to—"

"Of course," Malik responded. "Happy to help."

Sebastian shrugged. "There you go. And then we'll be back on Saturday and still have until Wednesday all together. Sound okay?" He looked at Cole. "You've got things under control . . . right?"

Cole's eyes met mine, just for a second, and then he said, "Of course. Everything will be fine."

"Okay. Thanks. I really am so sorry." Brynn sighed again. "I guess we'd better get home and pack."

Ah. Oktoberfest. As in the real, official, original Oktoberfest. In

Germany. Not in Washington Square Park or Jersey City or some-where in Pennsylvania. Gears were clicking into place slowly, but at least they were finally clicking. And as much as I believed Seb really did like us and enjoyed spending time with Cole and me, of course he didn't want to spend a week away from his new wife if he didn't have to. It all made sense and probably would have made sense sooner if I hadn't been so busy watching Cole, trying to figure out what he wasn't saying between the very few words that he *did* say. Why had Seb asked him if he had things under control? And more important, why had Cole looked at me like I was the unknown variable in that equation?

"But there's no reason this has to get in the way of your day," Brynn said with a little too much forced enthusiasm as she attempted to rally everyone's spirits. Mostly her own, I figured. "I'll call and make the reservation for two at Bar SixtyFive. And if you still want to go to the Guggenheim, I can call and ask for a curator to show you—"

"Thank you, but don't worry about us." Was I a horrible friend? Was it absolutely awful of me that I mostly just felt relief? Not that I wanted to get rid of Brynn and Seb, but I desperately wanted to get rid of Fodor's Guide to New York for the Social Elite. "In fact, can we reschedule the Rockefeller Plaza Rainbow Room thing? I'd love to experience that with you guys—"

"Yes!" Cole agreed emphatically and then reined his enthusiasm in a bit. Was it possible he was feeling the same strain of the day that I was? This might have been the best thing that could have happened. "I mean, yeah, from what you said, and a little bit of looking I did on my phone, it sounds . . . almost . . ." He looked to Sebastian. For as-sistance? "Romantic, maybe? I know you guys have been there before, but I think it would maybe be better for the four of us to—"

"I've got it!" Brynn squealed and clapped her hands. "Let's go on Saturday night and reserve private dining for Laila's birthday at the actual Rainbow Room! Yes! Unless there's a wedding or something, there's live music and dancing and stuff on Saturdays—and you re-ally are likely to see a celebrity on a Saturday night at the Rainbow Room."

I loved that she kept in mind how exciting it might be for us to see a celebrity while simultaneously forgetting that we were in the car with two of them.

"I thought for my birthday you wanted to go to the place with the hundred percent guaranteed Queen Bey sightings," I reminded her.

"No, this will be better. We can really do it up right." She was tapping away on her phone. "We'll need to get all dressed up." She glanced back at me. "Feel free to go through my closet. Or I should be back in time so we could go shopping, if you want." And then back to her phone. "It will be almost like . . . I don't know . . . double dates or something. Won't that be fun?"

"Or . . ." Sebastian dragged out those two little letters an awfully long time. "Maybe we should set them both up and make it a triple date."

Cole turned away from us all and faced front again before shaking his head and burying it in his hand.

Brynn stopped messing around with her phone at once and looked up at her husband like he'd grown another head. "What are you talking about? Triple date? With whom?"

Seb shrugged. "I don't know. We know lots of nice people. I just thought maybe it would be fun for them to meet some new friends and—"

"Yeah. Let's do that," Cole muttered. He was still stoically facing forward, and I could barely understand him from way in the back as he said, "That's a good idea."

What was happening?

And what made any of them think I wanted to spend my birthday dinner at some romantic NYC restaurant—where we might see *more* celebrities, none of whom were likely to be Beyonce and Jay-Z—with jet-lagged newlyweds just in from the largest beer festival in the world, my best friend who seemed more upset with me by the moment, though I had no idea why, and some rando blind dates from who knows where, just to make it all *more* uncomfortable?

"That seems a little unnecessa—"

"Ooh! You know who you'd really like?" Brynn asked in a flood of excitement. "Milo Ventimiglia."

"Hang on . . . *Jess*? You want to fix me up with Jess from *Gilmore Girls*?"

"I didn't know we were considering *Gilmore Girls* dates here," Cole said, turning around and no longer muttering. "Isn't that . . . I don't know . . . indulgent?"

"He's a great guy. He's in California most of the time, but I think he's here another few months filming. He comes on *Sunup3* whenever he's in town. He's one of my favorite guests. And he's single. A few years older than us, but not much." She looked at Sebastian. "Probably just a couple years older than you, right?" She didn't wait for a response before turning back to me again. "What do you say? Want to see if your favorite of all Rory Gilmore boyfriends is available for dinner on Saturday evening?"

I didn't understand how this thing she was asking me was an actual possibility, but even more than that, I didn't understand how or why anyone with even an ounce of sanity left in them would or could say no.

"Yes, Brynn," I replied as calmly as I could, since apparently this was no big thing to my famous friend. "If you would be ever so kind, I would very much appreciate you fixing me up with Milo Ventimiglia."

I may have spent most of my life blissfully (and, admittedly, sometimes less blissfully) unaware of the trends and practices of less rural, less isolated areas of the world, but by golly, we had the WB. And for those first few seasons, Brynn, Addie, and I had hidden ourselves away in the attic of my grandparents' house—the Clubhouse, we had called it since we were kids—and obsessed over every move Lorelai and Rory made. Obsessed over the banter. Obsessed over the music. Obsessed over the pop-culture references. And, oh yes, we obsessed over Rory's boyfriends.

Once it was just me left in the Clubhouse, Cole watched with me occasionally, but I didn't have the option then of saying, "You have to go watch the early seasons and get caught up," so he asked a lot of questions—*Does* everyone *have a child they didn't know about? Is that just a requisite of living in Stars Hollow?*—and never really got into it. And I couldn't blame him. *Gilmore Girls* said goodbye to its magic when it lost Amy Sherman-Palladino and moved to the CW, just like the magic of watching it was never the same once Brynn and Addie left. I watched the finale all by myself, sitting in the Clubhouse under a blanket crying, sad to be saying goodbye to more friends.

But now I was going on a date with Jess.

"Who do I get?" Cole had turned completely around in his seat as our surroundings became familiar and we pulled onto North Moore Street in Tribeca.

"Don't you think he and Greta would be fun?" Brynn asked Sebastian.

Seb laughed as the Escalade came to a stop. "I think Greta would eat him alive."

She winked. "And you don't think that could be fun?"

"Who's Greta?" Cole and I asked in unison, and when our eyes met, I smiled. He didn't.

"She does hair and makeup on *Sunup*. She's the cutest. Seriously. I think you'd really—"

"I want Zoe Saldana." Cole had blurted it out like he was stepping up to the counter at Burger King and ordering a Whopper without pickles, having already been promised he could have it his way. "Laila gets Jess Gilmore. I think I should get someone famous too."

Brynn's eyes grew wide as she looked from Cole to me and back a couple times, as if we were in the middle of a heated debate, but I hadn't said a word. I was just studying him. The way he once again wouldn't look at me. The way his brow was furrowing like he was angry, but he was biting his lips like he was nervous. And then there was Seb, leaning in and whispering something to him that seemed not to surprise him but caused the furrows to increase. Caused the teeth to bite harder.

"Well, I'm pretty sure Zoe is married with kids, but I guess I can reach out and see what sort of policy she and her husband have, if you want me to." Brynn smiled, trying to break the tension, and then looked at me and shrugged when the joke had no impact at all. "Alrighty, then. Um . . . Seb and I can brainstorm on the plane. I'm sure there are lots of celebrities who would love to go out with you."

"Good," he muttered. "Thanks." And then he turned back around and climbed out of the vehicle.

"What is that about?" Brynn whispered to me as she grabbed her purse from the floorboard.

I wish I knew. "You know Cole and his Zoe obsession. It's not a laughing matter." I chuckled lightly, hoping that would be enough for her.

It sure as snot wasn't going to be enough for me.

CHAPTER SIXTEEN

COLE

"Cole! Are you awake? Are you decent? Can I come in?"

He definitely had not been awake. And as for whether or not he was decent . . .

"Um . . . hang on." He couldn't quite remember what he'd gone to sleep wearing, so he lifted the sheet. Bottom half was fine. Joggers were present and accounted for. "Just a minute." Cole looked around the Sudworths' maidless maid's quarters and tried to orient himself again. He'd thrown a T-shirt somewhere at some point . . .

"Come on, Cole! Hurry up!"

He groaned softly as he spotted his gray shirt seemingly suspended in air on the opposite wall, and the memories of how that came to be caused the reorientation process to speed along nicely. "Be right there." He sat up and stretched his arms over his head, one way and then the other, as he lowered his feet to the carpet, then crossed the room and gingerly freed the ticking clock on the wall— there had been *so much ticking*—from its cotton prison. With a sigh he pulled the multipurpose T-shirt over his head and slipped his arms through.

"I'm coming," he called out one more time for good measure, though Laila had stopped knocking.

He paused briefly in front of the floor-length mirror and groaned again. There wasn't one particular thing causing the groan. It was just the reaction he had every time he looked in a mirror lately. He didn't think of himself as a vain person, but what could you do *but* groan when each new mirror in which you caught sight of yourself seemed to have advanced the film another year or two?

Taking a deep breath, Cole turned away from the mirror and faced the door. He couldn't remember the last time he'd done to Laila what he'd done to her the day before. Avoided her. Refused to talk to her—at least about anything real.

And then what had been that little outburst in the car? Had he seriously been so callow as to throw a temper tantrum because his blind date wasn't a celebrity? As if he cared. As if he had any interest in any of that.

Of course, that was the problem, wasn't it? He had zero interest in being set up. It really bothered him that he had zero interest. But not as much as it bothered him that Laila had been excited about the prospect. And, needless to say, none of that had bothered him as much as how bothered he had been.

He turned the doorknob and pulled the door open to see Laila beaming up at him with the biggest, most authentic grin on her face.

"Good morning." She was practically bouncing on her bare feet, her toenails painted the shades of various flavors of cotton candy. She'd gotten her contacts in, though everything else about her face was as fresh as if she'd just awakened. Without any makeup on she still looked like fourth-grade Laila to him, standing up to the fifth graders who teased Cole for not having a dad, threatening to "pummel" them, and somehow scaring them into believing that as little as she was, she could still do it. She was radiant—but she was also a mess. Her hair wasn't in its usual placed-and-perfected messy bun. There were loose strands everywhere, making their attempts at escape from Laila's carefully cultivated chaos. She was wearing a lilac scoop-neck Care Bears sweatshirt that said, "Friends Help Make Big Jobs Small!" and frayed denim shorts, and there were random streaks of who-knows-what across her neck, her clothes . . . you name it. And still . . .

Radiant.

"Good morning," he responded, grinning at her in a way he hadn't been able to yesterday. It was confirmed in his mind. He was a horrible human being. He'd done absolutely nothing to deserve this radiant beam of light and warmth in his life. Ever. Especially not lately. "You're awfully chipper this morning."

"I have a surprise for you." She reached out and took his hand and pulled him down the hallway, through the kitchen—*Oh gosh . . . what happened to the kitchen?*—and to the dining cubby, or whatever it was called. She stopped in front of the table, with her back to it, and positioned him in front of her. Then she squeezed both of his hands and released them, stepping to the side of him with a flourish. "Ta-da!"

A perfect flame burned from a taper candle in a silver candlestick next to an orchid in a silver bud vase, and on a dinner plate sat one egg, sunny side up, a couple slices of ham that had seen better days, and half a slice of charred toast.

"What's this? Did you order in, or . . ." *Oh! The kitchen. No wonder it's a mess. No wonder she is.* "You made this?"

The nervous energy that had been causing all the bouncing cumulated in a little bit of a squeal, and then she threw her arms around him. He didn't hug her back, only because she took him by surprise. But obviously sensing his lack of movement, she pulled away abruptly before his arms could catch up. The expression on her face didn't accuse him of a thing but displayed a new awkwardness he couldn't allow to go on any longer. And her eyes were lost to him—suddenly darting from side to side.

Fix this, Cole. Fix this now.

"This is amazing!" He leaned down and wrapped his arms around her and didn't let go until she had stretched around his torso again and snuggled in just as tight and comfortably as she always had.

"Okay, seriously . . ." He pushed back on her upper arms so he could look at her. "What is happening right now? Who are you and what have you done with my best friend?" She giggled, and he turned back to the plate of breakfast. It wasn't difficult to imagine most of what had transpired, and he would have given just about anything to watch it. The half piece of burnt toast was the best she could salvage, he was guessing. The ham had spots of black char on it but probably wasn't inedible. But the egg . . . The egg blew his mind. "Laila, that egg is perfect." He threw one arm over her shoulders. "I'm so impressed."

But not surprised. That was the rest of the sentence, but his instincts stopped his mouth from saying it. Of course he wasn't surprised. She could do anything. But right then it wasn't about how she could do anything. It was about how she'd done *this.*

"Hang on. Don't move. Don't touch any of it!" He pulled away from her and ran down the hallway to his room, unplugged his phone from the charger on the desk, and was back at the dining alcove— *Alcove! That's it. Not cubby*—in seconds.

"What are you doing?" she asked.

"Documenting this moment, of course." He snapped different shots from different angles as she giggled and blushed and then got involved by helping him set up the proper lighting as he activated the portrait mode on his camera. They stuck their faces in a couple shots and posed with the plate. "It's almost too pretty to eat, but I must admit . . . I'm dying to try it. Do I actually get to eat it?"

She reached for the fork on the table beside the plate and handed it to him before sitting down across from him. "If you're sure you're brave enough."

"Just try to stop me." He slipped into one side of the curved booth built into the wall and pulled the plate to him as he sat. He inspected it from a couple more angles—and took one more close-up photo of the egg yolk—before breaking into it with his fork. It broke perfectly. Cinematically, almost. He looked across the table at her in awe and saw her eyes frantically darting between his face and the plate. "Laila, I'm telling you . . . *no one* makes an egg this beautiful on their first try. You're a natural."

Color rose in her cheeks. "Well, technically, it was my seventh try. And then there were two eggs that I ruined before I even got them to the frying pan—"

"Makes no difference. No one makes an egg this beautiful on their ninth try either."

He cut into the white and scooped up a gorgeous bite, yellow dripping slowly back onto the plate, and put it in his mouth. And, truth be told, for as beautiful as it was, it just tasted like an egg. A bland one at that. She hadn't even salted it, he was pretty sure, and once he got inside, the white was a little undercooked. She'd used too much olive oil to keep it from sticking, causing him to believe that too little olive oil had played a big role in at least some of those other six attempts. But literally none of that mattered. It was the best egg he'd ever tasted in his life.

"Well?" She leaned in and rested her elbows on the table, though there was nothing else restful about her. She was jittery with anticipation. "Be honest."

Easy. "You're amazing."

"Oh, come on." She laughed. "You don't even have to eat the whole thing. I won't be offended." She reached across the table and tried to move the dish away from him, so he circled his left arm around the plate, lowered his head, and practically shoveled the rest of the egg into his mouth with his fork.

"You're such an idiot," she choked out through her laughter as Cole used the little bit of toast to soak up the yolk and then jammed that into his mouth as well.

He chewed and swallowed as quickly as he could and then stuffed the ham in before dropping his fork, raising his hands like he'd just been told time was up on *Chopped*, and attempting to say, "Compliments to the chef." He got about as far as "Comp—" before he started hacking from the saltiness of the (very nearly inedible after all) ham. Chunks of barely chewed pork started sputtering out as he coughed.

Laila was no help at all, of course. She'd completely lost it, and while Cole ran to the refrigerator to find something to wash the dry bites down with, she collapsed onto the cushions of the booth in a knotted-up, stomach-cramped fit of hysterics.

It was all worth it, he knew. Even as he downed a sparkling water so quickly his eyes sprang leaks and he felt as if holes were being burned into his esophagus, and even as he looked around Brynn and Seb's kitchen and noticed splatters of oil and grease and yolk in places the newlyweds probably hadn't even touched in their new home yet, and even as he realized that here in a second the laughter was going to start fading and the memories of the day before were going to rear their ugly heads again for both of them, he knew it was all worth it.

"You okay?" she asked a few seconds later, holding her stomach as she returned to an upright position and wiped freely falling tears from her face.

"Yeah, no thanks to you."

"I've always told you that if I ever cooked it would probably kill you. I just didn't know it would be because it was so delicious."

He smiled at her and returned to his side of the table. "I don't know what I did to deserve this, Lai, but thank you."

In an instant the humor was gone for them both as her eyes met his. "I told you. There isn't anything I wouldn't do for you, Cole Kimball. Not a single thing."

"Hey . . . hey, hey . . ." He started to scoot around to her but then realized how long it would take to get around the entire monstrous alcove. Instead, he climbed out and rushed over to scoot in next to her on her side. He wrapped his arms around her, and she rested her cheek on his chest. "I'm so sorry about yesterday. I was being a total jerk." Guilt washed over him, and déjà vu assaulted his senses. "And I'm sorry I've had to make that apology so many times lately."

She'd wanted to talk last night. After they got back to the condo and Brynn and Seb had given them keys and codes and phone numbers, thrown some things together, and headed to the airport with Malik, she'd tried to get him to talk. And instead, he'd focused far more effort than was required on moving his small amount of luggage into the now-devoid-of-wedding-gifts other room and settling in. Then he'd said he was tired and needed to rest. That had been . . . what? Six o'clock? Seven, maybe? He'd wasted too much of a day. A day he could have spent with her. They could have talked and sorted it all out, or they could have gone up on the roof and looked at the city, or they could have at least sat together in silence and pretended everything was okay. But he couldn't even pull himself together enough to pretend.

Not that he wanted to pretend.

What had she done for the rest of the night? He had no idea. He didn't know if she'd eaten dinner or been able to sleep. He didn't have any idea if her back had been hurting enough to need the pills that—*Shoot*. The pills he was still in possession of. He hadn't even thought about it.

And it wasn't that he thought Laila needed him to take care of her. He didn't. *She* didn't. She was just fine without him, and she always would be. But last night had been wrong. Everything about it had been so completely wrong. Nothing could be right with the world when he was focused on himself at her expense.

"Lai, look—"

"If you're really planning on leaving, then that's something we should talk about. I'm convinced there's no way on earth I can leave my dad right now, but if you can think of a way to make it work, we've got to be able to talk it through. And I need to be able to tell you why you shouldn't go, because I don't have the answers, Cole, but I know I'm not okay with that." Her hand flexed against his chest, balling up his T-shirt. "I know we're not supposed to talk about it. I know we made a deal. But I'm not okay with this deal anymore. We can't make deals where we don't talk about things. That goes against our original deal."

"What's our original deal?"

Assorted deals they had made through the years zoomed through his mind, bumping into and intersecting with memories and milestone markers. An insignificant deal not to watch season three of *American Idol* without each other. (And for twenty years their dismay at Jennifer Hudson coming in seventh, despite their calling in for her every week, had continued. How had the world not seen what they had seen?) Deals to notify each other as soon as possible if they ever had food stuck in their teeth. They'd made a deal to go to prom together, but when Laila struck up a spring break romance with Mrs. Stoddard's nephew, Drew, when he was visiting from Denver, of course Cole had stepped aside so Laila could ask him to go with her. He'd felt horrible when Drew couldn't make it, because Cole had already asked Brynn to go with him, thus sparking their short-lived attempt at romance. But ultimately the three of them had basically gone together anyway.

Some of the deals were more sacred than others, but he'd never taken any of them lightly.

"Our original deal is *us*, Cole." Laila pushed back from him and looked into his eyes as she clenched the front of his T-shirt in her fists. "*We're* the original deal. All other deals must work to support the original deal or they're not valid. And when we made the deal a couple nights ago to just take the pressure off and enjoy the trip, I guess I didn't realize all the reasons that wouldn't work. But any deal that causes you to avoid me is a bad deal. I would like to officially revoke the deal. Deal?"

What would happen if I kissed her?

He swallowed down the lump that had formed in his throat at the thought. Had it even *been* a thought? It felt more like a compulsion. A need. His arms were still wrapped around her, and her chin was tilted up toward him. And he was listening to and caring about every single word she said, and he was trying to sort it all out and figure out how to proceed, and how to clarify that it hadn't been *just* the (yes, he could agree, in retrospect) bad deal that had thrown him off his game (or, more accurately, had made him attempt to play a game in what had always been a game-free zone). But he was suddenly so distracted by her lips. He knew everything about her. *Everything.* So how had he never noticed that her bottom lip was always just a little pouty, even when she wasn't pouting?

He'd never noticed the little creases above her top lip, just below that perfectly centered dip between her nose and her mouth, but he didn't even have to think about it to have a complete understanding of what had caused the creases. Those were there because of him. Because of all the times she had contorted her mouth in reaction to whatever story he was rambling on and on about. Some ridiculous thing that had happened at Cassidy's. Something he'd been waiting all day to tell her. And the creases were there because of all the times she had held her tongue and funneled all her excess energy into puffing up and sucking her cheeks back in like a puffer fish while she put more effort than he deserved into finding a nice and supportive way to explain to him exactly why he was wrong about something.

What was the expression? That women's brains were spaghetti, able to mix everything together and get sauce on everything all at once, while men's were more like waffles, only able to absorb syrup in one grid at a time? Something like that. Even so, how had he been so distracted by everything else in life as to never notice that even her lips were a souvenir of the life they had lived together? What would happen if he leaned in, got closer than he ever had, brushed his lips against hers, and added one more stamp to the passport of their shared travels?

He cleared his throat and released her, then stood up from the booth. He had no idea what he wanted (well . . . he knew what he *wanted* . . .), and he certainly had no idea what Laila wanted. And it was that thought that forced him onto his feet.

"What do you say we go get ready and get out of here?"

Her shoulders fell. "Don't you think we need to talk?"

Of course he did. That was the point. And alone in that penthouse, suddenly hyperaware of her lips, he was afraid of the lengths he might go to just to avoid talking. "Yes. Let's talk. About all of it. I'm with you, Lai—that was a bad deal. I don't want to avoid talking to you about anything. Not ever again."

He felt his chest tighten and his heart speed up—or had it just stopped?—as he said those words. Because he meant them. They needed to talk. Although, right then, the only words coming to mind were all the curse words he never said. His grandmother had always told him foul language was a sign of laziness, but right then he wanted to run up to Brynn and Seb's terrace, turn away from Taylor Swift's roof (since Laila would never forgive him if he accidentally cussed out Tay Tay), and shout every last one of those lazy words at the top of his lungs.

"But let's get some air. Okay?" He didn't wait for a response before he turned and headed back to his bedroom, but he forced himself to stop as the kitchen mess entered his peripheral vision.

We'll clean that up later.

He took a deep breath and turned back again. "Thank you for breakfast. I can't . . ." It was possible his pounding heart was just going to keep climbing higher and higher up into his throat until it made an appearance every bit as appealing as that of the spewed ham. "I can't tell you how much that meant to me. You're . . ." Words were failing. Everything. Everything was failing. He brought his hands up and crossed them over his heart—or at least where his heart used to be before it began trying to make its escape—and whispered the only words willing to come out. "I love you."

Words he'd said to her pretty much daily for most of their lives. Those words would never fail him, but now he couldn't help but wonder if he'd failed the words by saying them so easily . . . so casually . . . so many times. For the first time, they felt inadequate.

She smiled at him and pursed those lips as she bit down on the inside and clearly compelled the tears to stay put. "I love you too. Meet you back here in a few?"

Cole nodded and grinned at her and then carried on to his room. But not before allowing his eyes a moment to linger on the stairs in the middle of the penthouse. *Nah. Not right now. Go get dressed.* He'd be back to give Taylor Swift an earful later.

CHAPTER SEVENTEEN

LAILA

Brynn and Sebastian had left us with Malik's number, and though he'd said it was absolutely no problem to drive us around or send someone else if the network had him driving some big shot around instead, and even though he'd insisted he'd bring something much less ostentatious for just the two of us, like "the Benz" or something (oh, *okay* . . . thanks for keeping it grounded, Malik), I'd never been so relieved as I was when Cole said, "Wanna see how lost we can get in New York?"

Even my suspicion that what he had in mind might entail some recreations of scenes from *Home Alone 2: Lost in New York*—a movie he had inexplicably counted as his favorite Christmas movie since we were eight years old—couldn't ruin my wholehearted approval of that plan.

"I feel so bad about how much I hated yesterday," I told him as we stepped out onto North Moore Street. "I know I probably should have been counting my lucky stars that we got to drive right up to entrances and avoid crowds and visit these amazing places, but—"

"Oh, I'm with you." He made sure he had all the keys and then checked that the outside door to the building was locked. Then he held his arm out for me to go ahead of him down the black corrugated metal stairs. "It felt like we were at New York-New York in Vegas or something. Like an *almost* lifelike version of the New York I'd imagined."

"Exactly!" We got onto the sidewalk and walked to the intersection of *Ghostbusters* and John-John. We looked to our left and then to our right, and then I pulled my phone out to look at a map.

"Don't you dare!" He grabbed my phone from my hand and held it over my head, out of reach. "See, that's the problem with you kids these days. This is why *Home Alone* would never work in the modern age. The McCallisters would have just called each other—or texted, probably. Problem solved. Or worse, someone would have gotten some notification that Kevin was no longer with them, and all they would have had to do was retrace their steps for a minute—no, sorry, ask Siri to lead them to his location—and boom. It's over."

"Yeah, that would have been just awful if the world's worst parents had found a way to keep track of their kid."

He lowered his arms but held on to my phone and yanked it out of reach when I tried grabbing for it. "Please don't degrade Peter and Kate McCallister like that in my presence. *They* weren't awful. Their big, extended family was awful." New Yorkers with their heads down and AirPods in their ears passed us on both sides, not paying any more attention to us than we were paying to them. "Their big problem was taking all those vacations together. Ludicrous."

I crossed my arms as laughter bounced in my chest. "Yes, I remember reading about that in your tenth-grade sociology essay. What was it called? 'I Can't Believe This Happened Again: A Case Study' or something like that?"

"I think you know very well that it was called 'And Yet They Never Lost Their Luggage: A Survey of Late-Twentieth-Century Parenting Styles.'" He smiled and handed me my phone. "The point is, modern technology has reduced the possibility of getting lost. And sure, whatever, I suppose an argument could be made that when it comes to ten-year-olds getting on the wrong plane and ending up wandering the streets of New York alone, befriending homeless bird ladies and the like, *maybe* technology is our friend. But for you and me, today, let's just wander. Okay?"

I was wearing high-waisted cargo pants I'd made myself. I'd sewn in extra pockets, beyond what the pattern called for, and I'd worn the pants today so that I didn't have to carry a bag around. Rather than put my phone in the usual pocket, I slipped it into a pocket above my knee and buttoned it up.

"There. Happy?"

He nodded. "I am. Thanks."

"So. Where to?"

"Here's what I was able to figure out about New York yesterday while we drove around: World Trade Center is south; the Empire State Building and other stuff is north."

"Wow. Impressive, Magellan."

It had been a while since we'd taken a trip together. I had forgotten how navigationally hopeless he was without mountains as his guides, and how much fun I always had at his expense as a result.

I spun around three hundred and sixty degrees. "Which way?"

He smirked at me. "You know exactly where we are, don't you?"

I shook my head. "Not exactly, but I glanced at a Manhattan subway map yesterday at MoMA, and I'm pretty sure 'other stuff' is this way." I pointed left. "More of the island available to get lost in, so . . ." I directed him with my head, and he laughed and repeated the gesture that I should go first and he would follow.

We began walking up Varick Street, and I was fascinated by everything I saw. I had to fight the compulsion to pull my phone out, not to get directions but to take pictures of every little thing. Signs directing toward the Williamsburg Bridge and the Holland Tunnel. NYPD cars. But I decided to follow his cues for now. We were wandering and disconnected. Together. And though we hadn't talked about the things we needed to talk about yet, we were talking. Laughing. It felt normal. Maybe slightly better than normal. I was in no hurry to put an end to that.

"Ready to talk?"

Well, so much for that.

"Ready when you are." I pointed straight ahead as a crosswalk light signaled for us to go across Canal Street, and he nodded. We looked both ways and jogged across as time ran out.

His hands were in the pockets of his jeans, and his posture seemed to be drawing him inward. We came to another intersection—a much bigger one at the entrance to the Holland Tunnel—and suddenly there were swarms of people and vehicle congestion where it had been relatively quiet. The countdown began on the walking signal, and Cole grabbed my hand and hurried across with me. When we reached the corner on the other side, there was a little park with some sculpture that looked like three giant red hex nuts stacked together, but I guess in New York it was art.

He kept holding my hand and pulled me over to the side by the park's fence. People we'd been hurrying across the street with passed us, and he watched them go. I just watched him.

"What is it?"

His eyes met mine then. "Is there anything you don't think we should talk about? Or . . ." He shook his head. "I mean, is there anything we shouldn't talk about? Anything off limits?"

"Of course not."

"No, I'm serious, Laila. I don't just mean because we say we can talk about anything, and because we always have. What I mean is . . . do you think we've ever avoided certain subjects? Maybe intentionally, maybe not. Do you think there's anything that . . ." He glanced down and realized he was still holding my hand and released it, and then he took a step back and crossed his arms. "Do you think there's anything we wouldn't recover from?"

I had no idea what was happening. I had no idea what had him spooked. But I knew the answer to that question.

"Absolutely not." I mirrored his posture and braced myself for whatever was coming.

He began walking again, and I stepped alongside. "Have you ever thought about us as an *us*?" His eyes darted to the side, but when he saw that I was looking up at him, he faced forward again.

I, meanwhile, was just going to have to trust that he wouldn't let me run into a light pole or step into an open manhole. There wasn't a single hope in the world that I was going to look anywhere but at him right then.

I'd meant what I'd said. I'd believed it. I *still* believed it, even now, knowing that *this* was the conversation he was wondering if we could survive. Yes. Of course. Of course we'd recover. I wasn't even going to let it get to that point. The point of requiring recovery. I didn't know what was causing him to ask the question, but it was just one more thing. One more thing we apparently *now*, for whatever reason, needed to talk about. One more thing in a lifetime of things.

I finally pulled my eyes away from him and looked ahead, not that I was really seeing anything. Buildings. People. Cars. It was the landmines of the conversation that terrified me. Why was he asking? Fear, probably. Fear of losing me. Fear of change. Maybe fear was causing him to think he was feeling things he wasn't.

Or had I somehow given him the impression *I* was feeling those things? Maybe that was it. And *that* was freaking him out because he thought I would do something desperate to keep him from leaving me. If that was it, how pathetic had I appeared that morning, telling him I would do anything for him? Cooking for him to prove that I meant it.

Focus, Laila. Focus. He asked a question. Just answer the question.

No. Eat. That would be better. We needed to start there.

I was suddenly starving. I had been fairly certain I wouldn't want to eat again for a while, after all the toast and eggs and bacon—yes, there had originally been bacon—I had nibbled on while watching YouTube videos of people cooking toast and eggs and bacon. By the time the last of the bacon was exhausted, I couldn't bring myself to look up videos on ham. I sort of phoned it in with the ham.

I stopped in front of a Shake Shack and called out Cole's name when he kept walking without me. Briefly confused, he turned around and spotted me and came jogging back.

"Hungry?" I asked.

"Are you serious?"

"Sorry. I'm not avoiding the question. I just—"

"No, I just mean after that breakfast I had?" The corner of his lips tilted up as I laughed. "Yes. I'm starving. No offense." He looked all around us—a Chinese food place, a pizza place, a bistro—then looked back at me, eyebrows raised. "You don't want Shake Shack, do you?"

"Why wouldn't I? It's synonymous with New York. Besides, it was delicious that one time we had it—"

"At New York-New York, Laila. Again, we're actually *in* Manhattan. Don't you want to experience—"

"I want fries."

He smirked at me. "There's a McDonald's right across the street. Why don't we just go there?"

"Look, they wouldn't have chosen Shake Shack as one of the restaurants to represent New York in Las Vegas, to lots of people who will never actually get to come to New York, unless it was authentic."

"You're right." He nodded. "Vegas is all about authenticity. Which reminds me, let's be sure to ride that roller coaster that circles over Grand Central Terminal, in front of the Empire State Building, and around the Statue of Liberty before we leave town. As cool as the one at New York-New York was, I bet the original is—"

"Hardy-har-har." I looked around at all the other options and then grabbed his arm and pulled him into Shake Shack. "Be a good boy, and I'll buy you a frozen custard."

⌒

We were loose and casual again as we waited for our food. We talked about passing the Holland Tunnel and spent far too much time trying to remember the title of the horrible nineties Sylvester Stallone movie where the Holland Tunnel was going to explode or something. (If I'd pulled my phone out, I would have been able to instantly clear away the earworm by figuring out the movie was *Daylight*. Of course I also could have found out that *Daylight* was about the Lincoln Tunnel. Not the Holland Tunnel.) And then we tried to remember Buddy the

Elf's quote as he recounted his journey from the North Pole to NYC, but once we nailed that down we remembered that *that* had been about the Lincoln Tunnel too.

Ultimately, we weren't sure why we were supposed to care about the Holland Tunnel.

Then, finally, we were enjoying our burgers and fries (and custard shakes, as promised), and I decided the time was right to take us back.

"How do you mean?"

He tilted his head. "I didn't say anything."

"No, I mean . . . your question. You asked if I'd ever thought about us as an *us*." I knew we needed to talk about it. I knew it would be fine. But all of that knowledge didn't stop my cheeks from getting warm as I repeated the words. "I'm just asking . . . How do you mean?"

"Oh." He set his burger down and started avoiding my eyes again. "You know. I guess . . . romantically. Or whatever. More than just friends."

"I wasn't asking what you meant by us as an *us*. I got that." I rolled my eyes. More at myself—I hadn't asked the question very well, I realized. But really, we were just both as awkward as could be about the whole thing. "I'm just wondering what you meant when you asked if I'd thought about it."

He studied me as he chewed on the ends of three fries. "I'm sorry, I guess I don't understand what you—"

"I mean, are you asking if the thought ever flitted through my brain? Like, incidental contact? Not incidental contact between you and me. I mean the *thoughts* being nothing more than incidental contact. In my brain, I mean."

"No, I get it. Like . . . thoughts just zipping through and not landing."

"Exactly. Or are you asking if I've ever considered whether it could work? Like, serious consideration. Pros and cons and weighing the repercussions and that sort of thing."

"Um . . ." He shrugged and grabbed more fries. "Either, I guess?"

"Oh. Okay. Then yeah. I have."

He groaned. "Which one?"

"We've been reading each other's minds and completing each other's sentences our entire lives, but we're not doing so hot today." I laughed. "This is awful, isn't it?"

Panic overtook him. "We don't have to talk about it. This is why I didn't know if we should—"

"No, Cole, I'm not saying . . ." I closed my eyes and rubbed my index fingers against my temples. "Both. It's zipped through. And, I guess, on occasion . . . it's landed. Yeah. Pros and cons, et cetera." I opened my eyes, and the panic was gone from his face. We were so out of sync right then that I wasn't exactly sure what the soft eyes and half smile represented, but I knew the telltale signs of Cole Kimball panic. Those weren't them. "What? Why? Is that bad?"

He shook his head. "Don't know why it would be." He picked up his burger again and took a bite.

Okay, so I'd thought about it. That was all he'd asked, and that was all I'd answered. I'd also thought about getting a tattoo and learning to ride a motorcycle and maybe someday getting something besides my ears pierced. (Admittedly that one had zipped right on by.) Now, of course, the moment was begging for a little reciprocation.

"And what about you?"

He stared at me with those same soft eyes and that same half smile and slowly chewed. Amusement? Was that what was happening? I just couldn't make sense of it.

Once he had swallowed, he set his burger down again and said, "What about me?"

Okay, *that* was amusement. Nothing cruel. Nothing teasing. But that twinkle in his eyes . . . Something had shifted. He was relaxed again. What in the world about this moment could possibly be causing him to relax? Or was *I* the one doing it wrong? Was I overthinking and internally freaking out over nothing?

Hang on, I'm not freaking out. No, I wasn't freaking out. But I needed his answer, and I needed it now.

"Don't be cute, Cole. Come on. Play fair. Same question. Have you ever had zooming-past and/or serious-consideration romantic thoughts about the two of us? And if so . . . you know . . . which one?"

He chuckled. "Way to remove the loopholes, Olivet."

"Thank you very much." *Now answer the freaking question before my head runs away with this any more than it's already beginning to.*

"Honestly?"

I threw a french fry at his face. Hit him right smack dab on the nose, causing him to do a stunned double take before he started laughing so loudly we got the evil eye from the people in the next booth. Didn't matter. I didn't take my eyes off of him.

"Okay," he said softly. "Sorry. The truth is I never really had any zooming thoughts. I don't think I ever allowed myself to go there when we were young because I had to be careful. You know? I remember always thinking how sad it would be if Addie and Wes broke up. I knew everything would have been ruined—not just between them, but between all of us. And then when Brynn and I sort of toyed with the idea of being together, it was just insane. So weird. So obviously not going to work, and that was fine. But I remember feeling like it could have been really bad if she and I had started to actually feel something for each other in that way, and *then* it didn't work out, as it inevitably never would have."

He picked up his napkin and wiped the salt and grease from his fingers—and from his nose—and then settled back into the booth. "And then Addie and Wes *did* break up, and it *did* ruin everything, just like I always knew it would. From that point on I didn't even have to try not to have those thoughts about you, because there was no chance I was ever going to let that be us."

I reached across the table and placed my hand under his. We instinctively intertwined our fingers. He studied them and then leaned forward as he turned his hand over so mine was on top, and then he began tracing the outline of my hand with the fingers of his other hand.

"I don't like the expression 'just friends,'" I whispered. "I don't like the implication that there's a hierarchy of relationships. And if there is a hierarchy, how dare anyone minimize friendship? Isn't friendship *everything*?"

His Adam's apple bounced up in his throat as he nodded. "Yeah," he said in soft, gravelly agreement. He lifted my hand and kissed my knuckles, and then he kept my fingers against his lips as they curved into a smile. "It's everything."

The warmth of his breath against my hand provided an unexpected spark in the core of my abdomen, and an involuntary intake of breath threatened to give it the oxygen required to burn the whole thing to the ground. My index finger twitched, errantly threatening to isolate itself from his grasp and brush against his still-upturned lips. But the rebellion was over almost before it had begun as I managed to recapture control of the finger and my breathing and the powder keg of emotions in the pit of my stomach and smile up at him with a status-quo smile that I was satisfied matched his to a T.

He closed his eyes briefly and kissed my hand one more time before releasing it and opening his eyes. "Well." He cleared his throat and began wadding up our wrappers and gathering our cups. "Thanks for having that sort of awkward conversation with me. I just thought maybe we should." He rubbed his eyes roughly and stretched his arms overhead as he said, "I think I can be normal again now. Sorry." He shrugged and rolled his eyes and then looked at his watch. "Want to get back on the road to 'other stuff'?"

I beamed at him. "You bet. I just need to make a quick bathroom stop first if that's okay."

He picked up our trays as we stood. "I think I'll do the same after I toss the garbage. Meet you outside?"

"Sounds good." I turned and began walking to the restrooms by the register, but then spun on my heel and hurried over to him, meeting him at the trash can just as he stacked the trays on top of it. "Hey, Cole, next time you want to say something . . . just go first, okay? That way I don't have to try to interpret what's happening and overthink everything in my crazy brain." I stuck my tongue out, crossed my eyes, and twirled my fingers out beside my ears, causing him to laugh as he nodded.

"Good note. Got it."

"Because this wasn't so bad, was it?" I threw my arms around his neck and forced him against me. And then I held on for dear life. The muscles in his arms and shoulders relaxed as they wrapped around me and then tightened as he pulled me in closer and raised me up onto my tiptoes. "See? There's nothing we can't survive." I released him from my grip, chuckling as he lowered me to my normal height. "This is nothing compared to when you forced me to admit I don't like *Die Hard*."

"Yeah . . . I'm still coming to terms with that one." He winked and then gestured toward the bathroom with his chin. "Go. I'll meet you outside."

"Okay. Meet you outside." I grinned and bounced away to the ladies' room, waving at him as I turned around and closed the gap in the door.

And then I pushed in the lock.

And then the grin gave way to a deluge of tears and the inability to breathe. The inability to think. The inability to make sense of any of it.

We had a deal to always talk things out. To not create answers for each other without giving each other the benefit of being asked the question. That may not have been a spoken agreement, but it was most assuredly our deal. So I knew that if what we'd just talked about was bothering me, I needed to ask him why *he'd* been thinking about any of that. About an *us*. Why that was a topic he needed to discuss.

But how could I do that? How could I bring it up again and force that awkwardness? An awkwardness that was now resolved on his side, it seemed.

And ultimately, what good could come from it?

All my life I'd assumed he'd never thought about it. There was something *beautiful* about thinking he had never thought about it. Something pure and absolute. Something that made me feel so special.

Maybe he would think of it someday, maybe he wouldn't. It didn't matter. Not really. Everyone else saw it, and of course I saw it. We were perfect together. Made for each other. Two halves of the same whole, yada yada—all that stuff that people talked about in lovey-dovey ways. It applied just as much to us. *More*, even. Best friends? Without question. Soulmates? Who knew what that really meant, but yeah. Absolutely. The only thing we didn't have was romance. And that was okay. Cole had just never thought about it.

Except, apparently, he had. And he'd ruled it out. And I loved his reason for ruling it out. It was perfect. It was *him*. It was because of how much he loved me. How much he loved *us*.

But now I knew. For the very first time in my life, I knew.

"Maybe someday" no longer existed.

CHAPTER EIGHTEEN

COLE

"And then yesterday morning a thought zoomed in, and rather than swat it away like a mosquito before it had a chance to get comfortable, I let it land on me. And rather than squashing it or flicking it before it could do too much damage, I just stood there watching it get fatter and fatter on the blood I was providing for it."

Okay . . . surely that wasn't how he would have said it.

"You've had those thoughts? Cool. Please teach me how to be as un-affected by them as you clearly are. What is this sorcery you practice?"

Nope. Still not quite right.

"I never had those thoughts. But since yesterday morning, they seem to be the only thoughts I'm capable of thinking."

Not perfect, but better.

Of course, it didn't matter. It didn't matter what he had wanted to say or planned to say or needed to say. He didn't say anything. When push came to shove and the opportunity for unstable-emotional-declarations-that-would-open-the-door-for-unpredictable-and-potentially-friendship-destroying-responses presented itself, he'd chickened out and not said a word.

Although had he chickened out? Really? Sure, right then as they continued strolling down Varick in silence, it felt like it. But he was pretty sure that the future of their friendship would thank him later. Their conversation had taught him two things he hadn't known before:

1. *Laila had already thought about it. Not only had thoughts zoomed through, but they'd also apparently landed. That was what she'd*

said, right? She'd done all the pros-and-cons lists. She'd weighed the possibilities. And if there was anything he knew about his best friend, it was
that she was a whole lot smarter than he was. She'd considered it and chosen not to pursue it. He wasn't going to question her choice or presume that
he'd thought of something in twenty-four hours that she hadn't thought of
throughout their lives together.

2.   It was normal that he was having the thoughts he was having. It
was normal that pesky images had infiltrated his unconscious mind and
caused him to consider possibilities and feel new things and think new
thoughts. There was a reason those rom-coms Laila loved used that sort
of tactic all the time. There was a reason that the one with Billy Crystal
and Meg Ryan was built around this exact same predicament of men and
women being friends—minus about thirty years together and adding in
a lot of Aqua Net. There was a reason that in that other one Tom Hanks
asked Meg Ryan if she thought something might have happened between
them if they hadn't met under the circumstances in which they had. And
it wasn't just that to know Meg Ryan was to love her.

We're obsessed with what comes next. We're obsessed with the idea that
there has to be more.

But Laila was right. What more could there possibly be than what
they already had?

"That sign says we're on Seventh Avenue," she said, breaking the
silence that had existed between them since leaving Shake Shack. She
looked behind her. "Did we get off of Varick somewhere?"

Cole joined her in looking back. He could still spot the green
Shake Shack sign. "No, I don't think so. Varick must have become
Seventh, I guess."

He had no idea when or how that had happened, but the day was
about getting lost, right? Finally, maybe they were on to something.

"Let's just keep going north."

She laughed. "Look at you. Pulling out big words like *north*."

"Sorry. My bad. I meant 'up toward other stuff.'"

They crossed a one-lane intersection and began commenting on
the architecture they were passing. Not in any refined, knowledgeable

ways. Laila was obsessed with the *Architectural Digest* videos where you got to look around celebrities' houses, but apart from that, they weren't architecture people. But every single building here was so unlike anything they could find in their tiny mountain town. In Tribeca—were they still in Tribeca?—they were surrounded by dark red and brown bricks, without any pinewood or Pro-Panel roofing in sight. And while you didn't have to look too hard in Adelaide Springs to find artifacts and even miraculously intact cliff dwellings and kivas from the Ute tribe migrating through in the 1300s, and the history of silver mining in the nineteenth century that was written across practically every acre of land, they still couldn't stop commenting about how so many of the buildings around them looked so much older than any they had ever seen back home.

"Do you think early Dutch settlers lived there?" Laila asked as they passed an old-looking redbrick single-level that now housed a sports bar.

"I don't think the early Dutch settlers built those kinds of structures, did they?"

"No idea."

Next to the bar sat a six-story gray structure that looked like it had been spliced down the middle, like a double-wide mobile home having to be split onto two separate trucks to be moved. But it had lost its other half.

She stopped and studied it. "Do you think that used to be a textile factory?"

He looked down at her and chuckled, and then looked up again and tried to give it serious consideration. "Yeah, I really don't have any idea. Could have been, I guess. Whatever it was, I like what they've done with their fire escapes. It's very, um . . . what's the word?"

"I think *Architectural Digest* refers to it as Neo-Gothic Survivalism."

Cole spewed laughter and then quickly swallowed it down and raised his hand to his chin, copying her serious-student pose. "Ah. Yes."

"Sarah Jessica Parker and Matthew Broderick have decorated their place in it, ground to roof."

She dropped the stoic expression and winked at him. They began walking again, Laila asking about nearly every building they passed if Cole thought it had some connection to early Dutch settlers or textile factories. As it turned out, she'd gotten through about two paragraphs of Tribeca's Wikipedia page before dozing off the night before.

At the mention of the night before, he finally got around to asking the question he should have asked her first thing that morning. "I'm sorry. I haven't even asked how your back's doing today. You *seem* better."

"Oh yeah, I'm fine. I can barely even feel it anymore."

"Um, that's called paralysis, Lai. You might want to have that checked out." Wow. Nothing like falling back on a dad joke when you're trying to avoid guilt. She was kind enough to respond with only a good-natured groan. "Seriously, I'm glad. And I'm sorry I had your pills. I hope you didn't need them."

She shook her head. "I didn't even think about them, to be honest."

Silence settled between them again. Of course it did. She still had to have questions. As masterfully as he wanted to believe he'd settled things between them at Shake Shack, she was still probably attempting to piece it all together. He had no doubt that she knew him well enough to be nagged by the feeling that she was missing something. And he knew her well enough to understand that the silence they were currently experiencing was a result of her mind going back to what she had been focused on when she wasn't thinking about her sore back. Yeah, it was just a matter of time before he had to—

Hang on.

Cole practically skidded to a stop in the middle of the sidewalk, and while he was too distracted to care very much, he was super impressed with the way New Yorkers with their heads down and hoods pulled tight or FaceTiming or pushing caravans of kids in strollers deftly avoided him without missing a beat. But he'd pass along his observations about that later. Right now . . .

Bedford. Bedford, Bedford, Bedford . . .

Why did he know that street name? And why did the indescribable feel of the neighborhood suddenly feel inexplicably familiar? Why did he have a feeling of déjà vu just looking at the name of that street on a sign?

He reached into his pocket and pulled out his phone.

"No way!" Laila protested at once. "We have a deal. We are right this moment completely lost in New York—"

"Really, Lai?" He looked up from his phone and pointed back the way they had been walking. "A little less than a mile that way. Take a right at *Ghostbusters*."

She crossed her arms and huffed. "Well, well, Mr. Navigator. Who's all big and tough and Wouter van Twiller now?"

He raised his eyes again. "*What?* What are these words you're saying?"

"Looks like *someone* needs to brush up on their Tribeca history."

Cole grinned and turned his attention back to his phone. "I'm sorry to break the deal, but I promise you . . . if I'm right about what I think I'm right about, you're not going to be upset for long." He typed a few more letters and scrolled down and then looked back up at her as his entire face contorted into a confident smirk. "Oh boy. Okay, ready to take a little detour?"

She shrugged. "Would I know the difference?"

"Come on." He grabbed her hand and began pulling her down Bedford. He couldn't believe he'd recognized the sign, and he hoped she wasn't looking up yet, because she would *definitely* recognize the sign. And she wouldn't have had to break their deal and pull out her phone to verify. A radar-esque sixth-sense tractor-beam thing was probably going to kick in any moment as it was, like the mother ship calling her home.

"That's really cool," she commented, looking down at how *20 MPH* was painted on the road as the street got narrower.

How much farther? How much farther?

And then he saw a cluster of tourists—scratch that, he saw multiple clusters of tourists—hanging out with cameras pointed upward at the next corner.

He stepped in front of her, in the middle of the street. There weren't any cars making their way toward them. It was as if everything had come together to allow him this perfect opportunity to make her happy. To *watch her* be happy. That was his favorite pastime.

"Laila Evangeline Olivet, how much do you love me?"

She snickered and held his eye contact. "You know—the normal amount."

Before he said another word, before he took a chance on her looking anywhere but into his eyes, he pulled his phone out again, clicked on his camera, and started filming her.

Her snicker turned into an embarrassed giggle. "What are you doing?"

Cole stepped to the side. She kept watching him, but out of the camera shot he pointed up at the tan brick building with the red-painted first level on the corner of Bedford and Grove.

Confusion and dismay remained on her face for about two seconds, and then her eyes grew wide, her hands flew up to her mouth, and she began hurrying forward to join the clusters of tourists.

Cole laughed and then regretted it. He didn't want the sound of his voice to interrupt the video of her, but he couldn't help it. He couldn't help but laugh at the excitement on her face and the wild pointing and the slack-jawed shock.

"Do you know who lives here?" she asked him in a way-too-loud voice, like when you're going over a mountain pass and don't realize your ears haven't popped. She managed to pull her eyes away long enough to look back at him and then run back into the middle of the street, grab the hand that wasn't holding the camera, and pull him to the corner with her. "Cole, do you know who lives here?"

"Of course I know." He just couldn't stop laughing. "That's why we're here, ding-dong."

"This is Monica and Rachel's apartment building."

"Yes, I'm aware."

"And Chandler and Joey. And . . ."

She faded off as she turned her attention to the other side of Bedford. The non-*Friends* side of Bedford. She stared at the plain white multilevel apartment building that looked like it had bars on the windows, and then her hands dropped from her face and landed on her hips, and she turned and faced away from him. She began staring at the building across Grove. It wasn't the moment to discuss it, but his first thought about that structure, with its beautifully out-of-place white panels and red shutters and ornate molding, was that maybe it had been at least inspired by the early Dutch settlers.

"What are you looking at?" he asked her, once again not loving that his voice would be in the video but desperate to get back to the part where Laila was giddy rather than contemplative.

"I'm trying to figure out where Ugly Naked Guy lived."

"We've been over this. Remember? They aren't real, Lai. Say it with me—"

"Shut up." She smirked at him over her shoulder and then turned back to face the main attraction. "Ooh!"

There we go. Her eyes were the size of beautiful, sparkling golf balls again. She grabbed his hand once more and pulled him a few feet to the curb.

"That's the sign. Bedford and Grove. Remember? That's the sign that they always showed when they were transitioning between scenes." She tilted her head and crossed her arms as her enthusiasm was somewhat muted once again by reality. "Well, that's disappointing."

He followed her gaze to the red first floor where *The Little Owl* was written across the awning.

"No big orange couch or anything, huh?"

"Don't get me wrong . . . I didn't think Central Perk would be here. But I didn't realize *anything* was here. Since it *is* a restaurant—maybe even a coffeehouse from the looks of it?—why would they not pay whatever they had to pay to get the rights to turn it into Central Perk?" She glanced at the tourists all around her. "People would come. Oh yes, Ray . . ." She adopted her version of a James Earl Jones voice. "People would most definitely come."

A laugh erupted from deep in his chest, and she beamed in delight. Cole had brought her to the *Friends* apartment, and Laila had pop culturally reciprocated in kind with a *Field of Dreams* reference. Who had a better best friend than he did? No one, that's who.

But suddenly her brows furrowed. "Are you still filming?"

"Of course I am."

She grew camera shy, as she always did. "You can stop now."

"Why would I do that?"

"If you're going to film, at least film the apartment building."

"I think the apartment building's been filmed enough. If the apartment building is filmed any more, the apartment building's going to develop a complex."

She snorted as she tried ducking behind him. "I see what you did there."

He whipped around and got her back in the scope of his camera just as she weaved herself out of the middle of a group of teenaged girls posing together, yelling out "Pivot!" instead of "Cheese!"

"I'm just saying, it's low-hanging fruit. Don't you think?"

"What is?"

She gave up on escaping his camera and began posing for it instead. It was a seamless transition—from trying to cover her face to acting like she was Marilyn Monroe standing over a subway grate—and one he'd seen countless times. He never got tired of it. There was probably more footage of flirting-with-the-camera Laila using up his iCloud storage than everything else combined.

"Central Perk." She began walking toward him like a runway model, standing on her tiptoes like she was wearing stilettos instead of high-tops and sucking in her cheeks like she'd sworn off smiling for Lent. "It's the lowest-hanging fruit of all time."

"It's pretty low hanging, I agree, but I have to beg to differ that it's the lowest." Cole crouched down in the street and aimed the camera up at her as she made kissy faces at him. "Yeah, work it . . . That's it . . . One more, just like that . . ." It was all being caught on video, of course, but he began making camera-shutter sound effects, and she struck a new pose with each click of his imaginary lens.

"Then what is?"

"Dunkin' Punkin'."

Her sultry stoicism shattered into giggles. "What's Dunkin' Punkin'?"

"Well, it's nothing, because the people at Dunkin' Donuts won't return my calls. But it *should* be the name of their pumpkin-spice latte."

She considered that for a moment. "That's genius."

He shrugged. "I know."

"Lowest-hanging fruit of all time."

"This is what I'm saying."

The photo shoot was over. She turned back to face the *Friends* building, and he stood from his crouched position and stopped filming. He'd captured some moments that he would treasure for a lifetime, and now he just wanted to be in *this* moment with her.

"Thank you for bringing me here." She squeezed herself in under the crook of his shoulder as he extended his arm around her. "Is it so much to ask that every day in my life exceeds my expectations, like it does when I'm hanging out with you?"

Cole chuckled softly. "That seems like a reasonable request." And he'd give anything to be able to honor it. He leaned over and kissed the top of her head and sighed. "We're good, right?"

He hadn't meant to ask it. He felt foolish for asking it, actually, apart from the fact that no filter between them seemed, at least to Cole, like a solid indication that they were, in fact, fine. He needed them to be fine.

"Of course." She wrapped both arms around his torso and looked up at him. "We're better than good."

He studied her face. Not for signs that she was hiding something. Not for indications that there was anything she wasn't saying. Maybe he should have been, but that just didn't occur to him right then.

Instead, he looked for more signs of their history written across her features. She was wearing a little makeup now, but he liked that she never wore too much. It would be a crime to cover up the freckles across the bridge of her nose. He'd consider it a personal affront if she somehow blended the tiny little scar above her left eyebrow—the one she'd gotten when they were in kindergarten and a mama magpie had misinterpreted her compassion toward her nestlings as a threat—out of existence. And if her lips were ever transformed into anything but that perfect pout . . . The one that made her bottom lip look like it was effortlessly reaching for him . . . The one that he hadn't noticed over the course of nearly forty years but that he couldn't stop obsessing over now that his eyes were open . . .

"Shall we carry on?" she asked. "Or should we try to get in there and see if there are any ridiculously oversize rent-controlled apartments we can move into?" She gave him one more squeeze and then began walking back onto Bedford. "Back this way, you think?"

She turned back and faced him when she realized he hadn't followed. "You okay?"

It was better this way. She was fine. They were good. He was . . .

Well, he wasn't quite sure what he was. Happy seemed like a bit of a stretch, with all he still had to figure out in his life. And the thoughts he was having about her—no longer the way-in-the-future thoughts his dream had forced upon him but the it-would-be-so-easy-to-kiss-her type that felt so much more dangerous—sort of deprived him of the ability to say he was comfortable and carefree. But he was having fun. He was savoring the moments. He was creating more memories.

He was with Laila.

"I'm great." He jogged to the curb after her once a bicyclist had passed in front of him. "Who should we go see next? Do Will and Grace live close by? Which *Law & Order* cops work this beat, do you think?"

"Ooh! Doesn't Carrie Bradshaw live in the West Village?"

Cole looked behind him—at what exactly, there was no telling. "Where's the West Village?"

"I'm pretty sure we're *in* the West Village."

"What happened to Tribeca?"

"It's still there. The *Ghostbusters* are holding down the fort while we're away." She stopped and looked up at him, and he shrugged, causing her to shake her head and laugh. "Your homework assignment for tonight is to at least look at a map."

And then they carried on toward other stuff, Laila wisely taking over and leading the way.

CHAPTER NINETEEN

LAILA

We only got lost—like, scary-and-we-might-get-mugged-and-or-eaten-by-rats lost—twice, and we felt pretty good about that. Of course that was just Monday. On Tuesday, after Cole took his homework assignment seriously and studied maps until he felt confident we could proceed safely, we decided to give the subway a try.

Here's what you need to understand about Adelaide Springs, Colorado. There's nothing wider than a two-lane road for miles around, and we refer to that two-lane road as "the highway." Not because we're trying to be funny or ironic or anything, but because it is the actual highway. It's also Main Street, and for the little chunk of space in which it cuts through the middle of downtown (for about four blocks), we call it that. And then the buildings go away and it's "the highway" again.

Remember in *Cars* when Sally took Lightning up to that higher viewpoint and showed him the big picture of what Radiator Springs had looked like in its prime? How cars used to have to drive through town on Route 66 in order to get to their destination? Well, that was basically Adelaide Springs too. Except instead of an interstate system giving everyone an easier and faster way to bypass us, it was mountain cut-throughs. And, of course, there was interstate, too, farther out, for those who wanted to avoid the mountains altogether.

And look, I get it. Think about how much easier it would have been for Maria and Captain von Trapp to escape the Nazis if they could have just gone around.

But I digress. The point is, in Adelaide Springs, our existence is not about getting anywhere quickly. Shortcuts consist of not stopping to talk to Maxine Brogan unless you have time to hear about the sweater she's knitting for Prince Charlemagne. Rush hour is actually rush three minutes, and it only occurs once or twice a year when Joan Parnell's precocious grandson, Hayden, is visiting from Oklahoma City. (Because Joan thinks it's adorable to let him hold her safety cop stop sign during morning drop-off at the school, you see.) And the only overpass in the county was built for wildlife. Seriously. It's about ten miles outside of Adelaide Springs town limits, and when you drive under it, you can practically hear the deer and elk lobbying for a new tax levy so they can put in a roundabout and maybe a Starbucks.

I say all of that to say this: while Cole and I were certainly more well traveled than a lot of people in our town, and I liked to think we were both pretty savvy, in general, nothing we'd experienced in our lives had prepared us for the New York City subway system.

"The local ones are faster," he told me as we stood by the rails, looking up at the signs in the Canal Street station.

We'd started out the same way as yesterday—past John-John, left at *Ghostbusters* toward other stuff—but with just a couple of non-*Friends*-related turns, we'd found ourselves in Chinatown. So we'd explored around there a bit and eaten at a great little Chinese restaurant where, sad to say, Cole ordered sesame chicken and I got the beef and broccoli, just like we would have at Panda Express in Colorado Springs. (We were both very disappointed in ourselves and our lack of adventurous spirit, though we had no complaints about the taste of the food.)

And then we decided to conquer the subway. So there we were. Staring up at signs as people all around us exhibited knowledge and know-how that the elk-traffic-is-crazy-this-time-of-day kids just didn't possess.

"I don't think that's right," I told him. "Why would the local be faster than the express? Doesn't 'express' carry an expectation of speed, right there in the name?"

He contemplated this. "Yeah, that makes sense. But I really think I remember reading that the local was the one you wanted to take if . . ." He stopped talking and turned around, looking back at the sign over the stairs we had just come down. "No. I take it back. I think you're right. But this one has us heading downtown. Do we really want to go downtown?" He looked back to me. "Where even *is* downtown in New York?"

I shook my head. "I don't think it's downtown, like the part of town where the city is. Not like downtown Denver is the part where the skyline is and stuff. I think it's down. Like, south. So if you're heading downtown you're going south, from wherever you are."

Again, he contemplated. "You realize this calls everything I thought I understood about 'Uptown Funk' into question."

I chuckled. "Absolutely. And don't get me started on 'Downtown' by Petula Clark."

"Although . . ." Cole held his finger up philosophically to signal the epiphany he was in the middle of. "'Downtown Train' by Rod Stewart makes much more sense now. In fact, if we were smart, we would have gleaned the lessons being taught by 'Downtown Train' and not even have to have this conversation right now. The Metro Transit Authority should just be piping it in over the announcement system."

He looked across the rails at the people standing on the other side, and then back up at the sign over the stairs. "So do we want to go uptown or downtown, local or express? J . . . Z . . . N . . . Q . . ."

Highlights of the next few minutes after that included Cole running up the stairs on one side of the tracks, intending to hurry down on the other to see what *that* sign said, but quickly discovering that the unlimited Metro cards we thought we'd been so smart in buying didn't allow us to use the same card at the same station for eighteen minutes. It was another day, another version of my fabulous multi-pocketed cargo attire, and his money was sealed up in my pants because we'd thought it would be too easy to pick his wallet out of his pocket. Cole's fear of being unable to get to me on the other side of the turnstile if a subway hoodlum targeted me while I rifled through all my pockets, trying to track down his debit card so he could buy a pay-per-ride pass, caused us to reevaluate our mugger-proofing strategies moving forward.

Anyway, he finally got to the other side, and we spent a couple minutes yelling across the tracks at each other, attempting to understand what the other was saying as trains rushed by and buskers busked. And then there was the classic moment when I had to take one contact out so I could pull my phone up as close to my eye as I could get it in an attempt to make sense of the subway map I was studying.

"It's possible . . . just possible"—Cole looked to me after we had both collapsed, winded, wide-eyed, and laughing harder than I could remember us ever laughing—"that after thirty years, your prescription needs updating, Sophia."

And then I popped my contact, which had been precariously balancing on my fingertip as life flew by all around us, back into my eye as we sped away on the N toward Astoria–Ditmars Boulevard, whatever that meant.

❦

And that's how we ended up in the Bronx. Well, not right away. The N took us to Queens, as some people may have already known it would. Needless to say, we had not known that. We mistakenly got out at Broadway, thinking it was *that* Broadway (it was not), and then got on the first train that was heading back the way we came, since as little as we knew about Manhattan, we knew even *less* about Queens. (Cole did not seem to think my ability to say, "Oh, Mr. Sheffield!" in a Fran Drescher voice was going to help us out.) At some point soon thereafter, we switched trains because our train was becoming another train, which made *zero* sense, but we decided it was a good moment to disregard our mothers' advice and carry out the New York subway equivalent of jumping off a bridge because everyone else was.

And *that's* how we ended up in the Bronx. It was a local train, so *not* the faster one, and stop after stop passed us by—or we passed the stops by, I suppose—until we'd been on the train so long that we were afraid to get off.

"It's like that episode of *Friends*," Cole said.

Now, just to be clear, Cole's relationship with *Friends* was not like his relationship with *Gilmore Girls*. He liked *Friends*. He may not have obsessed over things the same way I did, so he wasn't one to reference moments or throw out quotes very often, but in my opinion, that made it even better when he did. Like when Mr. Darcy told Elizabeth her good opinion was more difficult to get, and therefore more worth getting. Except less backhanded compliment-y.

"You mean when Ross was dating the girl from Poughkeepsie and fell asleep on the train and ended up in Montreal?"

He deflated. "Oh. That's good too. I was thinking of when the guy at Chandler's work thought his name was Toby."

I laughed. "Yes! No, that's better. This is exactly like that."

That was about the time we were ready to give up and commit to riding the rails for the rest of our days. We'd been on the train so long that it was too late to tell it our name was really Chandler.

And that we didn't want to go to the Bronx.

But then the train voice lady (whom we had named Dorothea) said something that caught Cole's attention.

"Did you hear that?"

"What?

He pointed up toward the PA system and whispered, "Listen."

I strained to hear as well as I could. "Next stop is 161st Street and Casey Kasem? Is that supposed to mean something to me? Apart from the obvious," I added. "That I'm going to be sending 'Downtown Train' out to you as a long-distance dedication."

He was too distracted to laugh at my joke. (It must have been the distraction. Because the joke was *hilarious*.)

"Not Casey Kasem. Yankee Stadium."

"Oh. Cool." And I guess it was. Cool, I mean. To steal a quote from *Sleepless in Seattle* and make it my own, I don't want to watch baseball. I want to watch baseball in a movie. Baseball movies are awesome. Baseball movies make me believe baseball is interesting and exciting and fun and romantic, and that the last play of the game is worth sticking around for because it will always win or lose the game and, quite often, determine whether or not the final batter retires as a legend / reunites with his true love / gets to be a father figure to some fledgling teen he may or may not have sired.

But *real* baseball? Real baseball sucks.

"Come on. We're getting off here." Cole grabbed my hand as the train screeched to a halt and pulled me toward the door and out onto the platform, through all the people who were pushing to get onto the train.

I stood close to him and tapped up and down my legs to make sure my phone and little zip wallet with my ID, credit card, metro pass, and twenty dollars cash were secure in my pockets, and then I looked up at him. His eyes were darting around frantically, trying to figure out where he was, I figured. Or maybe where he was going.

"Do you want to go to a game or something?" Were there baseball games in September? In the middle of the day? And could you just walk in? Kevin Costner had not prepared me for this moment. For that matter, a lifetime with Cole Kimball had not prepared me for this moment. I could remember when he and Wes wanted to play baseball and had begged their moms to drive them to Del Norte twice a week so they could join Little League. That had lasted about a month (I'm being generous) before they declared baseball to be boring and unworthy of stealing their precious bike-riding and video-gaming time.

"This way."

He began leading us toward the left, and I followed, and then there was a clearing in the trees and signs and people, and a giant ivory building that reminded me a little of the Roman Colosseum came into view, with *Yankee Stadium* in huge gold letters at the top. I have to admit, even caring as little about baseball as I did, there was a tiny bit of a holy-ground feel in the air. I may not have cared about being there, but I knew that Roy Hobbs from *The Natural* and Ray Kinsella from *Field of Dreams* and Crash Davis from *Bull Durham* and Dottie Hinson from *A League of Their Own* all would have stood there in reverence, so I sort of did too.

"My entire life he talked about coming to a game here."

I snapped out of my reverence and looked up at Cole, who was staring at Gate 6 wistfully . . . bitterly . . .

"Who?"

"My grandfather." He cleared his throat and kept his eyes focused straight ahead. "The man's entire life . . ." His voice trailed off, and he swiped angrily at his eyes. "In ninety years, he left the Colorado western slope once. One miserable road trip to Houston, and all he did the entire time was complain about how awful everything outside of Adelaide Springs was. I don't want that to be me."

"That's not you." I laced my fingers through his, and he held on tightly. "That's not you, Cole. Look where you are right now. You're at Yankee Stadium. 'The House That Babe Built,' right?"

He shook his head and chuckled, then looked down at me and smiled. "Close. 'The House That Ruth Built.' And it wasn't actually this Yankee Stadium, I don't think. I think they built this one in about—"

"Okay, I don't care."

He laughed, but I didn't want to make him laugh too much. I wasn't trying to make him laugh. It was the first time he had broached the subject of his grandfather, and I didn't want to lose the thread.

"You're in New York. You've traveled. And it was Bill's choice not to do that. That's not on you."

His smile faded as he sighed. "The thought of not seeing you every day kills me, Lai. It does. But the thought of leaving Adelaide Springs . . ." He looked away from me, back to Gate 6. "I'm not panicking, and I'm not having a midlife crisis. I'm ready. I'm pretty sure I need this. It's . . . it's what I want."

"Oh."

That was all I could really say. Because that changed everything, didn't it? He'd taken away my opportunity to playfully slap him and scream, "Snap out of it!" like I was Cher in *Moonstruck*. The pain on his face robbed me of my chance to play the martyr and beg him to stay for my sake if not his own. Any argument I put out there now would be asking him to choose what I wanted over what he wanted, and that put us in new, foreign territory. I couldn't remember the last time we hadn't wanted the same thing.

"Then I'll come with you."

At the words, he turned back slowly to face me again, and it was my turn to pretend I cared about looking at Yankee Stadium.

"Yeah." I nodded, diving straight into a fake-it-till-you-make-it approach. "It'll be fine. Surely fancy Brooklyn chef lady—what's her name again?"

"Laila . . ."

"No, that's not it." I forced myself to laugh at my lame joke. "Sylvia! That's it, right? Surely Sylvia needs servers, right? If she wants you so badly, maybe you can tell her we're a package deal? That's how Stevie Nicks got into Fleetwood Mac, isn't it? Lindsey Buckingham told them they were a package deal. Package deals can work. If not for package deals, we'd have no 'Landslide.' The defense rests, Your Honor."

"Laila!" His voice was behind me now, and his hands were on my shoulders, forcing me to stop walking. When had I started walking?

"I want to be where you are." The words caught in my chest as all the air propelling them escaped through my mouth. I pulled my eyes away from Yankee Stadium and turned to face him.

I'd always been indifferent to baseball. But suddenly I hated it. I wasn't even sure if I would like watching baseball in movies anymore. And that *really* sucked. Even more than the tedium of baseball itself. But from now on, when I thought of baseball, I would think of this moment. I suddenly and instinctively knew it, beyond the shadow of a doubt. This moment that, just a few minutes ago, had been laced with humor, buoyed by positive significance, and sprinkled with adventure. Now it was sad. Still significant—probably in positive ways that would reveal themselves later. But for now, the moment (and therefore baseball) was flashing big, neon signs of negativity.

Because there was no chance on God's green earth that he was going to sit back and let me sacrifice what I needed for *him* any more than I was going to ask him to sacrifice what he needed for *me*.

He shook his head slowly and smiled sadly down at me.

"I know." I stepped out of his grasp, needing just a moment of separation. "I really did mean it when I said there wasn't anything I wouldn't do for you, though."

"Right back at ya, Olivet." His voice was a croaked whisper.

I couldn't help but wonder if I would have fought harder before Shake Shack. Fought for him to stay in Adelaide Springs. Fought for us to stay together. But when possibility no longer existed . . .

It wasn't like I'd been working some long-con bait-and-switch sort of thing. My entire lifetime of friendship with Cole hadn't been based on a belief that someday he would see what had been right there in front of him all along and fall madly in love with me. I didn't think of it like that. Truth be told, I usually didn't think of it at all. He was my best friend. And had there been moments through the years when I had looked over at him and felt something in the pit of my stomach? Something akin to butterflies, but with a lot more weight. Like bats, maybe? Yeah. Sure. Of course.

And did I find him attractive? Well, duh. He was handsome. A good-looking guy. He was the most beautiful person I'd ever met, truth be told. In addition to the more superficial stuff that he didn't really have any control over—dark, soulful eyes and thick, gorgeous hair and other things that his mystery birth parents had left with him as a first and final gift—he always smelled really good. I liked that. And I already went into how much I always liked his style. And the way he looked at me—or whoever was talking, really, not just me—with his full attention. And the protectiveness that never made me feel weak but that somehow made me feel stronger, because Cole's strength was my strength too.

The way he laughed. That one was just for me, I was pretty sure.

He laughed with other people, but with me there was a freedom in it. And a history. Like every joke was layered upon another upon another, and ultimately, he wasn't just laughing at one funny thing I'd said but rather the backstory and warm-up act and the jokes yet to come, all at once.

People tried to make distinctions all the time. Attractive but not *attracted*. Love but not *in love*.

I'd never made distinctions with Cole. I'd never tried to justify or defend our relationship, and I didn't like that, for the first time in my entire life, I was finding myself doing that.

And for the first time, I couldn't help but think of how awkward it might be for him or for me or for some girl in Williamsburg. In our Williamsburg, all I'd have to worry about was one of the prison mannequins coming to life and going all eighties Kim Cattrall on me. But in Brooklyn Williamsburg? There were undoubtedly beautiful, sophisticated, living, breathing New Yorkers on every corner who would instantly recognize what a catch Cole Kimball is. If I was with him, and he met someone, I wouldn't be his friend who lived a few streets away in the same small town, and I wouldn't be his friend who occasionally visited on weekends while he was in culinary school. I would be the clingy childhood best friend who had followed him across the country, had no career of her own, and came over for breakfast every morning because she forgot to buy milk for her cereal.

I wouldn't want to be that other girl.

Of course, that wasn't the biggest problem, was it? The biggest problem was that now that I knew he'd ruled out the possibility of us together, I had to consider that *other* possibility. The possibility of there ultimately *being* another girl. And I hadn't had time yet to come to terms with being *me* when that happened.

"So that's it, then? You're really leaving?"

We'd had this conversation already. We'd had various versions of this conversation over the course of the past few days. But I knew this was the one that counted.

He stepped between me and Yankee Stadium so that I had no

choice but to meet his eyes. His red, strained eyes under those dark lashes of his. His jaw rippled and released as he chewed on the inside of his cheek and nodded. "And you're really staying."

Leaving and staying weren't the correct words to use as we stood on a sidewalk in the Bronx, but Adelaide Springs was at the center of our conversation, the center of our lives, and the center of who we were together. And as much as I knew we loved each other, and always would, for the very first time I wasn't sure that we would be okay if we no longer had *home* in common.

"Yeah. I am."

His eyes stayed locked with mine, and it was his turn to lead the fake-eventually-begets-make brigade. "It's not as if we'll never see each other, you know. Wherever I end up, it's not like I'll never go home."

Home.

"Brynn and Seb are only there part time, you know. I mean, you'll see them *here* more than you would see them at home, so—"

"I don't know for sure that this is where I'll end up. Look, I'll check out Denver too. Okay? And Boulder. I know it's been a while, but I got to know Boulder pretty well. I liked it there."

I began having to work a little more at getting each breath I took to fill my lungs. All those pretty little words coming out of his mouth—the ones meant to give hope of being able to count the miles between us in hundreds rather than thousands—didn't provide any comfort whatsoever. I could see the writing on the wall.

"This is where you're going to be, Cole." My brain was a confusing amalgamation of desperate desire to sabotage his NYC opportunities (an impulse I would never consider acting on) and the instinctive compulsion to make sure nothing stood in the way of him getting absolutely every good thing (an impulse I was pretty sure I'd been born with). "Have you called Sylvia?"

"I've texted her. Don't worry about that right now."

"Okay, but you need to make sure she knows you want the job so she doesn't give it to someone else."

"Can we just not worry about that right now?"

Not worry. Not . . . worry. Yeah, sorry. My self-destructing brain couldn't compute. "And even if you end up somewhere else—which you won't—it's not exactly easy to get back to Adelaide Springs, you know."

He sighed. "Yes, I know."

"And when you only have a weekend off of work . . . Although, come to that, I doubt trendy Brooklyn hotspots close on the weekends. And since your mom's never there anymore, and now that your grandfather is gone, and—"

"*You're* there, Laila." His brow furrowed as his elevated voice caused even a few usually impassive New Yorkers to glance our way. "Don't act like you don't know that's all I need."

If only it were.

"Yeah." I nodded, then turned and looked at baseball fans snapping photos. Of Yankee Stadium. Not us. "And now that I'm an expert traveler who has conquered all of New York City's boroughs—"

"Except for Brooklyn and Staten Island, of course."

"Those don't count."

Out of my peripheral vision I saw him tilt his head, and then his entire body swayed until he was in front of me again. "Because you haven't been there?"

"Exactly."

His brow relaxed, and a grin spread across his lips. "I'm sorry. I interrupted you. You were saying? Since your cumulative ninety steps in Queens and the Bronx make you an expert traveler . . ."

He was in my face, trying to get a smile out of me, and as much as I didn't want to give it to him, I couldn't help it. "I was going to say I could come visit you, but now I'm not sure I want to."

"As if you have a choice."

He nudged my elbow with his, and once again I resisted the relaxed environment he was attempting to create. Until he nudged again. And again. And then he had to wrap his arm around my waist and pull me back after an angry New Yorker yelled, "Hey, watch out! I'm walkin' here!" exactly as he would in a tourism commercial for New York if it were written, directed, and produced by a group of filmmakers from Provo, Utah. It was stereotypical, hilarious perfection in every way.

"I'm so sorry!" I called after the short, balding, heavyset man I was just *sure* made his living playing scummy landlords in Dick Wolf television shows. In response to my apology, he lifted his hand over his head and flipped me off.

I gasped, while Cole just started laughing.

"Did you see that?" Clearly he had. "I have half a mind to—"

"Not happening, tough stuff." He held on to the back of my jacket as I tried walking in the direction of the man, and his laughter grew as I continued walking in place. "I'm pretty sure that stories that begin like this end with the words, 'and she was never heard from again.'"

I stopped attempting to pull away but kept my eyes on my new Bronx nemesis until he got lost in the crowd. Then I sighed, turned back to face Cole, who had released me once he felt the danger had passed, and found him with his teeth holding on to the half of his bottom lip that wasn't turned up into a smile.

"What? Why are you looking at me like that?"

He reached out and brushed aside a strand of my hair that had fallen in front of my face. "We'll be fine, you know. A little distance is nothing. Nothing is changing between us."

I resisted the urge to lean into his hand and exhaled a held breath when his hand fell away. "Oh, gosh, yeah, I know. Nothing is changing." I smiled at him. "So what do you say? I don't know about you, but unless Yankee Stadium and Yankee Candles are part of the same co-op here or something, I've seen what I need to see. Ready to move on?"

He nodded and wrapped his arm around me as we walked back to the train station.

You know, it's funny. Until yesterday, I'd never imagined that there would come a time when I would keep things from Cole. Not until I did. And now, apparently, I didn't have any qualms at all about straight-out lying to him. Whether or not we'd be fine remained to be seen. But somehow, everything had changed. And the best thing we had going for us was that he didn't seem to have any idea.

CHAPTER TWENTY

COLE

Cole heard the doorknob to Laila's bedroom jiggle and immediately jumped up from the couch and ran to the kitchen. As he removed the plate from the oven and hurried it over to the marble island, the urgency of the jiggling increased. Then she began pounding on the door.

He chuckled. "Hang on just a second!"

"Cole, I can't get out!" she yelled in a bit of a panic. "The door's stuck!"

"It's fine!" He placed the candles in the chocolate-chip pancakes he'd had warming for the last twenty minutes as Laila slept longer than he had anticipated, quickly lit them, and took one more look around to make sure everything was ready.

"Why did you lock me in my room?" She twisted the knob again. "What are you up to? Are you doing something for my birthday?" Then, silence. "Sorry! I shouldn't have said anything. If you *are* doing something for my birthday, I hope I didn't ruin it!"

He shook his head and rolled his eyes as he began unfastening his belt from around the knob and the sconce beside the door that he had looped it through. He'd planned it as more of an advance warning system than a means of imprisonment—if she'd had the upper-body strength and determination of even a pigeon, she could have opened the door.

"First of all, we both know today's your birthday, so I don't think you could have ruined anything, really. And second, I'm not doing anything for your birthday. I was just in the middle of some classified business with the State Department. Needed some privacy. That's all." He looped his belt back around his waist and fastened it. Then he stood there and waited, but she didn't make any other attempts to open the door. "You can come out now, if you want."

The knob turned and the door cracked open, and she peeked out just enough that Cole could only see one eye behind glasses, along with her nose and half of her mouth. "There aren't other people here, are there?" she whispered.

"No. The Department of Defense does most of their top-secret stuff on Zoom."

"Cole!" His name was soft but still emphatic. She poked her head out a little farther. "It's just if it's a surprise party or something, I need a minute to get presentable."

"Laila, you know exactly two people in New York, and they're both in Germany right now. Who do you imagine I invited over for this surprise party?"

"Oh." She stepped back and pulled the door open the rest of the way, then inched out slowly, looking around on high alert as if she still suspected that a roomful of people were going to jump out and startle her.

Of course he wouldn't throw her a surprise party. He had, once, back when she turned twenty-one, and though they hadn't talked about it since, he'd promised himself he would never do that to her again. Cole would have liked to pride himself on knowing it was one of the few times in their lives he'd let what *he* thought she needed get in the way of what she clearly communicated she wanted, but there was no pride at all in it for him. Her parents had recently separated, and Laila had insisted that all she wanted for her birthday was a little peace and quiet away from their ongoing battles that she continually found herself in the middle of. He could have taken her hiking or for a long drive up into the mountains, and it could have been just the two of them, just like she wanted.

But what had he given her instead? He'd invited the entire town to Cassidy's, when it was still just a bar, thinking it would be fun for her to order a drink as a legal adult. Well, he'd invited the entire town apart from either of her parents. Both of whom, of course, knew every other person in town. None of whom ever imagined that the only two people who weren't invited were the warring Olivets. Both of whom showed up.

It had been a disaster. And the worst part had been the moment when everyone jumped out and yelled surprise and Cole had to watch the happiness vanish from her face, knowing that he had caused that.

He had known better anyway. Even if her parents hadn't been caught up in themselves and unable at that time to put their hostility aside for the sake of their daughter, he should have known better. Laila had always been someone who loved pulling out all the stops to make the people she loved happy, and she'd never had a shy bone in her body when it came to making Cole laugh or making sure customers had a great time at the Bean or Cassidy's. But she had no desire to ever stand in the spotlight alone.

Cole stepped behind her so she could see what he had done for her. It wasn't much. He'd used exactly thirty-nine chocolate chips, but he wasn't even going to tell her that part. She might have really appreciated the personalization and been extra huggy with him, and obviously that would have been okay. But there was also a chance she would view each chocolate chip, as she ate it, as symbolic of how quickly the years were passing, and that could spiral out of control very quickly. Overall, she hadn't been too maudlin about this particular birthday so far, but he didn't want to take any chances.

"Aww!" Her fingers formed a steeple over her mouth and tears sprang to her eyes. Big, magnified tears beneath the lenses. "This is so sweet!"

Oh, Laila. She was so easy to please, and that just made him want to work harder to blow her away. Some pancakes, a few candles, and streamers he had brought from home since he hadn't known what the party-supply situation was like in the Big Apple, and she acted like Oprah had just presented her with a minivan and new house for her and her six kids. "It's just pancakes. There are other things planned. This is just . . . breakfast."

He'd always loved going all out for her birthday. There had been a few isolated missteps here and there, like the surprise party, of course, and her thirty-seventh birthday when they'd gone white water rafting and alpine zip-lining even though they both had the flu and weren't quite sure how they made it out alive. (Literally. The last thing Cole remembered was being strapped into a harness, and then he somehow found himself in a tree that jutted out from the side of a mountain. Poor Laila had maintained consciousness and had the unfortunate memories of projectile vomiting while zipping into the wind at four-teen thousand feet.) But for the most part, her birthday was usually one of his favorite days. He got to pamper her and make her the focus of ev-erything in a way she would never allow the other 364 days of the year.

Strangely, though, he'd never felt any sort of pressure—certainly not from her, but not even self-imposed, which was surprising—to go bigger and better each year. That wasn't what it was about. He loved to catch her off guard, and every so often the way to do that was with some big gesture. (Their oft-referenced trip to Vegas had been a surprise for her thirty-second, and in 2010 he had taken her to see John Mayer at Red Rocks—a gift he would probably never be able to top in Laila Land, if bigger and better had been the goals.) But it really was just about making her feel special and loved. And though he had attained fluency in her love languages years ago, he tried never to take that for granted. It was all selfish on his part anyway, he knew. He lived for those moments of witnessing pure joy and delight on her face.

"Thank you." She turned around to face him and wrapped her arms around his neck.

Cole's breath caught as he enveloped her in his embrace and pulled her against him. Every muscle relaxed and tightened simul-taneously. How was that even possible? Physiologically, he knew it probably wasn't, but if it was impossible, then his body was apparently a scientific marvel.

"You're welcome," he breathed into her hair, delicately flowing against his lips.

He hadn't realized just how little he'd touched her over the course of the past few days, but he knew it now. He began breathing easier, even as the air felt thinner and the oxygen seemed in short supply. He hadn't known his body temperature had been abnormal, but now, as blood pumped through his veins with the intensity of those Colorado rapids that had become the final resting place of, he was pretty sure, some of their internal organs two years ago, he really couldn't understand how the coldness hadn't done him in when he wasn't holding her.

Snap out of it, Cole. If you don't let her go soon, you're going to make things weird, man.

He knew it was true. Very, *very* wise advice he was attempting to give himself. But as his fingertips twitched against the small of her back and she snuggled in closer in response, wise counsel wasn't what he wanted.

He wanted her.

He'd felt so confident that it had been a great few days. After fearing that things he'd said or, worse, things he hadn't said on Monday might have ruined everything, they'd actually had a really great few days. That little talk at Yankee Stadium sure had helped. Of course, there were still more things they were going to need to talk about, but there would be time for that, Cole had figured. At least they were talking. They weren't avoiding talking about the uncertainty of the future. She'd asked him which New York neighborhoods he might be interested in living in as they rode the Staten Island Ferry. (He genuinely had no idea.) He'd asked her if she was going to keep working at Cassidy's if she could, with the new owner, while they ate Black & White Cookies from William Greenberg, sitting on a bench in front of Belvedere Castle in Central Park. (She genuinely had no idea.) They'd rambled off top ten lists of their experiences together—ten best places they ever camped, ten best meals Cole had ever cooked for her, ten longest-running inside jokes between them—while they frantically searched for an open public restroom in Times Square. (A subject about which not a single person in Manhattan seemed to have any idea.)

But there had still been a little bit of distance between them.

Had Cole been avoiding touching her because he was afraid to conjure up the images in his mind again? The ones that hadn't gone away by a long shot, but with a little time and a little distance and a whole lot of effort had stopped being all he could see when he closed his eyes? Or had Laila shied away from her usual hugs and affectionate squeezes because she had sensed what he had stopped short of saying at Shake Shack?

He had no idea, but neither of them seemed to be concerned about any of that now. Her arms, which had been looped around his neck, lowered in front of her, her hands resting on his chest. Though who was he kidding? Her trembling fingers, drumming and flexing against him, weren't resting any more than his own hands, which had morphed from their casual, friendly position at her lower back into a desperate, hungry grasp at her hips. He lowered his eyes to look down at her. To gauge her emotions. He knew her better than anyone, but this—*this* . . . whatever this was—wasn't accompanied by any muscle memory or prior experience to draw from. If he got this wrong, he would ruin everything. He would ruin them.

"Hey, Lai?"

Her forehead was pressed against his collar, just above her hands. Still drumming. Still flexing. Occasionally curling his T-shirt into her fists in a way that made him more certain than he'd ever been about anything that he wasn't misreading a thing.

"Hm?" she asked. One syllable. Not even a word so much as a sound. But in it, Cole heard her staggered breath and her fear. *Fear.* They were each other's safety and each other's security. Laila's fear had always been a foe for him to vanquish. But this fear was exhilarating. It was theirs. Together. And the fact that she was just as afraid as he was, and yet she stood here . . . in his arms . . . attempting to pull him closer even though they were centimeters away from crossing lines they'd never even realized existed.

If he got this wrong, he would ruin them. But what if he got it right?

Cole tightened his grip on her pajama pants–clad hip with one hand while the other joined hers between their bodies, for just an instant, before brushing against her chin and tilting it upward. Her eyes rose slowly to meet his, heavy with all sorts of things he'd never seen there before. Fear, sure. Anticipation, maybe? Longing? Desire? If so, what did his eyes look like to her?

"Happy birthday, Lai."

He said it, and then he hated so much that he had said it. So much so that he had to close his eyes and imagine, for just a moment, that he hadn't said it.

He'd been preparing to kiss her. For the first time in the history of a friendship that was older than their memories, he'd been just about to kiss her. There were so many things he could have said.

"Is this okay?"

"You're the most important person in the world to me."

"I haven't been able to stop thinking about you."

As he stood there with his eyes closed, they all sounded stupid in his mind. But still. Any of them would have been better than "Happy birthday." What was that supposed to mean? What was she supposed to *think* he meant? Was that her gift? He'd promised her there was more in store than just pancakes. Was that what he'd planned for her? Chocolate chips and a little bit of lovin'?

"You okay?" she asked.

Okay . . . now his eyes were closed, and he was laughing. *Smooth, Kimball. Real smooth.*

His eyes shot open as he felt her posture change. He was horrified to think of what he would find in her expression when he looked at her looking at him, but much, *much* more horrified by the thought of standing there even one moment more, probably making her wonder if he was actually in the middle of a psychotic meltdown.

"Sorry." He laughed again and stepped back from her. It was the only natural thing to do since her hands had dropped to her sides and the moment was clearly so far beyond ruined.

She was staring at him, all longing or desire or whatever had been in her expression having been replaced by the look that accompanies mental recitation of the list of actions to take if someone in your presence has a stroke.

"For what? What's so funny? I . . ." She looked behind her and then took another step back as she pushed her glasses up higher on the bridge of her nose and then crossed her hands over her stomach. "I guess I don't understand what's happening." She fiddled with her glasses again and then returned her hands to her abdomen as she took yet another step back. "I'm sorry if I did something . . . or said something . . ."

Now *this* fear of Laila's Cole recognized. This was his foe. His adversary that he would march into battle against again and again, as many times as necessary, to keep her from ever feeling uncertain or unprotected or vulnerable. And he was the cause of the fear. *He'd* made her feel uncertain and unprotected and vulnerable.

Well, that's that, then, isn't it?

"I was about to kiss you, Laila."

She flinched, and then her eyes grew wide. Cole braced himself for whatever was to come. All he knew was he was so tired of skirting around things with her. It had been one week out of . . . how many? A couple thousand? A couple thousand weeks of not keeping things from each other. Of not shying away from the tough conversations. Of knowing there was nothing—*nothing*—that would ever be too much for them to overcome. And then not even seven full days of acting like he didn't know if that was true. But it *was* true. And he was exhausted from trying to sort it out without her help.

She had flinched, and her eyes had grown wide, but she was still looking at him. She hadn't run away. And if he'd read things wrong or had been about to make a mistake or whatever, they'd sort it out together. It wasn't a mistake to talk with her about it.

"Sorry," he finally got out after a couple of stammered attempts.

"I'm not trying to freak you out. I'm not *trying* anything. I just . . ." He ran his hands through his hair, and then his arms landed crossed on his abdomen, mirroring Laila. "So, here's the thing. At Shake Shack, when I asked you if you'd ever thought of us . . . you know . . . like that . . ." *Stop talking in code. Just say the words.* "When I asked you if you'd ever thought about the two of us together romantically, it was because I never had, Laila. Never. Not once in our entire lives."

She cleared her throat and looked down at her bare toes peeking out from under her long, blue-striped pajama pants. "I know. You told me that."

"Yeah. But I didn't finish the thought."

Her head snapped up so quickly that her glasses bounced on the bridge of her nose before landing crooked, and she had to straighten them. "Then finish the thought."

Cole exhaled slowly. "I never *had*. And then I did. I . . . had a dream about you. Sort of a . . . romantic one."

Her shoulders fell. "Oh. Well, that's not really a big deal, is it? I don't think that counts as thinking about it." She chuckled and began fiddling with the strands of hair near her face. She watched him for a moment and then cleared her throat. "Must have been some dream, though, to rattle you like this."

It was one thing to be open and honest with her. He was relieved to finally be doing that, no matter how awkward it was. But as memories of the dream—memories that were every bit as seared into his brain now as a lifetime of things they had actually done together—appeared before his eyes again and his pulse began to quicken, he knew that certain things were still better for him to keep to himself.

"It was. But that's not really the point. The dream isn't the point. The point is everything—every thought—has sort of been going through a different filter since then. I mean, you said you'd already thought about the possibility of us, over time, but I've sort of had all the thoughts in the last, like, five days or whatever. But it was still just thoughts." He took a step toward her and then wondered, for a moment, if that was a mistake. But she didn't step back or even seem to register the closer proximity. "And then I hugged you, like I've hugged you ten million times before . . . except . . ."

"Except it didn't feel like the last ten million?"

Cole shook his head gently. "No. It didn't."

They stood in silence, and the only thing awkward about it was that it wasn't awkward in the least. And it got even less awkward when she looked behind her at her melted candles that had long ago extinguished themselves and left wax across the surface of the pancake on the top of the stack. Then she did such a Laila thing that he couldn't help but smile. Without any pomp or circumstance or even a whisper of ruined birthday disgruntlement, she grabbed the second pancake from the stack and began tearing pieces apart and stuffing them in her mouth.

It was right then that he understood, for the very first time, that if she was any other woman in the world, he would be wildly, madly in love with her. If only she wasn't already the person he loved most.

"So why didn't you?" she finally asked, her mouth full of pancake.

He resisted the urge to laugh as he wondered how many of their most serious, life-altering conversations had taken place while Laila had a mouthful of pancake. "Why didn't I what?"

She shrugged. "Kiss me."

It was Cole's turn to flinch. And as for wide eyes . . . he was pretty sure he had become the personification of a shocked goldfish who had just had its eyes dilated at the optometrist.

In a Tim Burton cartoon.

"Um . . . because it's us, Laila. How could I—"

"No." She shook a strip of pancake at him before taking a bite of it. "I'm not asking the big, philosophical question. Not right now. Something happened and your mood shifted—"

"Oh." He chuckled and took a step over to the island and leaned against it. "I said, 'Happy birthday.' And I felt like such a dork. I don't know why I said it right then, but it got me all in my head. Like . . ." He adopted a deep Barry White sort of voice, except sleazier and with flashy finger guns to match. "Hey, baby, what are you wishing for when you blow out the candles this year?"

A half-chewed bite of pancake escaped from her mouth as a guf-faw erupted from her. That, of course, made Cole lose it, and by the time she was leaning over to try to find the spit-out food, she couldn't see anything because she was laughing so hard she was crying. She finally just gave up and collapsed onto the floor, curled up on her side, holding her stomach as she tried to catch her breath between gasping laughs. Cole slid down against the island until he was sitting on the floor and scooted over until his leg was by her head. Without a word or another look at each other, she rested the back of her head on his thigh and he began stroking her hair. Well, stroking her hair, wiping away the tears that were still streaming down her face, and occasion-ally picking off pieces of pancake and chocolate chips from various locations on each of them.

She stared up at him and he stared down at her, smiles on their faces, and finally Cole sighed and softly said, "You're just my favorite, Laila Olivet. I don't ever want to do anything to mess us up."

"And you think kissing me would mess us up?"

His cheeks puffed up with air and he shrugged as he let the air out. "I think there'd be no turning back."

"And you're sure you'd want to turn back?"

Cole opened his mouth but no sound came out, and she sat up beside him. He tilted his head so he could study her.

"Listen, all I'm saying is . . ." She lowered her eyes and began clasping the corner of her bottom lip between her teeth. "I was right there with you. I wanted you to kiss me, Cole." Her eyes met his again, and whatever had been there before—anticipation . . . long-ing . . . desire—seemed to be back. "And to even be thinking about this, much less talking about it, is terrifying. But what if it's something we need to think about? To talk about? And not just so we can deal with it and not have to worry about it anymore. What if . . ."

Laila rose up onto her knees, then grabbed his hands and used them to pull herself closer to him. In one deft move—so natural and seemingly practiced, as everything between them seemed to be, whether it had ever happened before or not—her left leg, bent at the knee, was resting on his thigh, and they were face to face. Eye to eye. "What if we're so afraid to mess up what we have that we're actually messing up the best stuff? The stuff we haven't even seen yet."

Cole leaned his head forward as she inched closer to him still. He could smell the sweetness of the chocolate chips on her breath, and he could see every dried, salty tear spot on those awful, enormous glasses that he loved so much. Laila seemed to become aware of her Sophia Lorens in the same instant he did, and she untangled one hand from his and raised her fingers to remove them. He reached up and caught her hand.

"Don't you dare."

She smiled at him in response, and he twisted his wrist to run his thumb along her jawline. She adjusted her grip to the top of his hand as his fingers fanned out across her neck before tangling in her loose waves.

And then his phone began vibrating in his left pocket, against her leg.

Of course it did.

"They'll go away," she whispered. "Ignore it."

She just about had him convinced—as if that took any effort at all—when they heard the ding of Brynn and Sebastian's penthouse elevator. They pulled apart and jumped up in instinctive panic, and when the elevator door opened and some black-haired woman in a red pantsuit, red heels, and red lipstick neither of them had ever seen before stepped into the foyer, Cole was reaching for the coffeepot to clean it and Laila was on her hands and knees looking for pancake chunks.

"Oh, sorry. I didn't realize you were still here. Brynn said the coast should be clear about now. You're Cole, I assume? I tried to call you."

His eyes flew open. "Oh! I'm so sorry. Drea?" Cole asked, rushing over to her with his hand extended.

"Drea." She said it in a way that sounded like she was correcting him, but he was pretty sure she was saying it exactly like he had just said it.

She did shake his hand, so he decided to take the win and just say, "Ah." As if he understood the difference. He dared not try again. "Yeah, I'm Cole. This is Laila."

Laila jumped up and shook Drea's hand. "Nice to meet you." Then she looked to Cole with a friendly and strained smile that he easily interpreted as "Who is this stranger who has a key to our friends' apartment, whom you apparently know and I do not? Also, are we cool? And where do we go from here? Are we going to go on as if we weren't very much on the verge of making out just now?"

It was entirely possible he was projecting some of his own concerns into his interpretation of her smile.

"Drea—"

"*Drea*," Drea interrupted him.

Seriously! They were saying the exact same thing!

"Right." Cole cleared his throat. "She's Brynn's personal assistant. She's helping me with . . . well, birthday stuff. For you."

"You're the birthday girl, huh? Nice. He has a pretty sweet day planned for you, so I should probably get out of here and let you get to it. I'll swing back by in a bit." Her red stilettos clickety-clacked back to the elevator, and then she turned back to them as she got to it. Drea looked first to Cole. "Between seven thirty and eight, right?"

His eyes darted to Laila and then back to Drea. "Yeah. I think so. If that works for you. I really appreciate your help."

"My pleasure. With Brynn out of town, I'm bored out of my mind anyway. And Murrow tends to get my seat on flights now." It *sounded* like she was making a joke, but her face didn't seem so sure.

She turned to Laila. "Happy birthday. Have fun, you two."

After the elevator doors had shut, Laila said, "I don't even know where to start on any of that."

Cole chuckled. "Well, let's start with her name. Am I missing something?"

"Yeah, you were butchering it. It's Drea."

"Drea?" he repeated, focusing on replicating the sounds exactly. He squinted to watch Laila's lips as she repeated it and they said it together. "Drea? Drea. Drea. Drea?"

She began giggling and walked the crumbs she had picked up from the floor over to the garbage can. "I'm messing with you. I can't hear any difference."

He picked up the dish towel from the island and swatted her with it as she passed. Then, as he tidied up the kitchen, she picked around the wax to eat a little more of the pancakes. He wondered how to proceed with the day he had planned.

The easy silence transformed into a weighty one.

Cole cleared his throat. "So, um . . ."

"Hang on." She sat on a barstool across from him with the island between them. "Before you say anything, can I ask you something?"

"Of course."

"Whatever you have planned for my birthday . . . How would it work as a date?"

He swallowed hard. "Oh . . . um . . . yeah, I mean . . . if you want, we could . . . I mean, I guess since we almost . . . you know . . . But at the same time, are we sure that we . . ."

"Hang on, hang on." She leaned her elbows onto the marble surface and lowered her eyes until she caught his gaze of avoidance. "Don't self-destruct on me here. Let's just talk. It's just you and me, pal. Let's not freak out. Okay?"

Those warm green eyes of hers that always reminded him of the freshly cut grass of a well-watered lawn certainly helped calm the rising panic. "Okay." He took a step back and leaned against Seb and Brynn's giant farmhouse sink so he could put a little space between the two of them but keep looking at her. As long as he was able to see her reassuring smile—which he *knew* to be genuine because her eyes were crinkled to match—he knew they were okay. And as long as *they* were okay, he was okay.

"Okay," Laila echoed and relaxed back into the stool. "So here's what I'm thinking. I obviously don't want to spoil whatever you have in store for today—you know I love your birthday surprises—so feel free to veto if this is a bad idea. Because of my birthday or any other reason. But I was just thinking, okay . . ." Her eyes were still warm, and so were her cheeks, if the rapidly spreading pink splotches were any indication. "Obviously something's happening between us that . . . well . . . hasn't happened before. And we're thinking about things we don't usually think about, I guess. And I understand what you were saying about being afraid to mess us up. I really do. And you know I don't want that either. So yeah, we need to be . . . cautious, I guess? And let's face it, it's probably for the best that Drea—"

"You mean *Drea*."

Laila snorted and raised her hand up to cover her nose for a second, causing Cole to relax even more. If she was still comfortable enough to snort in his presence, they were fine.

"Sorry. My bad. It's probably for the best that *Drea* came in when she did. Even if . . ." She looked at him for a second and then lifted her shoulders to her ears. "Even if this is maybe something, we probably don't want to start by kissing and jumping too far ahead. That would make everything super awkward if this *isn't* something. Right?"

"I agree that may not be the wisest place to start," he concurred.

She nodded once, sharply. "Okay, then. So what if, just for one day, we pretend we don't have a lifetime of history and shared memories?"

He tilted his head in confusion. "How are we supposed to do that?"

"Um . . ." She chewed on her bottom lip and looked upward as she gave it more thought. "First date?" And then, more confidently, "Blind date. Set up by friends. We've never met." Her eyes rolled upward again, and she bobbed her head from shoulder to shoulder as she played it out in her mind. "Yeah. It could be fun. You know . . ." A huge, giddy grin broke free as she looked at him again. "What if you weren't Fox Books and I wasn't The Shop Around the Corner?"

It sounded insane to him, but when she was looking at him like that—with happiness that he figured had a *tiny* bit to do with him, laced with a fair amount of excitement that stemmed from the possibilities of the day but that was overwhelmingly based in thoughts of *You've Got Mail*—what was he supposed to do?

"I don't know your stories, and you don't know mine?"

"Right."

"And I just treat you like a woman I'm trying to impress on a first date?"

"Exactly."

"And you'll act like—"

"Okay, Cole, the rules aren't that difficult." She smirked at him. "Are you in?"

Either this was going to be a Laila birthday to beat all Laila birthdays, or he was going to be wishing for the good old days of the birthday when he nearly fell into the rapids trying to save her sunglasses after they fell off while she was vomiting over the side of the raft.

He looked at his watch and then back up at her with a matching smirk. "I'll pick you up in an hour."

CHAPTER TWENTY-ONE

LAILA

I really don't know why Cole and I had spent the better part of a week sharing a guest bathroom while we had the entire place to ourselves. Small-town rural manners, I guess. Even though Brynn's last words to us before they left had literally been, "Our casa is your casa." The kitchen and living room, our respective bedrooms, the guest bath, and a little bit of the roof. We hadn't explored any farther. But in our haste to get ready at the same time and my sudden desire to wear something—*anything*—that Cole hadn't seen me wear ninety times before, I had ventured into their master bedroom suite.

I had seen the promised land, crossed right on into it, and spent some time in its luxurious bathtub with more jets and candles and bath salts than I knew what to do with. And Brynn's closet? Holy haute couture, Batman. Not that fashion was my thing. Not in that way. No, I lived for cozy pants and flowing dresses and nearly threadbare sweatshirts. Brynn could have all those short skirts and sleek overcoats, and those entire walls of shoes. But to me it was sort of like opera. I didn't have to enjoy it to appreciate it.

I'd gotten Brynn's permission to raid her closet, but actually picking something out was a lot trickier. For one thing, she was America's Ray of Sunshine and dressed the part accordingly. She wore colors and patterns and flowers and looked amazing in all of it. And it wasn't that I shied away from any of that, necessarily, but the fact was, the most comfortable things I owned were wide-legged jeans and white T-shirts. Cole had told me to dress comfortably for our date, and that I didn't necessarily need to dress up for what he had planned. He was able to say that knowing that even though I was a casual dresser, I had a certain standard. I wasn't going to go out looking like a slob. (It was one thing to act like we didn't know each other for the rest of the day, but when it came to getting ready, I was really glad we had a shorthand.)

Like I said, I didn't want to dress in something he was used to seeing me in. But I didn't want to dress up too much and make him feel underdressed for . . . whatever.

Your closet makes me feel like I'm going to prom with The Wiggles.

Brynn responded to my text with a laughing emoji, followed immediately by a link to an article about the new purple Wiggle who was apparently a hottie beloved by Katie Couric. Then she said, Don't knock it. The Wiggles aren't just for kids anymore.

I was torn, of course. Not about The Wiggles. I'd moved on from The Wiggles before I even finished typing my jab to her—and before that, around the time I turned twelve. (Admittedly, I did hold on to my love for them a bit longer than I should have.) But I was torn as to whether I should ask for her fashion advice. I knew she could help me, and considering Drea was apparently involved, Brynn probably knew what Cole had planned for the day. But there was no way she knew the unexpected turn our plans had taken. She would *love* to know. That much was certain. And I would love to talk to her about it. Hopefully I would, soon. But whatever was going to happen needed to happen in the bubble of Cole and me first.

Still . . .

Okay, fashion guru. I can't believe I'm asking this, but what should I wear? Don't ruin any birthday surprises for me, but help! I wouldn't mind going a little outside of my comfort zone. #NYC But no Wiggle prom. Ideas?

Her face showed up on my phone a second after I sent the text, and I pushed the button to accept her FaceTime call.

Oh yeah. Technology.

"Hey."

"Hey, birthday girl!" she greeted me, and I immediately heard Sebastian shout, "Tell her I said happy birthday!" from another room. "Seb says 'Happy birthday,'" she obliged. "Have you seen anything you like?"

"Well, sure. There's lots of gorgeous stuff. But it's mostly gorgeous stuff that would look great on you. No offense."

She laughed. "Yeah, I'm super offended that you think I would look good in all those gorgeous dresses. How dare you!"

I rolled my eyes at her and then turned the camera into the closet. "Direct me. Is there anything . . ."

My voice trailed off as my attention was captured by the coziest-looking plain black sweater I'd ever seen, in a sea of dresses we only would have dreamed of for our Barbies when we were little. Actually, I was pretty sure I had made some miniature versions of these dresses for them, and that was when I just had a little beginner's sewing machine and had only mastered one seam, and our Barbies wore a lot of strapless pencil dresses and towel wraps. We were always pretending they were rushing out of the shower and getting ready for their big awards ceremony in the city, for which Ken would pick them up any moment.

Oh my goodness, Brynn grew up and became TV Superstar Barbie! We would need to discuss that scratching of the psychological surface later, but for now . . .

"I really like this sweater. I think it could look nice with some khakis or something. Do you think that would work?"

I pulled the hanger from the closet and held it in front of the phone for her to see. She gasped, and I assumed she was going to make some teasing remark about how positively *shocked* she was that I had chosen neutral colors. But I misinterpreted this gasp.

"Good choice, Lai! But it's not a sweater. It's a dress. And it will look amazing on you."

I was hearing her, but most of the words had been background noise that I would have to compute later. "This is a dress?" As a long sweater, I'd been dying to wear it. But, um . . . no.

"Okay, trust me on this. You have the cutest legs. Doesn't Laila have great legs, Seb?"

Sebastian let out one loud burst of laughter in the background. "What kind of fool do you take me for? I assure you, yours are the only legs I notice, sweetheart."

"It's just Laila. Her legs don't count as another woman's legs."

He deactivated his sugary, doting-husband voice and called out louder, "I honestly don't remember ever seeing you in anything that showed your legs, Laila. But I'm sure they're first-class legs!"

Brynn had been watching him over her shoulder and turned back to me as she snickered at him. "And I know it looks super short, but it's really not. It's about mid-thigh on me—"

"Mid-thigh!" I coughed. "I don't even like my bathing suits that short!"

"But that's on me! I'm taller than you, and my legs are longer. We're proportioned differently. Trust me on this. I think it will land just above your knees, and it will look great! And it's G. Label."

I tilted my head. "Is that supposed to mean something to me?"

"Goop. Gwyneth Paltrow's label."

"I do love Gwyneth."

"I know you do!"

My love for her had begun when she was dating Brad Pitt, though really that love had turned into more of an obsession over the way Brad's style and fashion always perfectly matched that of whomever he was dating, like he was *Single White Female*-ing them. Beyond that, I'd really liked *Shakespeare in Love*. And, of course, the television coverage of her ski-collision trial had been better than any limited-run series I had binged with my beloved Netflix subscription.

"Well . . . okay, hang on." I threw my phone across the room to the bed and quickly whipped my bathrobe—okay, *Brynn's* bathrobe—off and slipped the dress over my head. "This is so soft!" I called out.

"Let me see! Let me see!"

"Just a second." I pulled the ribbed material (wool/cashmere blend, the tag informed me) down along my curves (Yikes! I had curves in this thing!) until it landed just above my knees as Brynn had said it would.

"You shaved your legs, right?"

I laughed. "Yes, I shaved my legs." I jumped to the bed and grabbed the phone and then hurried back over to the mirror so she could see. "So? What do you think?"

She gasped again. "Oh, Lai. Yeah . . . you *have* to wear that. Seb, come give us a man's opinion."

I smoothed the material over my hips as Sebastian's face popped into view. "Yeah, that looks really pretty."

"And it's going to be seventy-one degrees there today," Brynn said from the corner of the screen. "A sweater dress is perfect for days like this. And it has pockets! It is truly a perfect dress."

"Thanks, guys. Better run. See you tomorrow?"

"Can't wait!" Brynn trilled. "Love you. Have fun!"

Once we'd ended the call I studied my reflection, looking for imperfections and not having to strain too hard to find them. Brynn had diplomatically said she and I were proportioned differently. Yeah . . . she was long and lithe while I'd always defined my legs as stumpy. My knees were sort of knobby and decorated by bruises and scratches and scars that were an unavoidable consequence of spending your life climbing things like trees and mountains and making your way back down to the ground with the help of harnesses and skis and sleds and, occasionally, a gunny sack and baby oil. (In a small town, children found all sorts of ways to entertain themselves.) I didn't have any desire to hide those imperfections from Cole. He was familiar with each and every one of them and had patiently listened to my complaints about all of them through the years. And of course there wasn't a scar he hadn't seen. In most cases he'd been there when I got it. In more cases than not his quick, thorough first-aid skills were to thank for those scars healing up as well as they did.

But I wasn't going to spend the day hanging out with my best friend. I had a date with a total stranger. And while I wasn't as confident about the cuteness of my legs as Brynn seemed to be, I had to admit the complete package I saw in the mirror came together pretty well. I almost always wore my hair up, but I was pleased with the way softer water, less humidity, and Brynn's fancy supersonic hair dryer had worked together to give me one of my better hair days, so I was just going to let it be. I'd tried to do my makeup like I would for a date, though it had been so long since my last date that I wasn't really sure if my face said, "First date! Nice to meet you!" or "What do you mean Adele doesn't still wear a beehive?" Now, all that was left were the shoes.

I pulled the bedroom door open and listened for a moment. "Are you out here?" I asked loudly enough for him to hear me if he was, but not so loudly that he'd hear me from behind closed doors. When I didn't hear anything, I ran on my tiptoes across the condo to my bedroom. I got inside and closed the door quickly and quietly behind me and then pulled my Cinderella pumps from my suitcase.

Okay, so there'd be a fair amount of walking. But I had spent countless hours in those shoes. My one elegant indulgence in a rough-and-tumble life. I'd be fine.

I slipped my feet into them, and everything in me went on high alert, all at once. My feet were so comfortable, and I *knew* my legs instantly looked longer, so I felt good about all of that. The only strange part was how—by simply slipping on those pink, glittery shoes that I had logged literal miles in since birthday number thirty-six—I suddenly felt ready to make a good first impression on the guy who'd bought me the shoes in the first place.

"This is weird," I muttered aloud to myself before slumping onto the edge of the tent bed and burying my forehead in my hands.

Were we making a huge mistake? I'd tried not to think too much about just how close we'd come to kissing—*so close*. But suddenly, without the clock ticking and without designer soap aromas clouding my brain and without the quietest hair dryer in the world causing me to question the little bits I had thought I understood about science, all I could see was the way his eyes had fluttered down to look at my lips as his head tilted toward mine, and all I could feel was his breath, warm and gentle, and all I wanted was—

"Ding-dong!"

"What do you want, blockhead?" I called out in response to his voice as I stood from the bed. I took a deep breath and glanced at my watch, grabbed my phone and little change purse from the dresser, and straightened the dress one more time. "Here goes nothing."

I stepped out of the room with a smile on my face and then looked around in confusion. "Where are you?"

"Ding-dong!" Cole repeated, though I couldn't quite compute where his voice was coming from. It sounded like a muffled shout from inside the wall.

"Cole? What are you—"

He altered his tactic. "Knock-knock!"

Just then, the elevator doors began opening, but he hurried to push the button to close them again from the inside and scooted over to get out of sight.

It finally dawned on me what was happening, and I hurried over to the elevator as I choked down the giggles that had begun bubbling up. I took a moment to compose myself again in front of the elevator—deep breath, straighten the dress, smile a normal smile rather than a "You're such a dork!" smile—and then pushed the button to open the doors. When they slid open, those giggles I'd choked down were replaced by a slight whimper, which I immediately attempted to cover, of course. All things considered, I think I did pretty well.

He was standing there in slim-fitting gray slacks and a V-neck black T-shirt under a black leather jacket. And he was wearing his wedding boots, of course. He loved those things. It was all his except for the jacket. When had he had time to get in there and raid Sebastian's closet? I'd been in their room almost the entire time.

No matter. *Wow.* He had shaved again, but his hair was loose and the waves were free, which I loved. I loved everything about the way he looked—always, but right then, especially. But it was the combination of all of that and the single red rose in his hand that had caused the whimper.

"Laila, I presume?" he asked, not moving from his position in the elevator. "I'm Cole. It's great to meet you."

"Um . . . yeah. You too."

"My friends told me you were beautiful, but you know how it is. They also said you're funny and smart and kind. All the things. You have to figure they exaggerated on some of it, right? They didn't prepare me for . . . *this.*" He held the rose out to me but still didn't take a step. "You're stunning."

Okay . . . apparently, we're doing this.

"And you . . . You look . . . great. *Really* great."

That was all I could manage to get out. For most of my life I had resisted any sort of attraction *because* it was Cole. It was going to be an interesting day, trying to resist all I was feeling and thinking and wanting because it *wasn't* him.

I couldn't move. I couldn't breathe. I hadn't even managed to reach for the rose. Bless him, he was doing a really good job of acting like I wasn't making things as awkward as I was. But then, a second later, when the elevator doors began closing again and his eyes darted to the side, unsure if he should push the button again or trust that I would do it (and that trust, of course, carried with it a very real threat of his arm getting crushed), I finally snapped out of it. He had committed fully to this silly idea I'd had. The least I could do was not leave him alone on the limb.

"I'm sorry! I'm being so rude." I pushed the button, and the doors opened again. "Would you like to come in for a minute?" I finally grabbed the rose and held it up to my nose to sniff. "And thank you for this, by the way. That's really sweet."

"My pleasure." Once he was free of the rose, he put both hands in the pockets of the jacket. "And thanks for the invitation, but we actually have some time-specific plans, so maybe we should . . ."

"Oh! Of course. Yeah . . . just let me . . . lock up?" I didn't want to break back into real life, but I had just realized that he had been in possession of Brynn and Seb's keys. I shrugged slightly, and I noticed his lip twitching.

"Great. Do you have everything you need?" I lifted the palms of my hands upward, and he nibbled on his lip to control the smile that wanted to break loose. "Are those your keys back there on the kitchen island? I wouldn't want you to forget those."

"Ah. Yes. My keys. I'll need those, won't I?" I spun on my heel and took a few steps until I could reach the keys. "Thanks." I spotted the bud vase I had used when I made him breakfast and impulsively grabbed it from the top of the fridge. "Sorry . . . just real quick . . ."

"Of course. Whatever you need to do."

I put some water in it and slipped the rose stem in. "There. I think I'm ready now."

"Um . . . those are some great shoes. *Really* great." His eyes were slowly making their way back up from my feet to my eyes, and my level of awkward self-awareness rose with them, like a thermometer on a telethon. "Just so you know, there is going to be a fair amount of walking today . . ."

"It's fine. I've logged a lot of miles in these shoes." *As you know very well.*

He shrugged. "I'm sure whatever you think is best will be great. But, you know . . . if you had a pair of Converse or something . . ."

I laughed. *Alright, then.* So much for subtlety and the ignorance of strangers. "Oh, well, now that you mention it . . ." I shook my head and hurried into my bedroom, kicked off my heels, and slipped on some socks and my pink high-top Chucks. At least we'd had one singular moment in our history in which my legs were dressed to impress.

"Better?" I asked as I reentered the space.

He smiled at me—mischievous, charming, and just so Cole Kimball. "You couldn't possibly go wrong. But I do feel better about not leaving you with blisters when I drop you off tonight." He gestured into the elevator. "After you."

"Thank you." I walked past him, his appreciative gaze warming me from head to toe and back again. Having to resist touching him, even in the casual, unthinking ways we always touched each other, was scintillating. Every breath had a different rhythm, and each word took careful consideration. Yet as he pushed the elevator button to take us to the ground floor, I was able to effortlessly interpret the twinkle in his eye.

He was having as much fun as I was.

"So, Laila . . . tell me a little bit about yourself."

CHAPTER TWENTY-TWO

COLE

He had planned such a Laila-specific day. Long—well, ninety or so hours—before they'd decided to play the game they were playing. The idea had begun percolating as he watched joy radiate from her at the *Friends* apartment building, and then every aspect of the maps he'd studied and the YouTube clips he'd watched late at night in his maid's quarters had been with the singular focus of creating a perfect day for her. At first, he'd been unsure whether the day could possibly translate to a first date sort of day, and the truth was that it wouldn't have if the date was with anyone in the world besides the one and only Laila Evangeline Olivet. He had no doubt there were other women in the world who would have enjoyed the things he had planned. But for a first date? For a first date, he would have been viewed as coming on way too strong. Or, quite likely, a needy psycho who was so desperate for love that he would accept nothing less than wearing the woman down into such a heap of exhaustion that she wouldn't notice when he moved a duffel bag of his stuff into her apartment at the end of the night.

But Laila? Laila was going to love it. True, he hadn't anticipated her wearing a dress when he first mapped out the day. He'd seen it as more of a jeans sort of day for them both, as most days were for the two of them. But now? Good luck ever convincing him that she hadn't been born to wear that dress.

As for all the other stuff, he knew that they would each choose to ignore the inconsistencies he'd created by morphing Laila's once-in-a-lifetime New York City birthday celebration with her best friend into a totally normal blind date with a stranger who probably wasn't a serial killer.

"I don't know if you're a big fan of romantic comedies . . ."

"Are you kidding?" They were hopping on the J train at Canal Street like it was the most natural thing in the world. He loved how good they'd gotten at riding the subway. "I love them."

"Can I tell you a secret?"

"Sure." They grabbed two empty seats in a mostly empty car. "Fire away."

She adjusted the hem of her dress and Cole fought the temptation to focus on her knees by observing and interpreting the smirk on her face. The one that clearly said, *Yeah . . . as if there's a secret I don't know.*

"I actually really love them too." Laila's eyes grew wide, and he delighted in being able to surprise her with something she hadn't known after all. "My best friend is obsessed with them, and sure, at first I was just humoring her, I think. She sat through movies I wanted to watch even if she had zero interest in them, so it was only fair. But somewhere along the line, I don't know what happened. So help me, it brings a tear of joy to my eye every single time Jennifer Lopez convinces some guy to leave his girlfriend for her."

Laila laughed. "Your secret's safe with me."

"I appreciate that." He looked up at the display screen to make sure he was keeping track of their stops. Only one more until they got off.

"What made you think about rom-coms?"

He shrugged. "I don't know. New York, I guess."

She sighed. "Yeah."

It would have been so easy to kiss her right then. To pick up where they had left off before Drea interrupted them that morning. There was room to spread out, but they hadn't made use of the space. They were side by side, arms touching, one more subway stop to go. But he'd only known this woman he was on a date with for approximately fifteen minutes now. It seemed a bit too soon for a gentleman to make a move.

They sat in silence to their stop, and then, as they began walking uptown, he asked her where she had grown up. Once again there was a slightly awkward smile as she thought through how to tell him about things he already knew. She began by telling him a few geographical specifics. The elevation. The location. An isolated area no one had ever heard of set between a bunch of places people paid a lot of money to visit. The population. The weather. She was in the middle of a sentence about Township Days when she stopped in her tracks on the sidewalk and her jaw fell open.

"Harry and Sally ate there."

Good. She'd spotted and instantly recognized Katz's Delicatessen. He'd been hoping it would happen that way. "That's right. Huh. That's pretty cool. Well, since we're here . . . what do you say? Want to go in and . . . grab a bite?"

He'd almost said, "Do you want to go in and have what she's having?" Thankfully he'd caught himself. That was another one of those fine-line things. To his best friend? Hilarious. To a blind date, twenty-five minutes in? Creep alert.

"I mean, I'd *love* to, but you said we have time-specific places to . . ." Realization dawned. She looked down at her feet and cleared her throat before whispering, "Yes, please." Her grin spread across her face as she raised her head to meet his eyes again. "Thank you," she mouthed to him.

"Hey, I hear they have good pastrami." He winked at her and she laughed—warm and rich and so full of joy.

Was it any wonder Laila's birthday was his favorite day of the year?

CHAPTER TWENTY-THREE

LAILA

"I think they're about to move."

Cole nodded. "Yeah, but Lady and the Tramp back there are gearing up to make a run for it. Do you think we can beat them?"

We were huddled at the table, Cole taking the final bites of his Reuben sandwich and me slurping my matzo ball soup. "Absolutely. Their lovey-dovey bit is ultimately going to be their downfall. Look at them. They can't stop touching each other."

"I see. You're proposing a little more man-to-man as opposed to zone."

"Exactly." I set down my spoon and took a sip of soda. "I think if you block them, I can use some offensive line to get in there and do some special-teams stuff before they even get out of the penalty box." Cole smirked at me, and I shrugged. "Whatever. Sports. Blah, blah, blah."

"Okay, then I'll deal with Lady and the Tramp while you go straight to Harry, Ron, and Hermione. Don't back down."

I stared at the three kids who had been in our crosshairs for nearly an hour. "They don't even know what they've got. It's just wrong."

The two boys and a girl (who actually looked like very nice kids whose parents I was half inclined to write a letter to commending them on raising such polite young people in this modern age) had been happily eating their sandwiches together, having a great time, about seven feet away from us. They were clearly Lower East Side kids who had walked there for lunch, lived in the neighborhood, and had an appreciation for delicious cured meats. But time was running out, and they were sitting at the *When Harry Met Sally* table. All I wanted was one decent picture at the iconic location and then Cole and I would be on our way.

But we'd figured out pretty quickly that almost everyone else at Katz's had the same aspirations. Most had come and gone. Many had just squeezed in a little too closely to our teen friends and snapped pictures anyway. But Lady and the Tramp, so named because they kept nibbling at dill pickle spears from opposite sides until they met in the middle, had waited it out.

But they hadn't been waiting as long as we had.

First date or no, Cole and I had been on the same wavelength longer than our friends from Hogwarts had been alive. That table would be ours.

"They're gathering their trash," Cole informed me through gritted teeth.

Of course they were. *Dear Professor McGonagall, or whoever is responsible for these delightful urban rats . . .*

"On it."

I picked up our tray and began heading toward the garbage can before turning back to ask Hermione if she knew where the restroom was. While she pointed to the back of the deli, I slid closer to their table to get out of the way of passing patrons. By the time I was thanking her and telling the kids to have a nice day, Cole was bending over to pick up a napkin he had dropped, providing me just enough time to slip into one of the chairs while Lady and the Tramp impatiently waited for him to stop blocking the aisle.

"Oh, pardon me," he said to them as he slipped into the chair across from me.

We both controlled our emotions and refrained from gloating apart from a soft fist bump under the table. Our rivals were fuming, standing there with their arms crossed, not looking too lovey-dovey at all.

"I almost feel bad," I whispered as I pulled my phone out of my pocket and began snapping photos. Cole leaned in and got his face in the pictures—over the table, in front of the neon sign, and with Lady and the Tramp in the background. I sat back in the chair and sighed happily as I flipped through the photos I had just taken. "This is amazing."

"Yeah . . . but I guess we should get going."

I stuffed my phone back into my pocket as Cole picked up our tray and we stood from our seats. We hadn't even stepped into the aisle before some totally new people swept in and stole the table out from under those we'd believed were set to inherit the Harry and Sally throne.

"Yikes." I spoke over my shoulder to him as we walked to the door. "Who knew romantic comedy was such a brutal blood sport?"

"Did you get some good pictures for your trouble?"

"I did." He held the door open for me, and I smiled up at him as we stepped out onto Houston Street. "If you want to give me your phone number later, I can send them to you."

CHAPTER TWENTY-FOUR

COLE

"This. Is. Incredible."

They'd hopped on and off trains like they knew what they were doing, walked like the city was theirs, and now they were standing in Central Park, staring at the Wollman Rink, one of the most famous ice-skating rinks in the world. Well, it would have been the Wollman Rink if it were winter. As it currently stood, at the end of September, it was the Wollman pickleball courts.

Cole couldn't help but agree. "The view's nice, that's for sure."

Laila turned her head and blushed when she caught him taking in the sight of her.

They were surrounded by the Plaza and Essex House and a whole host of other buildings he recognized without knowing what they were called, but he couldn't stop looking at *her*. She was leaning over the banister, looking down at the dozen or so pickleball courts where sweaty men and women of all ages and fitness levels were out there convincing themselves they were competing in a sport of champions rather than a friendly family game that he assumed was easier to pick up than Twister and that had less risk of injury. But Cole knew that in Laila's mind, she was seeing snow and gloves and John Cusack.

"This, of course," he said as he faced the rink again, "is the legendary spot where Harry and Marv hatched their dastardly plan to rob Duncan's Toy Chest in *Home Alone 2: Lost in New York.*"

Laila slapped him on the arm as she, too, faced forward. It was fascinating to him how more and more, the small, incidental gestures were impossible to discern as products of a lifetime of friendship or the best date either of them had ever been on. "Not you too."

"What?" he asked with a laugh.

"What is it with grown men and that movie?"

His pulse quickened again. That had been one of his favorite things about the day. They were doing a really good job holding to their personas as strangers, but he'd lost track of the number of times she had talked about him. Little things like that. *"Grown men." "My best friend." "This guy I know."* Even when they pretended not to know each other's stories, they were both part of all of them.

"It's a classic!"

"*Serendipity* is a classic."

Cole tapped himself on the forehead. "That's right. That was filmed here, too, wasn't it?"

She chuckled and began bouncing on her heels.

"Are you okay? Are you cold?" It was a perfect, beautiful warm day, but standing in the shade as they were now, there was a slight chill in the air.

"No. Just antsy."

"Antsy? Why?"

She shook her head. "It's stupid. I just sort of want to get out there."

Laughter exploded from him. "Out there? To play pickleball? In a dress?"

She shrugged. "Told you it was stupid."

He cleared his throat and shrugged his arms out of the leather jacket. He'd been too warm in it for most of the day, as he'd known he would be, but after a quick shower, he'd only had about forty minutes to run (literally) to the clothing store Sebastian had recommended. He'd used a credit card he had dutifully paid off every month since he was eighteen to buy a leather jacket in Tribeca, for heaven's sake. A leather jacket he would now be paying off for three to six months. And that was best-case scenario, considering he was now unemployed and adrift in his life.

And, sure, he probably could have borrowed something from Seb. But he knew there was a chance that Laila would get cold when they were walking home later that night. Actually, he was sure of it. And he would offer her his jacket as he had a million times before. And she would wear it. And then the jacket would faintly carry her scent with it. And there was zero chance he was going to let the scent of her on this day of all days die a slow death in Sebastian's closet or, worse, a fast one at the hands of a Tribeca dry cleaner. He couldn't think of a nobler reason to accrue a little frivolous debt for the first time in his life.

"No. It's not stupid." He folded the jacket over his left arm and stretched his right hand out to her. "Especially since we have a court down there reserved for the next thirty minutes."

She squealed and threw her arms around his neck, then jumped back once she realized what she'd done. "Sorry." She laughed, obviously trying to balance all the emotions and the rules.

"It's totally fine. I get excited about pickleball too."

CHAPTER TWENTY-FIVE

LAILA

An hour later, after I'd schooled my date in pickleball (or so I decided and Cole was too gentlemanly to argue about since, even after a delightful couple named Glen and Jeannie from Gramercy Park demonstrated more patience than we deserved in trying to teach us, we still didn't get it), we wandered through Central Park until we exited at Strawberry Fields on Central Park West.

(P.S. Pickleball is hard, and I am neither fit nor fierce enough to exist within its world.)

I just kept following his lead, having no idea where we were going and not caring one Ray Liotta.

Yes, I said "not caring one Ray Liotta." That was our blind date couple's first inside joke. It was strange being unable to make use of enough inside jokes to fill ten seasons of a sitcom, but when I said I didn't care one iota about *Breaking Bad*, and he misheard me, a new sitcom began.

As we walked across Seventy-Second Street, I asked him what he did for a living. It felt a little risky, because of course his best friend knew he didn't have a job at the moment. And his best friend was fully aware of the emotional landmine that existed within that topic. But to not ask would have been breaking the rules. Right? I'd chased off perfectly nice youngsters with this man I had just met. I'd traversed half of Manhattan with him. We'd taken countless ridiculous selfies together. And now we'd played pickleball under the watchful, bewildered, disappointed (though they were too kind to ever say it)

tutelage of Glen and Jeannie while I attempted to maintain my pro-
priety wearing a dress designed by Gwyneth Paltrow. (Maybe? I can't
honestly say I was clear about the role Gwyneth played in making
the dress.) In many ways it felt a little too late to find out if he was a
Chippendales dancer or bounty hunter or something.

"I'm a chef."

"Ooh, really?" I asked as we passed the Dakota. "Are you any
good?"

He gave this some serious consideration before answering, "Yeah,
actually. I am. I'm really good."

I bowed my head to keep my satisfied grin to myself. For so
long he'd insisted he was just a big fish in the small pond of Adelaide
Springs. He'd deflected praise by saying things like, "Beggars can't be
choosers." But I knew how good he was, and every satisfied customer
who'd ever eaten his food would only beg to differ.

"How'd you get started cooking? Is that just something you always did?"

"Sort of." He looked ahead of us and then behind as we came to
the intersection of Seventy-Second and Columbus Avenue, and then he
gently placed his hand on my back to usher me across the crosswalk. "I
was, um . . . Well, I guess my grandmother was my first teacher. And she
taught me that food is love." Our pace naturally slowed once we were
on the other side of Columbus, walking against the majority of pedestrian traffic on the sidewalk. "She used to tell me that when you didn't
know what else to do for someone, you should feed them. If they were
hungry, feed them. Cold, feed them. Sick, feed them. And sometimes
you just needed to feed them so they knew they weren't alone."

I smiled, remembering Eleanor. I hadn't ever heard her say those
exact words, but that was undoubtedly the code she had lived by.
I couldn't count the times she had gotten me to open up to her by
plying me full of cookies, or the times she had comforted me with a
bowlful of green chile stew.

"Were you raised by your grandmother?" I asked. And for whatever reason, it didn't feel awkward. It was the natural next question.

And for whatever reason, he didn't hesitate to answer it. "Mostly. Both of my grandparents, actually. My mom's mom and stepdad." I heard him release a contemplative breath as we walked side by side. "I don't know why I said that. The clarification of stepdad, I mean. He was the only dad she ever really had." He looked down at me and shrugged. "Sometimes the distinction seemed to matter to her, but I don't think it ever did to him."

"Why did it matter to her, do you think?"

"I don't know. But I always thought it was kind of sad. Because I'm pretty sure the distinction didn't matter to her when it came to how she felt about him. You know? He was her dad. But I think she always imagined that to him, she was only his stepdaughter. And I really don't think he ever saw her as anything other than his daughter." His voice was wistful. "And now he's gone, and I guess I wonder if all the worries are sort of frozen in place, for the rest of time."

I wanted to step in, knowing what I knew. I wanted to reassure him that Bill loved him and never thought of him as anything other than his grandson—because that was what we were really talking about, weren't we? He could see that pain in Cassidy, and he knew the truth in her situation, and he probably even knew the truth in his own relationship with Bill. But now Bill was gone, and the questions remained. I wanted to help him not be frozen there. But I couldn't do that today.

"Are you and your mom close?"

He chuckled softly. "I don't know. It's complicated, I guess."

"Sorry. If you don't want to talk about it—"

"No, it's fine." He nudged me gently with his elbow. "If you're sure you want to hear all of this."

A wave of nausea washed over me then. It was nothing major. Just an instant in which I felt clammy and had to focus on swallowing and breathing so I didn't hurl onto the steps of a brownstone on the Upper West Side. But then it passed, as quickly as it had appeared, and I was left to take stock of what had caused it.

The way he had nudged me just then—it was something he did all the time. It was something we did to each other on a daily basis, probably. And, I mean, it's not like I'm saying that was a special thing between us. It was just a nudge. Lots of friends nudge each other, I'm sure. I'm not claiming Cole and I had trademarked the elbow nudge and were going to sue Robin Thicke for elbow nudging Pharrell in the "Blurred Lines" video or anything. But it was so *us*. And right then, when he nudged me, it hadn't felt like us.

Again . . . sanity disclaimer: It hadn't *really* stopped feeling like us. We were playing a game. Conducting an experiment. Having a once-in-a-lifetime sort of day under unusual circumstances. At any moment I knew I could look at him and say, "Cole, I'm tired of this. I just need to hug my best friend," and he wouldn't hesitate to drop the pretense of being strangers and wrap his arms around me.

But when he nudged me as he was telling me his stories like couples in a new, exploratory relationship do, I'd felt something different for the first time. I hadn't felt like the girl he'd known since we were both in diapers, nor had I felt like the woman he'd nearly kissed this morning. I'd felt like some random woman in the future, on her first date with Cole Kimball. Some new, real, heretofore unmet woman whom Cole would tell his stories to. Whom Cole would share his pain with. Whom Cole would spoil with amazing surprises and open doors for and confide in and occasionally nudge with his elbow.

The nausea was gone, and it was the fear of an unknown future and jealousy of a thus far nonexistent great love that I had to swallow down. "Of course I want to hear all of this."

He looked ahead to the next intersection, just a few more rows of buildings away, and then stopped walking and pulled over to the side. He leaned his left shoulder against the beige bricks of an empty retail space, and I faced him, resting on my right arm just two or three feet in front of him.

"I'm adopted, right? And my mom . . . she's great. Seriously, she's a remarkable human being. I don't know all that much about my birth situation—I've honestly never had much interest in knowing—but I gather it wasn't so great. She saved me from . . . well, from who knows what."

I knew not to interrupt the silence as he watched people pass.

"But it's like *that* was her job. To save me from that other life. To bring me into a better one. And I'm so grateful she did that. But I'm pretty sure that was the end of the job for her. She didn't want to be a mother. She just wanted to do her part to make the world better, one person at a time, and once I was all squared away, she could move on to the next."

He scoffed and looked down at his feet. "What an awful thing, huh? Bless his heart, the poor little unwanted newborn who was given a home and loved and cared for . . ." He raised his eyes and met mine. "I've had a really great life so far, and I genuinely have nothing to complain about. I'm grateful for birth parents who, whatever the circumstances, made sure I had a chance at life, and I'm so grateful that my mother chose me—even if it was a choice between adopting a child or sending in a lot of money during the PBS pledge drive."

He chuckled and I joined him as I wiped away a forming tear as discreetly as I could.

"And I'm definitely grateful for grandparents who gave me the most loving home and friends who . . . well, who were closer than family, and a weird little town of some pretty strange people who helped make life pretty much as good as it can be. I don't know." He shook his head and rubbed his eyes roughly. "I guess it's just that I'm thirty-nine years old, and I suddenly don't know what I'm supposed to do with my life. And I want to blame other people for that. Somewhere deep inside, I'm *wishing* I could blame other people for that. But I have no one to blame but myself. I think I've . . ." His voice trailed off, and he looked down at his boots again. "I think I've always felt like I should be grateful. I just needed to be grateful. And I was. I *am*. But—"

"But it's hard to let yourself want anything when you've spent your entire life just counting your lucky stars for what you have."

His eyes locked with mine again as he breathed, "Yeah."

I offered him a half smile and just tried to stay present for him. To not think about how he had never said all of that to me before. At least not in that way. I guess if I'd been keeping better track—better records, maybe, to keep details and emotions from getting lost—the bits and pieces from an entire lifetime probably should have added up to knowing what he was feeling.

No . . . I *did* know. Knowledge wasn't the problem. But when a conversation about his mom took place weeks or months apart from a low day when he was really missing Eleanor, and then another year passed before he said something wistful about loving Adelaide Springs but wondering what life might have been like if he'd been able to forge his own identity away from an entire population of people who knew more about his past than he had ever cared to learn . . . And then when his grandfather died and he was suddenly robbed of the life that, in his eyes, he'd been gifted with, and which it would have been disrespectful not to want . . . And when his best friend could only think of how much she would lose if he were to explore any other possibilities for himself . . .

No. Knowledge wasn't the problem.

I reached out with the hand that was against the wall and wrapped my pinky and ring fingers around the same fingers of his as they dangled limp. "I know we don't really know each other, but do you mind if I say something?"

Cole smirked and curled his fingers into mine. "Are you kidding? After I just spewed my whole life story at you on our first date? You can say whatever you want."

I took a deep breath and looked down at our hands. "It sounds like there are a lot of people who really love you. And that makes sense. You seem to be a pretty great guy." I raised my eyes and peeked at him through strands of hair cascading over my face, and he smiled warmly at me before reaching out to tuck the strands behind my ear. I leaned into the palm of his hand and lifted my chin. "And it sounds like you've spent a lot of time taking care of those people. Between your gratitude and believing that food is love, and . . ." I sniffed. "And all those things. But I'm pretty sure none of those people would forgive themselves if they, even accidentally, held you back. From . . . whatever. From whatever it is you want."

"But that's the thing, I guess. I have no idea what I want. Not really. I know I need something different, but as for what that may be . . .'"

"And so *that's the thing*. It's time to figure it out. And I'm pretty sure the people who love you are still going to love you. And they're going to cheer you on. And they're going to be so proud . . ." I sniffed again and swallowed down as much of the emotion as I could. "They're going to be proud of *you*. Whatever you do. Wherever you do it. You're not betraying anyone by taking care of yourself for a change. I'm pretty sure that's exactly what everyone who loves you would *want* you to do. It's just that sometimes it's easy to lose track of where we end and someone else begins, I think. When we've never really known anything else except who we are together."

I knew I'd lost the blind-date thread. He knew it, too, if the smirky grin on his lips and the moisture shimmering in his eyes were any indication.

"Anyway, I'm rambling. Mostly I just want to say thank you for sharing that with me."

"Well, you're a really good listener. I couldn't help myself."

We stayed there a few seconds more, staring at each other until the awkwardness of being caught between not knowing what the blind-date version of us was supposed to do next and avoiding what the lifelong-friends version of us felt came naturally—hugs and food, most likely—became too much and we started laughing.

"Okay." Cole gently squeezed my fingers in his and then dropped my hand and stood up straight. "Shall we continue on?" He looked at his watch. "We have a little more time until we need to be at our next time-specific destination."

My eyes flew open. "Wow. So this really is an all-day thing you've got planned here."

He grinned at me and then chuckled softly to himself. "Coming on kind of strong for a first date, aren't I? I'm sorry."

I shook my head. "No. It's great. Best first date I've ever been on."

Best date, period. Maybe the very best day. Just when I thought Cole Kimball and I couldn't get any better.

"Same here." He caught his bottom lip between his teeth and eyed me inquisitively. "Are your feet doing okay?"

I glanced down at my pink high-tops and back again. "They're great. Though, again, this wasn't exactly the look I was going for."

"This look works for you. Though, really . . ." He whistled soft and low through his teeth, and an appreciate gaze traveled up my bare legs and back to my eyes. "It's difficult to imagine you wouldn't look great in anything."

I scoffed as we continued on Seventy-Second. "I don't know about that. My wardrobe of choice is usually a little more . . ."

So, that ellipsis up there indicates that my words drifted off. Just dissipated into the air like vapor. Yeah . . . that wasn't what happened as we reached the corner of Seventy-Second and Amsterdam Avenue and I spotted the Gray's Papaya sign. My words just kind of stopped. My words and my breath and time itself all just kind of stopped.

I hurried around to the Amsterdam Avenue side of the corner building and pointed at the window. "Tom and Meg had a hot dog right there. They stood *right there*, on the other side of that glass, and ate a hot dog. This is where Kathleen told Joe she was meeting NY152 in Riverside Park. You know? At the end? Almost the end. Like, this was the build-up to 'I wanted it to be you so badly.'"

I indulged in a little *You've Got Mail* freak-out and squealed right there in the middle of the sidewalk. Loudly enough that a passing group of tourists jumped and scurried down the street away from me. I called out, "Kathleen Kelly and Joe Fox ate a hot dog here!" as the only form of apology I could conjure. "Cole, do you remem—" *Blind date. Blind date. Blind date.* "I mean, have you ever seen *You've Got Mail*?"

Who knows? Maybe this man I had just met had also been part of a group of adolescent friends who had convinced one of their mothers to drive across the snowy mountain pass to drop them off at the movie theater two hours away on the day after Christmas in 1998 so they could watch *Prince of Egypt* and *A Bug's Life* back-to-back. And maybe when *Prince of Egypt* was sold out, my date's friends had gone to see *You've Got Mail* instead. And maybe my date was such a good guy—I mean, he *seemed* really nice—that when the other three friends decided to skip *A Bug's Life* and sneak into the R-rated *Bride of Chucky* instead, he decided to sit with his very best friend—who was a little younger and a lot more timid—through a repeat viewing of a romantic comedy he hadn't wanted to see in the first place.

And maybe he and his best friend had also had endless, ongoing, running-gag sorts of jokes about *You've Got Mail*. Maybe it was a Christmas tradition for them to watch it. Every single year for more than half their lives at this point. Maybe through the years he had given her bouquets of freshly sharpened pencils and copies of the Shoe books by Noel Streatfeild (S-T-R-E-A-T-F-E-I-L-D). Maybe they still occasionally complimented things by saying they were as frothy as a triple latte, because that had been some reviewer's quote on the VHS copy of the movie. And maybe he'd indulged in his friend's silly attempts to recreate the song where Greg Kinnear sang about the horn sounding so forlorn, all while acting like he'd never cared much for that movie. I mean, sure . . . it was a long shot. But maybe he, too, had done all of that.

If a guy really loved his best friend, that was just the sort of stuff he might do.

I turned back to face him, and of course he was watching me and smiling. *Of course* he had his phone out, filming my joy for his personal archives as he had for nearly as long as I could remember, beginning with an old Panasonic VHS-C camcorder. And of course he had brought me here on purpose.

"I don't even know what to say." I balled my hands into fists to try to keep from running and tackling him in a hug. "Other than 'Why are you filming me, you weirdo?'"

He laughed. "Admittedly what's happening right now could raise some first-date red flags, if not for a few very important details."

I crossed my arms and cocked my hip out. "I'm listening."

"Well, number one, I took you for a *You've Got Mail* fan from the beginning. And you just confirmed my suspicions, so I'm doing okay so far."

"True though that may be, I haven't heard any solid justification for the voyeurism yet."

He coughed out another laugh and then wiped the little bit of spit that had escaped from his mouth off of his phone and onto his pant leg. "Well, then you clearly aren't the *YGM* devotee I credited you with being. Either that or you haven't looked behind me yet."

I looked across Amsterdam Avenue, but I didn't see anything familiar. He tilted his chin the other way, to the other side of Seventy-Second Street. I noted an interesting-looking subway entrance. At least that's what I assumed it was. And a sign that said Verdi Square, but that didn't mean anything to me. Although . . . there was something sort of familiar about the tree in the corner of the fenced-in area, right where two sidewalks intersected . . .

In the nanosecond before my brain made the connection, Cole's phone began blaring music at full volume.

"No way!" I squealed, my recognition and comprehension complete. I grabbed his hand and performed a dangerously felonious amount of jaywalking, pulling him behind me, leaving a trail of ecstatic giggles (me) and "Dreams" by The Cranberries (him).

Though it's unfathomable to me, I suppose there might be some people in the world to whom all of that would mean nothing. People who (let's call it like it is) have more going on in their lives than I did and hadn't rewatched their five or six favorite movies literally to the point of having every line of dialogue and every note of the musical score memorized. But, again, I am not those people. The moment I heard the cymbal buildup at the beginning of "Dreams," I was picturing Tom Hanks and Meg Ryan just missing each other again and again and again as they traversed the same paths and basically walked the same steps on their respective journeys to work on Manhattan's Upper West Side. And the best shot of the whole sequence took place right where we were standing.

I caught my breath from the traffic-violating dash and stared with something akin to veneration at the spot where the sidewalk diverged. "Manhattan should rename this spot."

"The intersection of Joe Fox Lane and Kathleen Kelly Boulevard?"

I slung my hand over his shoulder and sighed. "Lowest-hanging fruit of all time."

CHAPTER TWENTY-SIX

COLE

They walked around the city for another couple of hours like that. Happy. Laughing. Uproariously so, really. Everything was fun, and everything was funny. Carefree. Giddy. From their attempts to film their recreations of the *You've Got Mail* sequence (which proved very difficult to do with neither the acting chops of Ryan and Hanks nor a separate camera operator) to their attempts to order hot dogs to their satisfaction (which proved impossible since the chaos of a crowded space and thick New York accents somehow resulted in their ordering sauerkraut, relish, and ketchup, which was pretty disgusting to a couple of Coloradoans), everything seemed sprinkled by magic dust.

So much so that by the time they needed to head back to Brynn and Seb's, Cole didn't want the date to end. He wasn't quite ready to say goodbye to their magical land of make-believe.

"So, I know this is awfully forward of me on a first date, but I was wondering if you might like to come back to my place." Even with all their joking and all of their suspension of disbelief (and never mind that they had shared a bed just a few nights ago, and a couple dozen times before that), he wasn't comfortable with the way that sounded as it left his mouth. "For dinner, I mean. I just . . . I thought I might make you dinner."

The sun had set nearly an hour ago by the time they stepped out of the Franklin Street station and began heading back to North Moore Street. Laila was wearing his new leather jacket, as Cole had predicted she would be, but she was still fighting a chill. The too-big jacket was wrapped around her as tightly as she could get it, and she was squeezing her arms while bouncing just slightly with every step.

"I'm not really the type of girl who goes back to a guy's apartment on a first date."

"And I'm usually not the type of guy who asks. But truth be told, I'm not quite ready to say good night yet. Besides, I'm famished. Who would have thought a disgusting hot dog would be so unfulfilling after walking about ten miles in a day?"

"And playing pickleball."

"Yes! Pickleball. Though I guess we did eat a mountain of actual pickles, too, not to mention enough deli meat to stock a Jimmy John's franchise for a week or so."

Their pace slowed as they turned left at the *Ghostbusters'* fire station.

"So what do you say? I promise to behave like a perfect gentleman."

"No funny business?"

He grinned. "No funny business."

Laila sighed dramatically. "Well, I guess I could text a friend or something . . . let them know where I am. Just to be safe."

Cole nodded. "That would be wise. I mean, *I'm* fairly certain I'm not a serial killer or anything, but you have no way of knowing that."

"Yeah. You can't be too safe." She stopped walking and released her arms from her hands' warming grips before reaching into the pocket of her dress to pull out her phone.

He attempted to keep a straight face as she was managing to do, but it wasn't easy. Not when she was making a point of turning her phone away from him and looking up over the screen at him on occasion as she typed, surveying him warily. And not when the truth was he was excited and terrified to be alone with her after the day they had had.

His own phone dinged in his pocket, making the first unsolicited sound it had made all day. In fact, he was somewhat confused as to why it was making its presence known now. He'd put it in Do Not Disturb mode before "picking her up" that morning, not wanting anything to interrupt their day. But he felt like he needed to look at it now. In Do Not Disturb, he had it set to receive only notifications from his emergency contacts. Now that his grandfather was gone and he and the staff at Spruce House wouldn't be calling, that left only Sebastian (not Brynn since she had delighted a little too much in her emergency-contact status and abused her unrestricted access), his mother, and . . .

Of course.

He swallowed down a chuckle as he pulled out his phone. And Laila, of course, remained stone faced and serious.

Hey, it's me. Soooo I'm on a date with this really great guy. Like REALLY great. He's super cute and nice, and we've had the best time today. And he wants to cook me dinner at his place, which is maybe not a great idea, but did I mention how cute he is? Anyway, I'm sure everything will be fine. I'll text you later and let you know I'm okay. I guess track my phone and call the cops if you don't hear from me. Love you!

Cole swallowed down another chuckle, but it became something else as it made its way back down. Some sort of heavy sentiment that made everything tricky and yet mind-numbingly simple, all at the same time. Her text was a joke, of course, but it was also the most significant thing in his life. He really was her trusted person. The one she really would text if she ever found herself in this sort of situation with some other guy.

But he couldn't reply like he would in that scenario. Actually, he had no idea *how* he would reply in that scenario. A week ago, what would he have said?

Have fun! Don't do anything I wouldn't do.

Not a chance. Or, who knows, maybe that was what he would have said. And then *he* would have abused *his* access and tracked her phone, right then and there, since they each had set up that ability for each other. He wouldn't have wanted to get in the way of her evening, but he would have needed to know she was okay. He sure wouldn't have gone to sleep until he heard from her again.

Funny, though. He was pretty sure he wouldn't have been jealous.

His problem, a week ago, wouldn't have been with the fact that Laila was out with some "cute" and "nice" guy with whom she'd had the best time. But now? Thankfully, the guy was him, but he couldn't ignore the tightening in his gut and the throbbing in his temples that accompanied the thought of it being anyone else.

Needless to say, he didn't know how to process any of that. He also felt totally fine about making that a future Cole problem. He was still on a date with a super-cute, super-nice girl with whom he was having the best time. So he sent the only appropriate response he could think of to his very best friend in the whole wide world.

New phone. Who dis?

Laughter exploded from Laila as her phone lit up, lighting up her face nearly as much as the smile itself.

"Okay, that's all squared away." She tucked her phone back into the pocket of her dress and stuffed her hands into the pockets of his jacket. "The cavalry has been notified. I would love for you to make me dinner, if you're sure it's not too much trouble."

"It would genuinely be my pleasure." They smirked at each other for a moment, and then she started bouncing again in an attempt to warm up. "We'd better get you inside."

They began walking the length of the remaining three buildings that stood between them and the Sudworths' (which had been Laila's place this morning when he picked her up and was going to be his now for dinner, but they would just ignore that little inconsistency), and Cole finally got the nerve to do something he'd been fighting the impulse to do since they sat on the downtown 1 train leaving Sixty-Sixth Street–Lincoln Center. He put his arm, bare below his T-shirt sleeve, around her shoulder and pulled her against him. She had the jacket, but he had the warmth, and though they kept their pace, he felt her melt into him.

He put his arm around her all the time. Often to help keep her warm. Sometimes for nothing more consequential than that after all these years, having his arm around her was every bit as comfortable as having it dangle by his side. She would usually wrap her arm around his waist in response. Sometimes, when the embrace was more temperature oriented, she would curl up into herself before curling up into him, and then he would wrap his other arm around her back and rub away the chill. But this was different. He watched, out of the corner of his eye, as she hesitated briefly, then pulled her opposite hand out of the jacket pocket and lifted it up to his hand resting on her shoulder. Instinctively they laced their fingers together and caressed the outlines of each other's hands with their loose thumbs.

They climbed the four steps of the black metal entry together and stopped in front of the building's locked door, illuminated by the streetlights and the lights of the city reflecting off the clouds in the sky. Cole's arm still around her shoulders, Laila pivoted toward him.

"Did I tell you it's my birthday?"

He swallowed hard as her breath danced across his chin and her body settled against his hip. "Today?" He cleared his throat as subtly as he could and was thankful when his voice came out stronger the next time he spoke. "No, you didn't. Happy birthday. I hope it's been a good one."

Laila reached into the pocket of her dress with her free hand and then slipped Brynn and Sebastian's key into Cole's free hand, since this was now his apartment.

"Possibly the best birthday ever," she whispered against him.

"Possibly?" Cole tilted his head toward her and rested his forehead on hers as Laila's eyes fluttered shut.

"Well, I haven't peed since the Upper West Side, so if that doesn't happen pretty soon, this birthday may be memorable for less enjoyable reasons."

Oh good grief. He chuckled and planted a quick kiss on her forehead before unlocking the door so she could run inside to the elevator. When he was a little too slow locking the door behind them, she called out, "I hope you don't mind catching the next one!" as the elevator doors shut.

Now there was the Laila Olivet he knew and loved.

CHAPTER TWENTY-SEVEN

LAILA

"Oh, Cole . . ." I stood in awe of the twinkly lighted wonder before me as I stepped out the glass door and onto the roof. "How did you . . . *When* did you do this?"

"Let's just say I have very important friends with at least one very bored personal assistant who was willing to spend her day—" He tilted his head and shook his hands in front of him. "Actually, now that I hear it aloud, scratch that. Since I just invited you to dinner about ten minutes ago, definitely a little problematic that there were preparations taking place all day. So, um . . . it's always like this?" The upturned hands accompanying the upturned lips and voice made me giggle.

"Nice save." I nodded and patted him on the arm. "Yep. Super smooth. *Totally* not giving me new-undercover-cop-being-thrown-into-the-deep-end-on-his-first-day-on-the-job vibes."

Wow. It really was breathtaking. We'd made it up to the roof once before, while we ate our breakfast on Tuesday morning, and even then, the view had captivated me. Much of the city was intentionally blocked by trees and shrubs and artistic gallery-worthy designs of . . . well, trees and shrubs, allowing for privacy and seclusion, right there in the wide-open spaces of the concrete jungle. But of course that only blocked out the buildings that were roughly the same height or shorter. Tribeca boasted and was surrounded by many, *many* buildings taller than seven stories high.

One World Trade, for one. It was as majestically displayed from

Brynn and Seb's home as Snowshoe Mountain, at just over twelve thousand feet in elevation, was displayed from the front porch of mine. But at night? At night my mountains were lost to me until the morning, while the wonders that surrounded me now, much like the city they inhabited, didn't really seem to come alive until the sun went down.

The night air had a party atmosphere to it, thanks in part to the music coming from . . . somewhere. It could have been from a local party or a nearby restaurant, but wherever it was, it sounded like the sort of party Cole and I wouldn't have hated going to. Ed Sheeran was blasting (as much as you ever really blasted Ed Sheeran) at that particular moment, so it didn't exactly sound like a rager. It was the perfect soundtrack for the atmosphere.

And then there were the decorations that Cole seemed to have had more of a hand in. Edison bulbs were strung from side to side and back again across the expanse of the roof, creating the perfect subdued lighting with a gorgeous yellow tint. Not the sort of yellow tint that made you wonder if someone's kidneys were failing. The kind that created that soft sepia hue that was so much more flattering than jaundice.

Brynn and Seb had more furniture on their roof than I had in my house. The space was clearly designed for entertaining, and it wasn't difficult to imagine the fancy, famous people who would inhabit the space as guests of our fancy, famous friends. But tonight the spotlight—metaphorical and literal, in the form of fairy lights suspended as if by magic—was on a table set for two. Nearby stood a giant stainless steel grill that looked ready to be put to work.

My mouth began watering at the thought of eating some of Cole Kimball's legendary BBQ, just as Cole had been drooling over the entire outdoor kitchen, with its rotisserie and smoker and wood-fired pizza oven and running water, since Tuesday morning. Outdoor heaters taller than either of us, with dancing flames creating almost a lava-lamp effect, surrounded the dining area, raising the temperature of the outside air enough even where we stood, still by the door, to chase away the chill. Although, who was I kidding? It wasn't propane that was making every nerve ending in my body tingle with warmth.

He'd done it for me. Okay, he'd gotten Brynn to get Drea to do it. But . . . for *me*. This was planned before we nearly kissed that morning. Before we hatched the blind-date plan. Before he picked me up and gave me a rose and snuck appreciative glances at my legs all day—some of which had been done for comic effect, but also sincere ones he'd thought I hadn't seen—and before our experiment of a day succeeded in, as far as I was concerned, the best ways possible. He'd done it for me.

And I was in love with him.

Not because he had treated me like a queen all day. Not even because he treated me like a queen most days. I was in love with him because this was who he was. I'd lived an entire life of all the good and all the bad with him, and even when he was feeling lost, and even when his heart was breaking, and whether he was treating me like a stranger or the person he knew better than anyone, this was who he was. He was wonderful and kind and caring and so selfless, and he had spent who knew how much time researching and mapping out movie filming locations to the point of knowing where he was going and leading me effortlessly through a city he didn't know any better than I did, all while possessing basic navigational instincts that were far inferior to mine.

Didn't that mean he was in love with me too? Not *because* he did that. Not exactly. But because . . . because . . . I don't know. Because how would any other woman ever be able to live with him caring about me that much? There was no point trying to insist to myself any longer that when some other woman came along, I'd be fine. It was *me*, right? For him, it was always going to be me. Just like for me, it was always going to be him.

"Well, happy birthday." He stepped toward the dining area, extending his arm to usher me forward. "I sure am glad I happened to have this all set up and ready to go. So, tell me . . . do you like steak?" He hurried over to the kitchen and began washing his hands. "You're not a vegan or anything, are you?" he asked over his shoulder. "I'd say I'm a relatively humble guy overall, but there's no point denying I grill a mean rib eye."

The playful grin was still on his lips as he turned around, towel in hand, but it fell away in pieces, like the way I cracked an egg. I still hadn't moved from the spot, having not followed his guidance to move farther in, and he hadn't noticed until right then. It was also right then, I assumed, that he noticed I didn't seem to be in the same playful spirit he was.

"Laila? You alright?"

I stepped toward him then. Slowly. One step. Another. One more. Did I dare take a fourth? Everything had changed and yet nothing had changed. At this point we could still wake up tomorrow morning and act like we were Bobby Ewing in the shower on *Dallas*. The entire season had been a dream. Or, more likely, we wouldn't pretend it hadn't happened, but we would be just scared enough by our feelings to try to minimize everything. He still hadn't touched me in any ways I hadn't been touched by him before. It just felt a little different. The pacing. The lingering. The fire beneath the skin. And we still hadn't said any new words, even if the words now possessed more complex layers.

"Will you do something for me?" I asked.

He twisted the towel between his hands, drying, and I watched his throat constrict, shadows of New York bouncing off him beneath the lights. "Who's asking? My date or my best friend?"

"Does it matter?"

He swayed his head gently from side to side and then set the towel down on the countertop behind him. "Well, sure."

"So what would you say if it's your date asking?"

"I'd probably say I'd be happy to, if I at all can."

Breath shuddered in my chest. "And if I'm asking as your best friend?"

Cole took a step forward. "There isn't anything I wouldn't do for you, Laila Olivet."

The force of his words—*my* words to him, less than a week ago—rushed at my senses, clearing away the muck and mire.

"Kiss me."

The two syllables were barely out of my mouth and I had not yet had the opportunity to inhale after them before his hands were cupping either side of my face, his fingers were spreading out into my hair, and he was pulling me to him. My head tilted as my lips parted for breath in the instant before my eyes closed, and then opened again. I wanted to see him. I needed to see how he was looking at me. I needed to know that he was sure and that there would be no regrets. I needed to know, as he had said only hours earlier and yet somehow a lifetime ago, that this wouldn't ruin us. I needed to know that we hadn't spent the day so far detached from our reality that the gravity of the situation had momentarily escaped us.

I didn't know what I was looking for, exactly. There wasn't a sign that I knew to be on the lookout for. We'd made a lot of deals through the years, but an escape plan for an errant, ill-advised kiss when we were pretending to be on a blind date was not something we'd prepared for. But when I saw the familiar smile creases appear around the outer corners of his eyes in the instant before our lips touched, I knew, and my eyes fluttered shut. My arms dangled at my sides, lifeless and numb, as everything changed and we passed the point of no return.

His mouth teased me, brushing against my bottom lip and then disappearing . . . again . . . one more time . . . creating agony and ecstasy that I knew I'd never recover from. I didn't know what to do with my hands, and I could hardly feel them anyway, but when Cole lowered his fingers and brushed them gently down my neck, followed the outline of my shoulders and down my arms, still covered in his jacket, and then slipped his hands under the jacket and around my waist, it was the most natural thing I'd ever done to place my hands on his chest. My fingers, of their own free will and suddenly very much alive, inched their way up to his shoulders, fascinated by the feel of him.

And still his lips teased mine with care and consideration, as if trying to make up for so many years of ignoring this previously unexplored part of me. A rare aspect of me that wasn't familiar to him. Again . . . torturous ecstasy. Exhilarating agony. I whimpered against his lips and dug my fingernails into his shoulders as a means of survival, and it suddenly seemed he had taken, in his view, an adequate amount of time introducing himself to and becoming acquainted with my lips. From that moment on, they were his.

His hands were in my hair again and I gasped—though I don't think the gasp ever made it into the open air—as he conquered the last vestige of uncertainty between us. I slipped my arms up, bending my elbows on his shoulders and hooking them forward until my hands were in his hair, cupped up over his head, pulling him down. I needed more of him. I needed to make up for lost time and store up for the uncertain future, and I *needed* him to never stop kissing me. It was like riding a frantically spinning ride at a carnival. You feel the damage being done to your equilibrium, but as long as you're spinning, you can ignore the effects you know are to come and just hang on for dear life and get lost in the explosion of your senses. It's not until the ride stops that you're unsure if you can still walk straight.

I needed him to never stop.

CHAPTER TWENTY-EIGHT

COLE

It was absurd to him now that he'd never imagined what it would be like to kiss her. At least not before this week. It was absurd to him now that he'd been walking beside her, eating beside her, offering a shoulder to her, laughing with her, living life with her for . . . what? Twenty-seven years since he'd really started caring about girls as a separate exciting entity? And never once had he imagined this.

Of course if he had imagined it, he was doubtful he would have imagined it quite like this.

Shouldn't it have been awkward? He and Laila were quickly approaching four decades of friendship, and the bond they'd developed in that time should have made him so tentative to skim her swollen bottom lip with his teeth as he was doing now. He should have wanted to dart his eyes away rather than study every tiny golden speck hiding in hers. He shouldn't have felt comfortable enough to make jokes, and yet the first words out of his mouth were, "You were asking as my best friend, weren't you? Because I'm really not the type of guy who makes a move on the first date."

She laughed, gently at first, and then they got lost in a fit of hilarity together. She lowered her forehead onto his shoulder, and he removed his hands from her waist, adjusted the jacket to make sure she was still benefiting from its warmth, and then wrapped his arms around her back.

No, he wasn't the type of guy to make a move like this on the first date, and until the thoughts and feelings for her began invading his brain against his will this week, he would have sworn he also wasn't the type of guy to make a move like this after nearly forty years. But maybe it was all about the glorious law of averages.

Not that the word *average* had any place in a conversation about what was happening between them.

Cole sighed. "As much as I hate the thought of talking about . . . well, anything, really, I suppose we should . . ." Laila raised her head and met his eyes, and he didn't have any difficulty recognizing the dread—fear, maybe?—in them. He really should have started that sentence better. "Eat. Food. Talk about dinner. That's all I meant. I suppose we should eat something."

She exhaled as relief flooded her eyes. "Oh. Yeah. Food would be good."

They were going to have to talk about other things. Eventually. Soon. And he didn't feel much hesitation about that. It was more that he genuinely had no idea where they would go from here. They couldn't go back as if it had never happened. At least he couldn't. He would never want to. But nothing else had changed. She needed to stay in Adelaide Springs. He needed to leave. She had contentment there. And family. He didn't. She saw home and happy memories everywhere she looked, and he was afraid he'd never again see anything but rejection and pain. Yeah, nothing had changed. Nothing . . .

Except for everything.

But for right now, he was still on a rather spectacular date with the most beautiful woman he had ever seen in his life. And he had promised her dinner.

$\sim$

"So here's a question for you," Laila began just after she swallowed her final bite of rib eye and washed it down with a sip of Pinot Noir Cole had grabbed from the Sudworths' wine refrigerator. He'd hesitated briefly, hoping it wasn't some vintage bottle that cost as much as his Jeep Wrangler, but he'd taken a gamble on how well he thought he knew his friends. Sure, he'd learned all sorts of things this week—Ryan Reynolds and maid's quarters and chauffeurs named Malik sorts of things—but he'd be less surprised to wave up to Ryan Reynolds and Blake Lively as they flew with capes overhead, checking in on their old stomping grounds, than he would be to discover that Brynn and Sebastian were wine-investment people. And of course he could have texted one of them and asked, but that would have required inviting other people into the world he and Laila had created, and there was no chance of that happening.

"Fire away."

"Were you attempting to murder me with the deliciousness of that dinner? I mean, you can be honest. Did you think that if you made it good enough, I would just keep eating until I exploded? Because if so, clearly your only miscalculation was in how much meat you needed to have on hand."

It was true that she'd eaten a lot. More than he had, truth be told. But that had come as absolutely no surprise to him. For one thing, walking around Manhattan all day, those spectacular legs of hers had taken double the steps to keep up with his longer stride. She had probably burned enough calories that the entire grilled cow wouldn't have replenished her. For another, Laila Olivet was the number one fan of his cooking and always had been. It would be impossible to calculate how much food he had prepared for her through the years and how much her input and approval had influenced his confidence, his cooking style, and even his menu at Cassidy's.

And on top of all of that, he had spent an inordinate amount of time this evening forgetting to eat because he was so busy watching her, delighting in how satisfied she was with every bite of steak and grilled asparagus and the antipasto salad he'd thrown together and stored in the fridge before she woke up that morning. Not typically one to daydream, on more than one occasion during their meal he had gotten so distracted by watching her lips from across the table that he'd had to hurry around and quickly merge the images in his head with reality.

"No murderous intent, I promise. I'm just really happy that you enjoyed it."

"Well, food is love, right?"

He smiled at her and nodded. "Yeah. Food is love."

She stood from the bench on her side of the table and began gathering dishes. Cole placed his palm on the top of her hand to stop her. To stop her and because he hadn't touched her in about three hundred seconds, and he was about to go crazy.

"What do you think you're doing?"

"Tidying up."

"Um . . . no."

"No?"

Cole shook his head. "No. It's your birthday. Besides . . ." He stood and leaned across the table until their noses were inches apart. "Don't you want dessert?"

He'd never seen her face turn so red so quickly, and it didn't take him long to realize what he had said to cause the reaction.

"I keep doing that, don't I?" He chuckled softly, though as she batted her eyelids in what he figured was a moment of self-awareness that he rarely witnessed her experiencing in his presence, and as she manipulated her bottom lip between her teeth, he found it all less and less funny. "I meant cake. I made you a birthday cake. But if there's some other sort of after-dinner delicacy you have in mind—"

Nope. He'd lost her to cake.

"When in the world did you have time to make me a birthday cake? Never mind. That doesn't matter. What kind is it?" The self-awareness was gone, replaced by the complete lack thereof that he treasured. How had he never noticed how sexy it was that she was comfortable enough with him to be completely herself?

"Red velvet. And, just FYI, I was up until about 1:00 a.m., thank you very much. Because I knew if I did it this morning, the smell of cake in the air would wake you up—"

"Yeah, don't care. Cream cheese icing?"

Cole laughed and collapsed back onto his bench, releasing her hand as he did. He gave up. "Obviously." But then his eyes flew open and he groaned as his head fell into his hands.

"What's wrong?"

"The frosting." He looked up at her through squinted eyes. "I forgot to make it. I'm sorry. I got tired and went to bed, and was going to do it this morning, but . . ."

She set down the silverware she had gathered in her other hand and walked around behind him. Soon her arms were around his shoulders and her lips were beside his ear. "That's okay. I'm sure it will be great without it."

He leaned against her arm and then tilted his head down and kissed her hand. Laila kissed his cheek, and then stretched over his shoulder more so she could reach his lips. Not that Cole made her work too hard, of course. He threw one leg over the bench and pulled her down onto his knee.

"Thank you for doing all of this today," she whispered as she leaned back across his lap, into the security of his arms, and her lips made a trail along his jawline.

Cole looked down at the bruises on her right knee, fading but still evident three full weeks after she'd crawled through gravel to reach Cocaine Bear, hiding under her car in her driveway, and circled them with his fingertips.

"You're welcome. Sorry again about the frosting."

"Are you kidding?" She planted a soft kiss on his lips, then pulled back to look at him. When she spoke again, her voice was as low as she could make it. "Don't you worry about it, sweet thing."

Cole's Barry White impression that morning had not been good, but Laila's was just pathetic. Made even more so by the fact that she couldn't get through a single word without having to choke down a laugh. And each time she laughed, her voice cracked, making her voice squeak between attempted bass tones, which of course made Cole completely lose it.

"Your sweet lovin' is all the icing on the cake I need," she squeaked out breathlessly, trying so hard to attain macho sleaziness and pulling off a lifelike impression of a soulful chipmunk instead.

"Alright. That's it." Cole scooped her up into his arms as he stood, then set her down, grabbed her hand, and began pulling her inside. "Let's go."

"Where are we going?" She kept laughing as she hurried to match his stride and wrapped her arms around his waist.

He threw his arm around her shoulders and kissed the top of her head. "I'll show you icing on the cake."

$\sim$

Earlier, he'd lost her to dessert, and now she'd lost him to his incessant need to convince Laila Olivet she could learn to cook.

"No, that's good, but you've got to make sure to get it from the sides of the bowl too."

"I am," she insisted, pulling the hand mixer up in the bowl— again—and flinging still-thickening frosting onto his arms, her apron, and the Sudworths' marble countertop. Again. "Sorry." She pushed the spinning whisks back into the depths of the bowl and grinned sheepishly.

"It's fine." Cole smiled and swiped some from his forearm before tasting it off his finger.

"How is it?"

"Really good, actually."

Laila chuckled. "You sound surprised."

He scoffed. "Of course I'm not surprised." For one thing, he'd taken advantage of the wine refrigerator to keep the cream cheese and butter perfectly softened (even if he had kept them in there a bit longer than he'd originally intended). He'd also discovered, un-surprisingly, that good-quality vanilla paste was easier to come by in Tribeca than it was in Adelaide Springs. But more than anything, he would never be surprised by her successes.

"Alright, give us a taste, then." She parted her lips and jutted the bottom one toward him.

Cole had spent the better part of twenty years trying to teach her to cook. It had begun as reciprocity, more than anything. Well, reciprocity and fear that if he ever moved away, she would sustain herself on a diet of chocolate chips, marshmallows, and coffee until he came home for Christmas. But mostly reciprocity.

She'd taught him to sew buttons back onto his shirts; he'd taught her to boil an egg. She'd taught him how to stitch up the pillows his grandmother had always kept on the couch, to keep the stuffing from oozing out, and he'd reminded her how to boil an egg. It was around the time he was hemming his own dress slacks and she claimed to have forgotten the hacks he had taught her to help the water boil faster at high altitude that he finally got her to confess she had no desire to learn how to cook. And from that point on, he didn't worry at all about her not knowing how. But he never stopped longing to share with her the joy he felt every time he stepped into the kitchen.

Cole swept his finger around the side of the bowl where she wasn't currently obsessing over one stubborn clump of cream cheese with the hand mixer—she was good at everything she set her mind to, but he still wasn't convinced she wouldn't accidentally chop his finger off—and scooped up a dollop. He brushed icing onto her pouty bottom lip and watched as she tasted and reacted. Yes, he couldn't deny he enjoyed watching her mouth as it manipulated the creamy mixture, but more than anything he was delighted by the unexpected pleasure of her own creation shining in her eyes.

"That's really good!"

He grinned and nodded as he licked his own finger clean once again and then instructed her to turn off the mixer. "*Before* you pull it out," he hastily added, and she complied.

"How did you know how to make this?" Laila asked, sneaking her finger in for another taste. "You didn't have a recipe or anything."

"I did originally." He grabbed her cake from the microwave,

where it had been hiding all day, and dug through drawers until he found an icing spatula. Drea had gotten all the wedding gifts put away, and the kitchen now resembled a Williams-Sonoma showroom.

"And you memorized it?"

He shrugged. "Sort of, I guess. I don't know. I don't really think about the simple things like cream cheese frosting anymore."

Or any of it. Though it wasn't that he didn't think about it, exactly, so much as he got to focus on the extra step or the surprising ingredient that would alter the recipe and make it his own. He knew what tasted good. He knew what worked well together and what didn't. He was skilled and devoted to his craft, and he loved the freedom that came from there not really being any wrong answer.

He'd miss that, he figured. The freedom. The ability to add something to the menu last minute or suddenly decide that tonight's chile rellenos would be stuffed with picadillo instead of chicken. He hadn't been a guest in another chef's kitchen since culinary school. It was going to take some adjustment.

"Simple?!" She looked around the mess that had been created with only a handful of ingredients. "This was simple?"

He set down the cake and chuckled as he ran both of his thumbs along her cheekbones, causing thin, dried layers of frosting mess to crumble and fall. "No. Of course not. Forgive me. Not even Julia Child could have done what you just did." He pulled her to him again and kissed her, something he'd only had the freedom to do for a couple hours, but the loss of which he knew he was going to mourn every bit as much as a lifetime in Adelaide Springs and an entire adulthood in the kitchen at Cassidy's.

Eventually, though, cake won the day, and after Laila spread the icing and Cole applied the candles, she carried the plates, utensils, and matches back up the stairs to the roof while he balanced the cake in one hand and her gift in the other.

"You shouldn't have gotten me anything," she complained. "This day was amazing and the food was amazing and—"

"You're amazing," he whispered to her as they set everything down on the table. "Now . . ." He struck a match and lit the candles. "Make a wish."

She smirked at him, and he knew they were thinking the same thoughts. Never in a million years, when they were joking in the kitchen that morning about how he'd unintentionally made things awkward when he wished her happy birthday just before not kissing her after all, had he envisioned they would be here, wherever "here" was, just fourteen or fifteen hours later.

Then she blew out the candles and he served the cake, and she made all sorts of low, satisfied, guttural noises that he'd heard countless times through the years and which he knew meant she was enjoying her food. But they were having a different effect on him this time than they ever had before.

He cleared his throat and pushed the wrapped package over to her. "Here. Open your gift." *Otherwise, I might actually lose the ability to function like a respectable human being.*

He didn't have to tell her twice. Her eyes twinkled as she tore into the pink wrapping and the pink bow. That was something he'd always appreciated about Laila—she knew that wrapping paper was meant to be ripped. Her grin of giddy anticipation remained as she opened the white box beneath the paper, but her jaw dropped instantly once she saw what was inside.

It hadn't cost him all that much. In fact, he'd picked it up on after-Christmas clearance when he and Seb ran to Colorado Springs for January's Costco run on behalf of all the business owners in town. Not that he'd found the little pink handbag at Costco. It had cost him a bit more than *that*. They'd stopped at Macy's because Seb needed to exchange a gift his mother had gotten him for Christmas, and Cole had wandered rather than wait in the vehicle. When he saw it, there was zero question as to whether to buy it, of course. It was a perfect match to her Cinderella shoes, down to the translucent quality and the hues of glitter, or whatever it was that caused the sparkly effect she said made her feel like a princess. The only challenge had been holding on to it in secret for eight months so he could give it to her on her birthday. (That and carefully packing his clothes in a way that would protect the box in his suitcase.)

"I love it." She mouthed the words to him, but no sound came out.

"I'm glad," he responded softly with a smile.

She stared at it and rubbed it and inspected every crevice and strap, and Cole couldn't help but think again of how unassuming she was. How easy it was to make her happy. But for the first time he wondered if Laila was truly that easy to please or if it just seemed so easy to him because he knew her so well. He suspected that was it, and he was suddenly filled with gratitude that he'd never taken that for granted. That he'd never rested on his laurels when it came to blowing her away. It would have been so easy to do.

He stood from his seat and offered her his hand. "Dance with me?"

She beamed up at him and set her handbag carefully back into its box. "It's really hard to imagine I'll ever say no to that."

The song playing somewhere in the distance transitioned from Lewis Capaldi to "Lover" by Taylor Swift just as Cole twirled her away from the table and into an open space beneath the Edison bulbs. Laila had left her shoes and socks inside when they came back out with the cake, and he relished the way he had to lean over to wrap his arms around her waist, and the way she leaned into him and stood on her toes as her arms encircled his neck. The way they fit so well together. The way each of their heads went to the right as they faced each other, just as they always did when they hugged or danced or whispered secret jokes to each other at inappropriate moments. The way she trusted her bare toes to his two left feet.

They'd danced together before, of course. Weddings, parties, school dances, random moments when great songs came on the jukebox at Cassidy's. He'd held her and swayed with her and dipped her and twirled her. But he hadn't felt anything he was feeling now. He hadn't ever been obsessed with the way her hair smelled like oranges. He'd never known her lips tasted like pomegranate. What a fool he'd been not to give any thought to the clues presented to him by the countless tubes of Burt's Bees lip balm he was always finding on the floorboard of his Wrangler or between the cushions of his couch or under the bar at Cassidy's. For years he'd held her and thought nothing of it, and now all he wanted was to find an excuse to hold her forever.

"I love this song," Laila sighed against his shoulder.

"I know you do." Then a thought occurred. "You don't think the music's coming from Taylor's roof, do you?"

She pulled back to look at him, her eyes frenzied. "I don't know. Do you think Tay Tay plays her own music at her parties?"

Cole shrugged. "Wouldn't you if you were her?"

She nodded in earnest. "I absolutely would." And then they were running over to the south edge of the roof, pushing each other out of the way and laughing as they squeezed between plants and shrubs to try to see the Franklin Street roof.

"I found them!" a voice called out behind them a few seconds later. Cole and Laila both startled and turned around. Sebastian stood smirking at them by the glass entry door and called down in response to whatever Brynn had said from inside the penthouse. "No, they're fine. Just stalking Taylor Swift."

Brynn stepped up the final stairs and out to the roof and Cole took a quick inventory of the situation and determined there was nothing there to raise suspicion about the day the two of them had had. It was a pretty romantic setting, sure, but that was Drea's doing, based on Brynn's suggestions, he assumed. So that was on her.

Satisfied that as long as they acted normal they'd be fine, he passed Laila a furtive glance and then stepped away from her and crossed over to them. "Hey there. We didn't expect to see you guys until tomorrow."

Brynn ran across the roof to Laila and threw her arms around her. "We took an earlier flight so we could make it back on Lai's birthday. We made it! With . . ." She raised her wrist behind Laila's back and looked at her watch. "Seven minutes to spare!"

"I tried to tell her that since she was born in mountain time we had an extra couple hours, but she wouldn't listen to me." Sebastian eyed the cake on the table. "Okay, not to be rude, but I haven't eaten since Munich—"

"We ate on the plane," Brynn interjected.

"Okay, I haven't eaten good food since Munich. Is there birthday cake to share?"

"Oh, of course!" Laila hurried over to the table. "Let me run in and get you a fork. Cole, why don't you help me. Brynn, you want some?"

"I don't mind using my hands," Sebastian insisted, cutting a piece and setting it on a napkin before lifting it to his mouth.

Brynn rolled her eyes and laughed at him. "My husband is not a fan of airline food, as you may have gathered. But I'm fine. Thanks. Now, birthday girl . . ." She sat down next to Seb and motioned for Laila to sit across from her. "Tell us everything. Cole wouldn't tell us anything he had planned. Sit, sit!" She motioned for Cole too. "Seriously, I want to know everything."

"He probably didn't trust you not to tell her," Sebastian mumbled with a mouthful of cake. "And I'm okay not knowing things. This is delicious, by the way."

Cole slid in next to Laila and noticed immediately how awkward it was to sit so close to her with Brynn and Seb right there. Although didn't they always sit that close? Why did it feel borderline salacious? And how was it possible that it was simultaneously awkward to be close to her and painful to be far away?

"Laila made the frosting."

Brynn and Sebastian looked in surprise to Cole, then to Laila.

"It's great," Seb praised before feeding a bite to Brynn, who concurred.

"Thanks. Cole's a great teacher." Laila became very interested in studying her fingernails all of a sudden. "It was a really great day."

It wasn't that Cole had been ignorant about how short lived the perfect little bubble they'd been living in all day would be—although, yeah, he'd expected to at least have the opportunity to kiss her good night. Not that he'd actually thought ahead to any of it. And then tomorrow? They'd figure that out tomorrow. But today, they'd been on a blind date. Though, come to think of it, that aspect of it all hadn't come into play very much since . . . hmm . . . When had they dropped the pretense? They'd eaten her birthday cake. She'd opened her present. They'd talked about that morning and the years before that morning. It had all been so seamless.

"Cole? Will that work for you?"

He'd been staring . . . well, at nothing, really. And he had no idea what he'd missed. Was that a second piece of cake Seb was almost done with? "I'm sorry, what? I must have zoned out there."

Brynn shook it off. "Oh, I know. It's super late. No, I was just saying we're going to need to do birthday brunch tomorrow instead of dinner. Milo has to fly back to LA for some press stuff, but we're going to meet at Bubby's—"

"Bubby's?" Laila asked.

"Yeah. It's the best. And it's literally just down on the corner. Not John-John corner. The other way. Milo's going to meet us there at ten thirty."

"Great." Laila turned her head toward Cole and then instantly back to Brynn after their eyes met briefly. "And what about . . . what's her name? Greta? Is she going to be able to meet us? Or did you manage to find him someone on the Hot Celebrities Only dating app?"

Laila briefly squeezed his knee under the table as Brynn laughed, and it took all the willpower he possessed not to hold her hand or put his arm around her, or do any of the things that would have felt so natural to do.

How was he supposed to act about all of this being-fixed-up stuff? All he knew was he had no interest in being set up on a blind date that would undoubtedly fall pitifully short of the one he'd already gone on today.

"Dude." He put his hand out and stopped Sebastian from going in for a third piece of cake and then walked over to the refrigerator in the outdoor kitchen and grabbed the bowl of antipasto salad from the second shelf. He looked around for an extra plate and utensil, but when he came up short, he dropped the serving spoon back into the bowl and handed the entire thing to Seb.

"Bless you," Seb muttered as he took his first bite.

"Greta can't make it, unfortunately," Brynn finally said, her smile becoming a grimace as she turned to Cole. "She has a family thing. And I didn't have a chance to call anyone else. I'm sorry. But I think we'll still have a blast."

"Do you want me to go invite Taylor to be your date?" Sebastian was still stuffing his face. "That's the least I can do for you now. This is so good. I can at least throw a rock with a note or something."

Cole chuckled. "Nah, I'm good. Thanks. It's Lai's birthday thing anyway. I can be a fifth wheel for Lai's birthday." He looked around at the mess to clean up. "I do think I need to start heading toward bed, though, if I'm going to be at my fifth-wheel best by brunch time." Thankfully he had long ago developed the habit of cleaning up as he went, so there wasn't too much, but he began gathering what was there. "I'll go get started on the kitchen."

"Let me help you." Laila stood and picked up the forks, and their eyes lingered for the first time since their hosts (whom they usually adored spending time with) had had the audacity to make themselves at home in their own home.

"That'd be great. Thanks." Cole turned to Brynn and Sebastian, who had finally stopped eating. "You guys must be exhausted. Jet lag, all of that. Go to bed. We've got this."

Laila inched just a little closer to Cole, and he hoped that meant she was as desperate to be alone again as he was. "Definitely. But can't wait to catch up tomorrow!"

"Are you kidding?" Brynn jumped up and took the forks from Laila's hands. "You're not cleaning up on your birthday."

"*We've* got this," Sebastian concurred, standing and taking the forks from his wife. But, unfortunately, the two Sudworths were not the "we" he was referring to. "There's no place for the two of you in the kitchen. Dishes are men's work." He smiled at Brynn and planted a loving kiss on her lips. "You two go. Happy birthday, Laila." He wrapped his forkless arm around her and gave her a hug.

"Thanks." She hugged him back and then stared at Cole and shrugged.

He shrugged back, trapped. "Um . . . yeah. Happy birthday, Lai." Cole opened his arms to her and was so relieved when she ran into them as she had a million times before—while also, of course, as she never had. Not once. Not like this. He inhaled the scent of her hair and caressed her back as affectionately as he could while still appearing normal. He thought he appeared normal, anyway. Strange . . . it was difficult to remember how he'd always hugged her before.

"Thanks for everything." She grabbed her gift from the table and then bounced up on her bare toes and kissed his cheek, and he wanted so badly to tilt his head and catch her lips as they passed. "You're not a bad date, my friend."

"You either." He winked as she pulled away, and he stretched out his arm to grab her hand before she walked away. Her fingers and her eyes lingered a moment longer, and then his arm dropped to his side when she was out of reach and heading to the door with Brynn.

"You look super hot in this dress, by the way," Brynn declared as they stepped away. "You should just keep it. Doesn't it look great on her?" She turned back to the guys.

Sebastian, who was in the process of wiping down the table, kept his eyes down and said, "I was a supportive attendee at the fashion show this morning. Please don't make me participate in the aftershow as well." He lifted his head briefly. "But yeah. Of course. You look beautiful as ever, Laila." Then he resumed his scrubbing.

Cole opened his mouth to jump at his opportunity to compliment her without raising suspicion, but Brynn spoke again before he had the chance.

"I'm surprised Cole managed to keep his hands off of you."

Laila's wide, frenzied eyes flashed back to him one more time, and they were filled with humor, causing Cole to cough out a laugh and then turn it into a full-out cough as subtly as he could. Then he watched her until she was out of sight—across the roof, through the glass door, down the stairs—and then cleared his throat before bracing himself and turning around to face his host. His trusted confidant. His dishes buddy, apparently. And, as he figured was probably most relevant in that moment, his astute, intuitive, Pulitzer-winning friend who never missed a beat.

"I didn't even ask, because I was so famished, but what was in that salad thing? It was killer."

Huh. Okay. Sure. Why not?

Of course *this* would be the one day that no one asked him if something had happened between him and Laila.

CHAPTER TWENTY-NINE

LAILA

I was incredibly proud of myself. I had made it through the entire night without any contact with Cole at all. I'd walked the twenty paces or so between my bedroom and the bathroom five or six times, each time slower than the last, stretching out my pre-bed routine as long as I could in hopes we would pass each other or maybe even share the sink while we brushed our teeth, but the door to his bedroom was closed and the condo was quiet every time I went through the common areas. At about two thirty I heard rustling in the kitchen and peeked my head out my door, but it was only Sebastian on the hunt for antacids.

It was around that time that I had stared at our ongoing text thread on my phone, watching for bubbles to pop up that would indicate he was thinking about me, too, but eventually I fell asleep reading through a text discussion we'd had in 2018 in which he had attempted to explain the rules of hockey to me.

Apparently in the present day, as in 2018, I really was just not interested.

But the pride I felt as my eyes fluttered open in response to the filtered sunlight streaming into the opening of my bed tent was quickly replaced by other emotions. Well, all of them, pretty much. I was feeling all the emotions. My heart was racing from the feeling that I had woken up in the middle of an exhilarating dream. My stomach was a plasma ball of activity, reacting to each touch and thought and memory with jolts of static electricity. And I felt like there was so much weight on my shoulders as I wondered if the romantic us was just a one-hit wonder.

Like, were we destined to be Fountains of Wayne? Was the entirety of our lives together going to be defined by "Stacy's Mom" blasting off right in the middle of it all, drawing in some serious big-time attraction before going back to our devoted but undeniably niche status quo and eventually fizzling out without fanfare and only reuniting for special occasions, like weddings and birthdays and to open for Soul Asylum or something?

Hopefully we weren't Snow Patrol, who'd worked hard and created so much solid material before and after their big breakthrough. Would we and the world pretend we weren't defined by that one thing, while secretly in the back of our minds we would always know that if we didn't close our concerts with "Chasing Cars" everyone would demand their money back?

Or, worst of all, would we go the way of Gnarls Barkley? How long would it take for us to realize that after "Crazy" there really wasn't any point in any of it anymore?

Only one way to find out.

Unlike a few hours prior, I eased my door open, careful not to make any noise, and darted to the bathroom as covertly as I could, with my clothes for the day tucked under my arm. I didn't even look behind me to see if anyone was present. There was going to be a lot to deal with today, and there was no chance I was dealing with any of it before I looked somewhat presentable and had minty fresh breath.

I took a quick, piping-hot shower but chose not to wash my hair, instead settling on a messy milkmaid braid to make the most of all the volume and texture that had resulted from a day of wearing it loose and free. Once my contacts were in, my teeth were sparkling, my makeup was minimal but made me look like I had slept more than the six and a half hours that I had, and I was wearing my wide-legged Banana Republic khakis that I had found at the thrift store in Pagosa Springs about five years ago and that I wanted to be buried in (I loved them so much) with a ribbed short-sleeved white sweater tucked into them, I took a deep breath and stepped out to face the world.

Sebastian was sitting on the giant horseshoe couch, reading the paper. Murrow was beside him, settled in and clearly happy to be home (though I'd actually never seen Murrow look anything other than content as long as Seb was around). And Brynn was standing at the kitchen island, coffee cup in one hand and phone in the other. Her thumb-only scrolling stopped when she saw me.

"Hey, you. Good morning! You look cute."

"Thanks. Is this okay . . . for brunch, I mean?"

"Perfect. You look great." She took a sip of her coffee and then set her cup on the island. "It will literally only take three minutes to walk there, but we can go anytime."

"Sounds good." I looked around the room as casually as I could. "Cole didn't oversleep, did he?"

Brynn shook her head. "Nah. He's ready. Said to just let him know when we're ready to go." She looked at her watch. "Seb, do you think we should go on now?"

"Yes!" I answered on his behalf. "I mean, I'd love to have a few minutes just to stroll, if that's okay with you."

And if Cole isn't coming out of his room until it's time to leave, that's a no-brainer. Don't you think?

CHAPTER THIRTY

COLE

Brynn knocked twice on the door. "We're ready to head out."

"Okay, be right there."

Cole sat up in the bed where he'd been lying fully dressed, his shoes dangling off the side, for the last twenty minutes and stretched his back and twisted his shoulders to get ready for motion again. He was glad he'd gotten up early enough to shower before Laila woke up so that he could have some time to himself before he had to act normal again.

Although that was the thing. Were they going to act normal? And for the time being, he wasn't even considering the deeper questions: What *was* normal? Were they even capable of that? Did he want to be normal with her ever again? But rather the most pressing question of all: Was she feeling, as he was, that everything had changed, or was she following the rules? Had it just been one day of experimentation and indulgence for her, and now they were back to ColeAndLaila, LailaAndCole? One inextricable unit, adding a really great day to a towering collection of really great memories that represented a really great friendship. A really great life together.

He hadn't shaved, and he was wondering if that was a mistake. Colorado Cole usually had facial hair, but so far New York Cole had stayed pretty smooth. Would that make a difference to her? And what did he even think any of that meant? It wasn't like he had tricked her into kissing him by shaving his face, like some ridiculous Lifetime movie except with less nefarious intent. But maybe Laila was only attracted to him clean shaven. What had she said? That clean-shaven NYC Cole was a "hottie"?

"Oh, please stop being crazy," he implored himself as he stood and grabbed his phone from the dresser, where it had been charging since just after dinner, and stuffed it into his pocket. His wallet was already in the back pocket of his jeans, which he confirmed with a quick pat, and all that was left was to go out there, face the truth, try to quickly assess and analyze a whole host of confusing thoughts and emotions, and walk his best friend / possible dream woman to her blind date with a Hollywood heartthrob.

Business as usual.

CHAPTER THIRTY-ONE

LAILA

"Good morning," I greeted as Cole stepped out of his room, causing him to startle a bit. In fairness, he probably hadn't been expecting me to be *right there*, looking like I had been listening through the door. Which I hadn't been, for the record. I'd only been *contemplating* listening through the door. I wasn't so unhinged as to go through with it, obviously.

"Oh. Hey. Good morning." He smiled at me as he closed the door behind him. "You look pretty."

"Thank you." I kicked my heel up behind me and balanced on one foot while lowering my new purse toward the raised shoe. "I have you to thank for that, I believe."

He wagged his head from side to side. "Nah. That's all you."

"Ready?" Brynn asked, peeking her head around the corner.

Cole and I nodded once at each other and both said, "Ready," then followed her and Seb to the door.

We stood behind them in the elevator and I was so tempted to grab Cole's hand or place my head on his shoulder. Just for a second. Just long enough to see how he reacted. But I spent too long building up the courage, and before I could do anything we were on the ground level. Still following. Still not saying anything. Not anything significant, anyway.

Brynn was doing most of the talking as we stepped onto North Moore Street, and I had naturally begun walking alongside her with Sebastian falling back to walk alongside Cole. But as we neared the corner, I felt Cole's hand on my elbow and I instinctively responded to his touch by stopping and turning to face him.

Sebastian passed me just as Cole said, "You guys mind going ahead? I need to talk to Laila for just a sec."

Brynn took a couple steps back toward us. "Everything okay?"

"Yeah. Fine. I just need a minute with her to . . . talk about something. We'll be right there, okay?"

"Sure. Table's under my name, but the place isn't too big. You'll see us." Seb wrapped his arm around Brynn's waist and led her away from us, and we were alone. On a crowded street, but I'd take it.

"Hey. You alright?"

"Yeah. Of course." He took a deep breath. "I just . . ." We were standing right in the middle of pedestrian traffic, and he waited for an opening in the crowd and then motioned toward the tan brick wall of the building, and we stepped to the side together. "I hate what's happening right now."

"What's happening?"

"I have no idea." He shrugged and ran his hands through his hair. "That's the problem. I don't know if we're supposed to talk about things or ignore them. I don't know if we're okay. I don't know how I'm supposed to act. And I feel like this is sort of where we were at the beginning of the week, and I hated that. I hated that feeling of not knowing how to *be* around you. You know? But this is worse. And also . . . better? I don't know if I'm making any sense."

"No, I get it. It's weird, huh?"

"*Super* weird. And I know this probably isn't the time to talk about any of it. Since you have a date and all . . ."

I laughed. "*Weird* is not even the right word for any of this."

"No." He shook his head. "It's not quite strong enough, is it?" He took another deep breath and let it out slowly, and then his eyes locked with mine. "I need to know we're okay. Even if yesterday was a huge mistake—"

"You think it was a huge mistake?"

"I didn't say that." He studied me. "Do you?"

I crossed my arms over my stomach and involuntarily took a step back from him. Why had I done that? "I don't know. I mean, I do if you do, I guess."

His eyebrow rose. "Well, *that's* definitely the conviction needed to, you know . . . dive into a relationship. Let's be sure to throw away a thirty-whatever-year friendship on the foundation of 'I don't know. I do if you do, I guess.'"

"Hang on." I lifted my hands between us and took another step back. That step hadn't been quite so involuntary. I felt heat climbing up my neck. I didn't even know what to react to first. "Who said anything about throwing away our friendship? Or diving into a relationship, for that matter?"

Cole cleared his throat and looked down at his boots. "Okay, see, that helps. If that's not what we're talking about here, it's good to know. That's all I needed for now. Awesome." He looked up at me again and then motioned forward with his chin. "I guess we should get in there."

He began walking past me, and I grabbed his arm. "Cole, stop. What are you doing? All I meant was that if you think yesterday was a mistake, then *of course* I do too. Not because I don't have my own thoughts and feelings about it, but because we need to be on the same page about . . . about whatever. It takes two to tango, and all that. That's all I meant."

"Okay, then. What are your thoughts and feelings?"

Huh. That was a fair question, and yet it felt like an attack. Or a trap, maybe. It felt sort of déjà vu-ish in a way I didn't understand. At least not at first. And then he kept talking.

"It just makes sense, at least to me, that if we're going to be on the same page, we have to start somewhere. So which is it? Just friends or something more?"

There it was.

"I told you I don't like that phrase. 'Just friends.' I also told you that the next time you wanted to say something, you needed to go first and just say it. Remember? So just say what you want to say." I didn't know what to do with my hands, so they went into my pockets, back to my stomach, back to my pockets as I waited.

We'll be fine. We'll be fine. We'll be fine. We'll be fine.

I repeated it over and over in my mind while I waited for him to say whatever was coming next.

"Yeah, I remember you saying that. Just like I remember saying this was the exact thing I was afraid was going to happen."

"What? What are you talking about?"

"Everything . . . yesterday . . . it threw us off. It's been less than twenty-four hours and we're already falling apart. We don't even know how to talk to each other anymore—"

"You need to slow down, buddy." *We'll be fine. We'll be fine.* "We just need to talk. That's all there is to it. But you're talking like decisions have already been made and everything's been sorted out, and like we're a mess and you know everything and I'm the problem, and . . . I don't know . . . I guess I just missed some things somewhere. We just need to *talk*."

He growled in frustration and threw his hands up in the air. "I know. That's what I'm trying to say. But it's difficult to talk about something like this while your date is waiting for you inside."

Okay . . . you've got to be kidding me. I didn't know whether to kiss him or slap him.

"Is that what this is about?"

"What do you mean?"

"Are you jealous?"

He scoffed. "No."

"Really?"

"Really." He squinted and a smile threatened to appear at the corner of his mouth. "Should I be?"

"No. Of course not." Even I wasn't buying that. "Okay, yes, actually! Why are you okay with me going out with some other guy after—"

"I guess maybe I didn't realize I had any reason to be jealous. This is some big-time movie star who's only here filming a movie or something, and you're going back to Colorado in three days. Are you expecting to discover Jess Gilmore is the love of your life?"

"First of all, his character's last name was not Gilmore and I think you know that. Please stop calling him Jess Gilmore. Second, no, I'm not *expecting* it. But it could happen, couldn't it? Or is the thought that a big-time movie star could fall for me so ludicrous—"

"Don't put words in my mouth, Lai. Don't do that. You know that's not what I'm saying."

"I don't know that. Frankly, I don't understand anything that's happening right now, except I think you're spinning out. I think you're scared, and—"

"I'm not scared." He scrunched up his face like he couldn't even make sense of the words. "Why? Are you?"

There was only one time in my life when I could remember Cole being mean to me. Not accidentally inconsiderate or a little too careless with my feelings or misguided in his earnest attempts, but straight-out mean. We were eleven years old and had been watching *The Exorcist* in the attic of my grandparents' house. Addie would put up with anything to hang out with Wes, even then, and Brynn just laughed at all the scariest parts, but I was terrified. Absolutely terrified. I tried covertly turning away and closing my eyes, and Wes and Addie and Brynn all said I should stop watching if I wanted to, but every time they gave me a way out, I insisted I was fine. And the only reason I kept insisting I was fine was because Cole had said earlier in the day, when he and Wes were hatching the *Exorcist* plan, that he loved scary movies and anyone who didn't was a coward, and he could never be friends with a coward.

That wasn't the mean part. That was just him being an eleven-year-old boy. But that night, as we watched, he kept teasing me and finding ways to spook me and make me jump. The girls were on his case from the beginning, of course, and even Wes, who typically acted as if Cole could do no wrong, told him to lay off. But he wouldn't. Not until I completely lost my composure and broke down crying like I had never cried in front of anyone before. Then, in addition to being terrified, I was humiliated.

They all left soon after that, and I didn't know if any of them would ever want to see me again. I was pretty sure, at the very least, Cole and I couldn't be friends anymore, since I had proven to be a coward.

That night he snuck through my bedroom window for the first of about a thousand times while I lived under my parents' roof. And while, in some ways, that was a textbook example of him being accidentally inconsiderate, a little too careless with my feelings, *and* misguided in his earnest attempts, considering I was already having to sleep with the lights on, clenching a rosary I had hastily made out of pony beads, a shoelace, and the water-spraying crown from my Fountain Mermaid Barbie (not Catholic . . . didn't matter), it was also one of the watershed moments of our friendship. He made me promise to tell him when he was being a jerk. And he told me that I could always tell him when I was scared because he knew I wasn't a coward, and anyway, he and I would always be friends, no matter what. So I'd told him I was scared, and he'd stayed there and read *Where the Sidewalk Ends* to me until I fell asleep.

"Of course I'm scared, Cole." I swatted at a tear tickling my cheek. "How could I not be? You literally just said that if we were to dive into a relationship we would be throwing away our friendship—"

"That's not what I said."

I scoffed. "That's pretty darn close to what you said. And you're talking about how we're falling apart and saying we don't know how to talk to each other anymore, and—"

"I just meant—"

"Shut up." I cupped my hand over his mouth. "I'm not done." But suddenly, as I felt his lips curl beneath my hand, I thought maybe I could be.

Nope, nope, nope. Things to say. Lots and lots of things to say. Did he just kiss my palm? Doesn't matter.

"And you're being a jerk." His eyebrows quirked downward like a sad puppy dog, and I wanted to take it back, but I couldn't. I'd made a vow twenty-eight years ago, and he'd given me very few opportunities through the years to carry out my commitment. The few isolated incidents in recent days had been easy enough to write off as him misdirecting his pain and grief, but this was different. This wasn't insignificant collateral damage. He was intentionally lashing out at me, and neither snow nor rain nor heat nor an overwhelming desire to feel his breath against my lips rather than my hand would keep me from the swift completion of my appointed rounds. "You made me promise to always tell you, so I'm telling you."

"Ahem."

With my hand still on his mouth and his fingers now on the high waistband of my slacks, I think preparing to pull me to him, we both turned our heads slowly to look at Sebastian. I didn't have any clue how long he'd been there, and I could only imagine what he thought might be happening.

"Sorry to bother." He looked at Cole and seemed rather nonplussed by it all, actually. "Doc just called me. I guess he's been trying to get through to you. Something about some papers they found when they cleared out your grandfather's room. And . . ." His eyes quickly darted to me and then back to Cole as he softly added, "I guess there's been an offer. On your house."

"What do you mean, 'an offer'?" I asked at the same time I felt Cole's heavy gust of breath on my palm.

I dropped my hand from Cole's mouth, which, admittedly, I probably should have done a few seconds earlier.

"That's all I know. He just . . . said he needs you to call him." Seb's eyes again passed from Cole to me and back again, and then he stuck two thumbs in the air and said, "Cool," before turning and heading back to the restaurant.

"An offer on your house?"

Cole sighed. "Lai, listen—"

"How can that be, Cole? How can— How can—" I stepped away from him and faced the wall for a moment, hoping just a second to breathe would help me calm down, but it had the opposite effect. "How can there be an offer on your house, Cole? Your house isn't for sale, is it?"

"All I did was ask Doc to maybe start putting some feelers out with people he knew. And he said he knew a Realtor in Alamosa—"

"I can't believe this." I began running my hand through my hair and then shouted, "Crap!" when my fingers got caught in the braid I'd forgotten about. I knew I was going to have to make a decision to either pull my hand out and allow the damage to be done, thereby accepting that my hair would spend the day emulating Jareth the Goblin King from *Labyrinth*, or just walk around like I was Mary Tyler Moore, preparing to throw my hat, but waiting for perfect thermal air pressure conditions.

"Here, let me help you."

Cole reached for my braid, and I slapped him away with my free hand and then welcomed the disarray and falling strands with indifference so that I could use both hands to shove him away from me.

Jareth the Goblin King it was.

"No. Stop!" I pointed my finger at him. "Don't touch me."

He released a frustrated growl as I continued backing away from him. "Laila, would you listen to me? I'm sorry I didn't tell you, but come on! It's only been a week since I even mentioned it to Doc. And that's really all it was. A mention. I thought it was going to be a long-drawn-out thing, if I was even able to find a buyer at all. How could I have known that—"

"Are you kidding me? With the way Adelaide Springs is growing? Someone bought Cassidy's out from under you, Cole. How much have we talked about how quickly the place is growing, and—"

"You're right." He nodded. "I'm sorry. Of course. I should have—"

"Did you really think that a great house on amazing land wouldn't be snatched up the instant you—"

"I said you're right!" he shouted, causing a couple and their children to hurry past us. "I said I'm sorry," he added more quietly. "I just didn't think about that. But it's not like I wasn't going to tell you. You know that. I wasn't keeping it from you. And I know that we canceled the deal. I know we were talking about things. But . . . I guess, maybe, that was a little too real. Too fast, you know?"

"Ya think?"

He groaned in reaction to the jab. "How many times do I have to tell you? I'm not having a midlife crisis here. I had no idea this could happen so quickly. Was that stupid of me? Obviously. You've made that very clear. But I genuinely didn't believe there was any urgency in talking to you about—"

"But Sebastian knew. Clearly. And I'm sure that means Brynn knows. You talked to Doc about it. I just can't understand why you talked to everyone except—"

"Because none of them have the power to make me change my mind!"

I scoffed. "Clearly I don't either."

"Are you kidding me?" He grabbed my elbows and turned me toward him. "Laila, you have the power to make me do anything you want me to do. You always have. And that terrifies me because I can't stay there. I can't stay in that house. I can't stay in that town and know that my grandfather cared more about freaking Township Days than he did me."

"That's not true."

"Isn't it?"

"No. It's not." It would be so easy to open my mouth and say all the words he needed to hear. Maybe he'd listen, maybe he wouldn't, but I wanted nothing more than to say them. "You just . . ." It wasn't fair that I couldn't throw everything else that also mattered out the window and unilaterally decide that nothing mattered as much as helping his heart to heal. "I promise you, it's not true."

"Whether it's true or not, every single block of that town holds a memory that I have to get away from now, because I can't look at the park where he taught me to ride my bike and wonder if that was the moment. If he stopped believing in me *then*, because it took me longer to learn than he thought it should have and he salved his conscience by reminding himself I wasn't a real Kimball, or even a real Dolan."

He swiped at his eyes and took a step back. "Maybe it wasn't until later when we were at the church for my grandmother's funeral and he didn't talk to me that whole day. Remember? You and my mom said he just didn't want to appear weak or too emotional with me, but who knows? Maybe that was the day he realized that with her dead, he didn't owe me anything."

"Cole, don't do this to yourself. I know he wasn't the most affectionate of men, but I promise you—"

"Or, I know—maybe it happened when I moved him to Spruce House. I was the only one left, and I couldn't take care of him the way he needed to be taken care of. I know that. But that doesn't change the fact that every time I drive by that place, I'm going to wonder if he felt like I had abandoned him—"

"He didn't."

"—and maybe that was why he didn't think he owed me so much as a heads-up that he had abandoned me too."

"Stop it," I whispered into his ear as I threw my arms around his neck and pulled him to me. "Stop it right now. He loved you. I'll never be able to explain why he did what he did, but he loved you."

"I'm still trying to convince myself I have the strength to leave you, Lai." He held me tightly. "Every other single thing in my life is coming together to lead me away from Adelaide Springs, but—"

"But nothing." I squeezed him against me and then lifted my head from his shoulder and held his face in my hands. "But nothing. Call Doc."

He leaned into my hand. "But we need to—"

"And we will," I assured him. Whatever he and I needed to do, we'd do it. Eventually. Somehow. "Right now, you just need to call Doc."

He nodded and rubbed his eyes again, then pulled his phone out of his pocket, began scrolling, and sighed. "I never turned off Do Not Disturb last night. Doc has called . . ." He kept scrolling. "Well, a lot." His finger stopped suddenly and his eyes began skimming the screen frantically.

"What is it?"

He kept reading for another couple seconds and then looked up at me. "A text from Sylvia. Her sous chef broke his hand, and the restaurant's soft opening is next weekend. She's . . ." His eyes went back to the phone. "She's asking me to start on Tuesday. As second sous chef." His eyes met mine again, and it was anybody's guess what he saw when he looked at me.

"Wow. That's . . ." *That's too soon. That's a horrible idea. That's the end of my life as I know it.* "That's amazing, Cole. What an opportunity. I'm so . . ." *Sad. Devastated. Heartbroken.* "Proud of you." I wrapped my arms around his torso and hugged him. Like I would have two days ago. Like I knew he needed me to. Like his best friend. It was time to focus on being his best friend, and that meant putting all of my own selfish desires aside. "I'm just *so* proud of you." I squeezed him one more time and then gestured over my shoulder. "You have a lot of calls to make. I'll let you—"

"No. Don't go. I'm sorry I'm handling all of this so badly. I'm not trying to be a jerk. It's just coming very naturally to me this week." His eyes were red and strained, and I wanted nothing more than to make it all better for him, no matter how miserable that made me. "Stay. Please?"

"Of course."

We'll be fine.

CHAPTER THIRTY-TWO

COLE

"Hey, Doc. Sorry. My phone was . . . Well, anyway. Sorry. So what's going on?"

"No, I'm sorry, kid. Sorry to interrupt your trip. I hope it's been a good one."

Cole could hear papers shuffling on the other side of the call, and New York suddenly seemed very loud in a way he'd mostly stopped noticing over the course of the week. He covered his other ear with his finger and closed his eyes to try to filter out everything pulling at him and fighting for his attention.

"It has, thanks. So, seriously, what's up with this offer?"

"There's a cash buyer making an offer of twenty percent over valuation."

His eyes flew open, and he saw Laila watching him carefully. Cole covered the phone and whispered, "Cash offer. Above value."

His heart pinched as he saw her eyes grow misty, even as she smiled and nodded and even clapped her hands softly in support.

"Who is it, Doc? I mean, I hadn't even officially decided to sell yet."

"Well, that's where it gets interesting. The offer's coming from that same company that bought Cassidy's."

"Great," he muttered. Nothing like having some stranger step in and make your life their own.

"Look, kid, I know this is quick and not at all how you envisioned this happening. It's certainly too big a decision to be pressured into. I needed to make you aware, but now I suggest you just enjoy the rest of your trip. When you get back next week, we can sort through—"

"Sebastian mentioned something about some papers you found?"

"Oh." Doc sighed. "Yeah, that's been interesting too. Honestly, I don't fully understand what we're looking at yet. Some documents that didn't get signed, I guess. Alpine Ventures is meeting with Bill's lawyer today, and then I'm supposed to get a call after that. Again, you need to be aware, but I don't think it's anything you need to worry about until you get back. Cassidy should be here this afternoon—"

The finger he'd had in his ear to block out background noise dropped like deadweight, and Laila, leaning against a brick wall with her "supportive friend" smile plastered on her face, took note. She stood up straight and took a step toward him.

"My mom? She's going to be *there*? In Adelaide Springs?"

Laila's eyes widened as Doc sighed again. "I assumed she'd told you."

When was the last time he had seen his mother? They FaceTimed on occasion, whenever she was somewhere that had any sort of internet or phone signal, but he was pretty sure it had been four or five years since he'd seen her in person.

"No. I haven't talked to her."

"Well, it's a long story. Basically, when we were cleaning things out at Spruce House, Jo and I found some notes Bill had made in a notebook. That led to us calling Cassidy with some questions we had, and that led to her getting in touch with Alpine Ventures, who immediately began panicking because this, that, or the other hadn't been signed or authorized or whichever. I don't know. Like I said, I should know more later today. And if there are things that affect you, you can deal with them later in the week. Lack of planning or preparation or whatever on their part or Bill's doesn't get to constitute an emergency on yours."

Cole wanted nothing more than to accept that. Few had been the times in his life when Doc Atwater's advice had led him astray. Truth be told, he couldn't think of a single time. And if he listened to him now, he could spend a few more days with Laila before everything changed even more than it already had.

But the writing was on the wall. He was going to take this job in Brooklyn, because he would be a fool not to. He was probably going to sell his house in Adelaide Springs, because he needed the money so he didn't have to live as a permanent resident in the Sudworths' maid's quarters. And if there were things he needed to sign and business he needed to take care of, it had to be now. His new life was suddenly scheduled to begin on Tuesday.

"Thanks, Doc, but I know what I need to do." Cole bit the inside of his cheek and studied Laila for a moment before reaching out and grabbing her hand. "I'll see you tonight."

CHAPTER THIRTY-THREE

LAILA

My hand dropped from his as he slipped his phone back into his pocket. "You're going home? Today?"

Cole sighed and rubbed his eyes and then spent a moment drumming at his temples before focusing his eyes on me. "Yeah."

"Why?"

He shrugged. "Because I won't be able to on Wednesday. Apparently my grandfather left some business messes for us to clean up. And I need to gather up some things, since this isn't just a vacation anymore. And, I guess, it will give us a chance to see my mother. Who knows when all the planets will align for that to happen again."

I loved Cassidy. Dr. Cassidy Dolan-Kimball. She certainly wasn't the most maternal of the mothers growing up, but she was kind to us all and loved us dearly. I'd asked her once, years after I became an adult myself, why she had hyphenated and kept her father's name after Old Man Kimball officially adopted her, since every story I'd ever heard about Eleanor's first husband had indicted him as a horrible father, an even worse husband, and just a despicable human being in general. One she had never once spoken to since she and her mother had broken free. She'd explained to me that for better or worse, her entire path in life—from leaving Indiana with her mom as a little girl to wanting to adopt a child to getting her PhD in some fancy societal-discourse thing I could never remember but which basically meant Cassidy was qualified to save the world—had begun in her biological father's broken home. She had told me that all the pain and all the heartache made just as much of an impact on who we became as the love and the joy and the happiness.

"I'm not going," I whispered, and then I planted my feet and forced the words out again with all the resolve I could muster. "I'm not going. I'm happy to help you get packed and book flights or whatever, but I'm not leaving until Wednesday. Like we planned."

His lips scrunched up toward his cheeks. "Huh. That's funny."

"What?"

A gust of air escaped from him, and his shoulders fell. "I wasn't imagining being on the flight home without you. I wasn't imagining doing any of this without you."

I suppose that was sort of funny. Not funny-ha-ha, of course. More funny-I-think-I-can-actually-feel-my-heart-cracking-apart-inside-of-me.

Was I making a huge mistake? Was it just my stubbornness causing me to be selfish and inconsiderate? If he needed me there, I needed to go. Right?

"You have the power to make me do anything you want me to do." I swallowed the lump in my throat. "But please don't ask me to say goodbye to New York Cole and Laila and then turn right around and say goodbye to Adelaide Springs Cole and Laila. I'm not sure I'd survive it."

He cleared his throat and looked down at the cracks in the pavement. "No. Of course."

"So you just focus on what you need to do for your family—"

"You know *you're* my family, right?" Cole took a step toward me and clutched both of my hands in his, then bent his knees to be on eye level with me. "And you're right. I was totally being a jerk." He inhaled his bottom lip in between his teeth and closed his eyes. "I'm sorry. I just . . ." His eyes opened again. "This whole week just came out of the blue, you know? For me, I mean. I know that you had already thought it all through and examined the possibilities, weighed the pros and cons . . . all of that. But like I said, until this week, I had just never even gone there." He shrugged. "I'm slow. Not gonna deny it. I mean, you had already ruled out the possibility of there ever being a future for us, in that way, before . . . I don't know . . . before I even realized you have better legs than Seb—"

"What are you talking about?"

He laughed. "I'm sure Sebastian has very nice legs, of course, but of all my friends . . ."

"No, I mean, why did you say I had already ruled out the possibility of there ever being a future for us?"

"Because that's what *you* said."

"No, I didn't."

"Yes, you did. At Shake Shack. You said . . . well . . ." He cocked his head to the side and furrowed his brows. "I asked if the thought of us had zoomed through or if it had landed, and you said—"

"I said yes to both."

He nodded. "Exactly. You said you had weighed all the pros and cons, and . . ." His voice, so strong and confident just a few words earlier, fizzled out. "But if you hadn't . . . Why didn't you ever . . . So what does that even mean, Laila? You weighed the pros and cons, and then what?"

And then what?

How could I explain it? How could I ever even begin to explain what came next in my mind? It wasn't about our friendship being ruined if we made the wrong choice, and it wasn't about waiting for him to fall in love with me. It wasn't about me pining after him or the two of us having some sort of "if we're not married by forty" pact.

"You know how everyone has always asked us why we aren't together? Or insinuated that we should be?"

"For our entire lives."

I chuckled and looked down at our hands—just one big jumble of fingers. "Yeah. A few years ago Sebastian asked me why you and I never dated. He asked if it was because we love each other too much."

"That's a nice way to put it," Cole murmured.

"You're right. It is. But I told him that wasn't it. I told him . . ." I sniffed and raised my arm to wipe my eyes, pulling Cole's hands with me. "I told him that you and I love each other just the right amount, Cole Kimball. And that's the best way I know how to answer your question too. I weighed the pros and cons, and guess what? No matter how you slice it, you and I *work*. As friends, as coworkers, as family . . . And, yeah, probably as, well, whatever we want to be to each other. You and I will always work. When you and I are together, there just aren't a whole lot of cons. Not with us. It's just . . . you know."

"Everything else."

"Yeah."

He released my hands and wrapped his arms around my shoulders, pulling me into him. "I just can't stand the thought," he whispered against my hair, "of us not being okay."

"You and I will always be okay." I slipped my arms around his waist. "Adelaide Springs Cole and Laila aren't going anywhere. They're not really saying goodbye. Just entering a new season." A new season with two thousand miles and an entire time zone between them. "I mean, you can feel free to call me. We can FaceTime ten times a day, if you want. Not that I want you to feel any pressure to do that. I know you're going to be busy with the new job and—"

"Oh, stop it. I probably won't be able to make it to the airport without texting you."

I chuckled. "Literally. But just remember, you won't have signal underground, so if you get lost . . ." Um, no. He was never going to be able to make it without getting lost. "On second thought, you should probably take a Lyft."

"Yeah. Good call." He kissed my temple before stepping back from me, and a million cherished memories fought to outshine the melancholy passing between us as our eyes remained locked. "I have to admit, I'm sad to be saying goodbye to New York Cole and Laila."

I smiled up at him sadly. "Me too."

"And this is why I'm scared, Lai. Like, right now, I need to go, and I don't know if I should hug you or kiss you or give you a high five. It's always been so easy. *You* have always been at the center of the most natural, effortless moments in my life. And now I don't know what I'm supposed to do."

I took a step toward him and ran my hands up his arms, to his shoulders. "Well, we sure as snot aren't going to say goodbye to New York Cole and Laila with an affectionate high five."

He grinned at me and brushed his thumb down my jawline. "Oh, thank goodness." And then his lips were on mine and his arms were around my waist, raising me to him and holding me like he wasn't sure he would ever let me go.

"What is happening right now?" Brynn practically squealed, startling us out of a goodbye kiss for the ages. Cole and I turned to face a gasping Brynn, a laughing Sebastian, and a very forgotten (at least by me) Milo Ventimiglia. Brynn covered her mouth before turning to Seb. "Did you know about this?" Before he could respond, her about-to-explode eyes were on us again. "How long has this been going on?" Another gasp. "While we were in Germany? And you didn't tell us? Oh, who even cares? I'm so excited. It's about time!"

I pulled away from Cole, not worried about having been caught but not wanting him to get freaked out by discussion and speculation about what any of it meant. "Chill, Brynn. Just . . . chill. We'll talk about it later. But, um, right now . . . Cole needs to go home." I did all I could to swallow down the sadness one more time. "To Adelaide Springs."

Brynn looked from me to Sebastian, and then her eyes landed on Cole. "Why? Is everything okay?"

"Yeah. Just some paperwork stuff relating to my grandfather's estate. I think." Cole shrugged. "And my mom's flying in. And I need to, um . . . Well, I'll be back—"

"Cole's going to be the sous chef at a new restaurant in Brooklyn!" I blurted out. He laced his fingers through mine, and I squeezed his hand almost hard enough to keep mine from shaking. "Isn't that amazing?"

"Wow. Congrats, man." Sebastian broke the painful silence that had lingered for several seconds. "Is this Sylvia's place?"

"Yeah. Thanks. I start Tuesday, so . . ." He didn't release his grip on me, but with his other hand he pulled his phone from his pocket and started texting.

"Just remembered you haven't actually accepted the job?" I asked him softly.

He grinned as his phone made the swoosh sound of a text being sent. "Yep."

Sebastian was talking to Milo about Sylvia being Sylvia Garos, and Milo was telling Seb that he had a reservation there in January, which was the soonest he could get on the list. And Brynn was . . . Well, Brynn was connecting all the painful dots of what wasn't being said by her lifelong friends.

"So I guess we'll see you soon," she said, her eyes brimming with tears as she embraced Cole.

He hugged her. "Take good care of our girl for the next few days. She's accustomed to a certain New York lifestyle now, you know. That includes Black & White Cookies at least twice a day." He pulled away from her and punched Sebastian on the shoulder. "I'll be talking to you."

"Do we need to call you a ride to the airport?"

"Yes!" I answered for him. I'd sort of forgotten, after our endless miles of walking and taking the train without them, that our friends were Escalade people.

"On it." Sebastian pulled out his phone and pushed a couple buttons. "Safe travels, pal." He returned the friendly punch and then turned away to talk, presumably to Malik.

It was while Brynn was staring sadly at Cole and me, and Cole and I were trying to pull our eyes away from each other in order to get moving, but not quite finding the strength to do so, that my jilted date broke up the heavy silence.

"Hey, I'm Milo." He stuck his hand out toward Cole and me, and his eyes darted between us. "Congratulations on the job and . . . something about paperwork and Germany, I think? I'm not sure I understand anything that's happened in the last few minutes, but, um . . . sorry for your loss. Maybe?"

Cole stuck his hand out to Milo. "Hey, I'm Cole. Sorry about all this."

"Laila." I jutted my hand out and smiled, manufacturing a bit of civility. A little bit of *anything* other than my desire to never take my eyes off of Cole. To never let go of him. What I wouldn't give to be able to go back in time and tell 2002 Laila Olivet that there would come a day when Jess Mariano would be nothing more than a handsome, charming, bad-boy third wheel to her.

"I'm Milo. Great to meet you."

Milo said something after that. Something about how he wished he could say it was the first time he'd walked in on his date kissing another man or something. And then something else that made Cole and Brynn laugh. And he was totally gorgeous, of course. I mean, he was Milo Ventimiglia. In the flesh. I heard him say something about how he was sorry he didn't have more time. Or did he say he was sorry he hadn't had more wine? No, that wasn't right. I could remember reading an interview where he said he didn't drink, so it must have been the time thing.

He was also a vegetarian. Admirable and all and, yes, he would probably live longer than I would. But seriously. There could be no future for me with a man who didn't eat bacon.

Pretty soon, after one more hug and insistence from me that if he was going to make it to Adelaide Springs today he had to get going, Cole was heading into Brynn and Seb's building, turning back and waving at me one more time, and then he was out of sight. And a few minutes later Milo was hopping on his motorcycle, very nice and forgiving about being stood up by the waitress from Colorado who had once had his face as the wallpaper on her Compaq Presario computer, and I could have followed after him. Cole, not Milo. That would have just been stalking. But I could have followed Cole. I could have spent a few more minutes with him. I could have helped him pack and booked his flight, and helped him process his emotions about everything that was happening. But that wasn't New York Laila's job. He'd said goodbye to New York Laila, and that was that. So now my job was to figure out where New York Laila ended and Adelaide Springs Laila began, so that by the next time I talked to my best friend, I would be in a better position to manage that nagging little crossover detail of being madly, completely, hopelessly in love with him.

CHAPTER THIRTY-FOUR

COLE

"Ah, there he is." Doc was the first to notice and turn as Cole walked in through the creaky screen door.

Jo scooted her chair back from the table and hurried over to him, her arms outstretched. "Bless your heart. You must be wiped out. Need some coffee or something? Have you eaten anything?"

"I'm fine. Thanks." Cole gave her a one-armed hug. Truthfully, he wasn't feeling very warm and huggy toward any of them at the moment.

Getting out of New York had been easy. You know, if you didn't take into account that every second he was getting farther and farther away from Laila, he was obsessing over his mistakes. He was pretty sure he had made the right decisions about the big things. He'd had to cut his trip short and go back to Adelaide Springs, and he still didn't see any realistic options, long term, that could keep him from moving away. Even if he could get over the pain of having Cassidy's taken away from him, facts were facts. Cooking was his only employable skill and his only passion (again . . . *employable*). It was all the little short-term things that he was pretty sure he was screwing up.

He should have asked Laila to come home with him. Right? Couldn't he have found a way to make sure their Adelaide Springs goodbye didn't really feel like a goodbye? Because it wasn't goodbye. Right? Regardless, why had he not made their New York goodbye better than that? As he'd left her there, only turning back long enough to smile and wave one more time, he'd been going for cool and casual.

See? No big thing. I'll probably see you at Christmas. But what had that left her thinking? Had cool and casual translated to indifference once exposed to the open air?

If she hadn't picked up an indifference vibe from that, she almost certainly had from, "Hey, Milo Ventimiglia, nice to meet you. You two kids have fun now," or whatever he'd said to her date. Her actual date. Her actual celebrity date who, Cole was not ashamed to admit, was the most attractive man he had ever seen in person (and he and Laila were ninety-six percent sure they had been seated across the aisle from Dermot Mulroney at the Australian Bee Gees Show in Las Vegas, so he knew a thing or two about good-looking celebrity men). But what could he have done? Was he supposed to pull Milo aside and explain the situation? Ask him *not* to be as enchanted and beguiled by her as he was of course going to be, because how could he possibly not be? And hey, while he was at it, could he be just a little less handsome? *That'd be great. Thanks so much.* Should he have slipped Sebastian a hundo and implored him to break things up if he spotted any sparks igniting?

It had been a very long day, and Cole was legitimately disturbed that thoughts about surreptitiously bribing his extremely wealthy friend to commit relational sabotage had become commonplace before he'd even crossed back over the Mississippi River.

He'd gotten to Denver by 2:30 p.m. mountain time, but mechanical issues with the commuter jet had resulted in the cancellation of the day's last flight to Telluride. And, of course, if he couldn't get to Telluride, he couldn't get to Adelaide Springs. At least not the relatively easy way. Rather than wait until morning, he'd rented a car and driven the 250 miles home. The 250 *mountain* miles home. So he'd had nearly five hours to come up with a bunch more things he should have done differently. That had been fun.

But still, none of that was what had caused him to greet everyone with such an un-huggy disposition. It was the most recent text he had received from his mother, just as he was pulling into town, that had done the trick.

We're at the bar. Can't wait to see you! xoxo

Whose genius idea had it been to meet at Cassidy's?

"You sure you don't want some coffee?" Jo asked again, ushering him to a seat at the big six-top in the center of the room. "Owen left it warming for you."

"Who's Owen?"

"Oh my goodness, would you look at my little boy? When did you become a full-grown man?"

Cole caught Doc looking at him as Cassidy made her way back in from the restroom, so he controlled the eye roll that was desperate to break free, but a little good, old-fashioned sassing his mother was unavoidable. "It's been about twenty years now, Mom."

She chuckled. "You know what I mean. Come here, you."

He stood from the seat he hadn't wanted to sit down in anyway and hugged his mom like a good boy. If he hadn't been so tired, and if every single emotional trigger he had hadn't already been set off, he probably would have been genuinely happy to see her. As it was, it wasn't that he was *unhappy* to see her. More just that he had bigger fish to fry, and very little oil left in the pan.

"Okay, Doc. Get me caught up."

Cassidy looked behind her toward the door as she sat next to Cole. "Shouldn't we wait for Laila?"

Cole's eyes flashed to Doc. "Was Laila supposed to come? You didn't mention that she needed to be here."

Doc shook his head slowly. "Nope. Not necessarily."

"Oh. Sorry," Cassidy said. "I just assumed, I guess. I'd love to see her before I fly out in the morn—"

Cole pushed away from the table, causing the chair—those stupid wooden chairs his grandfather had spent hours and hours carving spruce tree and antler designs into the back of even though Cole had wanted something simpler and had then been stuck with them for fifteen years—to fall backward to the floor as he stood. "She's not here. She stayed in New York. Now can we all please stop acting like Laila and I can't go anywhere without each other? I can function without her, you know. I'm a grown man who is perfectly capable of—"

He interrupted himself with an abrupt, angry groan. Even he wasn't buying it. He huffed over to the bar and squeezed the edge of it between his hands, pushing himself off of it and then lowering back down almost like he was doing push-ups. "This is my bar." He said it softly. To himself. And then he turned to face the six wary eyes looking at him like he was their rabid dog they were really hoping they wouldn't have to put down.

"This is my bar!" It was a shout, accompanied by a swift kick of the barstool next to him, causing it to clatter and roll until its journey was interrupted by the legs of a four-top. "This is my bar. My restaurant. And he just took it from me. And yes, yes, I know it was never really mine. But you begin to think of things that way. You know? And is that so bad? Isn't it a good thing to love something so much that you feel like it's yours, even if it never really was? It's good for the restaurant, right? Good for the business. Is anyone else ever going to love this place as much as I did?"

He kept facing them but pointed behind him to the kitchen. "Who else is going to spend hours upon hours every week making sure it's spotless back there? What, is *Owen* going to do that?"

Even Cole instantly knew that was a weak thread he was pulling at. Of course *someone* was going to clean the kitchen. Even business owners without a shred of love in their hearts don't want health-code violations.

"And the coffee?" *Yep. There we go. Much better accusation.* "He left the coffee warming? With no employees here? Who's taking responsibility for *that*? Is the insurance even in his name yet?"

He went behind the bar, switched off the burners, and carried the pot to the sink. As he watched the rich brown liquid circle down the drain and the aroma hit his nose, he sort of regretted that. But he moved on from regret pretty quickly when his eye caught sight of the lost-and-found bin under the bar.

"And this!" He grabbed the box after setting the hot carafe on the top, cooled burner out of habit and briefly wishing he had set it on the hot burner so someone else would have to deal with the scalded glass for once. "The way people leave stuff here." Cole rifled through the lost objects with his hand while staring emphatically at Doc, Jo, and his mother. "It's not because they're careless. Not usually. It's because they're so comfortable here that they don't think about checking their pockets to make sure they have everything before they go any more than they would make sure their books are still on the shelf at home each day. If they leave something, they'll just get it tomorrow."

He looked down at the objects and began lining them up on the bar top, one by one. "That's why Lucinda always has a pair of sunglasses in the box. She just switches them out and grabs them next time. It's why Fenton's keys are in here." Always. And that was in addition to the set Cole kept on a hook behind the soda machine. "Does *Owen* know to cut people off? Does *Owen* recognize when Fenton's had too much or when Roland's blood sugar is dropping and he needs some orange juice? Is *Owen* going to make sure all twenty or twenty-five of the PTA ladies get home safely on Tuesday nights?"

Truth be told, he'd been struggling with that one himself since Sebastian had been around less. *Owen* might want to put someone on the payroll, just to deal with PTA night.

He spotted Maxine's huge flip phone with the big, bold numbers on the keypad. The phone designed just for senior citizens. The one Cole had bought for her so she could call for help if she slipped and fell again when she was out walking Prince Charlemagne but which always seemed to be in the lost-and-found box, no matter how many times he returned it to her. He chuckled as he pulled it out, but the humor faded when he eyed a sliver of yellow plastic beneath it. He set the phone aside and tilted the box, and rolling down came three—no, wait, four—tubes of Burt's Bees pomegranate lip balm. He pulled one out and stood it on its end next to Lucinda's sunglasses. Then the second. The third. The fourth he kept in his hands a little longer, turning it over and over between his fingers before removing the lid and lifting it to his nose to see if it smelled as good as it tasted.

"Alright, son." Doc stood and slowly made his way over to the bar, returning the chair and the stool to their proper positions as he passed. Then he released a heavy sigh just as a compassionate hand landed on Cole's shoulder. "Why don't you come over here and tell us what happened with you and Laila?"

CHAPTER THIRTY-FIVE

LAILA

"And that was that. You guys got home, everybody went to bed, and we woke up this morning having no idea how we were supposed to behave in each other's presence. We ended things okay, I think. He texted me when he landed, and then again to let me know he'd decided to rent a car and drive home, so we're okay." It was like I felt a compulsive need to try to speak our okayness into being.

We were sitting on the wicker sectional, and the lights were still strung, and the propane heater flames were once again dancing, and the moon was reflecting off the city, and I had just tried pho for the first time, but Brynn and Seb's roof—and New York in general, really—had lost its magic. I had told them everything. And it was strange. I'd known Brynn since birth and Seb for almost a decade now. I'd talked to them both about lots of stuff. Personal things. Embarrassing things. Confidential things. Stupid, inconsequential things. And never once during those conversations had I thought of them as anything other than my dear friends whom I loved and trusted. But as I'd spilled my guts about the day Cole and I had had, the challenges I was facing with him, and the way it had all made me feel, I suddenly felt the full weight of them as a journalistic power duo. They were studying me so seriously and listening to everything I said so intently that I half expected the next question I heard to be a thinly veiled accusation that my failures of leadership had led to widespread corruption and a national crisis of confidence. (Or the Brynn equivalent of that—a confrontation about how I'd lip-synced during the Super Bowl halftime show or something.)

"So . . . that's it," I reiterated when neither of them took their eyes off me or opened their mouths to say anything.

"I'm really sorry, hon."

Let's be real, that hadn't been the reaction I'd expected from Brynn. Seb, sure. A resistance to overreaction was pretty much a guarantee with Sebastian Sudworth. But I'd expected Brynn to squeal and swoon and brainstorm plans to make it all work out. I would have placed at least even odds on her jumping up, throwing my things into a bag, calling up Malik, and initiating a *Notting Hill* sequence at the end of which I asked Cole a question at a press conference. Maybe something to the effect of "If you're determined to move away rather than stay with me forever, can you at least promise to never fall in love with some woman who, even if she lets us stay friends, I'll always know you like more than me?" Because that was something the readers of *Horse & Hound* and I were all quite curious about.

My most recent nightmare scenario involved him falling in love with a gorgeous culinary genius (probably named Charly with a *y* or Rian with an *i*) and getting married and moving to Italy, where they would cook and eat and make love under cypress trees, and the next time I saw him he would have children named Giuseppe and Carlotta and I would have to pretend to like the kids, especially Carlotta, whose middle name would be Laila, of course—except with a circumflex over the first *a* because what else would you expect from a pretentious, man-stealing, life-ruining harpy like Charly Kimball?

"That's it? You're not going to jump in and try to fix this?" The question to Brynn hung in the air, but surprisingly I hadn't been the one to ask it. "What happens next?"

We both faced Sebastian with wide eyes.

"I'm sorry?" Brynn asked him.

He scooted forward on the sofa, his head tilted toward her. "Look, you're the one who's been watching this thing play out since you were all on the playground together. They're your closest friends, and you've shipped them harder than . . . I don't know, Mulder and Scully."

Laughter burst out of Brynn. "Wow. Thank you for that very special blast from the past."

"Whatever. I'm just trying to speak your language."

"Masterfully done, dear." She peered over at me and raised her eyebrows. "And sure, no one wants this to happen more than I do. But I think Cole just needs some time to process everything. He knows how she feels now, and—"

"But does he?" Sebastian crossed over to the refrigerator to grab a bottle of water. He raised it questioningly, and I nodded, so he threw it behind his back and I caught it effortlessly—a little trick we'd mastered when I was waiting tables and he was working behind the bar at Cassidy's. He grabbed another for himself, unscrewed the lid, and took a long, leisurely gulp before speaking again. "I think you're forgetting the one common trait that all men share. *All* of us. Including the great Cole Kimball."

I took the bait. "And what might that be?"

He sat back down beside Brynn and shrugged. "Men are dumb."

Brynn guffawed as she leaned her head on Seb's shoulder and rested her hand on his knee, but I wasn't laughing. I was suddenly in studious scholar mode.

I leaned forward, across the patio table from them, and rested my elbows on my legs. "What do you mean?"

Seb stretched his arm around Brynn's shoulders, and the two of them leaned back. "He's confused, Laila. Everything that is happening between the two of you right now . . . You've already moved all the pieces around. If your relationship was a chess game, you're Magnus Carlsen."

I looked at Brynn, who looked as clueless as I felt. "Who?"

Seb exhaled and tried again. "Or what's-her-name in *The Queen's Gambit*. The one who saw all the chess moves on her ceiling."

"Oh! Beth Harmon?"

He smiled at me and nodded. "Yes. You're Beth Harmon. And Cole is some kid assuming he can play chess because he already knows how to play checkers. You know that if Cole makes *this* move, you'll need to make *that* move. And you've been doing it for years. Most of your life, I would guess."

"I don't think I do that." Even as I said the words, I thought of how I'd gotten us back into our comfort zone at Shake Shack. How I'd defused his panic after he almost kissed me in the kitchen. How I'd created a test tube for our emotions by suggesting the blind-date experiment. "I've never *meant* to do that," I amended, somewhat horrified at myself.

"No, it's not a bad thing." He removed his arm from around Brynn and leaned forward to mirror me. "I didn't mean it like you're strategizing or manipulating or anything like that. It's emotional intelligence. And obviously men as a whole aren't dumb. Cole's certainly not. But the fact is most of us run on a simpler operating system than most women. It's like the old stereotype of men refusing to ask for directions. More often than not, it's not because we're stubborn. It's because we don't know we're lost."

Silence filled the air, apart from the sounds of horns honking and people shouting and sirens zooming closer and farther away. The soundtrack to a life-changing week and a perfect day. Sounds that I had found charming and atmospheric in Cole's presence, but without him they were coarse and aggressive.

I reached across the table to grab Sebastian's hand. He brought his other hand in to envelop mine. "Thanks."

"Of course." He lowered his eyes, compelling mine to lock with them. "So what do you think? What happens next?"

"What happens next," I began, "is that I'm going home tomorrow."

"Tomorrow?!" Brynn nudged Seb out of the way and grabbed my hand in both of hers. "No! You can't! We have you until Wednesday. I thought you could go to *Sunup* with me on Tuesday. George Clooney is going to be on. George Clooney! And there's so much we still haven't had a chance to do and see. I was going to take you to see *Hamilton*, and you need to have frozen hot chocolate at Serendipity, and—"

"Thank you." I squeezed her hand, desperately needing her to stop talking before she mentioned any other things I wished I'd thought to do with Cole. "But I don't want to be here anymore." All day long I'd been fighting against the urge to give in to the sadness and misery by reminding myself I wasn't actually losing anything. It was going to be difficult enough to convince myself of that in Adelaide Springs, without him there. In New York, I didn't stand a chance. "The truth is, without him, I sort of hate it here."

And why wouldn't I? New York would always represent what could have been. At least in Adelaide Springs, I could start focusing on the future. There I could focus on what would always be. That was real. That was what mattered.

CHAPTER THIRTY-SIX

COLE

"I'm sorry." Jo was the first to speak several minutes later, after coffee had been refilled, tempers had been defused, and Cole had shared a brief synopsis of his torment with his mother, his former teacher, and the mayor. "What's the problem here?"

"Um . . . all of it," Cole responded, somewhat dismayed. He'd always known her to be an attentive listener, and he was pretty sure he couldn't have been any clearer. "I have no idea what to do now. I can't lose her. You know?"

Cassidy and Jo looked at each other, and Jo shrugged and then turned the other direction and looked to Doc—for answers, it seemed—and Doc just smiled and shook his head.

Jo turned back to Cole. "And why would you lose her?"

Why were they all staring at him like he was whispering Shakespearean sonnets in Klingon? What about any of this was difficult for them to understand? "Because I don't know how we're supposed to just go on with our lives like New York never happened."

"But . . . I . . . So why . . ."

Doc stepped into the middle of Jo's stammering. "Let me try a different approach, since I think Jo's kinda stalling out here a bit. Are you saying that before yesterday, nothing had ever happened between the two of you? No conversations about whether to be a couple? No chalking things up to bad timing? No jealous outbursts when you were dating other people?"

His mother decided to join in on this fun little game they were apparently all developing for Hasbro. "What about when you brought that girl from Boulder home with you?"

"And what about when Laila and Seb were flirty when he first moved here?" Jo pushed, leaning in. "I still think that one would have happened eventually if Brynn hadn't come back."

"What?!" Cole scoffed, and then it morphed into laughter. *Ridiculous.* "Laila and Seb weren't 'flirty.'"

Jo rolled her eyes. "You can't be serious, Cole."

Doc continued, "No *anything* when you'd had a little too much wine at a wedding?"

"No! Of course not."

Cassidy leaned in and tapped her knuckles on his arm. "You guys went to dances together. In school, I mean."

"Well, yeah. I mean, we all sort of went together . . ."

"And school trips. Camping trips. Vegas!" Cassidy slammed her fist on the table with a level of excitement that should only accompany the discovery of a new planet. "You mean to tell me nothing happened when the two of you went to Vegas? Nothing that you agreed would just stay there . . . ?"

Okay, this is madness. "Read my lips, you guys. Nothing. Ever. Happened. Not until yesterday." He glanced at his watch, still set on eastern time. "Day before yesterday. Why is that so hard to believe?"

Doc and Jo shared a few seconds of silent communication—mostly just Doc smiling and Jo rolling her eyes a lot—and then they turned in unison toward Cassidy.

"Do you want to tell him or shall I?" Doc asked.

Cassidy sighed. "I'm his mother. I should be the one to do it." She scooted her chair noisily toward him and then tapped on the side of his leg until he turned to face her. Once they were knee to knee and, apart from puzzled glances over his shoulder at Jo and Doc, she had his attention, she said, "You're in love with Laila. You always have been. And I'd be willing to bet the last dollar I have that she's every bit as much in love with you."

"Right." The corner of Doc's lips curled. He lowered his boot to the floor and opened up the file of papers in front of him. "Now that that's all cleared up, what do you say we get down to business."

⌐

Cole didn't have much time to try to make sense of what they were telling him about Laila. Not when the bombshells just kept coming.

"I don't understand," he finally said, for easily the hundredth time that day. "You're seriously telling me that Grandpa was just buying up abandoned buildings in Adelaide Springs for the better part of thirty years?"

"So it seems." Doc handed deeds to Cole one at a time. "The office space Spruce House rented to make room for more residents in the main building. Ken Lindell's insurance agency downtown next to the Bean Franklin. An entire strip of empty storefronts down on the south end of Main Street." Three more deeds in a row. "All owned by Bill, doing business as WECC Management Group, LLC."

Cole sighed and shuffled through the stack of papers, not that any of them made a lick of sense to him.

"I'm sorry, Mom, but I just don't understand how you didn't know anything about any of this. You're a member of the LLC, right? Isn't that what you said, Doc?"

Cassidy shrugged and pushed her chair back from the table. "You know . . . Dad handled it all. I didn't know that he'd bought up all those properties—"

"Weren't there board meetings or things you had to sign or—"

"I trusted him, Cole. I didn't ever worry about whether he was cheating me out of something or how much money I was going to make. It wasn't like that. He started this little LLC, and he and Mom were the owners, and when I turned eighteen, he let me sign something so I was an owner too. I figured he was just trying to help me feel like an adult. When Mom died, I remember he had me sign something to remove her name. It's not like we were staying up to look at profit-and-loss statements after you went to bed. I honestly hadn't thought anything about any of it in years."

"And Bill wasn't exactly one for open, transparent communication anyway, as we all know," Jo said as she placed her hand on Cole's shoulder and refilled his coffee. Coffee she had very kindly brewed without initiating even a single well-deserved guilt trip about the perfectly good pot of it he had poured down the drain. "It seems as if Owen was the only one who really knew anything."

Cole looked up at her. "Hang on. Owen? As in the new owner of Cassidy's?"

"Well, yes and no." Doc held his cup up for Jo to refill and then smiled at her as he thanked her. "This is where things get interesting."

⌒

Something smelled good. Food. There was food that smelled good. And Cole hadn't had anything to do with it.

"That can't be right."

He sat up in the king-size bed he'd bought himself when he moved back in with his grandfather. The bed upgrade had been Laila's idea, to help him combat the feeling that he was never actually going to achieve independent adulthood. As she'd said at the time, "Only big boys get to sleep in big-boy beds." There hadn't been space for much else in the room, but he liked it that way. Less space equaled less clutter.

"Are you up?" His mother opened the door a crack but didn't peek her head in, thankfully. Not that he was particularly indecent, with his T-shirt quilt pulled up halfway over his bare chest, but big boys didn't like their mommies barging into their rooms.

"Yeah. Sort of." He yawned and peered out the window to evaluate the positioning of the sun. "What time is it?"

"Nearly eight thirty. I thought we could eat some breakfast and talk before I have to go."

Ah, yes. That's right. It had just been a glorified layover in which she made a brief appearance in her son's life, brought clarity and confusion to crises both financial and romantic, and, apparently, made an omelet or something. All in a day's work for Dr. Dolan-Kimball.

"You bet. Be right out."

⌐

As it turned out, she'd done a little more than whip together an omelet. Eggs Florentine. His mother had made eggs Florentine. Perfectly poached eggs, homemade hollandaise, and all.

"That was delicious," he commended her. "No offense, but I did not know you could cook like this."

"Are you kidding? Where do you think you learned?"

"Um . . . culinary school? And Grandma, of course."

"Well, okay. That's true. But I've gotten better."

"Clearly."

She stood to gather the dishes, but Cole beat her to the punch. "Sit. I've got it." He took the plates and utensils to the sink and ran some warm water over the sticky yolk residue and then left them to soak. "So have you thought any more about, you know . . . everything? What are you going to do?"

"About the property?"

"Yeah."

She shrugged. "Sell it, I guess."

He grabbed the coffeepot from the counter and poured himself more. He moved toward her cup, but she put her hand over it and he returned the coffee to the burner.

"I'm not sure you understand, Mom. This is a big deal." He turned back to face her. "This isn't the Adelaide Springs you remember. It's growing. Quickly. All this property Grandpa bought—it's not worthless. And people are going to be willing to pay. But I think it's important that you sell to the right people. I feel like the decisions made today are going to determine the future of this town for a long time."

"I agree." She nodded. "So what do you say? Do you want them? I'll make you a screaming deal."

His lips flapped as a burst of air, carrying a laugh with it, escaped. But his mother remained sitting there, her eyes watching him over her coffee cup as she sipped, and she didn't seem to get the joke. "What, you're serious?"

"Of course I am. It seems like the perfect solution to me." She set her cup down. "How great would it be to open your own restaurant? And I was thinking we could give Ken the option to buy the insurance agency, sell some of the other properties to locals if they want them . . . Whatever. I'm sure we could get enough money by selling some others for you to renovate the building you want. Then you and Laila could settle down and—"

"That's a little premature, don't you think?"

"Well, whatever. But you don't want to leave this place, Cole. I know you don't."

"Would you please stop?!" He raised his voice more than he had meant to, but at least a decent night of sleep had put him in a better position to handle his frustration than the night before when he was knocking over every chair and barstool that dared get in his way. "Look, I mean no disrespect, but you have to stop acting like you know what I want. You have to stop acting like you know *me*, Mom. You only know about the Vegas trip because I told you Laila and I were going. Like, three months before we went. You never asked how the trip was, in the last seven years. For all you know, we canceled and didn't even go. And yet you spoke of it last night like it was something you actually have knowledge of. You have to stop acting like you actually know anything about me and my life anymore."

Cole closed his eyes and took a couple deep breaths. He didn't want to fight with her, but he tried to hear Laila's voice. If she were there, she would probably tell him what she had been telling him for years: *"You have to tell her how she's hurt you. You know she'd want to know. Just don't forget to also make sure she knows how much you love her."*

"Look, Mom, I'm sorry. I just . . ." He opened his eyes, and she was gone. "Mom?" He walked out of the kitchen and down the hall-way toward her bedroom after making sure she hadn't gone outside. "Mom? Where are you? I didn't mean to—"

"You need to see something." She sat at the foot of her bed in the room his grandfather hadn't made any changes to since she moved away. Her laptop was on her lap, and she patted the bed for him to join her.

"I shouldn't have said those things. I'm sorry if I—"

"Hush. It's my turn to talk now." She clicked around on the track-pad and then turned the screen for him to see. "Emails. From your grandfather." She scrolled and scrolled and just kept on scrolling. There were hundreds of them. Maybe more.

Cole took the laptop from her hands. "Grandpa didn't know how to email."

She chuckled. "Not so well, no. But I don't always have phones where I am. You know? So early on I tried to teach him the basics so we could stay in contact this way."

"Tried?" Cole was still scrolling. "It looks like you succeeded."

"Not really. For a long time he would go to the library, and Helen Souza would type for him. When her eyesight got too bad, he went to Laila."

He looked up from the screen. "Laila typed up emails to send to you?"

Cassidy nodded. "Yep. And helped him access the ones that I sent. Probably a couple times a week, on average. For the last . . . oh, I don't know. Eight years or so, I guess." She tilted her chin and studied Cole. "I'm a little surprised she never told you."

He looked back at the screen and resumed scrolling, mostly to keep his mother from seeing the emotion welling up in his eyes. He wasn't at all surprised that Laila hadn't told him. It made perfect sense. For one thing, she wouldn't have thought it was hers to tell. But he figured she also knew that if Cole knew his grandfather had gone to her for help, it would cause him to ask all the questions he'd instantly begun asking himself in that moment.

"I could have typed for him, Mom. Why did he . . ." He blinked feverishly until he could see clearly again. "Why didn't he ask me? Why didn't he want me to help him?"

"Cole Harrison Kimball, for as smart as you are, you're pretty slow sometimes. You know that? Of course he couldn't have you type them. They were all *about* you. If you came up with a new recipe, he told me about it. You took a trip somewhere, he told me about it. Sometimes the only thing in an email would be something funny or brilliant or kind that you'd said or done. Gosh, Cole . . . I'm pretty sure I knew every time your vehicle got an oil change. You were his pride and joy. Don't you know that?"

"Um . . ." He cleared his throat and pinched the bridge of his nose. "No. I . . . I guess I . . ."

Cassidy took the laptop and set it on the bed behind him, then wrapped her arms around him, her cheek on his shoulder. "You're my pride and joy, too, you know. Just . . . for the record. I'm sorry if I'm not any better at communicating that than my dad was." He felt her smile against him. "But it wasn't just platitudes, you know?"

"What wasn't?"

"When I would leave and tell you how happy I was to be able to go out into the world and show some love to people who don't have what we have. It broke my heart. Every single time I've ever walked away from you, it broke my heart. But I always knew you were so loved and so cared for. I'm sorry if I wasn't there all the time, but I hope you know that being your mom is the best job I've ever had. You're the most important thing in the whole wide world to me, and I never could have done the things I did if I hadn't known I wasn't the only one who felt that way. And, truthfully, if that wasn't *still* the case." She tilted her head up and whispered, "I'm talking about Laila."

He twisted and opened his arms to hug her as years of bottled-up resentment surrendered to the power of love and gratitude. "Yeah. Got that. Thanks."

He may have been slow, but he was finally starting to catch up.

CHAPTER THIRTY-SEVEN

LAILA

I hadn't exactly been conscious as we flew into New York, but I wouldn't have wanted to miss the first views of my mountains as we approached Adelaide Springs for anything in the world. So it was probably a good thing that new fears and concerns had made my fear of flying feel pretty minimal. (It was also probably for the best that Cole had absconded with my painkillers and never given them back.)

It was the most beautiful place on earth. It didn't even matter that I'd seen such a small amount of everything else that was out there. I knew it. The way the mountains from certain angles looked exactly like kids draw mountains, with sharp triangular peaks and Charlie Brown–shirt zigzags of snow marking a clear break in the elevation of precipitation. The way you didn't even have to refer to fields of wild-flowers *as* wildflowers, because it went without saying. Everything was wild. Even the way you had to keep your pets inside at certain times of year or day so that they weren't snatched up by a hawk or devoured by a mountain lion.

Oh gosh, that's horrible. That's not how I should have said that. *At all.* But, I mean, wasn't it kind of cool that the animals we had to watch out for were genuine high-on-the-food-chain sorts of preda-tors and not rats or possums or some other icky, pesky things that of course everyone feared but that no one exactly *bragged* about being scared of or having run-ins with? Colorado pests made you want to climb to the top of Pikes Peak and sing "America the Beautiful."

And then, of course, there were the people. I loved the people of Adelaide Springs. Now that all my grandparents had died and my mom had moved away, I only had my dad and Melinda, of course. But I also had an entire population of people who honked when they drove by if I was out on my porch, and who would bring me interesting material they found at a consignment store in Grand Junction, just in case I wanted to make some new clothes or curtains with it. There were generations of people who had watched me grow up and who I knew still saw me as a kid, but who never failed to treat me as an adult.

Whenever I missed my grandparents, I could swing by The Inn Between. It had been years since Jo had converted their house into a bed-and-breakfast, but she never even blinked when I walked in, ascended to the top-floor clubhouse, and sat at the bay window to catch the sunset.

There were things that annoyed me, of course. The amount of snow some winters. The way the ragweed pollen filled the air from August to October, making me essentially allergic to breathing. And it was a total pain to always have to make sure my cats were distracted when I opened the door.

Sometimes Dad would just drop by at the absolute worst times with complete urgency because he wanted to fix a hinge on my bedroom door or snake the drain in the bathtub, even though the door had been off the hinge for nine months, and I never shut it anyway, and the tub was draining perfectly fine.

But still . . . I was so grateful to be close enough to keep an eye on him, and to know there were a whole bunch of people who considered it their duty to keep an eye on me.

"You buckled in, Laila?" Steve, the pilot, called back to me in the second row. I was the only passenger on this particular flight.

"Yep!" I shouted to be heard over the plane noise and braced myself by digging my fingertips into the seat back in front of me and closing my eyes. "Ready!"

So . . . yeah. Still not a fan of flying in general, and definitely not a fan of flying on little death machines that seem like they're made out of aluminum foil and are roughly the size of a flatbed truck. But I also wasn't a fan of driving a few hours in a rental car over mountain passes when I hadn't slept a whole lot, wasn't really sure what time it was (no matter what my watch said), and couldn't focus for more than seven seconds on anything but how Adelaide Springs wasn't going to feel like home anymore without Cole. Even if I couldn't imagine ever being anywhere else.

Finally, a few of the longest minutes of my life had passed and we were bouncing and skidding onto the runway. I opened my eyes again for the first time since we'd begun our final descent. I loved looking at my mountains, but I knew they were a lot more beautiful when you weren't fearing your imminent death from crashing into them.

"Thanks, Steve." I stepped past him with my backpack and purse and he followed me out to retrieve my suitcase. "I'm sorry you had to make the trip just for me."

"No worries. I have an outgoing too. Worked out perfectly."

My breath caught in my throat, and I implored myself not to get my hopes up. It was probably just the Marksons going to visit their grandkids in Seattle. Or maybe some of the snowbirds were heading to Arizona a little late this year. I'd gotten on early flights and gained two hours crossing time zones, but still. It had never occurred to me that I might get here before he left.

"Thanks again, Steve. Say hi to Kathy and the kids for me."

I looked toward the parking lot to see if I spotted Cole's Wrangler, and that's when reality caught up with me. He'd rented a car in Denver, which meant he'd probably driven back to Denver and would be flying to New York from there.

Ah, well. What's a little more disappointment?

In a few days I'd be driving up to Denver myself. How easy it would be to ask Dad and Melinda to drop me off at the airport after Melinda's appointment with the neurologist. Then they could drive my car home, and I could be back in New York—back with Cole—in less than four hours, and then . . .

And then Dad and Melinda would be left to make sense of and

apply whatever inevitably life-altering instruction they received from the neurologist. Dad would bottle up everything he was feeling. Melinda would put so much emphasis on caring for him that she wouldn't take good enough care of herself. And I'd have added, "Please don't forget to feed my cats," to the burdens they were carrying.

I sighed and pulled the handle out of my suitcase so I could wheel it to— Ugh. Not to my car. I hadn't thought about the fact that I hadn't driven to the airport a week ago and therefore did not have a car waiting for me. I pulled my phone from my pocket and flipped it out of airplane mode so I could call my dad to pick me up.

"Hey there. Did somebody call for a Lyft?"

My eyes shot up from my phone. Twenty-four hours. I'd only gone about twenty-four hours without seeing him, and yet I could practically hear my heart sighing in relief. "What are you doing here?"

It doesn't matter why he's here, Laila. He's here. First things first.

"What am *I* doing here?" Cole asked with a chuckle. "What are *you*—"

He released an "oof"-like sound as I rushed into him. I stood on my Converse-clad tiptoes and wrapped my arms around his shoulders, desperately needing a proper hug from him. A hug that helped me know that with New York Cole and Laila behind us, we were still okay. I needed to know that even if I was never going to be permitted to fully love him in all the ways I wanted to, we were in it together. *Life.* We were in life together, for as long as it lasted.

I clearly took him by surprise, but he adapted quickly and leaned into me, his arms around my waist. "You okay?" he asked against my ear.

"Yeah." My chin bounced off his shoulder as I nodded. "I'm just so glad I got to see you. I'm sorry I didn't fly home with you. I hate that we lost that time."

"Laila?" The female voice behind Cole sounded familiar, but it wasn't until I opened my eyes that I knew who it was.

"Cassidy?" Cole released me, and his mother and I hurried to each other. "That's right! I forgot you were . . . I mean, I wasn't thinking about . . ."

Sorry . . . wasn't thinking about anything that wasn't your son and how much I love him, and a little bit (okay, a lot bit) about how my brain just sort of melted and felt like it was going to ooze out of my ears when he was kissing me. So, tell me . . . How are you?

"Ready when you are, Cassidy," Steve called out before climbing the steps back to the cockpit.

"I wish we had more time," she said to me as she pulled out of our embrace, and then she reached out and grabbed Cole's hand. He squeezed it and then leaned in and kissed her on the cheek. "You keep in touch."

He nodded. "I will."

She gave his hand one last squeeze and looked over to me. "Both of you. Okay?"

I said, "Of course," at the same time Cole said, "Pretty sure Laila has your email address."

My eyes widened slightly and Cassidy winked at me, so I looked over at Cole and saw he was smiling. Some things had happened in those twenty-four hours, and something deep inside reassured me they hadn't been all bad. That smile—warm and filled with humor and affection—reassured me things weren't all bad. All the same . . .

"You're not flying out?"

"I have some time."

"Well, if you're driving to Denver, you need to get going. You do realize you start work in Brooklyn *tomorrow*."

"I've got it sorted out. Don't worry." He smiled and shrugged. "Like I said, I have some time."

I shook my head and groaned. "I'm so happy to see you, but if you end up losing this job because I keep you here too long, do you know how guilty I'll feel?"

"Good grief, Lai. Would you just relax? I do okay in Colorado, you know. I don't need you to be my travel planner here, okay?" He put his hand over his eyes to look up toward the sun until the plane disappeared into the clouds, and then he reached out and took the handle of my luggage from me. "Now seriously, do you have a ride?"

I shook my head. "I guess I'm pretty hopeless on my own. I'll have you know *no one*, not a single person, offered to wheel me through JFK on a suitcase this time."

He *tsk*ed. "New Yorkers are so rude." We stood there smiling at each other for a moment until he gestured over his shoulder toward the parking lot. "Come on."

I savored a few minutes of silence with him as we drove into town. He and I had always tended to be pretty quiet together when we were driving. We always had things to say to each other. Never, in our entire lives, had we run out of things to say. But when it was just the two of us in a car, it had always seemed like just *being*—observing the world as it passed by, collecting our thoughts, sometimes listening to music but usually not, each of us relishing alone time *together*—was the most important thing we needed to communicate.

So when we pulled up to the old, abandoned, stone-exterior buildings on Main Street that used to house a credit union and, I think, a dry cleaners for a while, and about a million other things before the last tenants moved on about a decade ago, I didn't have any idea what we were doing there.

"Have a few minutes for me to show you something?" Cole asked, his hand on his door handle.

"I'm all yours."

I met him on the sidewalk and studied him as he pulled a key out of his pocket and unlocked the door. There must have been a million questions dancing in my eyes, but he just held the door open for me and ushered me inside. "After you."

I couldn't remember the last time I'd been in any of the suites, but a familiarity washed over me all the same. I knew exactly where the light switch was and reached for it but was still surprised when lights actually turned on. "Electricity's still connected?"

"Electric heating."

That explained it. It wouldn't take long for an abandoned building to become a condemned one if everything was left to freeze during the winter.

I followed him in and looked around at the dusty corners, the broken chairs stacked against the wall, and the hideous lime-green wallpaper with orange and yellow flowers. Ultimately it was the wallpaper that jarred my memory.

"Oh my gosh, this was the beauty parlor!" I laughed as I spun around, looking at it all with new interest through the lens of nostalgia. "Has it seriously not been anything since . . . When did Fern move to Florida?"

"Yeah, 1995. That's the last time there was a business in here."

"*Wow.*" I continued walking around the small space, peeking my head into closets and blowing away dust on windowsills. "Remember when we saw this exact wallpaper on an old *Brady Bunch* episode?"

"I do." He was still standing by the door, watching me. "I'm thinking of buying it."

My eyes flew open and instantly darted around the space again to look at it from yet another perspective. "This unit? What, like, as an investment thing or something?"

"I guess you could say that." He breathed in deeply and then let it out slowly as he scratched his jawline where his facial hair was growing back. "I'd sort of like to invest in *you*, Laila Olivet."

I tilted my head and tried to make sense of what he was saying. "What are you talking about?"

"Come here." He took a few steps in and grabbed my hand, then pulled me outside with him. We walked down to the next locked door in the plaza, which I was now recalling had housed a daycare back in the early aughts, and he opened it up and ushered me inside. He flipped on the light, and we journeyed farther in.

"I didn't realize there was so much space here."

"Yeah, neither did I." He flipped another switch, illuminating another room in the back.

This suite was much bigger. Three or four times the size of the old beauty parlor, at least.

"I'm not sure if you remember, but this was the daycare—"

"Yeah, I remember that."

He flipped on yet another light switch. "And it was where Juanita Marquez was preparing the meals for the hotshots and smokejumpers during the West Fork Fire back in, what . . . 2013 or so? And then she talked about opening a restaurant, and it just never happened."

"Cole!" I planted my feet and grabbed his arm as he began heading toward another doorway. He stopped and turned to face me. "You have to tell me what this is all about."

He looked up at the flickering fluorescent lights above our head. "I guess my grandfather had been secretly building some security into Adelaide Springs's future for a long time. And I guess he was building some security into mine too." He squeezed my hand before releasing it and then stepped back over to the doorway and leaned against it. "He owned this entire complex. And a lot of other properties too." He looked back at me and shrugged. "Well, he and my mother, doing business as WECC Management Group, LLC."

I squinted at him. "WECC?" I thought for a moment and tried to make sense of the letters.

"Yeah. William, Eleanor, Cassidy, and Cole. The letters weren't capitalized in those first documents Doc had, so he pronounced it *Weck*."

"Hold on. That doesn't make any sense. He sold Cassidy's . . . to himself?"

Cole shook his head. "He didn't sell it to anybody. He'd been methodically transferring all his personal investments over to the LLC for years, I guess, so that everything was separate and protected away from medical expenses and assisted-living costs and all of that. Grandpa's personal lawyer didn't even know. It was like he was two completely separate entities. And he almost got it all squared away before he died. The only thing that got lost in the shuffle was a new operating agreement for the LLC. It was dated October 1, the same date the deed for Cassidy's is set to transfer to WECC."

"And what was supposed to happen with the new operating agreement?"

He crossed his arms over his chest as his shoulders rose up to his ears. "I was supposed to become the managing member, if you can believe that."

Of course I could believe that. I didn't understand it, but I believed it. It took no convincing whatsoever for me to believe Bill Kimball had been stubbornly noncommunicative rather than intentionally cruel to his only grandchild.

"So you would have owned Cassidy's." I spoke the words softly, not in the form of a question but as a declaration. And even though the declaration carried with it layers upon layers of sadness and grief over the loss of an obstinate, frustrating old man, I mostly just felt grateful. So grateful that Cole could no longer question the magnitude of Bill's love and respect for him.

"Yeah." He sighed. "But since paperwork didn't get signed . . ."

"I'm so sorry, Cole."

"No, it's okay. At least it's still in the family."

My eyes flew open wide. "Your mom owns it."

"Crazy, right?" He looked up and ran his finger along the doorframe, then blew the gathered dust into the air. "She didn't know much more than I did, though. This guy, Owen—he seems to be the only one with the entire roadmap. The rest of us just got random scenic routes to abandonment issues and confusion." He laughed. Truly laughed. There was such a lightness to him that I'd assumed would never again be present in conversations about his grandfather. "But Owen was Grandpa's property manager. Well, not just his. This is what Owen does, I guess. So while I had medical power of attorney, Owen was power of attorney on the business side, acting through his own company, Alpine Ventures."

"And he was the one who made an offer on your house?"

"That was my mom. When Doc called her after seeing her name on the LLC paperwork he and Jo found, she remembered that, oh yeah, she *had* actually signed all sorts of legally binding paperwork." Cole rolled his eyes indulgently. "Doc also mentioned that I was thinking of selling the house, and I guess within minutes, she had gotten in touch with Owen, learned that she owned half the abandoned property in Adelaide Springs, and had Owen make an offer to expand the portfolio."

"Is she planning on moving back here?"

He shook his head. "I don't think so. I think she just wanted to keep the house in the family too." He rested his heel against the wall and leaned his weight against it. "Or maybe she wasn't too convinced I wouldn't change my mind down the road and want to come back."

Everything felt so positive. Everything felt like it was heading in the right direction. But feelings sometimes lead us astray.

"So you could go back there, couldn't you? I mean, to Cassidy's. Your mom owns everything. Even the appliances and everything you sold. Right? And now that you know Bill never sold it out from under you . . ."

"I could. Yeah." He pushed himself up with his foot and began surveying the dust over his head again. "There'd never been any plan except for Cassidy's to be mine."

"But hang on, then. Why *did* they buy the appliances from you? Why didn't Owen tell you any of this when you called the night of your grandfather's funeral?"

"Because I didn't talk to Owen," he responded with a chuckle. "I talked to some Alpine Ventures vice president who didn't have a clue as to my grandfather's wishes for Cassidy's. He just thought he was getting a screaming deal and saving the firm a lot of headache and work down the road." He looked at me and smiled. "Owen wasn't too happy."

"I bet not."

I stared at him, waiting for him to say the last piece. To say that he was staying. To say that he'd already called Sylvia Garos and told her he was grateful for the opportunity, but this was his home. Cassidy's was his restaurant. But he didn't say anything. He just stared back at me, smiling gently but giving away nothing.

"You're killing me here!" It finally burst out of me, and I laughed, if only to keep from crying. "What are you going to do, Cole? Are you . . ." I swallowed down the bitter taste of adrenaline and fear and maybe more than a little hope in the back of my throat. Right then, I was pretty sure it was the hope that was burning the most. "Are you staying at Cassidy's?"

His eyes moved to my lips, trembling between my teeth, and lingered there before returning to my eyes. "No. I don't think so. Owen tried to convince me, but in the end, I think this is a great opportunity for Adelaide Springs. I think it's time for some fresh starts." He took a slow step toward me, lowering his head to try to catch my eyes before they fell away completely. "Lai? Would you look at me?"

He took another couple steps and then reached his hand out to cup my cheek. A tear landed on his thumb, and he gently brushed across my cheekbone to gather up others that were pooling rather than falling. "Hey, I'm sorry. Don't cry. I'm so sorry. Come here." His hand slid into my hair, and he pulled me against his chest. I felt his heavy sigh as he deflated against me. "I'm sorry. I was trying to build into a moment. I didn't realize you . . ."

He kissed the top of my head and then pulled back and tilted my chin up so my tear-saturated eyes had no choice but to look at him. "I thought maybe you'd want to open a little shop or something. In the old beauty salon."

The crying halted abruptly. Even my tear ducts were confused. "I'm sorry, what?"

"Or you could do alterations, maybe? Seamstress stuff?" His confidence and enthusiasm began to falter as he dropped his arms and stepped away from me. "Or not. Obviously I'm not trying to tell you what to do with your life. If it's a stupid idea, forget it. I just know that you're always getting compliments on everything you make, and people are always asking you to mend things for them. And I swear, Laila, you could make a fortune on those cargo pants alone. They're, like, mugger-proof. But seriously, no pressure. I just thought—"

"You just thought you'd offer me a consolation prize?"

He shook his head, eyes wide. "No! Of course not."

"How many times do I have to tell you? I actually love being a waitress." I hated that I was picking a fight with him. I was keenly *aware* that I was picking a fight with him. That was not our way. But all my frayed emotions needed to be funneled into something, and anger was the nearest receptacle. "I'm a really good waitress."

"I know you are."

"Why wouldn't Owen want to hire me?"

"I'm sure he will. I mean, he probably needs a chef before that, but—"

"So I'll wait."

Except I didn't want to work at Cassidy's without him. It wasn't that I couldn't carry on day to day without him. I could. I didn't want to, but I could. But at Cassidy's? Not a chance. Not when some of the greatest moments of my life had been helping Cole build Cassidy's into what it should be. Without him, maybe it could still be great. But it wouldn't be Cassidy's.

And I'd never thought about selling clothes I made, but he was right. Maybe I should. Yes, I'd always gotten compliments from locals, but my cargo pants had also drawn the attention of a mom in Central Park, desperately searching through a stroller and a diaper bag and even some playground sand for her cell phone. If she was passing through Adelaide Springs, I bet she'd buy a pair.

But a generous, empowering, potentially genius idea from my best friend was, of course, powerless against a little brokenhearted stubbornness.

"I'll keep on working at Cassidy's." I balled my fists and planted them on my hips. "But thank you."

He nodded and looked down at his feet just as a smirk became evident on his lips. "That's too bad." He dug into his pocket and pulled out four tubes of lip balm. "I believe these are yours, by the way."

I opened my hands to receive them in utter confusion. "Thanks?"

"My pleasure." He headed back to the door and punched against the stone wall with the side of his fist. "You know, I was sort of hoping you'd come and work with me here."

My lungs became immobilized, and I attempted to appear normal in spite of that. In spite of the hope and happiness (and fear of hope and happiness) that were beginning to stack on top of each other like Tetris blocks when it all starts going too fast and you know you can't keep up anymore, so you just let them fall.

"Here?" My voice sounded so pinched. I would have to do better than that. "What do you mean work with you *here?*" Well, that was no good. The squeak had somehow gotten worse.

He turned back to face me, a huge smile on his face, and grabbed my hand to pull me through the doorway to the back room. "Okay, so I know it's nowhere near as big as Cassidy's, but there are the solid beginnings of a kitchen here. It's already got all the fixtures in place. They need some updating, of course, but I think it could work." He pulled me back into the main room. "And then I think we could seat about forty. Maybe forty-five. Again, not as much as Cassidy's, but maybe that's better. Make it sort of exclusive. Not pricewise, of course, but maybe after it takes off, and if people keep moving in—and especially during Township Days—maybe we take reservations. And then, look . . ."

He released my hand and hurried ahead to a separate room to turn on a light. "I thought this could be a private room for parties or meetings or whatever. We could probably get another fifteen to twenty people in here."

He switched off the light, leaving me in the dark in more ways than one. And immobilization had made its way to my feet. I heard him still talking as he went back into the main room and began laying out his vision for outside dining at a patio he could build in the back, overlooking the canyon, but eventually his voice faded out.

"Lai?" Footsteps made their way back to me, and then he poked his head back into the side room. "Hey, sorry. Are you okay?"

"What's happening?"

"I just think—"

"No, I mean, *what's happening?* I need you to say the words. Are you not moving to New York? Cole, if you're not moving to New

York, you have to tell me. You need to say the words. I need to hear you say the words, Cole Kimball. No more messing around. No more building to a moment. Are you saying— Are you telling me— I need you to clear this up for me. Right now." My lungs shuddered back to life and everything in me began trembling as one final word formed on my tongue. "Please."

His eyes glimmered in the unlit room. "I'm buying this building from my mom. I'm opening a new restaurant. Here. In Adelaide Springs. I don't ever want to be anywhere you're not, Laila. Not ever. I'm in love with you, and apparently I always have been." He reached behind him, without taking his eyes off of me, and turned the light back on. Just in time for me to see the twitch hopping around at the corner of his mouth. "Is that clear enough for you?"

Relief and joy—maybe as much joy as I had ever experienced—flooded through me, making me feel like I had the adrenaline to lift a car and the exhaustion to sleep for a week, before releasing in the form of choking sobs. His arms were around me then, and I was crying against his chest and breathing in broken, jagged, happy bursts. He stroked my hair and kissed the top of my head and whispered calming words and held me tighter and tighter until my breathing regulated under the influence of his.

"What do you mean, *apparently*?"

He tilted his head back to look at me. "Hm?"

"*Apparently* you've always been in love with me."

He laughed and tightened his embrace again. "Some friends of ours took it upon themselves last night to educate me. *Apparently* my lifelong obsession with you isn't just normal friendship stuff. Who knew?"

I traced the muscles in his back with my fingertips, something I was pretty sure I'd never done before. Something my hands began doing without consulting my brain this time. "And that doesn't freak you out?"

"Are you kidding me?" He chuckled. "It's nice that everything finally makes sense for a change. Or at least it's starting to." He pushed my shoulders gently back and then ran his fingertips down my arms.

"The only thing freaking me out right now, if I'm being honest, is that I'm sort of standing out here on the ledge alone. I mean, no pressure, obviously, but if you *felt* like returning the favor and, you know, bringing some clarity to the situation, I wouldn't turn it down."

"That's fair." I cleared my throat and attempted to swallow my heart back down into place as he reached out and delicately tucked a loose tendril of hair behind my ear. "I will give serious consideration to your generous offer to help me open a store or something. And yes, I will work at your new restaurant."

He nodded and studied me. About ninety percent confident I was messing with him, I figured, but hesitant to prematurely close the gap across the last ten percent. "Good. Yeah, that's good. That will help."

"Well, you know." I shrugged. "We make a good team."

His eyes made their way to my lips again as his teeth brushed up against his. "That's true. We do."

"But yeah . . ." I stepped away from him and began walking toward the door, looking up at the outdated light fixtures. "Some things need to change."

"Should I be taking notes?"

"It's pretty simple for now." I faced him again with a scrunched-up nose. "I don't think being just friends is working for us anymore. It's so . . . what's the word?"

"Gauche?"

"Yes! Exactly."

"But . . ." He took a step toward me, and I backed away from him. "I thought we weren't allowed to use that term. 'Just friends.'"

"I still stand by what I said. Nothing ranks higher than friendship. But I think if we're gonna be all dernier cri about this—"

"I'm pretty sure you're not using that properly at all."

"—then it's time to realize it's okay to add stuff *to* friendship. Right?"

"Right." The way he was looking at me, with tenderness and intensity, was setting my heart on fire. He took another step toward me, and this time my feet remained glued in place. "It's like springing for all the extra packages when you buy a new car and getting that thing fully loaded." Another step.

"Yes. Now you get it."

He nodded slowly, and I could feel his breath against me as he bent his knees slightly and wrapped his arms around my waist. He pulled me against him again, and I took in the feel of him and the scent of him and as much oxygen as my lungs could hold.

"Are you done now?" He breathed the words into my ear before planting soft kisses on my neck, the beginning of a trail across my jaw, toward my lips.

In the last moment before he reached his destination—one of the last moments before my brain forgot how to form words—as my head rolled to the side, my neck unable to support it while Cole was leaving his trail of kisses, I whispered, "I love you. Always have, probably. Definitely always will."

I felt him grin against me. "About time you figured that out."

"Sorry . . . I was just building toward a moment."

His lips were on mine then, and the desperation I felt to keep him there forever mingled with the peace and assurance of knowing that wasn't something I would ever have to fight for. I looped my arms around his neck as he cinched me tighter and lifted me to him. Then he abruptly separated his lips from mine, leaving me disoriented.

"That's three."

"What are you talking about?" I puckered up my lips and tried to reach him again, but he was lowering me back to my normal height and walking toward the doorway.

"You know . . . your grandma Hazel's rule of three. Three big, life-changing things, all at once. I'm staying, we're opening a restaurant, and now *this*. Us. That's three."

He switched off the light and headed back into the future main dining room of the restaurant. *Our* restaurant.

"Except what about my shop?" I followed after him. "That should count as its own life-changing thing."

"You haven't officially said you're going to do it."

I shrugged. "Okay. I'll do it. There. It's official."

Cole sighed. "Well, then that throws off everything."

"I came home early. That could probably count."

He shook his head as he backtracked to get a light he had missed. "No. Then we would have just done this on Wednesday."

I laughed at his nonchalance about all the life change that had occurred in such a short period of time. "So we need one more?"

He rolled his eyes upward and appeared to be doing the math. "Or one less. I'm not really sure anymore." He slung his arm over my shoulder and led me to the door and then released me to lock it behind him. "I guess we could go on a date or something."

"As just us? No alternate personas? No pretense? No one-day-only rules?"

"Just us."

"And you think a date will qualify as life-changing?"

He leaned down, right there in the open on Main Street in Adelaide Springs, and kissed me tenderly. "Yeah," he whispered against my lips. "I think it might."

He winked and grabbed my hand, lacing his fingers through mine. "So have you eaten?"

"I'll answer your question with a question: Have you cooked anything for me yet?"

"Fair point." He opened the door of his Wrangler for me and gave me a gentle boost as I climbed up. "Are you in the mood for chocolate-chip pancakes?"

I put my hand out to him. "Have we met? Laila Olivet."

"A pleasure to make your acquaintance, Ms. Olivet." He grinned and took my hand, then raised it to his lips and kissed my knuckles. "Something tells me you and I are going to be very good friends."

ACKNOWLEDGMENTS

Thank you to Kelly, Ethan, and Noah for putting up with me when I get stuck in whatever emotional trauma my characters are experiencing at the time. Thanks to my mom, dad, and sister for giving out copies of books to every medical professional in northern Kentucky. (A little additional thanks to my mom, who taught me to crack eggs with one hand, like in *Sabrina*.) And thanks to the nonfamily (but still family) people I do life with—LeeAnn, David, Jenny, Tonya, Robert, Anne, Caitlyn, Sharon, Laura, and probably at least one other person I'm forgetting to name, whom I shall refer to as Mildred. Thanks for everything, Millie!

Thank you to the amazing publishing team—Amanda, Becky, Leslie, Kerri, Taylor, Savannah, and so many others—who somehow make sense of my ramblings (and make my ramblings better) enough to create a book. An actual book.

Special thanks to my editor, Laura Wheeler, who (for some reason) keeps believing in me when I struggle to believe in myself and who, this time, miraculously, helped me believe in myself again.

Do you know what else helped with that? Therapy. And lots of it. (That's my not-so-subtle way of saying thanks to my therapist.) Seriously . . . one of the best decisions I've ever made. If there is some stigma or argument in your mind keeping you from doing some work (counseling, not facelifts) on yourself, I strongly encourage you to do what you need to do to get healthy. I promise you you're worth the effort, friend.

Thank you, NYC, for being my muse.

And, hey . . . Oscar Isaac? Ditto.

Thank you to the writers who inspired me and entertained me and challenged me and distracted me while I spent time with Cole and

Laila. Writers like Thao Thai, Delia Ephron, Janine Rosche, Annabel Monaghan, Martin Short, Gillian McAllister, Gabrielle Zevin, Elle Cosimano, and so many others.

And thank you, Jesus. Whatever measure of talent or creativity I may have as a storyteller on my best day starts and ends with you, and in writing this book, you helped me rediscover the joy of it all. Thank you for that gift.

DISCUSSION QUESTIONS

1. Let's start by tackling the age-old question: Can men and women be *just friends*?
2. When you're on vacation, do you prefer to map out a plan, or do you sometimes enjoy seeing how lost you can get?
3. Have you ever done something while out of town that you would never do at home?
4. Do you like surprises? Talk about one of the best surprises you ever received. How about one of the best surprises you ever gave?
5. Cole's grandmother taught him that food is love. Share a treasured memory you have in which food and love intertwined.
6. Is there a movie you love as much as Laila loves *You've Got Mail* or Cole loves *Ghostbusters*? Is there someone in your life you share that love with?
7. If you were set up on a blind date with *your* teenage celebrity crush, who would be waiting for you at brunch?
8. Who would you cast as Cole and Laila in a film version of the book?

ABOUT THE AUTHOR

Photo by Noah Turner

Bethany Turner has been writing since the second grade, when she won her first writing award for explaining why, if she could have lunch with any person throughout history, she would choose John Stamos. She stands by this decision. Bethany now writes pop culture–infused rom-coms for a new generation of readers who crave fiction that tackles the thorny issues of life with humor and insight. She lives in Southwest Colorado with her husband, whom she met in the nineties in a chat room called Disco Inferno. As sketchy as it sounds, it worked out pretty well in this case, and they are the proud parents of two grown sons. Connect with Bethany at bethanyturnerbooks.com or across social media @seebethanywrite, where she clings to the eternal dream that John Stamos will someday send her a friend request. You can also text her at +1 (970) 387-7811. Texting with readers is her favorite.

bethanyturnerbooks.com
Instagram: @seebethanywrite
Facebook: @seebethanywrite